PRAISE
FOR OFF THE RECORD

"Off the Record *was such a fun read. Full of interesting, colorful characters and places that I could easily picture in my mind. A great mystery story with a bit of an education into the court reporting profession. Most of us court reporters don't have as exciting adventures as our dear Shae! I can't wait to follow Shae through more adventures.*"

—Veronica Williams, RPR
COURT REPORTER, OHIO

"*Great plot! I loved it!*"

—Doreen Sutton, RPR, CSR, CR, FAPR
COURT REPORTER, ARIZONA

"*Wonderful story! I'd love everyone to read* Off the Record. *Readers are in for a treat as Diana Kilpatrick unfolds the layers of the court reporting profession in an entertaining and informative way. I found her characters so memorable and loveable that I feel like I've made new friends. I look forward to hearing more from Shae Rose in the future.*"

—Elaine Childs, CSR
COURT REPORTER, CALIFORNIA

"*I didn't want to put it down! The idea of writing portions of the book in transcript form was genius and I loved the informative parts about court reporting. It can't be easy to write a mystery book while working in this career of ours. Looking forward to more adventures with Shae Rose. Excellent job!*"

—Judy Pisani
COURT REPORTER, NEW YORK

DIANA KILPATRICK

OFF THE RECORD

A SHAE ROSE MYSTERY

SHAE ROSE MYSTERY SERIES
DIANA KILPATRICK

Off the Record

Verbatim

DIANA KILPATRICK

OFF THE RECORD

A SHAE ROSE MYSTERY

FSP
FIRST STEPS
PUBLISHING

OFF THE RECORD
A SHAE ROSE MYSTERY, BOOK 1
by DIANA **KILPATRICK**

Copyright © 2018 by Diana Kilpatrick
All rights reserved

First Printing © May 2019

Published by

FSP
FIRST STEPS
PUBLISHING

First Steps Publishing
PO Box 571
Gleneden Beach, OR 97388
541-961-7641

This story is a work of fiction. Names, characters, places, and incidents are either products of the author's imagination or used fictitiously. Any resemblance to actual events, locales, or persons, living or dead, is entirely coincidental.

All rights reserved. No part of this book may be reproduced or transmitted in any form without written permission from the author, except in the manner of brief quotations embodied in critical articles and reviews. Please respect the author and the law and do not participate in or encourage piracy of copyrighted materials.

Every effort has been made to be accurate. The publisher / author assumes no responsibility or liability for errors made in this book.

Cover image © Diana Kilpatrick
Cover design, interior layout by Suzanne Fyhrie Parrott
Map illustration, *Lockwood Estate*, @colinyeo, Fiverr.com

ISBN - 978-1-937333-78-2 (hb)
ISBN - 978-1-937333-53-9 (pbk)
ISBN - 978-1-937333-54-6 (ebk)

Library of Congress Control Number: 2019932561

Genre: *Mystery, Cozy Mystery, Legal, Women's Fiction*
Keywords: Court Reporter, Court Reporter Mystery, Legal Mystery

10 9 8 7 6 5 4 3 2 1

Printed in the
United States of America

NOTE TO THE READER

When I set out to write a novel about a small-town, freelance court reporter, I did so with a niggle of trepidation. I knew that my book would inevitably find its way into the hands of some of my fellow court reporters, and we can be a pretty particular bunch. Every one of us wears an invisible but very real "Grammar Police" hat. We are never without it. We proofread in our sleep! We all have our own way of doing things, but paramount in our profession is the desire to do those things *well*.

I also hoped to reach people who are unacquainted with the field of court reporting. My mission was to provide a peek into the world of deposition reporting, and to do so in a way that readers would find informative and entertaining.

Friends, it is my hope that with this story you can escape into a different world for just a little while, and perhaps be inspired along the way. The world needs more court reporters! If your curiosity is piqued, check the end of the book for information on how you can look into developing a fascinating career of your own.

With love and appreciation for every person holding this book in your hands, I give you my best.

Diana

Lockwood Estate

PROLOGUE
AUGUST 1975

The man stepped quietly into the mud room of the winter house, his boots dripping globs of mud onto the intricate stone flooring. He stood still for a moment, watching water slide down his slicker and pool around his feet. Jenkins would be displeased.

An unusually fierce Idaho thunderstorm gripped the August evening. Moments ago, half blinded by sheets of rain, the man's journey to the winter house had been guided only by frequent bolts of jagged, ferocious lightning. He'd held his hands to his ears as he stumbled through the streaming grounds, cringing against the ear-splitting thunder, praying to a God he did not know that he wouldn't be struck down by the storm.

Now, in the quiet mud room, the man heard the crackle of a welcoming fire as it blazed in the great room.

Not that it's welcoming me, thought the man sourly. *I don't feel appreciated here anymore.*

He removed his boots without a sound, avoiding the room-length bench with a particular creak that would give him away. The slicker he wore slid silently from his arms, and he carefully draped it on a coat hook.

The mud room served as a buffer between the elements of the outside world and the gleaming surfaces within the house. Trained from childhood to keep it as neat as possible, he took his muddy boots from the floor, placed them on the entry mat, and shrugged. The damage was already done to the floor. He stepped over the mess and padded to the door that led to the great room. Beneath the elaborate mantel, he halted and placed one hand on the door frame to steady himself.

Ten feet from where he watched, his elder brother stood before a marble bust of their father. His brother placed a hand on the top of the smooth head, staring at it thoughtfully.

I knew I'd find you here, brother. Seems like you practically live down here these days. He scowled. *Too good for the rest of us, eh?* His eyes flickered to his brother's well-muscled forearm and deeply tanned hand as it stroked the bust. He stared down at his own hands and considered his comparatively sallow skin, his resentment deepening. At thirty-one years old, while he hadn't attained his brother's lofty six-foot-three height, he knew he could trounce his elder sibling in any number of sports, given the chance. He stroked his slightly stubbled jaw and clamped his thin lips tightly. *I'm pale because I work every day.*

A moment later his brother squared his shoulders as he left the bust. Then he seated himself comfortably in his favorite chair and leaned over his favorite desk. Favorite *old* desk. Everything his elder sibling loved was either old, old-fashioned, or both.

We're in the newspaper business, cryin' out loud. The man got angry every time he thought of it. *Keep up with the times!*

A sharp pain stabbed his stomach as he rewound the tape in his mind and mentally hit play:

My brother will never modernize.

With Father gone, he'll drive our business into the ground with his namby-pamby, half-baked ideas. And don't get me started on his complete lack of follow-through and a bleeding heart for the employees!

As the man fumed, his brother tipped back in his chair and held a sheaf of papers in the air before him. He appeared to be carefully reviewing them, and the man craned his neck to see what they were. The chair groaned as his brother shifted slightly and elevated the papers even more. *He doesn't even know I'm here.* Peering across the span between them, the man could just make out the words, *Last Will & Testament,* in the upper portion of the topmost page.

What's he up to now? Bitterness edged his thoughts. His brother was only thirty-four years old. Why make a will?

Planning on dying soon, big brother? He clenched his fists and felt his face flush. *Planning to squeeze me out of the little that's left to me?*

Even as these thoughts took shape in his mind, he knew their sister would call them unfair. His brother's bleeding heart seemed to extend to her and the rest of the family, even to himself—a fact that enraged him all the more. Since when had spinelessness been a virtue? It was a dog-eat-dog world out there, and with his brother at the helm, the family's newspaper dynasty would surely crumble and die.

Or has he found Father's will at last? Typical of him to keep it from me!

As the man's thoughts darkened, his eyes slid unwillingly to the marble bust. It rested upon an antique, three-legged side table. The table itself was notable, with its glistening, ancient cherry wood shining in the firelight. But it was the bust that captured the man's attention, as it had captured his brother's. Their father had commissioned the creation of the bust over a year ago. Uncanny chance alone had dictated its arrival last week, just days before Father's unexpected death. They'd buried their father just this afternoon. Unlike his brother, he didn't contemplate the bust fondly. Rather, he imagined that his father's eyes were gazing directly at him. Accusing him.

What are you looking at, Father? His shoulders stiffened in familiar defiance. *Your forgotten younger son?*

He looked back at his brother, who was still studying his sheaf of papers. Frustration overflowed from the man's ever-boiling inner cauldron, and his heart pounded.

He'd come here for a reason. He couldn't let the unease created by the bust's unseeing gaze diminish his resolve.

* * *

"Step into the light and warm yourself." His brother's voice reached him from his place in the great room. It seemed he'd known of the man's presence all along. "I need to speak with you."

Leaving his place beneath the mantel, the man took three steps mutely forward. He'd lost his edge, his chance to surprise his brother and confront him when he was off-balance. No matter. He'd waited in the background long enough. Father was dead, and the burning demands of the man's mind could not be quieted. Propriety could go to the wind.

"I want you to leave!" he blurted. "You've been away for years, off in the Amazon or wherever it was you were working, if that's what you called it. Father summoned you home, but he's gone now, and things need to go back to how they were. I was running the paper just fine without you. It's time that you got yourself on a plane and flew back to where you came from." That was it. The man had never been one to give speeches. He slumped his shoulders, spent. He'd said what he needed to say, and had no clue how his elder brother might respond.

With a wide smile, his brother leaned back in his old-fashioned, creaky, favorite chair.

"Ah, I'm glad we're of one mind, then," he said cheerfully.

The man squinted at him, shifting from one foot to another. What was this?

"What?" he managed. "So you don't plan to stay and take on the business?"

"Nope." His brother's grin broadened as he looked around. Dimples, ever near the surface, deepened at the sight his dripping brother, but he made no comment. Blue eyes twinkling in the firelight, he ran a hand through thick, sand-colored hair. "Father doesn't need me anymore, and you can run the paper just fine with our sister." He reached out and idly began to spin an old black globe that occupied the upper right corner of his desk. Stopping the globe suddenly, he pointed to South America. The Amazon. Of course.

"I'm heading back. This is where I've been, and to there I shall return. I left the biggest part of myself there four months ago, when Father sent for me." He contemplated the great room. His eyes fell upon a stack of old newspapers near an armchair. Father's chair. He cleared his throat.

"My heart was never in the newspaper business. But then I expect you know that." He chuckled. "Or at least you *hoped* it. You never cared for my ideas." He set the sheaf of paper down. "I've left everything in order. I've booked a flight for tomorrow morning."

The storm raged outside, while the storm inside the man grew quiet. He smoothed his own hair now, dark and lank after his dousing.

"Please tell everyone I love them," his brother continued, "that I hate goodbyes, and that I'm off to my life's calling. The rainforest, indigenous tribes." His expression grew wistful. "I must go and do what I can. I'm sure everyone will understand."

The man looked down at his dripping clothes. His wet hair chilled him, yet his heart thrilled. He'd plowed through a fierce storm, snuck into the winter house, soaking himself through so he could confront his brother, and for *what*?

He'd already won. His brother was leaving.

CHAPTER 1

CHEEKY PEAKS
AUGUST 2016

Dear Cheeky,

I am thirteen years old, and I am the only person at my school who doesn't have their own cell phone. My parents say I have to wait until I'm sixteen, have a job, and have "learned how to use social media responsibly." Help me! How can I explain to my parents that I NEED to have a smartphone?! What if I have an emergency? This is a matter of life or death!

2 Old 2 B Cellfree,

Abigail

Dear Abigail,

I trust this letter finds you alive and well. Please provide this column with your parents' names and address. I would like to personally bring them a casserole and a nice Chardonnay. Bravo to parents who don't fear setting boundaries for their offspring. Be thankful, young friend, that your real needs, like food, clothing, shelter, and love, are well and truly met. As to emergencies, I see no cause for great alarm, since by your own admission all of your friends and acquaintances are, shall we say, wireless. Do be careful what you do on your own, of course.

 Freshly hopeful,

 Cheeky Peaks

--∞--

Dear Cheeky,

I recently had a baby and put on some extra weight. What with sleepless nights and two other small children to care for, I am struggling to get my body back. I'm afraid I'm falling into a deep depression about it. Do you have advice for this struggling young mom?

 Skinny Jean Dreaming,

 Colleen

Dear Colleen,

Darling girl, I was once your age. I, too, gave birth to a precious one. How well I understand the betrayal a young mother can feel when her body changes, often in spite of her own best efforts! But Colleen, step back with me for a moment and look at the precious cargo the good Lord has put in your care. Three beautiful children! I invite you to relax and enjoy these years, for they will fly by, and you'll wonder where your babies went! And when the sun is out, walk with that beautiful baby. I dare say there are other young mothers who would love to join you. And remember, friend, your children are far more concerned with your love for them than they are with the size of your thighs. Your husband is too, if he's worth his salt.

 Super Fan of Young Mothers,

 Cheeky Peaks

--∞--

Dear Cheeky,

I have a brother who has been missing for forty years. I believe he is dead. I want to move things forward and get his estate settled in accordance with our father's wishes, but my sister is standing in the way. Please advise.

 For the Dearly Departed,

 Anonymous

Dear Anonymous,

I'll see you in court.

 Your Affectionate Sister,

 Cheeky Peaks

--∞--

CHAPTER 2
EXHIBIT A

I stood in the small conference room and stared at Exhibit A. Two men watched me as I caught my breath. Five-foot-six on my tiptoes and 120 pounds soaking wet, I could have been intimidated by the tall, well-dressed men awaiting me, but I wasn't. I was used to attorneys. At thirty-three, I'd already been working closely with many of them for eleven years.

I had rushed to get here on short notice, but I'd kept them waiting all the same. I was forever fighting the clock and underestimating drive times. *This time, it wasn't my fault.*

Twenty minutes ago I'd received a phone call from Annie, my manager, scheduler, drill sergeant, and security blanket. Annie had a gift when it came to handling court reporters and law firms. She could arrange an interpreter here, a canceled deposition there. In her hands, a panicked court reporter could be juggled on Line 1 while she promised the impossible to a legal secretary on Line 2. Annie knew where all of her court reporters were at any given moment, and she'd even tracked me down on my day off. Her call found me checking my post office box in Ketchum, Idaho. I lived in Hailey, eleven miles to the south, but I liked having a professional presence in Ketchum as well, so I kept a box there.

When she'd told me what she needed, I laughed aloud.

"A *stipulation?*" The post office was busy, and a woman in yoga pants looked at me curiously. "You need me to get down to Hailey for a *stipulation?*"

"Yep." Annie chuckled. "The attorneys are waiting for you in Warren's office, Shae. They've agreed to let you take custody of an exhibit."

I nearly laughed again. *Take custody?* It was true that as a court reporter, I often picked up exhibits the day before a deposition. Sometimes people would FedEx a box of documents to a hotel or a law firm, and I'd swing by and grab them from the receptionist. But Annie had said, "The *attorneys* are waiting for you."

What could this exhibit be, that the lawyers wanted to be present for the hand-off?

I'd stepped outside into the bright, glimmering air. The day had peaked at a wonderful eighty-four degrees, a relief after yesterday's high of ninety-two. I'd been planning to find a soda and stroll through the shops on Ketchum's Main Street. I loved watching the town rosining its entertainment bow as the workweek waned and Friday evening beckoned.

It was just a deposition exhibit. Why couldn't it wait to be admitted into evidence in an actual deposition setting? Not that I was complaining. A local case was very good news. Maybe I'd catch Friday afternoon in Ketchum next week.

"What's the case, Annie? Is something brewing up here?"

"Oh, you could say that. Some of the paperwork is starting to come through now. Looks like the first of these will be on Monday. Between this and some other jobs that are lining up in the valley, you're going to be a very busy court reporter for a few weeks. Cry *uncle* if you need help. We can send reinforcements."

My firm was special that way. We were family. If I got swamped, someone would travel many miles to help cover jobs.

"What time are they expecting me?"

"Four o'clock today. So in, like, twenty minutes. Can do?"

"Bye, Annie!" I'd grabbed the keys out of my bag and dashed to my car.

* * *

Exhibit A looked innocent enough to me, sitting alone on the conference table. A simple, small Samsonite case lay open before me and held, admittedly, an unusual object. A single bead of sweat found its way down the back of my neck, a testament to my dash down the valley and the stuffy conference room air. Resisting the urge to wipe it away, I pulled my gaze from the exhibit so I could greet the attorneys.

One, I already knew. I'd worked with Coop Rickman many times over the years. Maybe six feet tall, Coop had ash blond hair and an open, no-secrets face. A powerhouse attorney was carefully concealed behind a warm and sympathetic demeanor. That's what his clients liked about him. He could do fierce legal battle while retaining his charm. He was popular in *my* book because he was friendly, professional, and didn't speak fast. Court reporters appreciate attorneys who don't speak fast.

The other attorney was clearly from out of town. No local lawyer would wear a tie to a *stipulation*.

A stipulation that was apparently no laughing matter to these two gentlemen. A large civil case loomed. "Important" people were involved. This exhibit was vital to somebody, and neither side would agree that the other side could hold onto it—not even for a few days. Today was Friday. Depositions were to begin on Monday. The parties had stipulated (legal jargon for agreed) that the exhibit must be placed in the care of the court reporter *now*. Fortunately, I'd only kept them waiting five minutes.

I tore my eyes from the Samsonite case as the out-of-town attorney addressed me. "Dominic Flynn," he gestured, but didn't extend his hand. A wiry man with a thin face and even thinner mustache, his movements were small and jerky. He displayed all the signs of a fast talker. *Oh, boy.*

"Shae Rose." Still short of breath, I hoped that I sounded more graceful than I felt. "Nice to meet you."

Mr. Flynn looked in my direction for only a moment before his eyes darted back to the exhibit. "I represent the plaintiffs," he informed me, "Dalton and Spencer Lockwood, and of course," he breezed, "the Lockwood Estate in general." He whipped a document out of his briefcase and placed it before me, but Coop caught my attention, smiled warmly, and held up his hand in greeting.

"Nice to work with you again, Shae. I'm representing the defendants, all parties Kensington. And we're not here to argue on the record," he said as he handed me a deposition notice. "But you'll see that while Mr. Flynn *does* represent the Lockwoods, he does *not* represent the 'Lockwood Estate in general.'"

"Improper, Counselor!" Dominic Flynn's face flushed instantly. "We are not here to decide—"

Coop waved him off. "Save it for the judge, Dom. But it's not fair to Shae if you incorrectly state who your clients are, and you know it."

"It's a question that will be settled very soon, Mr. Rickman," he growled.

Coop slapped Dominic Flynn on the back and laughed. "That's what we're here for, Dom. That's what we're here for. In the meantime, Shae..." He nodded toward Mr. Flynn's document. "...I'm afraid we're going to ask you to sign this receipt." He handed me the paper, a silent apology in his eyes.

This was Hailey. One of the nicest small towns in Idaho. It's been called one of the nicest small towns in the Continental US, often referred to as "Idaho's Hometown in the Mountains." This was a town where people knew their mail lady's cell phone number, and where the wait at the DMV was never very long.

It would be Coop's style to hand me the Samsonite case, complete with its contents, and trust me with it. There were other forces at work here, though. Big-city forces. They required me to sign that I'd received the item. I'd worked with high-end lawyers before. I didn't mind their extra precautions. I'd take care of the exhibit either way. I scrawled my signature on the document and handed it back across the table.

I reached for a pen, sure I had some exhibit stickers in my car. "Am I going to mark it?" Mr. Flynn gasped and his hands twitched. I thought for a moment he might clutch at his throat.

"Not necessary, Shae," Coop answered. "On Monday we'll explain everything on the record, and note that you have custody of Exhibit A. No stickers."

Coop closed the lid on the exhibit's case and offered to carry it to my car. Dominic Flynn kept pace with us on the way out. As we exited the building, his eyes quickly scanned north and south, lingering on each parked car. Did this guy represent the mob in New York or something? His spiffy suit, shiny shoes, and edgy personality belonged in a place populated by more than eight thousand people.

I lifted my car's hatch and watched as Coop set the Samsonite case inside.

After seeing the item tucked safely into my car, Dominic Flynn hurried back inside. I heard him muttering something about making copies of the document I'd signed. Coop closed the hatch on my shiny black Nissan Juke.

"Make sure you bring the exhibit with you, Shae, to the depositions. You won't have to bring it inside all the time, but it should always be available." He looked northward, gazing at the mountains.

"This case is a humdinger, Shae." Coop was smiling in that easy way that attorneys have when they are well paid and comfortable with their case.

"You'll want to show up with your proverbial running shoes on. The agenda's pretty aggressive." He took in my untidy mop of short blond curls, jeans, and white cotton blouse.

I squirmed. *This is my day off.*

"Don't let the location or the parties to the case throw you. They're rich, and the estate is huge, but they're just people."

I nodded thoughtfully. "I took a look at the notice, but I don't recognize any of the names."

"I'll bet you do." He smirked. "You read the *Valley Scribe*, I'm sure. Ever hear of someone named Cheeky Peaks?"

* * *

Back in my garage, I opened the hatch on my Juke and stared at the case inside. What secrets did it hold? Why had this particular object been singled out, set apart from all the other objects on someone's estate? Why had it been handed over to me for safekeeping? I reread the deposition notice, looking for clues. I didn't recognize the surname "Lockwood," but the other name, "Kensington," rang bells in my head. I knew that name was familiar to me, but I couldn't place just where—

My musings were cut short as I heard a door slam.

"Yoo-hoo! Shae, dear, is that you?" Clarabelle Darling, my seventy-one-year-old neighbor, friend, and landlady, was calling from the direction of the house. I smiled. She knew who had come home. Had I been anyone else, Hercules, my five-pound Chihuahua, would have sounded the alarm with maniacal barking and vicious growling. As it was, all of his noises were happy ones as he bounded toward me. I grinned at him and set down the depo notice.

"Come here, Herc." I opened my arms. "There's a good boy!" Scooping him up, I nuzzled into his soft neck, laughing as he squirmed his head to try and kiss me. "What have you been up to today, buddy, huh?"

Panting slightly, Clarabelle rushed into the garage, her plump face flushed. I took in her cheerful, flower-print dress, sensible walking shoes, and wide straw hat. A retractable dog leash dangled from one hand.

"Oh." Her free hand fluttered to her chest as she tried to catch her breath. "He's such a scamp! We were about to walk down to Nettie's for an iced coffee, and he heard you pull up. There's just no stopping him when he hears you come home!"

I hugged Hercules to my chest, scratching behind his ears. "Were you naughty, boy?" I murmured playfully. "Did you run away from nice Clarabelle?" Hercules squirreled around, trying for more kisses.

Clarabelle and Bernie Darling, two semi-elderly sisters (Bernie, at *seventy*-three, was more spry and energetic than I, at *thirty*-three), had created a duplex out of their large family home. They inhabited the larger unit, while I rented the smaller. Our spacious garage was home to my car, the ladies' fire-engine red Ford Focus coupe, and my mighty Harley-Davidson Road King. The garage sat on the front left side of the duplex, with a side door that opened into a warm, brick-paved courtyard. The Darlings watched Hercules for me when I was at work, and he felt as at home with them as he did with me. Having received his greetings from me, Hercules allowed himself to be led away for his walk with Clarabelle.

I turned again and contemplated Exhibit A. I flipped the latches securing the old Samsonite case. Opening it, I studied the object within. A faint, lovely scent arose from within the case. I tried to place it, but the scent drifted away. Had I imagined it?

Lifting my eyes, I looked toward the back of the garage. I allowed my gaze to linger longingly on my beautiful smoky gold motorcycle. The exhibit in my car was mildly interesting, but it was, after all, just part of my job. I had a ride planned for tomorrow, and my thoughts drifted forward in time.

I was eager to gear up and start the engine on the big bike tomorrow. Its rumble was so beefy, so powerful, that it was almost intimidating. When I'd bought it, the salesman had taken in my slender frame and unsuccessfully tried to steer me toward smaller bikes. I knew it was a large bike for a woman my size, but I loved how it handled the open road. I loved the feel of the grips, the mini-ape handlebars, the custom seat—well, everything. After my purchase I'd done all that I could to make sure my Harley and I were a perfect fit.

I'd need to check the weather, make sure the forecast remained unchanged and sunny for the weekend.

A car drove by, too fast, and shook me from my reverie. I realized I'd been standing before my car's open hatch for at least five minutes, daydreaming. I looked inside the car.

"You may have stories to tell," I spoke aloud to Exhibit A, "but they are not my stories. You're not up at bat until Monday, so that's that for now." With one last look, I grabbed the case's lid and closed it gently, obscuring from view the most unusual exhibit I'd ever been entrusted with—a beautiful, black, 1945 Smith-Corona typewriter.

CHAPTER 3

BERNIE AND EVENING

As I always lock my garage door, I decided to leave Exhibit A in the car for the night. I carefully closed the garage door and then exited from the side door, pausing to enjoy our courtyard's friendly warmth. My eye caught a movement on the far side, and I looked up just in time to see Bernie disappearing into her home, so I trailed after her to say hello.

There was no sign of her when I stepped through the front door. "Helloooo."

"In here." Bernie's muffled voice came from the direction of the kitchen. I rounded the corner into that warm and functional room only to find Bernie, in typical fashion, wearing denim overalls and working in the cupboard beneath the sink. A polar opposite to her fluttery, excitable sister Clarabelle, Bernie brought a hard-working and practical approach to life. Each new day found her ready to tackle one task or another, and she kept our building in tiptop shape.

Bernie was kneeling on a folded towel that provided some cushioning for her knees. Her head and shoulders were hidden, but a hand shot into view as she asked, "Hand me that wrench on the table, please, Shae."

I looked at the table and saw a solitary wrench lying on the far end. "It's a good thing there's only one tool here, Bernie," I said, stepping over to it. I laid the wrench in her outstretched hand, which promptly disappeared back beneath the sink. "I'm afraid I don't know a wrench from a pair of pliers."

"I'll be sure to show you later, then. Can't let you be so helpless. Not that I can talk, though. I know what a wrench is, but my brain is otherwise on vacation half the time." I heard clinking as Bernie worked. "I went out to the shed for that wrench, and when I got down here to work, I realized I'd left the darned thing up on the table." She sounded purely disgusted. "Way too much effort getting all the way down here to be so forgetful. Glad you showed up when you did."

With a final grunt of effort, Bernie withdrew herself from the cupboard and sat on the floor. "So that's done," she stated with satisfaction. "Pipe was dripping back there. I'll come check yours tomorrow, make sure it's not doing the same thing." She held the wrench out to me.

I took it and set it back on the table, then turned back and extended my hand to help her up. She accepted it gratefully.

Back on her feet, Bernie washed her hands and then flipped the switch on an electric kettle. "Got time for some tea with an old lady?"

I laughed aloud. "You're younger than I am, Bernie." I reached under a cupboard and took two cups from where they hung on little hooks. "And sure, I have time. No big plans for the evening. No plans at all except trimming Herc's toenails, and I can't do that until he and Clarabelle get back from Nettie's."

"You be sure and do that at *your* place, Shae. Makes me nervous."

"I use tiny cat clippers. I won't hurt him."

"All the same..." Bernie handed me my tea and we enjoyed a companionable hour together. She told me that old Frank Gruber had been by, complaining in his heavy German accent that Hercules had barked at his goat Ziggy again.

"Who has a pet goat anyway?" Bernie asked in exasperation.

"Aw, Ziggy's cute in his way."

"Ziggy is incapable of expression," Bernie asserted firmly. "He just stares at you, and I don't think Hercules' barking scares that goat in the least. You ask me, the *goat's* the aggressor in this relationship. He gets loose and comes here on purpose, just looking for trouble. I'll tell you, Shae, sometimes that Frank Gruber just makes me tired."

She waved a hand through the air as if to dismiss Mr. Gruber and Ziggy from her mind.

We moved on to other topics, and in what seemed only moments Clarabelle and Hercules returned home.

"Ohhhh, I'm glad you've been visiting with Bernice, Shae, dear," Clarabelle fairly gushed. "Do stay to dinner, won't you?"

"Can't, Clarabelle," I said regretfully. "I have a pedi appointment with Master Hercules here, and I need to get my bike shined up." I grinned. "Going for a ride tomorrow."

"Oh, you be careful on that motorcycle, Shae." Clarabelle had long held my Harley in fearful fascination. "I just don't know *how* you find the courage to ride it."

"I'll be careful. But tonight I'm just cleaning it. Rain check on dinner?"

"We'll count on it," Bernie affirmed.

I gave Clarabelle's shoulders a squeeze and said goodbye to Bernie. Herc, knowing it was dinnertime, followed me home happily.

* * *

Some hours later, I was tucked in bed, reading. Though the day had been quite warm, a typical mountain briskness had chilled the air at dusk, and a cup of hot cocoa rested within easy reach. Herc had already crawled into his own bed. I looked down at the floor next to me and couldn't even see him, so deeply was he burrowed within his blankets.

It had been a pleasant evening. I'd polished my bike until it gleamed and laid out the leathers I planned to don in the morning. I'd then changed into comfy sweats, made some dinner, and eaten it slowly while getting some work done on a transcript.

Life was good. I loved my job, my home, the Darlings. I wasn't one to go out clubbing, and I rarely dipped my toe into the local singles' scene, but I was content. *Yawwwwwwn.* Bedtime.

I set my book down and traded my sweats for a T-shirt to sleep in.

"Night, Herc," I said as I closed the bedroom door and turned off my reading lamp. "Sweet dreams, buddy."

Not two minutes had passed before Coop Rickman's parting words revisited my drowsy brain, and I popped up in bed again. While on the very edge of sleep, I'd somehow made a connection that, while wide awake, I had failed to make. As with so many people, most of my best thinking happens just as I'm drifting off at night. And of course most of those great thoughts have vanished long before the sun has peeped into the morning sky.

Not so this time. Switching the light back on, my now wide-awake eyes darted straight to the corner of my room—a corner in which sat my beloved grandmother's rocking chair. That chair and a stack of old newspapers were the only possessions of hers that I had, and as I gazed at the chair I could almost feel her joyful presence. I absently fingered the amethyst seahorse necklace she had given to me on my eighteenth birthday. It warmed my skin as I thought of her. I never wore other necklaces, and I never took this one off except to clean it.

What interested me most right now, however, was the stack of papers that lay on the floor beneath the chair's seat.

Kneeling in front of the chair, I pulled the pile of newspapers toward me, thinking back again to Coop's words.

"*You read the* Valley Scribe, *I'm sure. Ever hear of someone named Cheeky Peaks?*"

I ran my hands across the words, *Valley Scribe*, on the topmost page of the first newspaper. Taking the paper with me, I rose and then seated myself in my grandmother's rocker, thinking back to all the times we had shared the weekly paper together. When I was young she would read to me, assuring herself that I was well-educated in the doings of our nation and local community. As she aged our roles reversed, and the paper transferred naturally into my willing hands.

We loved to laugh at funny articles, grieve at sad obituaries, or express mutual outrage at the day's political maelstrom. Above all, we loved to read *Cheeky Peaks* together. We enjoyed her wit, her no-nonsense replies that had kept her advice column in high demand for years. With practiced hands I quickly flipped to the column in the edition I held. I smiled quietly. This was the final paper I'd shared with my grandmother. She had passed quietly in her sleep shortly after its issuance, and I'd found no heart to read the *Cheeky Peaks* column on my own since that time. Ten years. I'd held on to these papers for ten years.

Grandmother loved to remind me that she'd known Cheeky Peaks, aka Aurora Kensington, in school. "Of course," she would invariably remind me, "she was Aurora Lockwood then. Even as a young girl she possessed a self-confidence that I envied, and now look. Her column is so wise and witty."

Aurora Kensington—formerly Aurora Lockwood—a member of the newspaper family and an heiress of the grand Lockwood empire.

My breath caught as my skin erupted in goosebumps. *Why hadn't I put two and two together sooner?* My new case held the caption of *Lockwood v. Kensington*. My eyes traveled to my closed bedroom door, my every fiber demanding that I charge out into the living room to double check my notice. But to do that would be to rouse Herc, and he might not settle back down easily.

I remembered that one of the Kensingtons listed was Aurora. I would read the notice tomorrow more carefully and see who the other parties were. I might even be able to get an idea of what the case was about.

As I slipped into bed again my thoughts jumped ahead to Monday. A legal battle was brewing within one of the valley's most prominent families; I would probably meet *Cheeky Peaks* in person; and an ancient typewriter was Exhibit A. The *Lockwood v. Kensington* case had definitely grabbed my attention. What would the coming weeks hold?

CHAPTER 4

INTRUDER!

A dog was barking. More than barking. The dog was going bananas, snapping and growling viciously. My eyes opened slowly, my groggy brain struggling to comprehend that I wasn't dreaming. Hercules was going completely nuts. When I'd gone to bed, he'd been burrowed snugly beneath the layers of blankets that topped his bed. What could have drawn him out of his cozy nest?

"What's going on, buddy?" Hercules was furious, repeatedly throwing all five pounds of himself against my bedroom door. "Hey, Herc, you're scaring me!" He'd never acted like this at night before. I tried to listen for unusual sounds, but at first all I got was an earful of frenetic barking. At last, Herc paused and stood at rigid attention.

What was that? Wide awake now, I heard muffled thuds and bumps beyond my closed bedroom door. *Intruder!* The word hit me like a wrecking ball. Adrenalin surged through my body, and my heart jolted, pounding wildly.

What was the rule when one was alone during a nocturnal invasion? Pretend to sleep through it, hoping they only wanted stuff within easy reach? Call 911 and risk being heard?

There! I heard a crash and a whispered curse coming from the living room, followed by footsteps crunching on what sounded like broken glass. Hercules resumed his clamor, and it occurred to me that his efforts might be the reason my bedroom had remained undisturbed.

I had no weapon, not even a lock on my bedroom door. One thing was sure, though. I couldn't stay in my room, pretending to sleep through the ear-splitting cacophony my Chihuahua was producing. I grabbed Hercules, clamped his mouth shut so my own voice could be heard, and in my best outside voice yelled quickly, "Grab the gun, Frank!"

A crunching sound and then the slamming of a door, followed by the thunking of heavy footsteps as they hurried through the courtyard. The sound faded as the intruder fled out into the street. As my heart's pounding boomed in my ears, I was only vaguely aware of another door slamming; other, lighter footsteps racing away; and the sound of one of Clarabelle's flowerpots crashing to the ground. Setting Hercules on the floor, I tugged on some sweats and shoved my feet into slippers.

"It's okay, Herc," I said to steady myself. "Good job, boy! Wow. I think you scared someone off. Good dog."

I didn't really expect my words to *work*, but Herc grew calmer, and I released the breath I'd been holding. Whoever had been here was gone. Hercules would know. Cocking his head to one side now, he only whined plaintively and scratched at the door. I heard a scuffle, and my knees nearly buckled, but Hercules was no longer alarmed. He scratched at the door again. I heard knocking and the sound of Clarabelle's voice.

"Shae, dear? Shae? Are you all right? We heard Hercules, and then it sounded like there was someone—"

I pulled the door open, and there stood Clarabelle, trying desperately to button up her bathrobe in between knocks. What was that on her head? Did Clarabelle sleep in a *bonnet*?

"Oh, there you are!" She sounded relieved as she hurried into the room, glancing all around. "Oh, we've had such a fright! Is everything okay over here?"

Hercules had charged right through the living room and out into the courtyard, the hairs on his back bristling straight up. Apparently assured any strangers had left, he came inside and stood on his hind legs, dancing around in front of Clarabelle, seeking reassurance and attention. She absentmindedly picked him up and squeezed him to her chest, whereupon he obligingly licked her cheek once. I wasn't sure who was comforting whom.

"Let's turn on a light," I said. "Someone's been in here." I reached for the hallway light switch, flipped it on, and gasped. The sofa's end table lay on the floor, its resident ceramic lamp broken in pieces. That was the crash I'd heard.

I glanced at Clarabelle's feet and was relieved to see shoes. Mismatched, unlaced walking shoes, hastily thrown on, but shoes. I grabbed each of Herc's paws to inspect them for damage, but he'd apparently hopped right over the breakage.

Clarabelle sucked in her breath, and I lifted my eyes from the mess on the floor. Papers were strewn across my dining room table, a box was tipped over, and three of my larger kitchen cupboard doors hung open. My laptop lay amidst the scattered papers on the table, and I marveled that it hadn't been stolen. I looked around more thoroughly, relief washing over me. Nothing obvious was missing. It was the scene of a burglary interrupted.

Someone had entered my home and searched for—valuables? In his haste, he—*should I assume it was a he?*—had apparently knocked the lamp over. He had then run off when I'd yelled to a fictitious Frank that he should grab the gun.

"They didn't take the laptop," I said, dazed. "They didn't take the TV. Goodness, they didn't even take my cell phone!" It was right where it should be at three o'clock on a Saturday morning—on the kitchen counter. No wake-up alarms needed on weekends. What crook would leave a cell phone behind?

My gaze traveled back to the cupboard doors, flung wide open.

"It's almost like they were searching for something specific."

"I'd say so," replied Bernie grimly, startling me.

She hadn't been there a moment ago. Speech left me as I took in the sight before my eyes. Bernie, her hair in wild disarray, stood just inside the front door wearing a three-quarter-length Boise Broncos nightshirt. Her hands were gripping a baseball bat so tightly that her knuckles threatened to pop right through her skin, and her stick-thin white legs led my eyes down to the pink bunny slippers Clarabelle had given her last Christmas—the slippers that had embarrassed her, and which I'd been sure she would never, ever wear.

"Big guy," she continued, unconcerned by my staring. "I didn't get a good look at him, 'cause he lit out so fast that he was rounding the corner before I got out to the street. He dropped this." She held out a crowbar for my inspection, and my heart skipped another beat. Bernie stood aside so I could see the damage done to my front door.

"Don't know if he meant to use it on *you*, Shae, but from the look of your door, he certainly used it to get into your *place*. You'd best call the cops."

Before I could assimilate all of this information, Clarabelle began fluttering around. "Oh, Bernice!" she cried, plunking Hercules unceremoniously down onto a chair. "It's three in the morning. I've had such a fright, and I can't possibly have *visitors*. You'll have to take care of it. What if that nice young officer comes…what was his name? I can't face him in this state! Oh, you stay with Shae, Bernice dear, I simply can't."

"Clare," Bernice sighed, "the police are hardly *visitors*, but all right. Off you go." Bernie set the baseball bat in a corner near the door and shook her head in mild exasperation while I gawked. How could Clarabelle be concerned about her appearance right now?

Well, she was *wearing a bonnet...*

Bernie turned to me, eyebrows arched as she took in my empty hands. "Shae, aren't you calling yet? I'd say time is a factor, in case someone is still lurking around."

A chill shot up my spine. "Right." This crisis wasn't over. Indeed, unless this had been a random break-in attempt, it seemed *likely* that the intruder would return. My mind finally kicked into gear, and I went to the kitchen for my phone. I unlocked it and opened it to the keypad, then paused.

Should I call 911 or the Hailey Police Department? I settled on 911, unsure about whether the police desk was manned at this hour. My call was answered immediately.

"Nine-one-one Dispatch. What's your emergency?"

"I've had an intruder." Darned adrenaline. Why did my voice have to shake? "A burglary, maybe, though I don't know if anything's missing. Someone forced my door open with a crowbar."

"Are you certain the intruder is gone?" asked Dispatch.

"Fairly sure for now." I took in deep breaths. "My dog scared him off, and my neighbor chased after him." I omitted the part about the baseball bat. "She saw him going around the corner a block away."

"All right," said Dispatch, "I've got an officer responding now to 235 Antelope Way in Hailey. Is that your correct address?"

"Yes."

"Thank you. He'll be there shortly. You mentioned a dog that scared away the intruder. Please shut the dog in a room somewhere. We don't want our officer threatened by a guard dog."

Ah. Something to smile about. "Well, I can send him over to stay with my neighbor, but he really isn't as much of a threat as he thinks he is." I wanted to ask who was coming, but somehow that didn't seem professional. Jackson Landers, the sergeant whose name had escaped Clarabelle, already knew Hercules.

Sergeant Landers' Aunt Nettie and the Darlings were friends, and he'd been known to stop by occasionally, just to check on their welfare. I'd been told that whenever he did, they plied him with coffee and cookies while Clarabelle did her best to coax interesting police stories out of him. Bernie had told me that when he visited them, Hercules would curl up on his lap for the duration of his stay. He always came by during the day when I was at work. I hadn't met him, but I'd heard all about him.

My mind snapped back to attention as I heard Dispatch's voice saying, "I'll stay on the line with you until help arrives. What kind of dog did you say you have?"

"He's a five-pound Chihuahua. He's very friendly, except to strangers."

"All the same," Dispatch carried on briskly, "even small dogs can bite, so if you'll put him—wait. Did you say *five pounds?*"

I managed a chuckle. "Yeah, but he knows how to sound mean when he wants to. I'm sure he's the reason the intruder stuck to my living spaces and didn't come into my bedroom." I reached down to rub Herc's head affectionately. He immediately flopped onto his back so I could rub his belly too. Touching Hercules was good therapy. *Normal.*

I hadn't noticed that Bernie had slipped out, but she

reappeared, fully dressed in an old flannel shirt and blue jeans. No bunny slippers in sight.

"Shae, you can let the dispatcher know that Sergeant Landers has just arrived. I'll go tell him we're all okay."

"Did I just hear that Sergeant Landers is on scene?" Dispatch asked as Bernie headed through the courtyard.

"Yes." I scooped up Hercules and poked my head out the door, looking toward the street. "He's just getting out of his car."

"All right then, I'll sign off. All the best to you." There was a click, and that was it.

I held the phone as if there should be something more. She'd been so professional, so anonymous, that I'd almost expected her to say, "And thank you for calling nine-one-one."

Sergeant Landers approached my front door as I was still staring dumbly at my cell phone. He was speaking with Bernie and hadn't noticed me yet. I knew from the Darlings that he was only a few years older than me. The sergeant sure looked smart in his uniform. He also looked very *awake*.

I suddenly became keenly aware of my hastily donned sweats and mussed hair. I probably looked like I'd just rolled out of bed, mostly because I had. *I'll bet there are sheet marks denting my face.* I moved behind an armchair to gain distance, hoping he had poor eyesight.

As they entered through my damaged front door, Bernie gestured toward the sergeant. "Shae, this is Sergeant Jackson Landers, Nettie's nephew. We looked inside the garage, and nothing looks disturbed. It's still locked up tight. It looks like someone was only after something in here. I'm sure Jax will get to the bottom of this."

Sergeant Landers had been taking notes as Bernie spoke. Well over six feet tall, Sergeant Landers had broad shoulders, an attractive square jaw, and liquid brown eyes. My heart stuttered in a reaction that had nothing to do with the frightening incident. *Shae! Who cares if he's gorgeous? Get a grip.*

He slowly surveyed the damage to my apartment, then turned the full force of his deep brown eyes upon me. I dropped Hercules. Thankfully, he only landed on the armchair's cushion.

"Ms. Rose? I'm Sergeant Landers with HPD. I understand there's been a break-in." His eyes never lost contact with mine, and yet I could tell he was also taking in the whole scene, missing nothing. "Any harm done to anyone that you're aware of, ma'am?"

Ma'am? I considered myself to be too young to be ma'am to anyone but a Southerner, and this guy had no accent.

"No," I answered, slightly miffed by the "ma'am." "No one's hurt, unless you count my poor neighbors' peace of mind."

"Bernie seems to be holding up." He smiled at her. "And I'll speak with Clarabelle in a few minutes. But first, ma'—"

"Shae." *Enough with the formalities.* "Just Shae."

"Got it," he said, jotting something quickly in his small notepad. "Maybe you'd like to sit down, Shae. I have some questions for you, and it looks like your peace of mind took a hit, too."

"Yeah, okay. I didn't see anything, though. Bernie ran after him. She's the only one who saw him."

"Yes, she told me about that. I sure don't like the idea of her chasing after an intruder, baseball bat or no."

So the bat was out of the bag. My omission of its use to 911 seemed suddenly silly. Still, when had she told him? They hadn't spoken for *that* long before they'd reached my door.

"Bernie has my private cell number, in case of an emergency." He tapped his pen on his notepad and eyed me as though reading my mind. "She gave me a call as I was on my way over here."

It sounded suspiciously like Bernie hadn't thought I'd actually get the call made on my own.

"I guess she spooked him some, though, because he dropped his crowbar. We'll be able to dust that for prints."

Wow! This was really happening. There was a cop in my living room, talking about dusting for prints.

"We take this kind of thing very seriously, ma'—Shae," he said sternly. "I need your complete attention." Apparently, he'd noticed that my mind had wandered off. "We'll dust the whole door, too, and the cabinets. We don't know what this guy's intentions were, but a crowbar can be a lethal weapon, so we'll be very interested in finding him. I need to ask, do you have any enemies? Anyone at all who may have something against you?"

"No-o-o-o," I said slowly, trying to match his tone. "No one comes to mind. I'm a court reporter, but I'm always just a neutral party in depositions. I rarely go to court where criminal activity is actually tried. I can't think of anyone who's angry with me."

But even as I was speaking, my mind traveled to the old Smith-Corona typewriter sitting in the cargo area of my car, safe and sound in the locked garage. Could *that* be what the intruder had been after? Only large cupboard doors had been opened. Cupboards that were potentially large enough to conceal a typewriter...

I spoke none of these thoughts aloud. If I mentioned the exhibit, Sergeant Landers might ask to see it—might even want to *dust* it for comparison prints or something. That possibility appalled me far more than keeping such an idea to myself did. I was responsible for that typewriter. It was mine to guard, to keep in a pristine and confidential manner. Nope, I wasn't going to say a word.

More people arrived and began the laborious process of investigating my crime scene. Bernie brought a huge thermos of coffee over and handed cups around to grateful recipients. Clarabelle, dressed and ready for the day now, arrived and offered to take Hercules over to her place. He'd been making himself known to all the nice police people, with no idea he was actually underfoot.

Just then it dawned on me that I was probably underfoot too. Sergeant Landers had long since taken my statement, and there wasn't anything more for me to do until everybody here finished their work. Bernie caught me eyeing the broken lamp and took hold of my arm.

"No cleaning up yet, Shae," she said, her voice understanding but firm. "Soon as they're finished, Clare and I will help you get everything back in place. I've already called a repairman to come fix your door, and he'll be here this afternoon. Jax thought it would be okay to do it by then."

I smiled gratefully as she led me out of my apartment and through the courtyard. It was nearly 7:00 a.m., and the sun was debuting its glorious self, casting back shadows and bringing forth promise of the sunshine and clear skies that had been forecast.

"I've put more coffee on, Shae," Bernie continued, putting her arm around my shoulder, "and Clare's making breakfast. Come sit down and rest a bit. You look done in."

I peeked at the sky once more and followed her inside. Coffee and breakfast sounded wonderful, but first I had to make a phone call. There would be no motorcycle ride for me today.

* * *

Forty-five minutes later, replete with strong coffee and Clarabelle's delicious, oven-baked, cheesy egg dish, I felt the early-morning fright begin to ease from my shoulders. I still had a mess to deal with in my apartment, but here, in the bright light of day, fear seemed a distant thing.

This was Hailey, after all. Beautiful, quiet, safe Hailey. Possibly we had experienced a random break-in to a relatively unprotected home. Even Hailey had people who found themselves desperate for money. My place was often empty as I traveled far and wide for work, and even if someone had cased the place while I was at home, they'd have seen a single woman living there with only a small dog. Easy pickings.

Nothing had been stolen. If the burglary had gone as planned, the intruder could have grabbed anything of worth after he'd searched the cupboards. One quick look would have told him I didn't have any valuables. There was no reason for him to return. *Stop being a scaredy-cat, Shae. It may not have been about the typewriter at all...*

I began to rummage through cupboards in search of a storage container for the remainder of Clarabelle's egg dish.

"And just what are you doing, Shae?" asked Bernie.

I jumped guiltily. Should I not have rummaged? Their chatter halted; both ladies were looking at me in disapproval.

"Um..."

"You'll leave this to us, and no arguing," said Bernie, steering me into their living room. "Take a nice nap while the police finish up at your place. We'll have plenty to do later when they leave."

She had already laid a pillow and a cozy, red plaid comforter on the couch. Pushing me down into their midst, she simply said, "We'll take Herc for a walk shortly and let you get some sleep. It'll be good for you."

I nearly argued. I nearly pointed out that I'd just had two cups of coffee, and sleep would surely be out of the question. *Nearly.* But the couch was comfy; the pillow and blanket were soft. I lay down and pulled the blanket over me, snuggling it up right underneath my chin. I should take the weekend to rest up, clean my home, and ready myself for early depositions on Monday morning. Depositions in the very matter tied to Exhibit A—evidence the crook may have been after. As I grew sleepy I knew further denial of that possibility was foolish.

My stomach fluttered. What if the very person who had attacked my front door with a crowbar would also be seated in the room with me on Monday, innocuously blending in with the other parties around the deposition table?

CHAPTER 5
FIRST DAY DRIVE

On Saturday, Clarabelle and Bernie took Herc with them while they hit the local garage sales and I snoozed on their couch. They returned some hours later in victorious possession of a lovely blue ceramic lamp, slightly larger than my own that had been shattered, but perfect just the same.

The police finished their evidence gathering and departed by early afternoon. It was only a break-in, not a murder scene, so I was allowed to go in and start cleaning up. Clarabelle kept Herc at their place so he wouldn't get hurt in the debris, and Bernie and I set to work. I cleaned up the broken lamp and pulled out the vacuum, while Bernie donned rubber gloves and set to cleaning off the cupboard doors. At 2:30, a knock on the damaged doorframe announced the repairman, and he began repairing the door jamb and installing new hardware, complete with a new deadbolt.

On Saturday night, I allowed Hercules to sleep in my bed with me, hoping his presence would soothe my restless jitters. So much for telling myself not to be a scaredy-cat. But whoever had entered my home on Friday night was still at large. I didn't feel safe falling asleep, even though Bernie had arranged three ladders, a wheelbarrow, and thirteen empty paint cans all along the entrance to our shared courtyard.

"If someone wants back in," she had stated, surveying her work, "they're gonna make a racket fit to wake the dead."

Comforting as that was, it had been nearly dawn before sleep found me, and I'd struggled into Sunday morning feeling like my head was stuffed with cotton wool. Halfway through my third cup of coffee, Sergeant Landers called to check on things and to report that, as yet, they had no leads as to who my intruder might have been. He also told me they'd found no prints on anything but my own and the Darlings'. The intruder had clearly been wearing gloves.

On Sunday night, Bernie doubled down on her fortifications, and I felt better on the whole, until Clarabelle helpfully pointed out that the fence was quite low in the back and someone could just hop over and smash a window.

Bernie all but rolled her eyes, saying only, "Come with me."

Clarabelle and I followed Bernie through their portion of the house (my section had no egress into the backyard), and we stood on the patio to survey Bernie's efforts. She had hung every wind chime that Clarabelle owned at intervals all along the back fence.

"The fence isn't *that* low, Clare," said Bernie. "It's five feet high, and if someone *does* try to climb it, we'll be able to hear him."

"Oh, clever you, Bernice." Clarabelle clapped her hands. "A musical alarm system! How ever did you think of it?"

Rather than reply, Bernie simply surveyed her handiwork with grim satisfaction. Walking to one of the sets of chimes, she tried to untie the line from which it was suspended. The chimes started chiming like mad as she tugged at the knot, and Bernie turned back to us. "See? Can't even try to remove them without getting them going."

She patted my shoulder and told me we should be quite safe,

and she hoped I'd be able to get some sleep. My nerves returned, however, as soon as we said our good nights. When I went to bed, I left the kitchen and living room lights on. Once again, I hugged Hercules throughout the night and jumped at every sound—particularly when the sound had been made by a wind chime. Turning over restlessly, I began to question the wisdom of turning a normally soothing sound into something ominous.

I finally drifted off sometime after 2:00 a.m. when Hercules, also acting edgy, had finally settled down and relaxed.

* * *

Monday morning found me sleep deprived and in no way ready for a new work week. My alarm sounded, and I rolled over in denial, burying my head beneath my pillow. Then I remembered the exhibit still waiting in the back of my Juke and the job before me, and I squirmed out from under my pillow. There had been two undisturbed nights since the break-in. That should strengthen my belief that the exhibit and the intruder were not linked.

Then why is your heart pounding, Shae?
Shush!
Suddenly wide awake, I scrambled out of bed. I padded through the living room, unlocked the deadbolt, and opened the door so Herc could go out. Normally, I'd have grabbed a leash and walked him around the block, but I knew that today he wouldn't leave if I gave him the freedom of the courtyard. He wouldn't go near Bernie's fortifications. Rather, he eyed them distrustfully, occasionally growling at some of the stacked paint cans.

I'd made coffee the night before and set the brewer's timer for 6:00 a.m., so now I held a steaming cup while perusing my deposition notice. Frowning at the notice, I swallowed some coffee. Agh! Hot! I dropped the papers and rushed to the sink. I swigged some cold water around my mouth in hopes that the burn was a temporary one. I wanted to finish my coffee.

I retrieved the depo notice from the table, frowning at it yet again. The deposition was to be held at a private residence. Depos at private residences can be complicated, and I felt a nervous tickle in my stomach. It listed an actual street address, but it also specifically stated, "North of Ketchum."

That could only mean one thing, and that was why I felt apprehensive. This place was going to be hard to find.

* * *

Several years ago (before everyone had GPS) I'd been sent to a private residence north of Ketchum. I'd wandered around the highway for half an hour before I found the obscure, gated entrance. By the time I had gained admittance and found the right room in the right building, I was late.

This time, I punched the address into my phone and hoped it would send me to the right area. Given the rural nature of "north of Ketchum," I didn't think my GPS app would be exact. I did hope it would let me know when I was close, or whether I had overshot the place entirely.

I set the phone where I could see it easily and headed off into rush hour traffic. The 9:00 a.m. start time of the deposition guaranteed that I would be competing for highway space with the masses heading north to work. And there are always *many* others. Ketchum is where the jobs are, and people drive from many different locations to fill those jobs. The commute doesn't consist of crowded twelve-lane freeways, but if you find yourself behind the wrong school bus, or on the south side of an elk herd, you'll wish you'd skipped that second cup of coffee.

I left the outskirts of Hailey and proceeded toward mid-valley. It was a beautiful day, so I blasted the radio and opened the sunroof. Summers are short in the valley, and I'd already missed a day on my motorcycle. I wasn't going to miss out now on the feeling of the wind in my hair, even if the morning breeze was a bit chilly.

I made it to Ketchum in fairly good time, yet still gripped the steering wheel impatiently as I hit red at every one of downtown Ketchum's three traffic lights. I couldn't afford to get behind schedule. I was heading to an *estate*. Unknown territory.

Out of Ketchum at last, I crossed Saddle Road and took a look at my phone. I didn't know if I would need to travel one mile more, or five. As feared, my app was uncertain as well. It once informed me that I had two miles to go, but then it reset itself and the display said I must go not two miles, but ten.

I crept along Highway 75, looking in vain for addresses. Homes in this area are large, beautiful, and private. You would never see a mailbox out on the road with "Miller Family" stenciled in large blue letters on the side.

Most of the houses were set back, away from the highway. I squinted at each one I could actually see, hoping in vain for a number of some kind to direct me. Such was my concentration that I jumped when a car swerved wildly around me, horn blaring. I checked my speed. I was going twenty-five miles per hour in a fifty-five zone. I pulled to the shoulder and consulted my GPS. It had settled down and now told me that my destination was one mile ahead. Holding the phone in my right hand, I checked my mirror and pulled back onto the road.

One mile farther down the road I checked my mirror again. No one behind me. I slowed again just as something caught my eye slightly ahead and to the left. Oh, how lovely! Someone had lined their private drive with beautiful boxes of perfect white roses. Remembering the angry driver, I peered quickly into the rearview again. No one back there. I slowed even more, hoping the driveway might have more than flowers to reveal.

And so it did! I was looking for numbering on the rose boxes, but what I found was a graceful, hand-carved wooden sign. It reminded me of a small, two-foot-high version of a Realtor's sign, the kind that resembles an upside down L. From the upper, horizontal bar, Realtors often hang a placard that declares a property for sale. It might also contain their headshots and contact information.

This little beauty was no temporary real estate advertisement. It was a sturdy post and arm, made from what looked to be oak, burnished to gleaming perfection. Words had been burned into the signage portion of the wooden placard, and the whole structure had been overlaid with soft, shiny lacquer. Having been driven into the ground next to one of the boxes of roses, it gleamed softly in the morning light.

It was so low to the ground that a casual passerby might miss it entirely. If, however, a person were looking for the entrance to a remote, hidden-away location, that person would not fail to see it. With a smile, I clicked on my left turn signal. Easing my car onto the narrow drive between the rose boxes, I reached for my phone and stopped the GPS app.

The charming little sign post by the road held not numbers, but words. Just two words. They were all I needed.

Lockwood Estate

I proceeded up the drive and soon found myself facing a massive double gate. There was a small, snug hut near my side of the gate, and I approached slowly, hoping to see someone in the hut. Short of that, I would have to get out and look around for a buzzer. I didn't see one in plain sight, but I needn't have worried. As soon as I rolled to a stop, a man emerged from the hut. He looked to be in his mid- to upper sixties and had a rugged air about him. His lean frame was clothed in denim, top to bottom. He wore his cowboy boots and hat as naturally as if he'd just stepped out of a Louis L'Amour novel. His friendly face carried a myriad of deep lines, no doubt a consequence of many years spent as one with the elements.

As he sauntered around the front of my car, he tipped his hat back to afford himself a clearer view of me. Now exposed, his white forehead made the rest of his leathery face seem softer somehow, less rugged, more friendly.

I rolled down my window as he approached. "Hello. I'm here for a deposition. I'm the court reporter."

"Been expecting you," he said easily. He nodded in the direction of the highway. "Hope you didn't have any trouble finding the place."

"Not at all. It's beautifully marked. Was that your work?"

The gatekeeper just hid a smile and stuck a toothpick in his mouth. The toothpick immediately became as much a part of him as his cowboy boots and hat.

"I'll open the gate for you, miss, and you just drive right on up to the big house. You'll see other cars, and you can park right there with them. Everyone is expecting you."

Everyone? There were two depositions set for today. A more careful perusal of my depo notice had revealed that Aurora Kensington herself was to be my very first deponent, and curiosity raged within me. What would *Cheeky Peaks* be like in person? The other parties to the lawsuit were also free to attend if they chose to. My shoulders tensed slightly. Were *all* the named parties waiting at the house? What would this day hold?

Before I could think to ask his name, the friendly gate man had moved back to his hut and activated the gate's mechanism. I watched in awe as the two sides of the gate opened silently from the center. They moved inward, toward the estate and away from my car. I put the car in drive. Time to go.

CHAPTER 6

LOCKWOOD ESTATE

I've never been a fan of private residence depos. It's mostly a question of ergonomics. I have a better chance of setting up my workspace to my liking if the job takes place in a law office or a hotel conference room.

My needs are few, but they're pretty non-negotiable. I need space to set up my laptop—somewhere I can see it, preferably. I need space to set up my steno machine. I need electricity. My laptop and machine have batteries, but we wouldn't want them running out of juice right when the testimony got tantalizing.

And here's the biggie. I need a chair without arms. I find it hard to write with no elbow room. In my experience, private homes don't have many chairs with no arms.

I have often arrived for depos in private homes to find friendly but uninformed residents who were awaiting *lawyers*. If someone had mentioned to them that a court reporter would also be attending the proceedings, that person probably hadn't mentioned seating requirements.

I have found myself, on more than one occasion, seated on a low, squashy sofa, my laptop on the floor, and my machine at its lowest setting on the tripod. Even then, in said lowest setting, the machine's keys were too high. I couldn't reach them properly from my sunken position. It's difficult to write at the speed of speech when you're holding your arms too high and your fingers are going numb.

Dining room chairs aren't always helpful, either. Many of them have arms. Even armless dining room chairs can be heavy, which I find awkward when I'm trying to *not* scratch a beautifully finished hardwood floor.

I have therefore taken to carrying a padded folding chair with me whenever I see a private residence on my depo notice. I don't always *need* it, but I sure always *have* it.

I left the gated area and the little hut. After I traveled about thirty feet, the trees began to thin out. I lifted my foot from the accelerator. The gated area had been densely wooded, and I had assumed I would find a nice house closely shrouded by trees and all manner of foliage. Instead, the woods were left behind, and as the narrow road widened, I emerged at last into a breathtaking scene.

The estate's grounds were vast, dominated by a huge front lawn encircled by a drive that went clear around it and back to this beginning point. Three separate homes had individual access to the drive.

To my immediate right, barely set back from the road, stood a long, single-story structure with a wide veranda that ran along all three sides visible from my vantage point. Its front deck boasted a porch swing and a small wooden table and chairs. The furniture looked handmade, and its luster reminded me of the darling little *Lockwood Estate* sign implanted at the road.

Directly in front of me, on the far side of the rounded lawn, sat a massive log home. The house featured huge picture windows *everywhere*. I imagined the light—the *views*—that could surely be found within.

Off in the nine o'clock position sat a lovely, smaller log structure with a steeply sloping roof. The roof overhung the porch in the front and protected a nice little walkway. I imagined the convenience of snow sliding off the roof and *not* landing on or near the porch. It was an ingenious design that bespoke not only efficiency, but privacy. A person would have to be right in front of the house to know if anyone was on the porch.

The house faced the drive, and on the right side (as I faced it) an obvious mudroom jutted out from the rest of the building. It too had a steeply sloped, overhanging roof. Though I was only fifteen miles or so north of Hailey, those miles all led *upward*. The snow load here would be far greater than I was used to; thus, the need for steeper roofs.

The smaller house was just far enough from the mansion to guarantee its occupants some personal space. It was ringed with widely spaced trees, and beautiful flowerbeds adorned the lawn surrounding the home. It looked unbelievably cozy. *Guest quarters?*

The drive was a well-maintained, smooth gravel, and I had no trouble pulling up to the house and finding the parking area. I parked next to a large SUV and switched off the ignition.

I was here to do a job, but I felt suddenly awkward, out of place. This was an elite home for elite people. People who valued their privacy and their majestic views. People who were perhaps unaccustomed to hosting tawdry legal proceedings within their walls. What would they make of me if they saw me struggling up their steps with my heavy equipment and my folding chair? My mind conjured an image of *Downton Abbey*, and I imagined a disapproving butler directing me to the servants' entrance.

I then cringed at the thought of searching for an electrical outlet in some refined and artfully appointed room. I thought of my old, tacky, twisted white extension cord, and shuddered. I hoped I wouldn't need it.

"Well, Shae," I spoke aloud, "get moving. And leave the darned chair in the car! You can come back if you need it."

That decided, I stepped out of the car and raised the rear hatch. I was reaching in to grab my steno case when a tanned, muscular arm snaked in and snatched the handle away.

"Agh!" I cried for the second time that morning. I jumped so high that I smacked my head on the raised hatch. I turned, one hand on my head and the other clutching my chest. It was the man from the gate. I'd been so taken by the breathtaking property that I hadn't noticed him following me in a golf cart. A silent golf cart.

He was grinning as he pulled my equipment from the car. "Sorry, ma'am." He actually tipped his hat. "I couldn't let you lift that out by yourself. Those are steep stairs you've got to climb. I'll take you in through the kitchen."

The servants' entrance!

But this was no disapproving butler. I couldn't remember ever seeing a kinder face. I smiled, catching my breath.

"Goodness, you startled me." I shut the hatch. "I had no idea you were there."

"Wouldn't leave you to fend for yourself on your first day, miss." He threw me a sideways glance. "There's a pack of people coming. Didn't think you'd want to arrive winded and out of sorts."

How thoughtful! I liked him immediately. "Shae Rose," I said. "Call me Shae."

"Pleased to meet you, Shae. I'm Hawk. I take care of the place. I'll hoist this up for you, and when you're finished, just wait and I'll carry it back down." He hefted my steno bag. "What have you got in here, anyway?"

"Just my work stuff." I laughed. "I'm used to it." I followed Hawk around to the north side of the house and a smaller parking area. *Note to self—remember this next time.* Hawk led the way up a flight of stairs, then through a small, unassuming door. Surprised, I stopped and surveyed the largest, loveliest mudroom I'd ever seen. I let that thought sink in for a moment. A lovely mudroom.

To my left hung a row of handmade coat hooks, with each upturned hook carved into different animal faces. I was happy I wasn't wearing a coat. I wouldn't want to hang it up and conceal a perfect lion, or an incredible bear, moose, or eagle. I'd never seen anything equal to the tiny, intricate pieces of woodwork.

To my right sat another masterpiece in the shape of a shoe-changing bench. Inlaid into the bench's backboard was an exact replica of the entire Lockwood estate, complete with trees, views, and flowerbeds. The artist had somehow managed to capture the main house's windows, so even though they were carved in wood, they still shone.

Winter gear was stashed in cubbies built on both ends of the bench. Neatly matched gloves, gators, and hats were stored on one side. Winter boots in a variety of sizes and styles filled the other.

I was wrong. This was clearly no servants' entrance. This was the *main* entrance, at least for informal occasions.

The room was easily twenty feet square, and so immaculate that I didn't want to step into it since I'd only just walked on the gravel drive. Hawk didn't seem concerned, though, as he rolled my steno case through the mudroom and into the room beyond. I couldn't stand there like a star-struck teenager, so I hurried after him.

I followed Hawk into the "kitchen," although the cooking area—vast and shiny and coppery—was off to our right. We passed through an open area that held, to our left, an opening into an oversized pantry. Beyond that, on the other side of a pony wall, was a cozy breakfast nook. The nook's table held a large bowl filled with a variety of fruit.

Toward the back of the table stood a single-cup brewer, complete with an assortment of coffees, teas, and chocolates. Two place settings were laid out, ready for anyone who fancied a quick meal or a hot drink. I could easily see myself curled up there with a book and some hot chocolate. And speaking of books, above the nook were recessed shelves chock full of them! I was falling in love with this house.

Hawk had left the kitchen and turned a corner. With a last glance at the little nook, I rushed to catch up. I passed through a grand archway that opened up into a formal dining room and found Hawk waiting for me. The vast table was covered with an immaculate white linen tablecloth. A quick count showed me eleven heavy chairs—five per side and one at the far end. The chair that interested me the most, however, was the one on the end nearest where I stood.

What caught my eye was a luxurious black leather secretary's chair—with no arms. It looked brand new. I could smell the rich, soft leather from where I stood. Was that for *me*?

As if he could read my mind, Hawk touched the back of the chair, swiveling it around. "Will this work out for you, miss— Shae? Coop said you reporters like simple chairs, but we don't have anything like that in the house." He squeezed the seatback. "Picked this up yesterday down in Twin Falls, and I thought it might work for you, but you'll have to say for sure. I can always trade it."

I was both horrified and thrilled.

"Hawk, it's gorgeous! Don't even *think* of trading it. But I have a chair. You never, ever should have bought a new chair just for these depositions."

He chewed his toothpick and pushed his hat back, a grin splitting his face. "Saw that little chair in your car." His eyes twinkled, and I could feel a blush rising up my cheeks. "Coop seemed to think that with, what, at least seven depositions coming up over the next little while, the court reporter ought not to be miserable. Mrs. Kensington agreed. I did too, comes to that."

What a wonderful work environment. Hawk had even placed an area rug beneath my fabulous new chair, no doubt to protect the hardwood floor's perfect sheen.

Now I looked around the lovely room for a power source. In a space this large, I doubted even my ugly white extension cord would reach an outlet. But Hawk was ahead of me here, as well. He pointed to a surge protector lying unobtrusively under my end of the table. He had run it from an outlet and had covered its cord with a second decorative rug so no one would trip on it.

"You can plug your equipment in right here," he said as he nudged the power strip with his toe. "I tried to think what else you might need, but I guess you'll just have to speak up if you think of anything."

I was feeling pretty bad about all of my private-residence trepidations earlier this morning. Never, in fifteen years of court reporting, had I encountered such thoughtfulness.

"It's perfect!" I smiled up at him in appreciation. "I just can't believe the effort you've gone to."

Hawk nodded and chewed his toothpick, surveying the room. "Okay, then. I guess you'll want to get set up. There's water and coffee there in the middle of the table. I expect the family will all come on down pretty soon."

With that he left, and I was alone in the beautiful room with the beautiful chair. I took hold of the back of the chair and spun it around playfully. No wobbles. Perfectly balanced. I seated myself to check for height. It was a little high, so I found the lever under the seat on the right side and lowered the chair a couple of inches. *Ah. Just right.* Now to business.

I could have done this part in my sleep, so my mind wandered as I unpacked all of my equipment—laptop, steno machine, tripod, power cords, depo notebook, exhibit stickers, pen, notice, and the realtime cable that would connect the machine to my computer.

* * *

"*Real time?*" I could hear Clarabelle's voice in my head when the unfamiliar word had come up months ago.

"Oh, Shae," she'd said, "that sounds so interesting! What is real time? Is that when something is really *happening* in the deposition, even as you are typing it all down?" She'd fairly bounced with curiosity.

"Writing, Clarabelle," I had corrected gently. "Remember? I told you, we don't *type* on our machines. We *write*."

"I *do* remember now, Shae! And you poke them! I'm catching on, really. Now, what happens in real time?"

"Stroke." She looked confused. "As opposed to *poke*. Each time we press the keys down, it's called a stroke."

Unruffled, she'd waved her hand. "Everyone has their own little way of saying things. Now, you were going to explain. What on earth happens in real time when you are in a deposition?"

"Realtime," I'd explained, "is one word, not two. It's what we call it when our steno strokes travel to the computer via cable or Bluetooth, bounce off our personal dictionary—" Clarabelle looked blank, so I rephrased. "Our steno strokes are read by our personal *database*, and they translate immediately into English."

"I saw you do that once!" Clarabelle had suddenly remembered. "I came to get Herky and you were listening to someone talk, and you were typing on your machine—"

"Writing."

"—and the words were all coming up on your computer screen. I remember! It was so mysterious! Who was talking? I never did ask. I hated to interrupt, of course."

"I was practicing. I do that so I don't get rusty between jobs. Anyway, it's not officially realtime unless the attorneys have a separate device linked to mine, so they can see it too. A lot of my friends have iPads they bring to depositions when attorneys request that additional service." I'd smiled ruefully. "I don't have an iPad yet, but one day I will."

"Oh, Shae, aren't you just the cleverest thing! Wait till I tell Nettie. It's all so smart and foreign!"

By then Clarabelle's attention span had reached its limit, and she'd turned away.

"Herky! Here, boy! Let's go walkies to see Nettie and get the paper. I want to see what Cheeky Peaks has been up to!"

CHAPTER 7
SETTING UP

My grin widened at the remembered conversation with Clarabelle, and as I leaned down to adjust my tripod, a chuckle escaped me. Clarabelle's wide-eyed, innocent fascination about every topic under the sun never failed to cheer me.

"I'd love to hear the joke," said an amused voice, interrupting my happy flashback.

Brought back to reality, my cheeks flamed at the sight of a gorgeous young man standing in the dining room's opposite archway. I'd been bent over my machine, laughing to myself, off in la-la land.

My humiliation doubled when I realized the young man was not alone. His ridiculous good looks could certainly justify my tunnel vision, but when at last I noticed his companion, I couldn't notice anyone else.

Standing next to him, her hand resting on his outstretched arm, was a statuesque woman, tall and striking in an ivory ensemble. She had to have kissed her seventieth birthday goodbye long since, but she was obviously on friendly terms with that fact. Her slim figure was elegant in slacks and lightweight, cream-colored cashmere. Glistening pearls graced her neck, with a smaller, single strand dancing lightly at the wrist near the young man's arm. In her other hand she held a cane embossed in white mother-of-pearl.

At the sound of the young man's voice, she had cocked her well-coifed head, turning sightless eyes in my direction.

The young man guided her forward as my breath caught in my throat. This lovely woman looked to be the same age my grandmother would have been had she lived longer. I felt sure I was truly meeting *Cheeky Peaks* in the flesh.

"Levi Kensington." Her young companion grinned at me. "And this is my grandmother, Aurora Kensington." He turned to the older woman. "Nana, I do believe we've found the court reporter."

I tightened the knob on my tripod and stood, hoping my cheeks had simmered down.

"Shae Rose," I warbled awkwardly as my face reheated. "Pleased to meet you, Levi, Mrs. Kensington."

"Ah! The court reporter." Aurora Kensington's voice was as elegant as the rest of her. Smooth, assured, no nonsense, she seemed to take no notice of my voice's quaver. "Depositions in the house, I ask you. I can't say I didn't see this day coming. Very well, Ms. Rose. I'm told I'm to be your first victim. Direct me to the hot seat, if you will."

"You'll be sitting right next to me, Mrs. Kensington." Slightly better. "Here, on my right."

As Levi began to escort her toward her chair, she patted his arm. "I'll be fine now, Levi. I know this room well."

Levi remained motionless as she released his arm and moved toward me. Her right hand rested lightly on the top of each dining chair, as though she were silently counting them.

"What's this?" Her cane had reached the throw rug that lay over Hawk's extension cord. Aurora had instantly noted the difference in floor elevation and texture and stopped.

"It's a rug Hawk's put on top of an electrical cord, Nana."

"Hawk's a good man," Aurora affirmed to the room at large. "I imagine he didn't want to see Ol' Granny Goose trip on a wire and have a great fall like Humpty Dumpty. Ha!"

Levi laughed as I stared. I was unaccustomed to finding deponents in such good spirits. And how delightful that Aurora Kensington exhibited traits of the fictional but beloved *Cheeky Peaks* in her real life.

"We'll make sure you don't sit on any walls, Nana." Levi had a charming, easy laugh. His manner was utterly unpretentious. He was not an unusually tall man; I guessed his height to be approximately five-eleven. His features were strong but not hard, his air confident, but not arrogant. He wore chinos and a casual, black, short-sleeved Henley.

Like so many men in our resort town, his frame was well-muscled and lean. It was easy to envision him enjoying any number of outdoor activities that Sun Valley offered. Skiing, biking, hiking, snowmobiling…my thoughts trailed off. So many men in Idaho enjoyed hunting. He didn't look like a hunter to me. I couldn't imagine his tousled brown hair squashed beneath a camouflage hat, or his deep blue eyes squinting into a rifle sight.

Stop staring, Shae. I turned my attention back to my equipment just as another slim figure entered the room.

"Ah, Amy," said Levi, "this is Shae Rose, our court reporter for these dismal proceedings. She's already brightened things up a bit." His eyes focused on me. "Shae, my elder sister, Amy Kensington."

Is there no end to the beauty found in this house?

Amy Kensington was easily as tall as her brother and equally athletic. Youthful strength oozed from her sinewy frame, and I imagined hundred-mile bike rides, yoga, Zumba classes, and of course, skiing. Lots and lots of skiing. Her shoulder-length, light brown hair was glossy, her cheeks chiseled, her skin translucent. She was a vision in designer jeans, navy tank top, and a carelessly draped silk scarf.

I felt frumpy in my stretchy black work pants and nylon blouse. At least I'd had my nails done recently. I raised my hand in greeting.

"Hi, I'm Shae."

"Amy." Her voice sparkled. I hoped there weren't more like her. I was going to get a complex. "I see you've met Nana. She runs the show around here."

"Hardly," Aurora murmured drily. "If I ran the show, we certainly wouldn't be embroiled in a legal battle."

"It'll be over in no time, Nana." Amy touched Aurora's elbow lightly. "I've got your chair pulled out for you. Just here. Let's get you settled before Dalton and his dreadful attor—"

Amy glanced at me and grinned. "Sorry." She didn't sound sorry. "I know you don't pick sides in these things, but that attorney has been hounding poor Nana to death with interrogatories and document production requirements. Honestly, Levi," she said, squaring her lovely shoulders, "Dalton is the one who brought this awful lawsuit. I can't think of any reason why *we* have been required to spend so much time dealing with it."

I was struggling to keep up. It's difficult in large cases to meet and remember multiple parties all at once. I mentally reviewed the names of the four people I'd already met so I could cement them in my brain. Hawk, who worked on the estate. He was not a party to the lawsuit, but I knew I'd be seeing more of him. Then there were the Kensingtons—the very stately Aurora and her grandchildren, Levi and Amy. I wrote their names in my book. They were the defendants in the lawsuit and clearly not happy about it.

But who was Dalton? I looked at my notice again. Ah. Dalton Lockwood and his son Spencer were the plaintiffs. They were suing the Kensingtons, and they weren't here yet. I carefully wrote their names in my book as well.

"There's no 'poor Nana' element here, Amy, and you well know it," said Aurora. She drew herself up grandly, but Amy's grin only widened. "And there's no need to 'get me settled.' I'm old, but I'm hardly feeble. Plunk me in my chair, and we'll see what's what. And I know what you're up to, my dear." Her tone softened. "You'd like to make me angry at this whole business so I'll be firmer in the deposition. Well, I am sure I shall be quite firm, indeed. It's a pity I need to be. This is family business. It's beyond my most infinite cognition how Dalton thought he could bully us this way."

"Are Dalton and Spencer Lockwood related to you?" I wasn't just curious. It always helped to know where everyone fit.

"Yes, Ms. Rose." Aurora patted Amy's hand where it rested on her elbow. "Dalton is my younger brother, and Spencer is his son. His late-in-life son. Spencer is of a similar age to Amy and Levi."

Amy guided Aurora slightly forward so she could determine her chair's position and lower herself into it.

I opened my laptop and set my steno machine on its tripod.

"I do have another brother," Aurora continued conversationally, "named Otto. He's the eldest. He's been away. At times like these I do miss him." She turned her face to me. "But then, if Otto were here, you would not be, Ms. Rose. There would be no lawsuit."

"Yes, I think I saw something on the notice about—"

"Otto being dead?"

"Y–y–yes." I wasn't sure where this conversation was heading.

"That's certainly what my younger brother, Dalton, is trying to prove." She lifted her chin slightly. "But I don't believe it. We've never been contacted with any bad news about Otto. I believe he's immersed himself in some reclusive Amazonian tribe and is doing good work among them."

"We're here, Shae," Amy said, picking up the story, "because my Great Uncle Dalton wants to have his and Nana's brother Otto *declared* dead." Her tone sounded disgusted. "He has no proof, and we're fighting him on this. Like she said, Nana believes Uncle Otto is still alive."

"But who is right?" Levi shrugged. "You'll hear all this anyway, Shae, so you may as well know. This case is about my Great Uncle Otto, who I've never had the privilege of meeting, and the fact that he's been missing for over forty years."

A chill traveled up my spine and my skin tingled with goosebumps as I thought through the implications. We were going to spend entire days together, days where people would either be discussing a dead man as though he were still alive or talking about a living man as though he were dead.

Court reporters hear an awful lot, and throughout my career I'd heard many things I wished I could erase from my memory. But never, in eleven years of reporting, had I sat in a room where half the parties hoped another human being was alive, while the other half were trying to prove that he no longer drew breath. And because depositions are only a *portion* of the litigation process, I might not hear the outcome of the case.

What if, after hearing all the depositions, I never learned what happened to Otto Lockwood? I took in each face gathered thus far around the table, and decided then and there that I couldn't let that happen.

CHAPTER 8

DEPOSITION OF AURORA KENSINGTON

Aurora's deposition was scheduled to begin at 9:00 a.m.

At eight forty-five, Attorney Coop Rickman breezed through the archway from the kitchen, clearly at home here. He made his way to his clients' side of the table with a handshake for Levi and a warm peck on the cheek for both Amy and her grandmother. I knew him well and didn't ask him for a business card. He pulled one out for me all the same, and I returned the favor.

I'd met Dominic Flynn at the "stipulation," last week, and when I heard his voice added to others approaching the dining room, I plucked out another business card. I needn't have bothered. Mr. Flynn cruised right by with nary a glance in my direction. A dour-faced man followed close on his heels, and he took his lead from his attorney. I could see a strong resemblance to Aurora in this man's face, but where her face exuded good-natured strength, his face had sagged into a permanent petulance.

This could only be Dalton Lockwood, plaintiff, who had brought suit against his sister Aurora and her grandchildren. I knew Kensington to be Aurora's *married* name. It was all starting to make sense. Dalton and Aurora were siblings in their seventies. Dalton was suing Aurora because she wouldn't agree to have their eldest brother Otto declared dead. I added a brief form to this job's particular dictionary. D * D, for "declared dead." If the term came up I could now tap it instantly and it would translate appropriately.

The last to join us was a thin man with sand-colored hair who I judged to be about my age. I'd never met him, but his expression seemed wary to me as he slouched quietly in through the archway from the living room. He made his way to a chair that sat in the back corner of the room beneath a large hanging fern. I glanced at my notes. This could be Spencer Lockwood, co-plaintiff with his father, Dalton. I was about to ask, but Levi made my query unnecessary.

"Hey, Spencer," he said.

Spencer raised a hand in greeting but said nothing.

That was it, but that was enough. I checked off Spencer's name in my notebook. My transcripts must reflect every person present in a deposition, so I needed to take good notes. So far this job had been easy, because everyone who was present was also a named party. That meant their names were on my notice. Why did that matter? Spellings. Court reporters obsess over spellings. Knowing who he was and how to spell his name made me happy.

After greeting Spencer, Levi stood and walked toward me, taking care not to jostle his grandmother as he passed her chair.

"So, Shae," he said, gesturing to all of my equipment, "how's it work?"

Nice. I like it when someone takes an interest. "It's shorthand."

Levi eyed my steno keyboard closely, his eyes fairly dancing. "You gotta give me more than that. I've always been so curious. You always see the court reporter in movies and stuff. Sometimes their fingers barely move, and I'm baffled. Are they really taking every word down?"

"Most of them are actors who don't know how it works."

"Wow!" I could literally *see* the wheels churning in his brain.

"That explains it! So tell me something. Why have a laptop if you're taking it down on the – your – "

"Writer."

"Writer. Cool. What's the laptop for?"

I placed my hands on my steno keys, and Levi immediately saw his name, Levi Kensington, appear on my laptop screen.

"Hey! How'd you do that?"

"My machine is linked to the laptop. My software reads my steno outlines and translates them into English on the laptop screen."

"Okay." Levi grew more animated by the minute. "So write what I'm saying now."

It was already written.

"This is *awesome*. So you buy software that has all this stuff already on it?"

"It's pretty incredible software." I grinned at his enthusiasm. "But each court reporter is responsible for his or her own personal dictionary. I created each entry in my dictionary from word one. I've told my software how I write every word, every prefix, every suffix, every number.

"And my name, Levi, was already programed in?"

"No, but it is now. I made a special dictionary for this job. I included all of your names and made them short, easy to write. When we make a short form, we call it a brief. I have a bunch of briefs for this job."

"What's the brief for Levi?"

"L, long E with an asterisk, F."

"F? Levi has a V in it."

"Steno has no final V," I explained, enjoying myself. "The final F does double duty. It's a V when that's what we need it to be."

"And why did you put an asterisk?"

"Because L long E F spells leaf. Think about it. Leef. It's all phonetic. I put in the asterisk to differentiate it from leaf."

Levi's eyes had started to glaze over when I'd mentioned the long E, and my explanations about the final F and the asterisk had sealed the deal. It happened sooner or later with every interested person, and Levi had hung in there longer than most. I was about to give him an excuse to exit the explanations when he voiced a final question.

"Soooo, I have to ask." I looked up and caught him searching for the right words. "With all the voice recognition software and everything these days, I mean, could any of that ever replace you?"

A grin split my face. I got that question a lot. "Nope. Court reporters are in higher demand than ever. In fact, there's a shortage."

"Really?" I could tell my answer pleased him. "Why is there a shortage?"

"Because people have the same question you had, about voice recognition, or even digital recordings. But a machine can't decipher a heavy foreign accent or ask someone to repeat themselves if a slamming door drowns out the answer."

"That's really cool, Shae. Thanks for explaining."

"Sure," I grinned again. "I was about to create some more briefs for this job, Levi. More about the machine later?"

"Okay. I'd better get back to my seat." He made his way back, sat down, and began telling Amy how his name had magically appeared on my screen.

I turned back to the task at hand, but there would be no time for more briefs. Though it wasn't yet nine o'clock, Mr. Flynn cleared his throat.

"Looks like everybody's here," he said with a clipped tone. "So, Madam Court Reporter, go ahead and swear in the witness, and let's get started."

He grabbed one of my business cards from the table and studiously began peeling the back off of it.

I looked at Aurora Kensington. "Will you raise your right hand for me, please?"

Turning in my direction, she complied. I lifted my right hand as well.

"Do you solemnly swear or affirm that your testimony today shall be the truth, the whole truth, and nothing but the truth?"

"I do," she said, then nodded firmly and lowered her hand.

I poised my hands above my keys and began to write.

AURORA KENSINGTON,

First duly sworn to tell the truth relating to said cause, testified as follows:

EXAMINATION

QUESTIONS BY MR. FLYNN:

Q. Mrs. Kensington, my name is Dominic Flynn, and I represent Dalton and Spencer Lockwood in a lawsuit they've filed against you. Do you understand that?

A. I do.

Q. How would you prefer I address you today? Aurora? Mrs. Kensington?

A. Mrs. Kensington will do nicely.

Q. Very well. Mrs. Kensington, where were you born?

A. Helena, Montana.

Q. Beautiful area. And what is your date of birth?

A. Saturday, July 4, 1942.

Q. I find it striking that you should mention that it was a Saturday. Can you tell me why the day of the week is significant to you?

A. It was the Fourth of July, of course. My birth interrupted a barbeque, such as it was, being war time. My mother never forgot, and it became one of those childhood stories that sticks, if you will.

Q. I see. So, today you are seventy-four years old, if my math is correct.

A. Your math is correct. And I've seen more than my share of fireworks since that time, I'm sure.

Q. Yes. And your father was a bit of a newspaper tycoon, was he not? Myron Lockwood?

A. Oh, he'd certainly be pleased with your description, Mr. Flynn. Father did well in the newspaper business, yes.

Q. Well, Mrs. Kensington, let's not mince words. Your father did very well in the newspaper business. I'm told he founded and owned newspapers in no fewer than ten cities.

A. That's true, and I won't downplay his success. Frankly, several of those "cities" were towns, but let's not quibble. The word "tycoon" amused me, but he did very well indeed. He'd have enjoyed your terminology.

Q. As you know, Mrs. Kensington, we're here today to discuss that very newspaper business, along with its considerable subsidiary assets.

A. I am all too aware of what gathers us together today.

Q. When your father died, Mrs. Kensington, were you able to locate a copy of his will?

A. I was not. We knew father's wishes, of course. Otto, being the eldest, was the most familiar with how Father wanted things arranged. He told us Father's wishes shortly after Father's death. Well, he gave us the broad strokes. As to the finer details, I'm afraid all Otto ever said was, 'You know how Father liked to keep everything in his head.'

    Q. Mrs. Kensington, if your father had in fact prepared a will, do you know the name of the attorney whose services he would have engaged?

    A. Tut, tut, Mr. Flynn. Has Dalton not told you? Father abhorred attorneys. I'm afraid he lumped the lot of you in with door-to-door insurance salesmen.

    Q. So then, if your father had left a will, and considering his aversion to those in my humble profession, do you think he would have drawn it up himself, perhaps?

    A. No, I'm afraid not. For a newspaper man, Father was terrible with his own paperwork. He would have asked Otto to draw it up or type it out. Whatever the terminology is.

    Q. And by what means would Otto have produced such a document, if indeed one existed?

    A. He'd have typed it up, of course, as he did with all of Father's necessary paperwork. His own paperwork too, for that matter.

At this point, Mr. Flynn reached for a small stack of papers. He looked briefly in my direction. The normal course would be for him to hand me a document, and I would put an exhibit sticker on it. It would be marked and admitted as a deposition exhibit. The document would then be handed to the deponent, who would be asked questions about it. Had Mr. Flynn ever encountered a blind witness before? He seemed a bit lost.

    He leaned over and held a whispered consultation with Dalton, his client. I was under no obligation to write their conversation down, for the simple reason that I couldn't *hear* it. The conversation lasted for more than a few seconds though, so at last I was compelled to add a parenthetical into the transcript.

                (Inaudible Conversation.)

I didn't write who was having the conversation. I didn't say how long it lasted or that I could hear every sixth word. The conversation as a whole was inaudible to me. If Coop didn't like their whispers while we were on the record, he could certainly do something about —

I scrambled to my keys.

         MR. RICKMAN: Dom, if you need a break, take a break. I'm tired of trying to not overhear your consultation over there.

         MR. FLYNN: We're ready to continue.

BY MR. FLYNN:

    Q. Are your ready to continue, Mrs. Kensington?

    A. I am. I should think these interruptions will only prolong the day.

Mr. Flynn shot a last worried glance in Dalton's direction, but Dalton waved his hand as if to say, "Just get on with it." Mr. Flynn then handed me a document, perhaps three sheets thick and stapled together.

         MR. FLYNN: Madam Reporter, will you please mark this as Exhibit B?

My thoughts flew to Exhibit A, sitting outside in my car. No one had asked to see it yet. I wrote a "B" on a blue sticker and placed it in the bottom right corner of the document. Three strokes on my steno machine inserted a parenthetical neatly into the transcript:

>(Exhibit No. B Marked.)
>
>BY MR. FLYNN:
>
>Q. Mrs. Kensington, I'm handing you a document that I will represent to you to be the Last Will & Testament of Myron P. Lockwood. I will likewise hand you –

He handed me another document, and I scrambled to mark it and return my hands to my keys.

>(Exhibit No. C Marked.)
>
>BY MR. FLYNN:
>
>Q. – a second document, which has been marked as Exhibit C. I will represent this to be the Last Will & Testament of Otto F. Lockwood. I know, Mrs. Kensington, that your granddaughter, Amy, is seated next to you. Perhaps she can be of assistance to you in examining these documents. When you have identified them, I will ask if you are familiar with them.

Aurora lifted the documents, one at a time, and fanned them carefully in front of her. She held them near her face, each in turn, as if her dull eyes could somehow see the small print from close proximity. At last she laid them on the table and faced Mr. Flynn, shoulders squared.

A. Mr. Flynn, I shall not require Amy's assistance to assure you that, beyond any doubt whatsoever, these documents are false. I am familiar with what they purport to be, but that is quite impossible. They are not documents that were prepared by my brother Otto.

Mr. Flynn paused for a moment, seeming to gather his thoughts. Aurora hadn't run her hands over the documents, seeking lumps or bumps or indentations. All the same she, completely blind and seeking no outside input, had decried the documents as false. By his expression, Mr. Flynn didn't believe her, but was struggling with some inner turmoil. I decided that he didn't want to be too brusque in his questioning of an elderly blind lady, and that he was holding his blunt New York personality in check.

Aurora gazed serenely into space while Mr. Flynn pursed his lips.

Q. I will represent to you, Mrs. Kensington, that your other brother, Dalton, provided me with these documents, and he assured me of their authenticity.

(I hate that word, *authenticity*. Too many syllables. I wrote a note to myself in the transcript to find a brief for it. I'd delete the note later.) Aurora was answering.

A. I should think every person in this room knows that I dispute my dear brother's so-called evidence. If I agreed with him, that these documents were indeed Father's and Otto's long-lost wills, we wouldn't be here today.

Aurora lifted her chin slightly, and Amy's lips curved into a secretive smile.

Q. Mrs. Kensington, has Dalton explained to you how he came to be in possession of these documents?

A. Yes. Some drivel about cleaning out a cupboard in the winter house. I'm sorry, Mr. Flynn, but it's quite far-fetched. Dalton's never cleaned a cupboard in his life.

Q. Let's say, hypothetically, that this one time Dalton did clean out a cupboard, because he was desperate to find his father's final documents. Wouldn't that be plausible, Mrs. Kensington? I mean, surely you can see –

A. I can't see anything, young man.

(*Choke!*)

Q. And I meant no disrespect, Mrs. Kensington. But perhaps we can agree that Dalton was highly motivated. Let's be frank, ma'am. Your brother, Otto, has been missing for more than forty years –

A. And now we come to the crux of it. Dearest Dalton wishes to have Otto declared dead.

(D * D—declared dead. I remembered just in time to use it.)

Q. There's no question pending, Mrs. –

A. He hopes that, with a death certificate, obtained by legal if not physical means, he can enforce the terms of these fallacious documents you've handed me. Well, not while there's breath in my body.

You can't declare a man dead who is quite alive. A man who wrote to me, in care of my Cheeky Peaks column, not more than five years ago.

Dalton's hand slammed down on the table, his face purpling. *Uh-oh.* He was about to talk. So inconvenient when people talk when they aren't supposed to. I have to write every word said in a deposition, and I didn't have a speaker I.D. set up for Dalton. I scrambled to identify him now as DA*LT. I'd worry about a proper dictionary entry later. He was already talking. I had to catch up.

  DA*LT: Now look here, Aurora, I'm not going to sit and listen to some fairy tale you and Amy cooked –

  THE WITNESS (Aurora): You'll leave Amy right out of this, Dalton.

Aurora rose to her feet, regal, bristling.
I'd caught every word and sat at rigid attention, waiting to see who would speak next. The attorneys knew their attempts to regain control of the proceedings would also be on the record. Coop caught my eye.

  MR. RICKMAN: Off the record.

Everyone stood up and began talking at once.
My mind was racing. So Otto *wasn't* missing? He'd communicated five years ago and then disappeared again? *Why?*
Dalton pounded his fist on the table again, furious at this turn of events. I overheard him speaking with Dominic Flynn in not-so-hushed tones. "She's been torturing this story to death for the last five years, Dom! She never showed *me* that letter. No. I've let it go on this long, but no more. I've got the law on my side…" Dalton's voice faded out of earshot as Mr. Flynn rushed him from the room.
And then the juicy part. Otto had written in care of *Cheeky Peaks*? Did something in the greater family dynamic concern

him such that he hadn't just sent his letter directly to Aurora? This case was becoming more intriguing by the moment, and now my ears were burning. I was fascinated.

Also, how could Aurora be so sure the exhibits were false? She couldn't see them. Had Otto said something when he'd written five years ago?

Amy stood and helped her grandmother out of the dining room. Coop was leading them to another place so they could confer in private. I sat down at my computer and added DA*LT to my job dictionary. Now if he spoke it would look like:

DALTON LOCKWOOD: Blah, blah, blah, et cetera.

Normally I would call him MR. LOCKWOOD, but there was another Mr. Lockwood in the room—Spencer. If he, too, decided to say something on the record, I needed to avoid confusion.

That done, I sat back in my comfy chair. No guessing how long this break would be. No one had officially called for a "break," so I just had to wait. When tempers flare in depositions, my wait can be one minute or half the day.

CHAPTER 9

COFFEE AND AN IPAD

"Do you like coffee?" whispered a conspiratorial voice.

I turned slightly. Levi was leaning against the broad doorway through which I'd entered the room. I hadn't noticed that he was still there.

Coffee sounded good, so I didn't get a well-mannered, "Oh, I'm fine, thank you," out of my mouth before he was motioning to me. I stood and followed him in the direction of the lovely nook.

"Coop says you're not to appear biased toward one side or the other, so I can't sit and have coffee with you," he said, smiling. Oh, lord, a dimple in his left cheek, and he seemed to be about my age…

He's too young for you, Shae. He's too RICH for you, Shae!

"But there's no reason you can't enjoy yourself during breaks. Pick your poison." A gesture took in the assorted drink options, the single-cup brewer, and the place settings. *Clarabelle would love those mugs.* "As you can see, we've got coffees of varying flavors. We've got tea, Chai, Chai Latte, hot chocolate. Lots to choose from."

I felt suddenly bashful at the thought of sitting there alone, hot drink in hand as I stared silently at the gleaming kitchen. I also didn't want to carry a coffee back into the spotless dining room, so I finally opened my mouth to decline his kind invitation.

But Levi wasn't finished. Leaning in with a grin, he said, "You probably don't want to get wrapped up in a book since you don't know when we'll be resuming."

I raised my eyebrows. "You've done this before."

His laugh was quick and easy. "No, but hopefully I have some common sense." He pulled open a drawer tucked beneath the nook's table. Withdrawing an iPad, he asked, "Have you ever played The Vessel?"

Who has spare iPads lying around? I don't even own one.

"No, I don't think I've ever played a game on an iPad."

"Well, here you go, then. Fair warning – it's addicting." He tapped on the app's icon and a welcome screen opened up. "Just enter a user name and you can play during all the breaks if you like." He passed me the iPad. "I'll just go and find Nana and Amy now. Be sure you make yourself a drink."

He was off, and I was intrigued. I chose a nice vanilla latte, started the brewer, and sat down to explore the game.

* * *

Forty-five minutes later found me completely engrossed in The Vessel. My coffee long finished, I'd kicked off my shoes and curled up on the cushioned bench, feet tucked beneath me. Brow puckered, I turned the iPad this way and that. I found that here, just *here*, if I zoomed in…*ah! Yes!* Objects found their place, codes revealed their secrets. I learned how to use the game's bionic abilities to see invisible objects and to lift heavy items. Soon my vessel was nearly seaworthy. I just needed to find the navigation equipment…

"Shae, how many times do I have to say your name to get your attention?" I heard Coop ask.

I looked up sheepishly. "Give a girl an iPad…"

Coop laughed out loud. "Glad you found something to do. Our schedule may be a little unreliable throughout these depos. Come on in, we're ready to get back to it."

I followed him back through the doorway and took my seat. The parties had reassembled and were waiting only for me. I'd have to try not to become so absorbed when I resumed The Vessel later.

I hovered my hands over my steno keys and nodded to Mr. Flynn. With a curt nod back at me, he picked up his questioning again.

BY MR. FLYNN:

Q. Mrs. Kensington, are you ready to continue?

A. Indeed, I am.

Q. Very good. I want to return to the subject of the authenticity of Exhibits B and C. I noted that when I handed you the documents, you were quite sure that they are not the final documents of your father, Myron, and your brother, Otto. I am going to re-hand you what we've marked as Exhibit B, and I will represent to you that the title of this document states that it is the Last Will & Testament of Myron P. Lockwood. I would ask that you take another look – that you re-examine the document. After you do that, I'll ask you whether or not you still believe that it is not real.

Aurora graciously accepted the stapled pages from Mr. Flynn. Again, she fanned the pages in front of her, and held them closely to her face. Then she set them down.

A. Mr. Flynn, these documents are not my father's.

Q. Forgive me, Mrs. Kensington. I must ask a difficult question. Are you able to see, Mrs. Kensington?

A. I am not.

Q. How long have you been unable to see, Mrs. Kensington?

A. It came on gradually, Mr. Flynn, but to your question, I lost all vision perhaps ten years ago.

Q. Are you able to tell me the cause of that, Mrs. Kensington?

A. I am not. I saw doctors, of course, but I'm afraid they lost me at "congenital." One doctor told me my condition was "present at birth," and that I should be thankful I had many good, full-sighted years tucked away before the full onslaught of my defect took hold.

Q. Your courage is admirable.

I looked up. I doubted whether Mr. Flynn admired this lady one bit. Nice of him to say it, I supposed.

However, Mrs. Kensington, the fact that you can't see the documents raises the following question. How can you identify that the documents are not real?

A. Simple, Mr. Flynn, and the answer is the same for both Exhibits B and C. My brother, Otto, had a particular fondness for a very thick vellum paper. He'd never have trusted an important document to paper as flimsy as the sheets you handed me. Additionally, Otto had a cedar box that he kept his writing paper in. He loves trees, my Otto.

He loves to be outdoors. When he absolutely had to be in the house doing paperwork, he made sure that he brought some of the outdoors in with him. Thus, his cedar box.

Because Otto didn't really type that many documents, his supply of paper always lasted quite a long time. When he finally used a sheet of paper, the smell of cedar was noticeable. I have fanned these documents. I have held them to my nose. There isn't the faintest trace of cedar clinging to them. They are not Otto's papers. And because Otto handled that sort of thing for Father, and would have used his paper for Father's affairs as well, I can say that they are not Father's papers, either.

Q. Mrs. Kensington, do you really expect us to believe that your nose can ferret out the authenticity of a document some forty years after its drafting?

A. That is precisely what I'm telling you, Mr. Flynn.

Mr. Flynn reached over and slid the documents back to his side of the table. He raised the pages up to his nose and sniffed. He sniffed every page of both documents. Coop had opened his mouth as though he wanted to object to the last question, but instead he waited while the sniffing commenced and Mr. Flynn resumed.

Q. Mrs. Kensington, were you present when your brother, Otto, created a will for your father?

A. You know that I was not.

Q. So you really have no way of knowing what type of paper he did or did not use.

A. Only in that I know my brother.

Q. Ma'am, I've now smelled the documents for myself. I will admit to you that they do not smell like cedar. They do, however, smell like storage. Will you agree with me that papers that have been stored in a forgotten cupboard can lose their, um, fragrance, and pick up an ordinary mustiness?

A. There lies your problem, Mr. Flynn. I know some people think of Otto as forgetful and careless. I assure you, nothing could be further from the truth. He would never have hidden important documents away in a forgotten cupboard. I will not change my mind. These documents are not real.

I do not smell cedar, Mr. Flynn, but I certainly do smell a rat.

CHAPTER 10

LUNCH, DAY 1

"Lunch hour" are two words that freelance court reporters hear all too infrequently. I carry granola bars, trail mix, and water everywhere I go. If I'm feeling particularly ambitious, I may even use a thermal lunch sack and carry a salad or a sandwich with me. Even those go to waste, often as not, when everyone in a deposition agrees to "push through lunch" and get the thing done.

Today, I'd been in a hurry because I thought I'd have trouble finding the estate, so I'd thrown a hard-boiled egg and some carrot sticks in my lunch sack and hoped the day wouldn't go long.

I was greatly surprised, therefore, when Hawk reappeared as everyone stood and agreed to take an hour for lunch.

"Lunch is available down at my place for anyone who's hungry."

"Sounds wonderful, Hawk," Amy said, "but we can't. We're meeting with Coop over the lunch hour. Jenkins is bringing us some sandwiches."

Hawk nodded agreeably to her and looked at Dalton, but that gentleman was already pulling his attorney from the room, whispering fiercely into Mr. Flynn's ear. Spencer had melted away without my even noticing it. Suddenly, I was alone in the room with Hawk, and he raised an inquiring brow.

"Hungry, Ms. Rose?"

"Shae," I said. "And I don't want to be any trouble…"

"Only trouble will be if no one comes to eat." His tone was friendly, humorous. "Got a nice spread set out. Right this way."

Normally, I would have felt awkward following a new acquaintance to lunch in the middle of a deposition, but Hawk's manner was so relaxed, so easy, that I told myself to unwind and enjoy an entire hour off. I followed him past the nook, through the kitchen and back out the mudroom door. We descended the steps and made our way down to the residence nearest the trees, where the road opened onto the estate's gardened property.

As we drew nearer I again admired the wide veranda that encircled – I could see now – the entire cabin. For that's what it was, really. A lovely cabin, as opposed to anything one might accidentally call a "house." I stepped onto the deck and saw that it truly was a shame no one else had been able to come. A scrumptious feast was set out upon warm-colored, solid, handmade tables. The thick wooden chairs shone and looked almost *soft*, though they held no cushions.

"Help yourself, Shae. Don't be shy." He removed his hat and gestured with it up to the main house. "Since none of them could come, I'll join you myself. I don't get many visitors. You're a welcome sight, young lady. Plates are down at the end."

My stomach rumbled and I laughed, grabbing a plate. "Hawk," I said, eyeing all the food, "you have *no* idea how rare this is. What a treat!"

Hawk beamed and blushed all at once, and he watched me as I surveyed the entire table. He'd provided chicken salad, with nuts in a side bowl, probably in case anyone was allergic. Further along sat a mouthwatering spinach, bacon, and egg salad that still looked warm. Next to that was a plate filled with grilled zucchini and summer squash, with glazed, grilled carrot slices arranged prettily throughout. Fresh pumpkin bread, regular bread, and a huge bowl of fresh fruit completed the spread. Hawk had made plenty for everyone.

I grinned at him and dished up helpings of everything. Hawk followed suit and filled a plate, and we each chose seats facing outward toward the grounds. Before he seated himself, Hawk poured large glasses of ice-cold lemonade for each of us from a chilled pitcher. I stared at my plate, hardly knowing what to try first. I finally stabbed a glazed carrot slice and closed my eyes, in heaven.

The food was all delicious, and as we ate, Hawk eased us into some light chit-chat. I found him comfortable to be around.

"So, Shae," he began, digging into his chicken salad, "how long you been doin' this?"

"Court reporting?"

"Yeah."

"Eleven years. Hard to believe it."

A relaxed half hour ensued as he asked about my profession. What had made me choose it? How long did school take? Did I ever work in court?

I queried him as well and learned that he'd been working on this estate for over fifty years. He'd been hired on by Myron Lockwood in 1965, and Dalton had all but begged him to stay after his father's passing and Otto's disappearance. Hawk had agreed, largely because he hoped Otto would return, and also because he felt heartsick for Aurora. She'd lost her father and her brother within a week of each other.

My curiosity ramped up as I realized there had to be more to the story. Had Hawk not *wanted* to work for Dalton? Questions clamored for attention in my head, but since we were dangerously close to talking about issues associated with the case, I silenced them.

He leaned back and stuck a toothpick in his mouth. "Eleven years as a court reporter, eh? Don't seem possible. Thought you were about twenty-five when I first saw you."

"I'd say you can keep thinking that, and thank you, but I don't think I want to be twenty-five again."

"Never heard a gal say she don't mind getting older."

"I never said that, *sir*." He threw me a sidelong glance at the "sir." Half playfully, half seriously, I continued. "I only said I didn't think I'd want to be twenty-five again."

"Something bad happen when you were twenty-five, Shae?"

Hawk was peaceful to talk to, as well as pleasant to be around. I rarely opened up to people, especially *new* people, but his manner was irresistible.

"My parents died when I was twenty-five," I said simply.

He grew very still. "I'm so sorry, Shae. I oughtn't to have pried."

An all-too-familiar lump threatened to rise in my throat, and I deliberately imagined twelve frolicking kittens on the grass before me. The lump receded, just enough. This was not the time for a visit with grief.

"It's okay, Hawk." I took a deep breath. "They were doing what they loved. I was grown, and they traveled as often as they could. They were in a bus accident in Patagonia, believe it or not." Another breath. "And now I live with two ladies who treat me like their own daughter."

He looked worried, so I held out my glass for more lemonade and changed the subject.

"Hawk, this furniture is gorgeous. I've never seen anything like it."

A shy, pleased smile crept over his face. "My daddy taught me how to work with wood when I was no higher than his knee."

"*You* made all of this?" I ran my hands over the warm, smooth arms of my chair, astonished.

"Yep. Glad you like it."

"I *love* it! And the little sign by the highway?"

"Made that last week, and them flower boxes. Otherwise, picking out where to turn in can be tricky."

"Last *week*?" A thought struck me. "Hawk, did you make them so we could all find the drive for these depositions?"

"Well, now," he drawled, looking back out over the grounds, "maybe not so much as *all* find the drive. Family lives here. Attorneys have been here plenty."

Surely my jaw was gaping by now.

"Hawk," my voice a whisper, "you surely didn't make a sign and build flower boxes and fill them with white roses just for *my* sake…"

"Seemed like the hospitable thing to do. Coop said you were real nice, and he asked if I could do something to mark the entrance to the place."

"And you chose roses." My words were barely audible, even to me.

"'Course." He chomped his toothpick and cast a bashful glance in my direction. "See, Coop also told me your name."

CHAPTER 11
AURORA PART 2

My name. Hawk had chosen roses because of my name, Shae *Rose*. His weathered appearance nearly masked the creativity and kindness that defined the man beneath. Nearly, but not quite. One had but to look into his eyes to see the twinkle there.

I trailed slowly back up to the main house after lunch, still marveling at all of his thoughtful efforts. He'd carried my equipment, provided a special chair and electricity, hosted a wonderful lunch – and before any of that, before he'd even met me, he'd built pretty wooden planters and placed roses in them, in keeping with my name. I had never met anyone like him, and I savored the memory of a very nice hour that had, I thought, created a new friendship.

As I walked along, I enjoyed the crunching of the warm gravel beneath my feet. Driving in this morning, I'd been focused only on finding the house. Now, however, I was delighted to find more evidence of Hawk's handiwork. Hand-carved flower boxes, much like the ones at the road, lined the drive. Benches, each as intricately designed as the one that graced the main house's mudroom, offered places to rest and enjoy the estate's beauty. Even the handrail leading up the steps to that same mudroom was a masterpiece of knobby, lacquered wood with smooth, rounded edges that made for a sure grip. Details that I'd overlooked that morning now stood in beautiful clarity. Hawk's touch was everywhere.

Upon entering the dining room, I found that almost everyone was present. Aurora looked as confident and serene as she had this morning, and she smoothed her sweater as she seated herself. I took my place at the head of the table just as Spencer snuck through the archway and resumed his seat. I'd yet to hear him say a word.

Dominic Flynn adjusted his tie and sat down, one eyebrow raised at me. I nodded, fingers poised above my keys, ready to begin.

BY MR. FLYNN:

Q. Mrs. Kensington, do you understand you're still under oath?

A. I do.

Q. I neglected to ask earlier. Do you have children?

A. Yes. I have one daughter.

Q. And her name and age, please?

A. Lorelai Kensington, and she is fifty-four years old.

Q. I know, Mrs. Kensington, that your grandchildren live with you. Is Lorelai their mother?

A. Of course.

Q. And what is their father's name?

A. I believe Lorelai called him Jimmy. I'm afraid that's the extent of my knowledge. She left with him without my permission.

Q. When did that happen?

A. In 1980. Lorelai was just eighteen years old.

Q. Do you know if she and Jimmy are still a couple?

A. I do not.

Q. Do you know of any way we can get in touch with her?

A. I do not. I believe Levi and Amy have had some correspondence from her over the years, but I have no knowledge about from where it was posted.

Q. Very good, madam. I'll leave that subject alone for now and switch gears, if I may. I understand, Mrs. Kensington, that the valley has you to thank for the Cheeky Peaks column in the Valley Scribe.

A. Very kindly put, Mr. Flynn. Yes, I manage that column with the help of my granddaughter, Amy.

Q. And what are your respective roles in that effort, Mrs. Kensington?

A. Amy opens and organizes the mail, and I respond to as many letters as I can.

Q. Does she read them and only provide particular pieces of correspondence to you?

A. No indeed. She sorts them by topic, and then she reads every one of them aloud to me. She then takes down my replies and submits everything to the paper's editor.

Q. Cheeky Peaks is an unusual name for an advice column.

A. Thank you.

Q. If I might, may I ask how you came up with it?

A. I thought it sounded better than Audacious Mountaintops.

Levi snorted, and Mr. Flynn's lips twitched. I stared, wondering if I'd catch him in a smile, but he controlled himself quickly.

    Q. Let's return to the subject of your father, Mrs. Kensington. Did he approve of an advice column finding its way into his publication?

    A. Not at first, Mr. Flynn. His favor grew in equal measure with the valley's reception of it.

    Q. And what did you perceive the valley's reception to be?

    A. Tolerant at first, then warm, and eventually quite enthusiastic.

    Q. Mrs. Kensington, did your brother, Otto, ever talk to you about the will your father asked him to create?

    A. Never once.

    Q. Did you believe, at the time of your father's accident, that they had failed to complete a will at all?

    A. I did believe that, sir, because we searched and found nothing.

    Q. I'm sorry if this is painful to revisit, Mrs. Kensington, but I have to ask for some details about your father's accident. Can you tell me where you were at the time, ma'am?

    A. I was here in the main house, going over some details of the upcoming edition…

    Q. With whom were you going over the details?

    A. Pardon? Oh, with Dalton, of course. Do you know, Father's fall was so violent that they found his dentures right across the room… He didn't just tumble down the stairs, they said. They believed he tripped on the rug at the

top landing and was...launched...clear to the bottom....
Forgive me. This is very difficult to talk about.

I looked up. Aurora was struggling to remain composed. I remained very still, fingers poised. My own father had died in an accident, and my heart surged with empathy. I knew all too well that time didn't heal wounds this deep. Speaking about them brings sleeping wounds awake, where their pain can be felt afresh.

Mr. Flynn paused long enough for Amy to press a tissue into her grandmother's hand, and then continued.

> Q. And the fall happened in the winter house?
>
> A. Yes, yes. The winter house. We never heard a thing. He – he broke his neck, you see. But for one undoubtedly terrifying moment, he didn't suffer...
>
> Q. Would you like a break, Mrs. Kensington?
>
> A. Yes, I believe I would.
>
> (A break was taken.)

I sat quietly while the parties rose as one and left the room. Depositions have surely got to top the list of things that trigger a person's grief – even forty-year-old grief. If Aurora needed a moment to gather herself, it was quite understandable.

Alone in the room, I scrolled through my transcript, tidying things up along the way. The word "dentures" hadn't translated, so a green steno outline drew my eye at once. Every deposition, it seemed, revealed words that had yet to make their way into my dictionary. I highlighted the word and hit the proper keyboard command, and ta-da, I had a new dictionary entry. Henceforth, "dentures" would always translate into English.

I didn't leave the dining room to resume my iPad pastime. To have done so would have felt disrespectful just then, somehow. The two attorneys stood in whispered consultation just beyond the archway. Mr. Flynn shrugged and waved his hand in a "no biggie" gesture. Coop motioned to someone, and Aurora, Levi, and Amy followed the two attorneys back into the room. Dalton and Spencer, likewise, entered and resumed their places.

"Ms. Rose," said Mr. Flynn, "Mr. Rickman's got one or two questions, and then we're going to close the deposition for now. Then we can begin his deposition of Dalton. Ready?"

"Yes," I said.

MR. FLYNN: I'll pass the witness for now, Mr. Rickman.

EXAMINATION

QUESTIONS BY MR. RICKMAN:

Q. Aurora, are you okay to continue for just a few more minutes?

A. Yes, Coop. I'm fine.

Q. I wanted to return briefly to the letter you received from your brother, Otto, five years ago.

A. All right.

Q. You said he sent it in care of your column. Do you know why he didn't send it to your personal post office box?

Had Coop read my mind? My ears burned as my fingers flew.

A. We have a shared family post office box. As you know, there is no mail delivery in Ketchum. Everything goes to a post office box. I believe he sent it care of my column's box to ensure that I would be the one to receive it.

Q. Do you still have that letter, Aurora?

A. Sadly, I do not.

Q. Do you know what happened to it?

A. I don't, and it's quite a mystery. That letter, along with the other two that Otto sent, disappeared from a locked drawer in my desk at the office.

Q. When did Otto send you the other two letters, Aurora?

A. I received the first letter six months after Otto left in 1975. The second arrived approximately two years later. Those letters were very different from the one I received five years ago.

Dalton was fidgeting around in his chair, and I reminded myself of his I.D. outline, DA*LT, in case he said something again. Coop ignored him.

Q. In what way were they different, Aurora?

A. Well, the first two were quite happy, really. He'd found a group who funded medical visits to remote villages, and he'd joined up with them. Oh, Otto's had no medical training. He isn't even all that skilled in woodwork or practical matters. But Otto can comfort a child, or read to people, or pitch in with cooking, things like that. He is also very good when things need smoothing over with authorities. I imagine that asset is very useful.

Q. And how, then, was the letter of five years ago different?

A. Oh, I don't know. It seemed rather lacking in information. It had none of the detail of the first two letters. He said he just wanted me to know that he loved me and thought of me often, and that he was glad I had my grandchildren for company. There wasn't much else. No return address. No foreign stamps. I assumed he'd asked someone traveling Stateside to post it for him.

Q. And again, all three letters have vanished?

A. Yes. Broke my heart.

Q. When did that happen?

A. It had to have been at least a year ago. I never understood it. They were in a locked drawer.

DALTON LOCKWOOD: I didn't take your darned letters, Aurora.

I knew it! He just couldn't seem to stay silent.

THE WITNESS: And I have never accused you, Dalton.

MR. RICKMAN: Aurora, those are all the questions I have.

MR. FLYNN: That will end the deposition of Aurora Kensington for today, but I want to leave it open in case we need to visit with her about anything in the future. Is that agreeable, Mr. Rickman?

MR. RICKMAN: No objection. We'll read and sign all of these, Shae.

(Deposition was adjourned at 2:15 p.m.)

(Signature was requested.)

* * * * *

I checked the transcript to be sure I'd written that the depo was "adjourned" rather than "concluded." Satisfied that all was in order, I surveyed the room, stopping when Coop caught my eye.

"Ms. Rose," he began, pulling some notes from his briefcase, "I wonder if I could trouble you to go out to your car and bring Exhibit A inside, please."

"No problem."

"And then you might want to hunt down another cup of coffee. I need to speak to my clients before we begin Mr. Lockwood's deposition."

"Okay. You know where to find me."

I always found it interesting when we "switched sides" in a depo. Where Mr. Flynn had taken the lead in Aurora's depo, now it was Coop's turn, and he brought an entirely different style to depositions. He didn't usually spend time with some of the historical questions other attorneys employed. I'd often found him to be laser-like in his questioning. Precise, to the point. Get in, get out.

I hurried through the kitchen and out to my car. Retrieving the heavy typewriter case, I slammed the hatch and lugged the exhibit back up the stairs and into the room. Coop motioned me to just set it on the floor beside him. Then he and the three Kensingtons departed. Dalton, Spencer, and Mr. Flynn had left while I was outside.

I returned to the nook and chose a nice Chai Latte. It was too late in the day for coffee. I dug the iPad out of its drawer. I'd found Aurora to be a forthright and convincing witness, but after the break I'd get to hear the other side of the story. Would Dalton's testimony be as compelling and believable?

CHAPTER 12

DEPOSITION OF DALTON LOCKWOOD

It was late afternoon before Coop came to tell me that they were ready to begin. His timing was unfortunate, really, because after nearly three hours of Vessel development, I'd only just unlocked the door that revealed my ship's captain. He was a cheerful fellow, and his arrival had signaled the fact that I'd achieved a new level of the game. A dialog box had popped up explaining that I'd have extra help from this point forward. My captain would also be my guide, it said, and he would help me discover not only our destination once we were underway, but also the whereabouts of the rest of the crew.

Ah, well. I ruefully tucked the iPad back into its drawer. I was here to work, and games could wait. I shook myself a little to re-enter the present and headed to the dining room, where all parties were already present and accounted for. I double checked the back of the room to see that, sure enough, even Spencer lurked ever silently beneath the hanging fern.

I was happy that everyone had stayed on their own side of the table. Sometimes people inexplicably move around when a new attorney takes over the proceedings. In court reporting school, we are taught to identify speakers using a "round robin" technique, whereby each speaker is identified by where they sit. Since I'd already identified my attorneys, it would get confusing if they played musical chairs on me.

Fortunately, Coop stayed on my right, only shifting to the seat nearest me so he could be directly across from Dalton Lockwood, our new deponent. Dominic Flynn edged down the table one seat to make room for Dalton next to me. I asked Dalton to raise his right hand as I administered the oath.

DALTON LOCKWOOD,

First duly sworn to tell the truth relating to said cause, testified as follows:

EXAMINATION

QUESTIONS BY MR. RICKMAN:

Q. Good afternoon, Mr. Lockwood.

A. May as well call me Dalton.

Q. Thank you. Will you please state your name for the record?

A. Dalton Victor Lockwood.

Q. And your date of birth?

A. August 1, 1944.

Q. You are seventy-two years old today?

A. I am.

Q. Dalton, I'm going to get right to it. Why do you want your brother Otto to be declared dead?

A. Because I believe that he is.

Q. And why do you believe that?

A. It's the law. No word from him in five years, if even that word is to be believed.

Q. And have you made a diligent search for him, Mr. Lockwood?

A. Say what now? He left. Went to the other side of the world. Wouldn't have known where to look.

Q. I'm going to hand you a book, Mr. Lockwood. I won't make it an exhibit, but I'd ask you to read the portion I've highlighted. It's Idaho Code § 15-1-107 (c). I imagine you've seen it before.

Dalton reluctantly received the heavy Idaho Code book from Coop and perused the page.

A. I've read it.

Q. I'm sorry. I'd like you to read it aloud for the record. And read slowly, please, for Ms. Rose's sake.

A. "A person who is absent for a continuous period of five years, during which he has not been heard from, and whose absence is not satisfactorily explained after diligent search or inquiry is presumed to be dead."

He shoved the book back across the table.

Q. Thank you. I'll repeat my question. Have you made a diligent search for your brother Otto?

MR. FLYNN: Objection. Asked and answered.

MR. RICKMAN: He hasn't answered it.

MR. FLYNN: He said he wouldn't know where to look.

BY MR. RICKMAN:

Q. Did you try, Mr. Lockwood?

MR. FLYNN: Objection. Coop, he said he didn't know where to look. Phrasing your question in a different way just because you didn't like the answer isn't getting us any further down the road. The world's a big place. I don't know how anyone would begin to look for someone they haven't spoken with for forty years.

MR. RICKMAN: Oh, I don't know, Dom. I can personally think of a number of ways I'd go about trying to find my brother if I really wanted to. And we're going to have trouble here if you keep coaching the witness. Make your objection as to the form of the question, and that's it. No more speaking objections.

BY MR. RICKMAN:

Q. Mr. Lockwood, did you try, in any way at all, to locate your brother before asking that he be declared dead?

MR. FLYNN: Objection. Form. Go ahead and answer if you can.

THE WITNESS: I didn't know where he was. I didn't know where to look or who to ask. He vanished forty years ago. It's been five years since Aurora said she got a letter. Five years is the law.

BY MR. RICKMAN:

Q. You filed over a year ago. It had only been four years then.

A. I knew these things take time. It's a formality anyway. I never saw that letter Aurora supposedly got five years ago. Otto's been gone forty years. It's time this family moved on and complied with Father's wishes.

Coop reached to the center of the table and pulled Exhibits B and C to himself, studying them carefully before passing them to Dalton.

Q. Mr. Lockwood, you were present during your sister, Aurora's, deposition. Is that correct?

A. Yes.

Q. I'm going to hand you what was marked in her deposition as Exhibit B. Have you seen that document before?

A. I have.

Q. Will you identify Exhibit B for the record, please?

A. It's my father's Last Will & Testament.

Q. And it's dated when?

A. July 30, 1975.

Q. Do you happen to know the date of your father's accident?

A. I recall it vividly. It was August 12, 1975. As to your reference to an accident, though, Father's death was always questionable, in my mind. I never felt I got a proper explanation for the events of that day. It's hard to credit the falling-down-the-stairs story. Father knew those stairs like the back of his hand.

Q. What are you implying, sir?

A. I'm not implying anything. But Father was still a strong, sure-footed man. Can't imagine how he took such a dive off those stairs.

At this, Aurora made a sound that sounded remarkably like a hiss.

Q. Where were you when your father fell, Dalton?

A. Here, in the main house with Aurora. Otto was in the winter house with Father. It was Otto who heard him fall.

Q. Do you know if Otto's first call was to emergency services or to you?

A. I never asked him. An ambulance arrived quickly, though.

Q. Okay. Thank you for that. I want to return, now, to the subject of Exhibit B, your father's alleged will. Is it safe for me to assume that you've read that document thoroughly?

Dalton had *harrumphed* at the use of the word, "alleged," and now he fairly growled his response.

A. I have.

Q. In the name of saving time, please paraphrase, or summarize, whatever you like, your father's wishes as he set them down in that document.

A. Sure. The long and the short of it, Father left the estate and the business to both Otto and me equally. Fifty-fifty shares.

Q. And your sister? Did your father leave anything for Aurora?

A. He left her a modest stipend and said that she and her family were to live here on the estate for as long as they liked.

Q. Why a modest stipend, if you know?

A. I don't know. But if I had to guess, I would say it was because she was married by then and raising Lorelai. If I had to guess further, I'd say that perhaps Father didn't leave substantial assets to Aurora because he didn't want them passing to Lorelai. Even then, at age fourteen, Lorelai was fly-by-night and unpredictable.

I dragged my attention away from the primary speakers and peeped at Aurora, but she hadn't fidgeted at all during any of this. I guessed she'd heard it all before.

    Q. Dalton, I'm now showing you what's been marked as Exhibit C. Do you recognize this document?

    A. I do.

    Q. Please identify it for the record.

    A. It's my brother Otto's Last Will & Testament.

    Q. And in the same fashion, if you would, please paraphrase the contents of this document for us.

    A. It's a simpler document. Otto just says that if he should pre-decease me, that his 50 percent of everything would go to me.

    Q. At which time you would own 100 percent of both the estate and your father's business, which was comprised of several dozen highly successful small-to-mid-sized town newspapers. Is that correct?

    A. That's how he laid it down in the papers, yes.

    Q. And no mention of Aurora in Otto's will?

    A. Just the same, that she be allowed to live here and continue to receive her stipend.

    Q. And that's it?

    A. It was all she needed. She'd married a wealthy man.

    Q. Had Aurora shown any interest up until that time of being involved in the business itself?

    A. Well...

    Q. Please answer the question.

    A. She'd shown some interest.

Q. And you heard her testimony earlier that she was, in fact, going over the paper's next edition here, with you, when your father had his accident?

A. I heard her.

Q. Isn't it true, Dalton, that Aurora was heavily involved in running the paper, and had been since she was fifteen years old?

MR. FLYNN: Objection. I'm not going to allow you to badger the witness, Coop.

MR. RICKMAN: No need to raise your voice, Dom. Let's keep the decibels down.

MR. FLYNN: I'm not yelling, Coop.

And he wasn't. Coop had thrown that in for the record. Mr. Flynn had mentioned badgering the witness. Coop's question hadn't been a badgering one, in my opinion, and Dominic Flynn hadn't yelled. I could only surmise that the lawyers were showing themselves to be diligent in front of their clients and were creating a record for a jury to hear later. Coop casually flicked a piece of lint off his sleeve and resumed. He'd gotten what he wanted on the record.

BY MR. RICKMAN:

Q. Returning our attention to Exhibit B, Dalton, which is your father's will, it looks like the will was dated just two weeks prior to your father's death.

A. Yeah.

Q. Fortuitous timing.

MR. FLYNN: Objection. Is there a question there? Now what are you implying, Coop?

Coop ignored him and leaned down to open the old Samsonite case. Lifting the lovely little Smith-Corona from within, he gently placed it on the table in view of all.

BY MR. RICKMAN:

Q. Dalton, do you recognize what we've marked for deposition purposes as Exhibit A?

A. Looks like Otto's typewriter.

Q. Do you believe that this typewriter was used to type up both Exhibits B and C?

A. Had to have been. It's all Otto ever used.

Q. And do you believe that Otto used this typewriter to create Exhibit B, your father's will, on July 30, 1975?

A. I do. That's why Father called Otto home from wherever the heck he was, to create Father's final documents. Otto did so, fortuitous or otherwise.

Q. All right, Dalton. Thank you. I'd like to switch gears and talk for a moment about the Valley Scribe, and then we'll get you out of here.

A. Fine.

Q. You and your sister, Aurora, have been running the paper jointly since the death of your father over forty years ago. Is that true?

A. Yes, that's true.

Q. And would you describe your working relationship with Aurora to be compatible?

A. I guess it was at first. Not so much anymore.

Q. Can you tell me why?

A. I like things as they are, as they've always been.

Aurora has brought her grandkids into the business, and they keep wanting to change things. I don't think the paper needs changing, and I wish they'd all leave well enough alone.

Dalton was fairly growling, and I thought Coop had struck this nerve deliberately.

Q. What kind of changes are you talking about, Dalton?

A. Oh, it's the whole internet thing. We already publish most of the paper online, but they want more. They want things that would be specific to the online version.

Q. Such as?

A. Oh, blogs and interactive weather and searchability. Who knows what all they'd include.

Q. What is your specific objection to these things, sir?

A. The Valley Scribe is a news source, not a video game. Most people want the actual hard copy form anyway. Why pour money into modern gimmicks that no one's even asking for?

Q. I see. I suppose then, Mr. Lockwood, that having 100 percent control of the paper at this time would suit your purposes very well.

A. I'm only looking to have my Father's wishes implemented. Otto's too, since his will agrees with Father's. I found these wills more than five years ago. Father had been gone thirty-five years at that point. I think forty years is long enough to wait to execute a will, don't you?

MR. RICKMAN: Thank you very much, Mr. Lockwood. Unless your attorney has some follow-up questions for you, this deposition can be adjourned.

MR. FLYNN: No questions. We'll read and sign all of ours, as well.

MR. RICKMAN: As with Aurora's deposition, I'd request that this deposition also remain open, in case we need to return with more questions. But for now, we're done.

(Deposition adjourned at 5:30 p.m.)

(Signature was requested.)

* * * * *

I never shut things down without making at least one backup of the day's testimony. I saved my file and inserted a flash drive into a USB port, my mind a flurry of thought. From his testimony, it seemed that Dalton was just as sure that the two wills were *real* as Aurora was certain that they were *false*. Each of them had everything to gain and even more to lose should their side of the case not prevail.

No wonder they were fighting! How would they ever get to the truth of it? And where was Otto? Vaporous thoughts flitted through my mind and I knew I had no real sense of the case yet. I found it strange that Otto had written but had left no return address. *Where are you, Otto?*

Distracted, I went about reversing my setup process and began packing things away. I finally zipped my steno case closed and gasped as a lean and leathery hand reached to take hold of it.

"I got it, Shae."

"Hawk!" I put my hand on my pounding heart. "You move like a freaking shadow! Please…make some noise or something next time." *Anyone would jump if they'd recently had an intruder in their home.*

Hawk, who knew nothing of my break-in, only chuckled. He easily lifted my case with one hand and stuck his toothpick more firmly between his teeth with the other.

"Make some noise, eh? I'll try and remember that. I did tell you this morning I'd be back to help you get your gear back out to your car, though." Still chuckling, he waited while I gathered up the three exhibits. Coop had replaced the typewriter in its case, so I only had to pick it up. Heart still thudding, I followed Hawk back out to my car. He lifted my steno case into my car, and I bid him a good night, watching him head toward his own cabin with the beautiful veranda.

* * *

Because our first day of depositions had run late, the sun had dipped behind Bald Mountain, and the sky was already darkening. As I eased the exhibits into the cargo area, my skin suddenly prickled. Was someone watching me?

I looked around to be sure Hawk had truly gone. Shadows lengthened as early evening drifted toward starlit night. The vast expanse of lawn seemed peaceful and non-threatening, but the distant woods – indeed, even the windows in any of the estate's structures – could easily conceal watchful eyes. I glanced down at Hawk's cabin in time to see a lamp switch on, warming the interior. Hawk had gone home, and I was being paranoid. The main house loomed to my right, vast, yet serene. There had been too much talk of disappearance and death today. That was all.

I slammed the hatch and fished my car key out of my bag. I thought about home, suddenly eager to see Hercules and the Darlings. A mug of tea and a tale of Clarabelle's latest escapades would soothe my nerves.

Settled into the car, a movement caught my eye just as I reached toward the ignition. A lone figure stood near the darkened, partially obscured porch of what I had initially thought was the guest house. I'd learned, during the course of the day, that the family referred to the cozy smaller residence as the winter house. I squinted in the increasing gloom. Definitely a man – a stranger. He hadn't been present at the day's proceedings. The movement I'd noticed had been the swinging of the mud room door. The man himself was now motionless as he stared across the grounds – directly at me. As he watched me steadily, my stomach clenched. Who was he?

I fastened my seat belt, reversed out of my parking spot, and moved slowly back to the main drive. A furtive glance toward the winter house confirmed that the stranger was still there, and a trickle of fear traced my spine. Why would someone come outside, stare, and not at least wave a hello? And why was I covered in gooseflesh? It would have been simple enough to drive right past the winter house, roll down my window, and introduce myself. Under normal circumstances I would have done just that. Something about the man's stillness stopped me.

Disappearance and death. Events forty years in the making. A lone, still figure in the distance, watching me in the gathering darkness. I shivered and double checked that the car doors were locked, then headed toward the highway and home.

CHAPTER 13

NEW GATE

What was up with the bright lights and activity at my house?

I'd turned onto my normally quiet street, my thoughts only on comfy sweats, a hot drink, and an evening visit with the ladies. But there, right in front of the house, sat a panel van of some sort. The vehicle's headlights blinded me as I drove down the street toward it. The van was blocking access to the garage, so I parked at the curb.

Voices reached me as soon as I opened the car door. Male, female, and – what? German?

I got out and approached the courtyard to find a hefty construction-type male pointing with his hands and trying to out-speak old Frank Gruber, who had apparently come to complain again. Mr. Gruber, not to be outdone, raised his hands in the air, then poked Construction Dude's chest, and carried on in ever-increasing volume in an ever-thickening German accent. His words were nearly unintelligible. Bernie was trying to insert herself between the two men, demanding that they calm down. Clarabelle held Hercules as she rocked up and down on the balls of her feet.

"Well, Shae, surprise," Bernie said, sardonically.

"Oh, bother," fussed Clarabelle. "We wanted this to be finished before you got home."

Mr. Construction turned away from Frank Gruber and puffed out his chest. "Hi, there!" He was very friendly for someone who had appeared to be arguing a moment ago. "You must be the little lady this gorgeous new thing is for." He beamed at me, waving his arms to direct my attention to a brand new, six-foot high, wrought-iron fence.

I was stunned. Our courtyard was semi-private, enclosed on three sides by the house and garage. The garage and the house, taken in total, formed a U. As one faced the property from the street, the garage was on the left. The center portion along the back of the courtyard belonged to the ladies, and the right side of the premises had been converted into a separate apartment, a dwelling I happily called home.

The structures were set back from the street, and due to the fully matured trees that lined the courtyard's entryway, a person had to actually *enter* the courtyard to see the residences within. The trees had done nothing, of course, to prevent someone from breaking into my side of the house a few nights ago.

What stood before me now were decorative iron bars, painted white, that stretched from one side of the U to the other, completely enclosing the courtyard. In the middle of this decorative white fence opened a gate, and it was near this gate that I'd seen all the commotion.

I looked from Bernie to Clarabelle in disbelief. How much had this cost? And how had they found a contractor on such short notice?

"Shae," said Bernie, "meet Sam Ivory." Mr. Construction stuck out his hand, but I just nodded to him, still in shock.

"How did you ladies do this?" I sputtered. "You must have spent a fortune…" I trailed off, lost for words.

Clarabelle appeared to be bursting with the story, so I looked to her and waited.

"Ohhhh, Shae! Isn't it the prettiest thing? And now no one can break in ever again! It was Bernie's idea, of course. She spent simply *ages* on the phone. But finally someone told her poor Mr. Ivory here had an order cancel, and ohhhh, I don't know everything, Shae, but this lovely fence had already arrived in his shop! He only had to modify it a little."

I took in the rather large construction scene and considered the piles of unused wrought iron, the welding equipment, and the late hour. I smiled. Would Mr. Ivory agree with Clarabelle's assessment on the size of the task?

"And now we are safe." Clarabelle's eyes danced. "What do you think, Shae? It's been so hard to keep the secret. We found out it was available on Saturday, and Bernie wouldn't let me say a word."

"I tell you vat I zink," spat Mr. Gruber. "I zink my Ziege vill come through these bars, he is so small, and von't be able to get out. I zink zis gate is bad, bad. I zink you must take it down now, or I vill complain!"

Bernie raised a tired brow in my direction. This argument with Frank Gruber had been ongoing for years. His pet goat regularly got loose and charged into our courtyard, hoping to chase Hercules around. In the past, it had been a simple matter to walk the goat home, or to call Mr. Gruber to come and fetch him. Now, rather than offering to keep a tighter watch on his goat, it seemed Mr. Gruber was accusing the ladies of creating a trap for him.

It seemed to me that if Ziggy could get *in*, he could surely get *out*, but Clarabelle just hugged Herc tighter and tried to mollify Mr. Gruber.

"Frank," she said excitedly, "that just won't happen. See, Sam has a smaller grill he's attaching to the lower portion. I mean, Herky's so small too, smaller than Ziggy, and, you know, we don't want him getting through the bars, either."

Mr. Gruber's eyes strayed to the pieces lying on the sidewalk. He must have interrupted Sam before he could attach the finishing touch to the gate's lower portion. Suspicion etched his face as he thought that through, and his eyebrows furrowed deeply.

"I vill come back tomorrow," he said at last, still cross. "And I vill see. But I don't like it, and I don't like zat dog. He alvays barks at my Ziege and frightens him. Zis is wrong." He pointed a bony finger at me. "You should train your dog not to bark and frighten ozzer animals!"

I said nothing. I wanted none of this.

Turning on his heel, Mr. Gruber left us and headed to his home, a mere five houses down but on the other side of the street.

"Um, ladies?" Mr. Ivory pulled our attention from Frank Gruber.

"Yes?" We all chimed at once, and laughed.

"You all ought to go on back inside now. I need to weld this grill into place, and it's best you're not around while I'm doing that kind of work."

"Of course, Mr. Ivory," Bernie said briskly, clearly happy that Mr. Gruber had gone home.

"And it's dark now, so I'll be back first thing in the morning to weld the decospikes along the top of the back fence, and get that all painted up too."

"Decospikes?" *What on earth?*

Mr. Ivory reached into his van and withdrew an ornamental, slightly bulbous iron object with a three-inch high, pointed spike extending from its narrow end.

"I'll weld these on top of the wrought-iron fence that's already in the back." He held one up proudly. "They have pretty designs in the round part at the bottom, see? That's the deco. But no one's going to want to climb over these pointy things that'll be sticking up. That's the spike." He beamed again, clearly pleased with the opportunity to explain his work. "I'll weld these in place every six inches along that whole back fence. Ain't no one gonna want to climb over that. You won't have to think twice about intruders."

Front gate, back fence. They'd covered everything. No one could catch us unaware again.

"Let's go, Clare, Shae," said Bernie. "The windchimes will keep the backyard safe for tonight, and then we'll have a nice secure fence right round the place tomorrow when Mr. Ivory finishes up."

We all turned to Mr. Ivory as Bernie extended her hand to him. "Thank you, Sam, for coming at short notice, for staying late to finish, for your kind and cheerful nature. I apologize for our neighbor, Mr. Gruber. I'm afraid he was a little ornery, but I hope you won't take it personally."

"Yes, he can be curmudgeonly," helped Clarabelle. "But we think he can't be all bad, because he named his little goat Ziggy. Isn't that cute? And Ziggy really *is* kind of cute." She glanced at me, and then added guiltily, "Except when he's chasing Herky, of course."

"It's okay, Clarabelle." I smiled. "Ziggy is a cute goat with a cute name, even if he does have a grouch for a human."

With a last look at our wonderful new cold metal fortifications, we bid Mr. Ivory a good evening.

It was with a lighter heart that I stepped for the first time through that lovely, safe, white, decorative, magical gate. I couldn't imagine the strings Bernie had pulled to bring this together so quickly, but one thing was sure. Tonight, at last, I would sleep. I was tempted to skip the evening hot drink I usually shared with the ladies and just go to bed, but I'd been looking forward to visiting with them after my long day.

Bernie cocked her head. "Coming over for a bit, Shae?"

Decision made.

"Counting on it." Herc had been trying to reach me from his place in Clarabelle's arms, so I embraced him now and relished his kisses as I followed the Darlings into their cozy home.

I always enjoyed our nightly drink ritual in the ladies' cozy living room. I chose my customary spot on the sofa and tucked my legs beneath me as Clarabelle handed me a steaming mug of peach tea. Bernie told me she had spent the day repainting Clarabelle's favorite garden bench. They'd found it at a rummage sale years earlier, thinking they would refinish it one day. It was a wooden affair with decorative, hand-carved frogs clinging to all four of its legs. I hadn't noticed its fresh look in all the excitement caused by the new fence, but the ladies assured me that it had now been transformed from a grungy, old-wood gray to a bright and cheerful white.

When Bernie had finished explaining her tarping and sanding and prepping and painting, it was Clarabelle's turn to tell us about *her* day. She and Herc had gone to see Nettie, of course, and there had been some great commotion when a neighbor's cat had zoomed through Nettie's yard, riling Hercules to the point where he upset the coffee tray and sent the ladies' afternoon treats splashing and crumbling to the floor. Clarabelle held Hercules and stroked his head throughout the telling and I smiled, perceiving that the ladies had laid the blame for the catastrophe squarely on the cat.

As for me, I couldn't go into details of the depositions, but I shared with the ladies that my job had taken me to a grand estate that day, and I told them all about the special leather chair that had been provided for me. I rhapsodized endlessly about the amazing lunch Hawk had prepared as Clarabelle and Bernie drank in every word. But I said nothing of the stranger who had stared at me from across the vast lawn. Who was he? Why had he stared so intently at me, offering no form of greeting?

The memory of the incident sent a chill through my body.

CHAPTER 14

DEPOSITION OF LEVI KENSINGTON

On Wednesday morning I arrived for Levi Kensington's deposition feeling much more confident than I had on my first day. I'd had a day off in between the depos, and I'd spent the time cleaning up Monday's transcripts and honing my job dictionary. Coop had told me that the depositions in the case would be spread out over two or three weeks so that Aurora wouldn't be overtaxed as she participated. Aurora Kensington seemed a quietly formidable force to me, but hey, I didn't mind a day in between to get my work done.

A second day in a new place is always easier. I knew how to find the drive, and I knew Hawk would be waiting to let me in. I was familiar with the parking nearer to the mudroom entrance, and I was ready for Hawk to follow me up the drive in his silent golf cart and carry my steno bag inside. I didn't know what to expect, but I knew all the players. I was constantly adding to my dictionary for this job, so dialog was translating more and more cleanly.

Levi's deposition was to begin at ten o'clock, but when I stepped into the dining room at nine thirty, I found that Levi had also arrived early. He was uncharacteristically relaxed for your average deponent, with his chair tipped back, his feet up on the dining room table, and a newspaper obscuring all but his shins and loafers.

I was about to say good morning when he laughed aloud and called, "Amy, you've gotta come read this. This guy's great!"

Amy swept nimbly into the room wearing bicycle gear, her windblown hair caressing each bright cheek. She tossed it carelessly out of the way and approached her brother.

"You should have come, Levi," she said reprovingly. "It's a beautiful morning." Amy glanced my way. "Oh, hi, Shae."

"Hi, Ms. Kensington."

"No, no. Amy will be great. And Levi, Nana may be blind, but she'll feel the grime from those shoes of yours on the tablecloth. Feet down!"

"My shoes aren't grimy," Levi retorted cheerfully, complying all the same. He brought his feet to the floor and brushed off the table. "Happy?"

Amy shrugged. "Your funeral when she catches you. So what did you call me in here for?"

Levi's face split into a grin. "It's this Badger Thicket guy again. Blogger."

An iPad had been propped up by his legs and hidden from my view by the paper.

"I've got today's paper," Levi continued, "and this Badger dude has played devil's advocate with most of today's content. Ha! He must have stayed up all night blogging from what he found in the online edition. He's spinning stories in different directions just for public amusement. And he's really good."

Amy whisked the pitcher from the center of the table and poured herself some water. "Like what?"

I was setting up my equipment while enjoying their banter.

"Well, you remember that the airport announced it was going to reduce the number of flights due to the slack season coming up?"

"Yes." She shrugged, sipping her water. "I think we all get it. Not as many tourists, not as many flights required."

"Yeah. But Badger asserts that the number of flights won't be reduced at all. He claims to have inside information. He says the now unavailable flights will still fly, but they'll be filled with local hotel and restaurant employees who are being spirited away for their yearly jaunt to the Bahamas." Levi grinned. "Man, I wish *that* were true. They work pretty hard during the season." He was thoroughly enjoying himself. "I mean, I'm not doing it justice. You'll have to read it, but this is great stuff. Laughter for the sake of laughter. We could all use more of it."

"What did he have to say about the Mine Shaft Hotel in Hailey finally being condemned and torn down?" Amy seemed to be getting into the Thicket spirit.

"He claims the Mine Shaft's sad demise had more to do with numerous ghost sightings within its eerie walls than it had to do with poor plumbing and a corroded electrical system."

This time Amy laughed aloud along with her brother. "Good for him, whoever Badger Thicket is. I'd love to meet him."

"Can't see that happening, Sis. I mean, you know these bloggers," he said, nodding sagely. "They generally live in basements and survive on pizza and corn chips. Ol' Badger probably doesn't even own any outdoor shoes."

Amy grabbed the paper and swatted him with it as his eyes twinkled. He was fully aware that Amy worked diligently on her own blog in addition to helping Aurora with the Cheeky Peaks column.

"Well," Amy tossed her hair and re-opened the paper. "I like Badger Thicket, and I expect I *will* meet him one day. And make sure you don't throw out the paper when you're finished with it. I expect Jenkins will want to read it."

Jenkins? Amy had mentioned Jenkins yesterday in reference to someone who had prepared sandwiches, but I hadn't seen anyone in the house apart from the parties to the case. *Who is Jenkins?*

Amy turned her head to the archway that led in from the living room. "Oh, good morning, Nana."

Aurora had arrived in the dining room just in time to hear the swat of the paper, but not the gist of the conversation.

"Good morning, you two." She grinned impishly. "Levi, sounds like you're in fine fettle. Ready to go nine rounds with Mr. Flynn, are you?"

Levi stretched back, but stopped short of tilting his chair. "Oh, I think I'm game for my time at bat. I'd rather answer his questions than watch you have to deal with them. Can't imagine what he wants to ask me, though. I'd love to have met Uncle Otto, but since I didn't, I doubt I can contribute much."

Coop Rickman strode into the room and plunked his battered briefcase down on the table.

"It's because you're a named party, my man," he said, clapping Levi on the shoulder. "Shouldn't take too long, though, I wouldn't think. No promises, though. You never know what the other side has planned for a deposition. Isn't that right, Shae?"

"Pardon?" I sputtered and dropped my pen. He'd distracted me by including me in the conversation.

"You never know how long a depo may go. Can't give any assurances."

"Seems like yours are usually fairly short." I bent down and retrieved my pen. "But you're exactly right. I never know what a day will hold. I travel around with a stash of protein bars just in case we work through lunch or stay late."

"See?" He raised his eyebrows at the others as though I'd proven his point. "Court reporters know they have to travel with water, food, and overnight supplies." He grinned at me. "Totally unpredictable, this profession you've chosen, Ms. Rose."

"Yep." I'd always thought Coop Rickman was an observant person. "And I wouldn't change a thing."

At this Coop began withdrawing his pen and yellow legal pad from his briefcase. He told Levi to take the chair next to me as Dalton and Mr. Flynn filed in through the archway opposite to where I sat. As they took their seats, Spencer slouched quietly to his chair beneath the hanging fern, his face in shadow. Everyone was present. Mr. Flynn nodded to me, and I administered the oath.

LEVI KENSINGTON,

First duly sworn to tell the truth relating to said cause, testified as follows:

EXAMINATION

QUESTIONS BY MR. FLYNN:

Q. Good morning. Please state your full name for the record.

A. Levi Peregrine Kensington.

Q. How old are you today, Levi?

A. I'm thirty-one.

(Okay, just two years younger than I. But still too rich.)

Q. Is Peregrine after your grandfather?

A. Yes.

Q. But your father's name wasn't Levi, and his surname wasn't Kensington. Do you know why you don't share his name at all?

A. There's no drama here, Mr. Flynn. Nana and my grandfather, Peregrine, had one daughter. When she was eighteen, she fell in with some of the artsy crowd in Ketchum, and she ran off with one of them. She was away for six years, during which time she produced Amy and me. Her fellow decided that fatherhood cramped his style, so Lorelai, my dear mother, dropped us here with Nana and ran off for good. They were never married, so she gave us her name, Kensington. I think she middled me with Peregrine as a peace offering of some sort to Nana.

"Hmpf!" snorted Aurora. Coop patted her arm.

Q. Is your mother still alive?

A. Oh, yes, I believe so. She sends the occasional Christmas card.

Q. Would you prefer me to call you Levi today, or Mr. Kensington?

A. Levi, absolutely.

And away we went. Did you graduate from high school? When? From what school? Did you go to college? Did you obtain any degrees? What is your relationship like with your grandmother? Your sister? Your great uncle? Your cousin, Spencer? What is your involvement with the *Valley Scribe*?

We battled on for over two hours before things got interesting.

Q. Levi, before this litigation, had you ever seen the two wills we've produced as Exhibits B and C?

A. Never.

Q. Were you, though, familiar with Exhibit A, the typewriter?

A. I've seen it, certainly. But way before I was born, Nana had put all of Uncle Otto's things in his room, and we weren't allowed to touch them.

Q. Why would you have had cause to enter his room, if it was off limits?

A. I never said off limits. We weren't told to never go in there. We were just asked to leave his things in peace. I entered the room one day to comfort Nana. She was in there, sitting on the bed.

Q. What was she doing, that you felt she needed comforting?

A. Crying. This was before she had received his letter of five years ago. She missed him. I think she was worried about him.

Q. Was she doing anything else?

A. Yes. She was holding some of his old stories. Uncle Otto used to write short stories for the paper, mostly about some of the local color. Nana told me his drafts were always typed up on the Smith-Corona, on his special paper. When I went into Uncle Otto's bedroom, Nana was holding his stories near to her face. She said she could still smell the cedar on the pages.

Mr. Flynn's eyes flashed, and I sensed this was not a road down which he wished to travel. He changed tact abruptly.

Q. Levi, did you see the letter your uncle purportedly wrote to your grandmother five years ago?

A. I never did. I spent far too much time at college, Master's and whatnot, so I wasn't home at the time. I heard about it, but by the time I came home to visit, it had vanished.

MR. FLYNN: Levi, those are all the questions I have for you today.

MR. RICKMAN: I have some follow-up questions.

I readjusted my machine slightly so that I was facing only the right side of the table. Coop leaned back in his chair and set his note-taking pen casually next to his legal pad. I often thought Coop Rickman was the most relaxed attorney I knew.

EXAMINATION

QUESTIONS BY MR. RICKMAN:

Q. Levi, could you smell the cedar scent on the papers your grandmother was holding in Otto's bedroom that day?

A. Not at first. When she mentioned it, I held them up close to my nose and could get an idea of it. It wasn't strong, but it was there. The papers had been put away in a box, nothing that was cedar lined, so the scent had faded.

Q. Would you say that your grandmother has a good sense of smell, Levi?

A. She has an extraordinary sense of smell. Freaky sometimes.

Q. Not uncommon, perhaps, in a blind person?

A. Okay. I'll go with you. But I think she's unusually gifted, even considering her blindness.

Q. Can you give me an example of her smelling superpower, Levi?

A. Sure. Everyone loves In-N-Out Burger, right? And everyone in Ketchum knows there isn't one around here. We're deprived. Anyway, one summer we were down in California doing the tourist thing. Well, Amy and I were doing it. Nana didn't much want to walk around Disneyland.

So, as a treat to her, we decided to take her to the beach one day so she could put her feet in the waves. We'd arranged for some old friends of hers to meet us there.

MR. FLYNN: Object to the narrative. Move this along, Coop.

MR. RICKMAN: Just following up on your questions, Dom. You didn't let Levi finish explaining Aurora's sense of smell, so I will.

BY MR. RICKMAN:

Q. Go on, Levi.

A. We didn't tell Nana where we were going, because it was a surprise. But as soon as I pulled off the freeway, Nana exclaimed right away,

"We're on Beach Boulevard! Oh, how nice. Are we going to the ocean? I do love Huntington Beach."

At this I nearly lost it, so perfect was Levi's impersonation of his grandmother. I swallowed a giggle and kept writing as Levi continued.

So of course I asked, "Nana, how can you know we're on Beach Boulevard? You been fibbing to us all these years about your sight?"

She says, "No, you goose. Can't you smell it?"

"Smell what?" I asked her.

"In-N-Out," she said. "I always know when we get off the freeway at Beach Boulevard, because I can smell the In-N-Out Burger. I'm hungry. Let's stop and treat ourselves."

Q. Levi, how far away is that particular In-N-Out from the freeway off-ramp?

A. I'd guess at just under two miles.

Q. And your grandmother had no clue where you were going that day?

A. None. She sure surprised me by figuring it out that way.

Q. So when your grandmother says she can tell the truth of a matter from her sense of smell alone, do you believe her?

MR. FLYNN: Objection. Form. Coop, this goes far beyond what I –

THE WITNESS: Can I answer?

BY MR. RICKMAN:

Q. Yes.

A. I believe her with every fiber of my being.

MR. RICKMAN: No further questions.

(Deposition concluded at 12:05 p.m.)

(Signature was requested.)

* * * * *

I stretched back in my chair and stifled a yawn. Ahhhh, stretching felt so good. We'd been going for two hours with no break, and I was definitely ready to *move*. And to eat! Levi's mention of In-N-Out Burger had reminded my tummy that it was lunchtime.

Hawk appeared on cue and watched as all the parties melted away as they'd done yesterday at lunch. I couldn't blame them. Had I been a party to the case, I'd have wanted to confer with my attorney over the lunch hour too.

I saved my job and locked my laptop screen. I'd developed that habit after a particular job where I'd returned from a break to find an attorney and his client scrolling through my transcript. Since every letter in a transcript is my responsibility, and since they could have, even unwittingly, changed something, I'd gone a little nutso. A sympathetic reporter friend had told me later that I could hit the Windows icon and the letter L, and it would lock the screen. Brilliant!

Screen safely locked, I turned and smiled at Hawk.

"Lunch?" he asked.

"Thought you'd never ask."

We ambled down the drive even more companionably than we had the day before. The lunch was just as great, the conversation even better.

This was an unusual case in an unusual setting, and I was being unusually spoiled. I sat on Hawk's welcoming veranda and knew it was time to firmly put to bed any suspicions that someone here had broken into my home in search of the exhibit in my care. No one I'd met thus far seemed at all capable of such doings. No one had shown the least bit of interest in the typewriter when it had been produced in Dalton's deposition.

The break-in had surely been a coincidence, and the intruder had not returned. Even if he had, he'd have been stymied by the now impregnable Fort Darling.

I stopped short, my musings stifled as the winter house caught the edge of my peripheral vision. The stranger I'd seen had been *here*, not in Hailey.

CHAPTER 15
DEPOSITION OF AMY KENSINGTON

No one else had yet returned to the dining room as I took my place and unlocked my screen. I did a test stroke on my machine to make sure it was still communicating properly with the computer. When that checked out, I began scrolling slowly through the transcript. I was searching for any little thing I could clean up in order to save editing time later. A comma here, a dash there. Anything I could do now would help.

Amy was to be our deponent that afternoon, so when I heard her voice I looked up. I wanted to be sure she knew she should occupy the chair to my right, but I shouldn't have worried. Amy and Levi were chatting amiably together as they entered through the archway, with Coop following close behind them. When they reached the table, Levi bowed slightly to Amy and swept his left arm forward in a grand "after you" gesture.

Amy, having changed out of her bicycle gear, was a vision in skinny jeans and a light-weight, cream-colored knit tunic. Nodding regally to Levi, she glided the length of the table and found the correct seat. Of course she had.

She turned to me and smiled. "Nana won't be joining us this afternoon, Shae. She needed to meet with the paper's editor about next week's edition."

"Got it." I made a note in my depo notebook. "Thanks."

I'd barely set my pen down when Dominic Flynn, Dalton,

and Spencer all flowed into the room. Spencer slunk off to the rear, while Mr. Flynn and Dalton resumed their seats to my left.

"Ms. Rose, I'm told Mrs. Kensington will not be joining us this afternoon." Mr. Flynn's voice was clipped and fast, as usual.

"Yes, I've been informed."

"Very well. We're all here, so let's go ahead and swear in the witness."

I turned to Amy to ask her to raise her right hand, but she'd already done so. I mentally added *cooperative* to the list of attributes I'd subconsciously been compiling for Amy. Smart, beautiful, athletic, good-humored, *rich*, likeable, and now cooperative. The fact that she managed all of that so effortlessly hardly seemed fair. *Sigh*. I resisted the temptation to smooth down my own unruly curls, raised my hand, and administered the oath.

AMY KENSINGTON,

First duly sworn to tell the truth relating to said cause, testified as follows:

EXAMINATION

QUESTIONS BY MR. FLYNN:

Q. Good afternoon. Please state your full name for the record.

A. Amy Lianne Kensington.

Q. And what is your date of birth?

A. December 4, 1982.

Q. So you are thirty-three years old today?

A. That's right.

Q. Do you mind if I call you Amy today, or would you prefer Ms. Kensington?

A. Amy is fine.

Q. Thank you. Amy, you've been present for the depositions of your grandmother, your great uncle, and your brother. Is that correct?

A. It is.

Q. So you've seen how the process works?

A. Yes, I have.

Q. And your attorney has explained the rules of a deposition to you?

A. Yes. I'm to answer audibly, and I'm not to interrupt you.

Q. Very good. Amy, you heard your brother's testimony regarding the Smith-Corona typewriter this morning. Correct?

A. Correct.

Q. Is your memory the same as his, that the typewriter was kept in Otto's room after his disappearance, and you were asked not to touch it?

A. Yes, that's right.

Q. Weren't you ever curious about it?

A. Of course I was. It's a beautiful little 1945 typewriter. I wanted very much to play with it.

Q. But you didn't?

A. I never did.

Q. It sounds like your grandmother did a very good job raising you.

A. She was our world. We had our reckless moments as kids, as teenagers, but we never wanted to hurt her. We knew Uncle Otto was a tender subject for Nana. She asked us not to disturb his things, and we did as she asked.

At this, Amy shrugged and folded her hands, a picture of serenity. Mr. Flynn shuffled through his folders and withdrew both of the wills, Exhibits B and C.

    Q. Amy, I'm handing you two documents that have been previously marked as exhibits in this case. Are you familiar with these documents?

    A. Only because I saw them in the prior depositions. I haven't read them.

    Q. It really isn't necessary to read them now, Amy. My questions only have to do with whether you have personal knowledge –

    A. Excuse me, Mr. Flynn. Are you going to ask me questions about these documents?

    Q. Well, yes, but only as to what you, yourself –

    A. Then I would like to have the opportunity to read them.

    Q. In truth, Amy, I won't be asking about the contents as much as –

    MR. RICKMAN: Dom, you handed her the documents and said you're going to ask questions about them. If she wants to read them, she gets to read them. We can go off the record.

I looked at Mr. Flynn to see if he would object to going off the record. When he didn't, I added my parenthetical.

    (A break was taken.)

It wasn't a get-up-and-move-around kind of break, so we all sat quietly while Amy read each document through. The wills were brief, just three pages each. Really only two pages, because the third page was the signature page. Amy was finished in under five minutes.

THE WITNESS: I'm finished, Mr. Flynn. You may ask your questions now.

BY MR. FLYNN:

Q. As you know, Amy, we are trying to discover the origin of these documents. My questions, again, will be directed only to the origin, and not the content.

A. But why not the content, Mr. Flynn? That was what brought these documents into question in the first place, even before anyone thought about the paper they're written on.

Q. I'm here to ask questions, Ms. Kensington. Not to answer them.

MR. RICKMAN: Just go ahead and answer his questions for now, Amy.

THE WITNESS: Very well.

BY MR. FLYNN:

Q. Do you know who created these documents, Amy?

A. No, I do not.

Q. Do you believe them to have been typed on your Uncle Otto's old typewriter?

A. I have no idea.

Q. Because you have never, as you said, "played" with the typewriter before. Is that correct?

A. That's correct.

Q. So if your Uncle Dalton says that he found these wills in a cupboard in the winter house a number of years ago, why would you have any reason to doubt his word?

A. Because of what the wills say, Mr. Flynn. I'm afraid we're back to that.

But Mr. Flynn refused to be drawn in, and he changed the subject abruptly.

Q. Switching gears, Amy, were you aware that your grandmother received a letter from her brother Otto five years ago?

A. Yes. I opened the letter.

Q. Do you still have the letter?

A. No. I read it to Nana, and she kept it after that. I haven't seen it again.

Q. Do you happen to remember what the postmark said? Was it mailed from South America, for example?

A. As Nana has already said, it was not. Naturally, I looked at the postmark, Mr. Flynn. Sadly, it was of no help. The letter was mailed from Atlanta, Georgia.

Q. Did you find that strange, Amy?

A. Not at all. Uncle Otto had explained that he was giving the letter to a colleague who would soon be traveling to the States.

Q. You heard your grandmother's testimony about the contents of this letter. Correct?

A. Correct.

Q. Do you remember anything about it that she didn't include?

A. No. She described it accurately. I remember feeling a little sad, at the time, that Otto said so little. But Nana was just thankful he'd finally written at all. It had been so long.

MR. FLYNN: Amy, thank you for your time. Those are all the questions I have for you.

MR. RICKMAN: I have a few.

Amy, who had already seemed quite relaxed, exhaled slightly and smiled at Coop. She must have known that the hard part was over and that answering questions from her own attorney would be easy.

EXAMINATION

QUESTIONS BY MR. RICKMAN:

Q. Hi, Amy.

A. Hey, Coop.

Q. I'd like you to take another look at Exhibits B and C, if you would, please.

A. Certainly.

Q. Amy, what is it about the contents of these documents that troubles you?

MR. FLYNN: Objection. Irrelevant. These documents are older than the deponent, Coop. She is entirely unqualified to testify as to whether Myron and Otto Lockwood approved these wills and signed them.

MR. RICKMAN: That's fine, Dom. Your objection is noted.

BY MR. RICKMAN:

Q. Go ahead, Amy.

A. I'm troubled by these documents for the simple reason that Nana says these weren't her father's wishes. And since Uncle Otto's will simply agrees with my great-grandfather's will, then I don't think Exhibit C can be believed either.

     Q.   Can you give me a specific example of what you mean?

          MR. FLYNN: Objection.

BY MR. RICKMAN:

     Q.   You can answer.

     A.   Nana told me that her father always encouraged her interest in the newspaper. He'd allowed her to start working there after school from the time she was fifteen years old. He taught her all he knew about running a paper. He told her she should never let anyone try and push her out of the business just because she was a woman.

     Q.   Lots of women run businesses.

     A.   Yes, now they do. But Nana's father told her such things fifty years ago, at least. So for me to read here, in this alleged will, that her father left her no share in the business, well, it's inconsistent with all he'd ever said to her.

     Q.   And you feel the same with regard to your great-uncle's will?

     A.   Perhaps even more so. Nana has always told me how close she and Otto were, how much he encouraged her to be independent. Even if my great-grandfather had left her nothing, but had, as these papers suggest, left everything to his sons fifty-fifty, I believe Otto would have rectified that in his own will. I think he'd have left his sister, and not his brother, his half of everything.

          MR. RICKMAN: Thank you, Amy. I have no further questions.

Mr. Flynn looked long and hard at the table before him, then he leaned in and whispered a consultation with Dalton. Only moments later, he managed a half smile at Amy.

> MR. FLYNN: I have nothing else for you, Ms. Kensington. You're free to go.
>
> (Deposition concluded at 1:50 p.m.)
>
> (Signature was requested.)

* * * * *

And that was that. Two days of depos for this week were a wrap. I noticed none of the usual chitchat as everyone rose from their seats. Amy's deposition had been somber, somehow, and even Levi forewent his usual banter. We were really getting down to the bare bones of the case. Dalton placed no faith in a five-year-old letter that he had never seen. The Kensingtons placed no faith in wills that set forth wishes contrary to what Aurora remembered her father expressing. With what seemed to be so little proof on either side, who could ever hope to untangle this mess?

Everyone quietly exited the room with their respective attorneys as I began packing up. I had no further depositions scheduled until Monday and Tuesday of next week, and those were on different cases. My Monday job was to be held in Ketchum, but Tuesday would find me out the door bright and early, heading to Pocatello. Coop had told me he was starting a trial on an unrelated matter, so we would have nothing more set for this case until two weeks hence.

I was going to miss Hawk and his excellent lunches. I was going to miss my iPad game. I was going to be haunted by the elegant and terrible mystery of this case. What if someone was lying? What if no one was?

Hawk was waiting for me by the time I finished packing up. Without a word, he picked up my machine case and headed through the kitchen. I grabbed my tiny exhibit folder and followed him. Exhibit A, the typewriter, had stayed in the car today. Outside, I looked around surreptitiously. It was still broad daylight, but even so, if I saw the mysterious stranger again I wanted Hawk nearby. Surely, he'd recognize the person.

We saw no one else, however, as we opened my car's hatch and put everything inside. Hawk simply stood for a moment, hands in his pockets, as he chewed his toothpick.

"Guess we won't be seeing you for a couple weeks, then," he said.

"Nope. I'll be busy scoping these transcripts, and then I have work on other jobs next week."

"Scoping?"

"It's the word we use for editing our transcripts. What I do here is only a fraction of my work. I do the rest at home."

"How long's it take you?"

"Usually two to three times the length of the actual depo."

His eyebrows shot up. "Really? You manage to keep on top of it okay?"

"Not always." I laughed. "But I have the rest of today and all of tomorrow and Friday to get these done. It won't be a problem."

"Well, okay then." He reached out awkwardly and patted my shoulder. "You take care then. I'll be here to help you with your stuff in two weeks."

"I hope so, Hawk. I'm sure you already know that the next deposition in this case will be your own."

He turned and spat and I laughed again. "See you then, Hawk. It'll be okay."

"If you say so. I'll go and get the gate for you." He sauntered away.

 I wanted to put Hawk's mind at ease that he had nothing to worry about, but really, how could I know what kind of questions was Dominic Flynn cooking up for him?

CHAPTER 16

FARMERS

The following Monday morning I pulled up next to the building in Ketchum known as "The Complex." It was an older, two-story building located centrally in town. People in need of office space could rent small or large offices, depending on their requirements. In addition, the second floor boasted a medium-sized conference room, and that was my destination this morning.

The conference room had been reserved for today's depos, and I'd arrived early so I would have time to set up and settle in for the day's work. Nobody here was going to hand me iPads to play with, and there'd be no yummy lunch provided. I was back to reality. No frills.

I parked right next to the front entrance. Fortunately, the early hour meant that there was still lots of parking available. That wouldn't be true later when the day really got going and Ketchum's summer visitors ventured forth. By mid-morning the streets would be congested with people. Streets and sidewalks would be filled with automobiles, bicycles, and pedestrians while visitors enjoyed a beautiful summer day in the mountains.

I heaved my heavy machine case out of the Juke's cargo area. No Hawk to help me today, and this building had stairs but no elevator. Extending its pull handle, I turned to slam the hatch door closed. My case bumped along behind me across the uneven bricks as I approached the front door and pulled it open.

The stairs were, mercifully, not terribly steep. After I greeted the building's receptionist I lowered my pull handle, picked up my case, and lugged my gear up to the second floor. The conference room I sought was located near the landing at the top of the stairs. I could see that someone had been there ahead of me and turned the lights on. I entered and surveyed the room casually.

It was a rectangular room, with a table and chairs dominating most of the real estate. I decided to set up at the end nearest the door, though I knew that the power outlet at this end had widened with age. My plugs never fit snugly. Sitting at this end meant running the risk that my plugs would fall out completely, my batteries would drain, and at just the wrong moment in the depo my computer would beep and cry for juice.

As I began pulling my equipment from my steno bag I allowed my thoughts to wander. I thought longingly of my perfect setup in the Lockwood mansion, with my leather chair and a power strip right at my feet. *I wonder what they're up to? What's it like, living in a home where the inhabitants are at war with each other?*

I inserted my laptop and writer plugs into the outlet, and then jammed my machine case against them so they'd stay put. My computer was humming to life even as I heard some commotion downstairs and realized some of the parties had arrived. A quick perusal of my notice reminded me that the plaintiff was a man named Lester Sutt, and he was suing Calvin and Cordelia Breedlaw. The Breedlaws had retained the services of Doug Harkins, an attorney well known in this entire region for his defense work. Smart, attentive to his clients, and unrufflable.

It was Doug's voice that I heard as he and his clients ascended to the conference room. The Breedlaws were a couple in their mid-sixties, and that couple made such a sight I caught myself staring – and not just at the people. Loping up the stairs beside them was a huge, young, frisky Rottweiler. He caught sight of me and was about to lunge in my direction, stumped-tail wagging, jowls drooling. Mr. Breedlaw caught him just in time with a soft command, "Stay, Hooch." I'd been ready to whisk my machine, tripod and all, out of harm's way, but the dog stopped in his tracks. He sat down on his haunches and looked at me hopefully.

I smoothed out my papers and smiled at Hooch, but I wasn't about to move from my seat. The dog might take that as an invitation to play.

Satisfied that Hooch was obediently staying put outside the conference room door, Mr. Breedlaw turned to me. "Good morning, young lady," he said in his quiet voice.

Calvin Breedlaw was perhaps six feet tall, rail thin except for an *enormous* belly. He looked like a string bean who'd swallowed a pumpkin. He had mid-length gray hair and a well-groomed goatee, and my mind immediately conjured an image of him as an officer in the Confederate army. *A well-fed officer,* I thought, *considering the size of his tummy.* The thought must have made me smile, because he smiled back, his eyes twinkling with merriment.

He turned to his wife. "Looks like we've found the right place, Dee-dee."

"Good morning," I returned pleasantly, making a mental note that Cordelia actually went by the name "Dee-dee."

"Well, Cal," his wife returned, "were you thinkin' Doug steered us wrong somewhere? Of *course* we're in the right place. Now quit talkin' and let me catch my breath. I ain't used to climbin' stairs at this altitude. Where are we sittin', Doug? I want to get settled before Lester shows up, or I just may poke him in the eye for causin' all this fuss."

Cordelia Breedlaw was a short, comfortably rotund woman with an unmistakable no-nonsense air about her. She carried a huge quilted satchel in one hand, and her other hand held an oversized, overstuffed, brown leather handbag. It looked heavy. Small wonder that she was out of breath!

Her face softened as she pointed a short finger at the Rottweiler. "You stay right there, Hoochie. There's a good boy."

The trio, unable to get past me and my gear in the tiny space, circled lengthwise around the conference table. "Cordelia," said Doug, "you're up first, so you'll sit nearest to the court reporter. I'll sit on your other side. Cal, you can pick any chair further down the table, but remember, you don't get to talk during Cordelia's deposition. You'll get your turn later. But when it's not your deposition, I don't want you saying anything at all, okay?"

"Aye, aye, Cap'n," returned Mr. Breedlaw softly. "I'll sit quiet and keep an eye on Hooch." A sudden stirring. "Oh, now, Hooch, I didn't call ya, buddy. Watch yourself, missy."

Too late. Hooch leaped into the room, whining as the table and chairs prevented access to Mr. Breedlaw. He turned my direction, thinking to find a way through. I barely had time to grab my machine as a huge wet nose ran up my arm.

"Hoochie!" cried Mrs. Breedlaw. "You go lay down! Leave the nice lady alo – "

I closed my eyes just in time as the enormous Rottweiler licked my face from chin to hairline. Something cold and gooey landed on my arm as I tried to shield my equipment from Hooch's enthusiastic romping.

"*Cal*vin!" squawked Cordelia, as Hooch left me and resumed his quest for his master, "get Hoochie-poo settled, or they'll make him wait in the car!"

"That'll do, Hooch," breathed Mr. Breedlaw. Hooch

immediately sat, grinning round at all of us. "You go on now," Calvin Breedlaw all but whispered. "Get yourself on out that door and lay down. There's a good boy."

That dog obviously lived for the word of his master. Good as gold, he stepped outside the conference room door and lay back down. I slowly withdrew my hands from their protective position above my steno machine, feeling a chill as a blob of drool rolled off my arm and plopped onto my leg. Ew!

I stood up and scanned the room, hoping to catch sight of some extra-strength paper towels. Just then I heard more footsteps on the stairs, and knew other parties were arriving. Desperate to wipe the remaining slobber off my arm and slacks, I nonetheless stopped in my tracks, staring once again. A giant of a man who could only be Chance Adams ascended the stairs, his 10-gallon Stetson and booming voice leading the way. He was followed by a wiry, angry-looking man who I assumed must be Lester Sutt. Bringing up the rear was Jed Barnes, local co-counsel from Twin Falls.

Chance Adams surveyed the situation. His eyes took in Doug Harkins, the Breedlaws, a gigantic Rottweiler, and me. He seemed to notice everything in that order, and when his eyes fell at last on me, his face lit up.

"Well, you must be our court reporter!" he beamed. "Chance Adams! Call me Chance. Pleased to meet you! One second now." He was carrying a banker's box full of files, and as he made haste to deposit the box on the table, I got a good look at his massive hands. I promptly dove for a business card, hoping to offer it and avoid a painful handshake. By the time he'd turned back to me and extended his right hand, I was ready. I held out my business card hopefully, but just as I began to reply, "Nice to meet you, Mr. Ad – " his left hand swooped in and plucked the card away, even as his right hand grabbed mine in a bone-crunching grip. I swallowed a yelp just in time. As Chance Adams turned to greet the others in the room, I surreptitiously inspected my throbbing right hand, wondering if the damage would be permanent.

"Well, looks like we're all here!" announced Mr. Adams, taking the seat nearest me and removing his hat. "Everybody ready to start?"

Cordelia Breedlaw had settled herself comfortably in her chair, and she now reached into her gargantuan quilted bag and withdrew the biggest knitting needles I'd ever seen. After then extracting a massive ball of thick, soft, ivory-colored yarn and a partially completed afghan, she looked around.

"I like the super bulky yarn, myself," she announced, looking my way. "Warmer. Got to get three more of these finished by winter. Alpaca, that's all I use. Family expects 'em for Christmas. Wears me out, but never mind. I'm the only one's got the skill anymore, seems like, in this family. Everyone else is on the computer, or lookin' at the TV, so it's up to me to keep 'em warm. Ain't that right, Cal." It was a statement, rather than a question, and Mr. Breedlaw only smiled in reply.

Nor did Mrs. Breedlaw look worn out in the slightest. Clearly in her element, she settled the afghan project on her lap and began clicking away with her needles. "Best get this show on the road," she asserted to the room at large. "I have things to get back to, and this is a pure waste of time." She jabbed a fat needle in the direction of Lester Sutt. "You can bet your bottom dollar, Lester, that I'll be writing to *Cheeky Peaks* about this nonsense."

My head snapped up.

"Yes, sir," *click, click, click,* "I'll write to her column, and then everyone who gets the paper will know how you sued us because *your* no good, thievin' horse kept stealing apples right off my tree.

It's not *our* fault your horse hurt his foot trying to pound down our fence – "

But Doug Harkins laid a calming hand on Mrs. Breedlaw's arm and she clamped her lips together, probably remembering an earlier admonition to answer questions simply and volunteer nothing. As she quietened I imagined Amy Kensington reading Aurora, aka *Cheeky Peaks,* a letter from an upset Cordelia Breedlaw. I found myself looking forward to whatever response *Cheeky* would proffer to the outraged farm wife. For now, time to put Cordelia under oath. I stuck my right hand in the air.

"Will you raise your right hand for me, please?"

Mrs. Breedlaw's hand shot up like she was swearing to defend the country.

"Do you solemnly swear or affirm that your testimony today will be the truth, the whole truth, and nothing but the truth?"

"I do," she nodded once and dropped her hand back to her knitting.

CORDELIA BREEDLAW,

First duly sworn to tell the truth relating to said cause, testified as follows:

EXAMINATION

QUESTIONS BY MR. ADAMS:

Q. Mornin', Mrs. Breedlaw. State your full name for the record, spelling your last.

A. Cordelia Olive Breedlaw, B-r-e-e-d-l-a-w.

Q. How old are you, Mrs. Breedlaw?

Shocked, Mrs. Breedlaw turned to face her attorney.

THE WITNESS: Can he ask that, Doug? I mean, he may as well ask my weight. There are things you never ask a lady.

MR. HARKINS: Counsel, you have all of our discovery responses, and you know full well what my client's age is. For the sake of moving things along, though, how about if you ask her when she was born.

BY MR. ADAMS:

Q. Ms. Breedlaw, when were you born?

A. That's the same thing, but fine. I was born Christmas Day, 1945.

Q. Making you 70 years old today. Thank you.

THE WITNESS: Doug, can we take that out? He just had to say it.

MR. HARKINS: It's okay, Dee-dee. No one will read this part of the transcript if we go to trial.

BY MR. ADAMS:

Q. What's your physical address, Mrs. Breedlaw?

A. You have my answers to all those horrid questions you sent us. You know where I live.

Q. Mrs. Breedlaw, this is going to be a very long day if you refuse to answer even basic questions.

A. I need a break.

Q. We just started. We can take a break soon, but I've only asked two questions. I'll repeat, what is your address, Mrs. Breedlaw?

A. I want to talk to my lawyer. I need a break. You're prying.

MR. HARKINS: Here's a Kleenex, Dee-dee. Let's take a break.

MR. ADAMS: Not when there's a question pending.

MR. HARKINS: I'll allow my client to take a break whenever she wants one. Plus, you never gave her that instruction.

MR. ADAMS: I didn't have time to.

MR. HARKINS: Come on, Chance. It's an address. She lives at 173 Chestnut in Filer. We're taking a break.

(A break was taken.)

CHAPTER 17

CLARABELLE'S DISCOVERY

Driving home later, I was eager to get into my apartment and change clothes. I'd never had an opportunity to find a wet cloth and wipe Rottweiler drool from my skin and pant leg. Cordelia Breedlaw's testimony had continued as it had begun, with frequent emotional break-taking and even more frequent baleful glares in Lester Sutt's direction. Our brief lunch break had been interrupted by Chance Adams asking me to help him sort through some of his exhibits. We'd finished Calvin Breedlaw's deposition – far friendlier but less entertaining than his wife's – an hour after the lunch break, during which I'd eaten nothing. Chance had asked if I would stay and help him organize the rest of his exhibits. I would have refused had I known it was going to take two solid hours. It was late afternoon by the time we finished and went our separate ways.

The blob of drool on my pants had dried and bore a close resemblance to a dirty snowball stain. It was obvious there had been a mess there, but the only thing visible was a white outer ring. What wasn't visible was the dried-on gore within the ring. *Yuck.*

On my arm, the goo had hardened into a stiff patch of skin that I chose not to investigate too closely. My right hand still ached from the knuckle-crunching it had received. Shower. Hot shower. Minutes away. That would fix everything.

As I parked my car, I let myself imagine the hot water and steamy bathroom. Pulling my machine out of the cargo area, I wondered if Herc would be patient enough to wait an extra thirty minutes for his dinner.

I raised the handle on my steno case and pulled it along behind me through the courtyard. As I approached my front door, I reached for my keys, then frowned. The door was slightly ajar. Only an inch or two, but I was certain I'd left it closed and locked this morning. My heart thudded. Someone had been in my house. Were they still there? A sickening sense of *déjà vu* threatened to overpower me.

No way.

I glanced over at the Darlings' door. Closed tight. It didn't look like they were even home. A second glance, this time at our new gate. Shut and locked.

Shower forgotten, I released my grip on my steno bag and lowered the handle. I set my purse down on top of it. I wanted both hands free for whatever was facing me inside my apartment. Holding my breath, I quietly stepped closer to the door and nudged it open with my toe.

Suddenly I was surrounded, what felt like on all sides, by five pounds of excited Chihuahua. Hercules had flown off the couch and made a run for me. He was scampering around my legs, leaping as high as he could, in hopes that I would bend down and catch him.

And why had he been sitting on my couch while I was at work, rather than staying with the ladies in *their* home? Well, because the ladies were *here*. Bernie and Clarabelle were uncharacteristically seated right there, on my sofa. Bernie looked like she'd been interrupted in the midst of some outdoor task. She was wearing faded blue jeans and her favorite flannel work shirt. Oddly, I noticed a soft leather folio resting near her feet. I noted her tightly folded arms and grim expression.

Seated at the other end of the sofa, Clarabelle looked – no other word for it – *embarrassed.*

She sat on the edge of the couch, wringing her dimpled hands nervously. I spotted the remains of a crumpled tissue on her lap, and when her red-rimmed eyes rose to meet mine, she nervously reached for another from the side table. Whatever was wrong with Clarabelle, I was relieved that at least it hadn't been another intrud –

Then it caught my eye. The side table held more than a simple box of tissues. In mute horror, I observed my Lockwood exhibit, *the* Lockwood exhibit, resting quietly on the table next to the tissue box. Small and sturdy, the lovely little 1945 Smith-Corona sat as though it were part of the decor.

I swallowed hard. *It shouldn't be sitting there.* I'd tucked it carefully away in a box labeled, "Lockwood Exhibits." Its existence was a secret. Deposition proceedings are confidential. And yet, there it was, out in the open, with the ladies.

I took in Clarabelle's evident discomfiture. My stomach churned as I held to the doorknob for support. Whatever had happened, I mustn't overreact.

"I can see from your face, Shae, that you've spotted the problem." Bernie folded her arms, her countenance resolute. "Your apartment, I'm afraid, has witnessed some unfortunate shenanigans this afternoon."

Bernie shifted slightly so that her folded arms and stern countenance were directed at Clarabelle, rather than at me. Clarabelle squirmed all the more and patted her legs in invitation to Hercules. He happily complied and hopped onto her lap. Fortified, Clarabelle drew a deep, shuddering breath.

"On you go, Clare," said Bernie. "Don't keep Shae waiting. Best tell her quickly what you've done, and what you found."

Clarabelle stroked Herc's head and neck over and over. At last she looked up, attempting a tiny, Clarabelle-like smile. Guilt oozed from her, as though she were a schoolgirl who'd been caught smoking with a boy in the woods after midnight. Even so it was impossible to keep her naturally cheerful nature suppressed.

"Now, Shae," she said, wavering slightly. Then she took another breath. "I promise I didn't mean any harm." Clarabelle's voice cracked on the final word, and Bernie stood up to get her a glass of water.

I carefully lowered myself into an armchair, hands trembling, wishing she would spit it out. I only cared about one thing right now, and the slow pace of this explanation was maddening. I tried to keep my external features calm while my inner self implored, *WHY IS THE TYPEWRITER OUT OF ITS BOX?*

Bernie handed Clarabelle the water, and Clarabelle took a delicate sip. She set the water down and squared her shoulders. She patted Hercules on the head.

"I wanted to take Hercules out," she resumed. "It's just so pretty outside."

I nodded what I hoped was encouragement.

"I couldn't find his leash anywhere. I tried to think where I put it yesterday, but it just wouldn't turn up! You know how I usually have a spare in my kitchen?" she asked, her eyes begging for understanding.

Another nod from me.

"Well, that one wasn't there either. So I thought I'd just sneak in here and see if you had an extra somewhere." She reached for another tissue and blew her nose. "I knew you wouldn't mind, Shae dear, since I'm in here all the time after all, watering your plants and everything. You know, when you travel." Sniff. Deep breath.

"So here I was, and I couldn't see a leash anywhere. And I thought that was really such a shame, because Herky was restless, and it truly was *so* nice out…" she trailed off, appearing to think.

"Best get to the point, Clare, for Pete's sake!" Bernie scolded. "Just tell her what happened and have done with it!"

"I'm *trying*." Clarabelle wrung her hands, crumpling her tissue further. "I've got to say things in my own *way*."

My head started throbbing at the temples, but I held my tongue for now. I would need to keep my voice even when I did speak to Clarabelle. If I startled or tried to hurry her, she'd become flustered, and I wouldn't get any more out of her.

"Go ahead, Clarabelle." I hoped I sounded gentle, patient on the outside. My trembling hands became clammy though, as my inner voice grew deafening.

The typewriter is out of its box!
The typewriter is out of its box!
The typewriter is out of its box!

Nothing good could come from such an important exhibit being mishandled.

Exhibits are the responsibility of the court reporter. He or she is to keep them safe and untampered with – period. The exhibit buck stopped with me, and I couldn't afford to mess up something this important.

Clarabelle correctly interpreted the signs of panic in my face. She fussed with her tissue and said she needed tea before she could go on. She refused to be hurried, and Bernie wasn't going to cover for her.

Rather than tear my hair out, I decided to leave the ladies for a few minutes and get cleaned up. My shower was an abbreviated version of the one I had planned, but it was soothing all the same. I felt much better after I threw my soiled clothes in the hamper, slipped into my comfy sweats, and poured a cup of tea for myself. I heard Hercules munching down his dinner in the kitchen. My own appetite had vanished.

Within twenty minutes, tea in hand, I had resumed my position in the armchair, ready to take up where we'd left off.

"Okay, Clarabelle. Let's try this again." I set my cup down. "You couldn't find a leash, and you came over here to look for one." Her head bobbed up and down. "You know that's okay with me. Right?" Another bob. "So just tell me what happened next."

"Well," she began, "I was looking around the kitchen, and then I saw a box by the dining room table." She glanced over to where the box still sat. "I didn't remember seeing that box there before, so I thought, you know, that maybe you'd been doing some cleaning, sort of clearing things out. I promise," her eyes begged me to understand, "I just took a peek inside in case you'd maybe thrown away an old leash. I wasn't prying, Shae, dear."

She stopped again.

"And you saw the Samsonite case?" I swallowed hard. My encouraging expression could slip at any moment.

Another nod. "I couldn't think what it was, but it seemed such an odd place for you to keep such a nice little suitcase."

I forced a smile. "So you lifted it out?"

"Well, yes, Shae, and it was so *heavy*! I – I *had* to see what was in it. So I put it on the table and opened it up."

At last we come to it. "And saw the typewriter."

"Yes!" Her eyes lit up. "Oh, the lovely thing." She leaned forward, comfortable with her story at last. "It's just like the one I learned to type on when I was in school. Oh, such memories at just the sight of it."

Bernie cleared her throat and crossed her arms again.

Clarabelle glared at Bernie, then smoothed her skirt. "You understand, Shae, dear. It just looked so perfect, sitting there on its little platform. I couldn't think why you'd want to throw it away."

"Stop it, Clare. You knew full well it wasn't trash." Bernie was losing patience.

"I'll tell it as I remember it, Bernice," Clarabelle huffed. "I'm the one inside my own head, after all." She turned to me again. "So I couldn't see any harm in seeing if it still worked, considering that it was probably headed to the garb – " she threw a look at Bernie, "Good Will."

"Okay." I wanted to keep my tone reasonable. My head throbbed again. Was this what high blood pressure felt like? "You took it out to see if it worked. How did you do that, exactly?"

"Oh," she waved her hand through the air, "I simply put it on the table, got some paper out of your printer, and rolled it right in."

My jaw dropped open. I didn't know Clarabelle even knew how to discern a printer from any other machine. I couldn't imagine how she'd located the paper tray.

"And guess what!" She clapped her hands in delight, forgetting that she was officially in trouble. "It worked. Beautifully. Oh, it took me back, I tell you, Shae. I always loved the feel of those round keys."

I sighed. Maybe this wasn't the end of the world. It sounded like Clarabelle had simply typed a few lines on the typewriter. She hadn't taken it apart or anything. My shoulders relaxed. Clarabelle had just been Clarabelle. Curious, carefree, excitable Clarabelle. No harm, hopefully no foul.

I put my hands on my legs, ready to ease her mind and

push myself to a stand. It was getting late in the afternoon. I needed to walk Hercules. Just as I opened my mouth to assure her that things were going to be fine, I noted that Bernie wasn't moving. She was waiting for more. Apparently, I hadn't heard everything yet.

Bernie remained silent for another full minute, then gave up. "Shae, Clare didn't just type a few words on a page." Bernie reached down and retrieved a pile of papers she'd placed in the leather folio at her feet. "Clare, it seems, was having a typing party over here." Bernie was exasperated, it was plain to see, but not angry. It was hard to be angry at Clarabelle.

Bernie pointed to my old copy of Agatha Christie's *Murder on the Orient Express*. It was lying on my table, held open with a stapler.

"There are ten sheets of paper here, filled with portions of that mystery novel." Bernie waved the papers in my direction a bit wildly. "I counted them. But that's not the full story. Go on, Clare. You're nearly done. Finish up so we can get out of Shae's hair."

Clarabelle straightened her shoulders again. "Yes, well…" She sipped her tea. "I was having *such* good fun, typing away. Oh, I do enjoy the carriage return."

"Focus," I breathed.

"Of course, dear. A *teensy* bit of patience might be in order. So, there I was, typing on this black beauty, imagining that I was Agatha Christie, coming up with such wonderful stories. The only trouble I encountered was when I had to type a Q." She seemed puzzled. "It didn't seem to matter whether it was an upper case Q or a lower case Q, either. It wouldn't type them properly. None of the Qs lined up. All the Qs were higher than the other letters, like they were superscript."

Clarabelle was full of surprises this evening. She knew about superscript?

"Anyway," she went on, "I didn't let it bother me. No one was ever going to see my pages, after all. It didn't matter to me if the Qs were too high.

"I finally remembered poor Herky. I knew he'd be anxious for his walk, and I realized I'd left his leash in the car when we'd run out for coffee this morning. By then I'd had enough fun for one afternoon. I stood, planning to put the typewriter back in the box, just as I'd found it."

My breath caught at the sound of a subtle shift in her voice. She'd grown quieter and far more serious than I'd ever known Clarabelle to be. I sensed we'd come to the crux of it at last. I gripped the edge of my seat cushion.

"Go on."

"When I picked up the typewriter..." Her voice was hushed. "Something..."

She looked desperately at Bernie, who nodded at her.

"Something – something fell out of it!"

I felt the blood drain from my face. *Something fell out of it?* The exhibit was now altered. *Forever.*

I didn't waste time hoping that the object that had fallen was insignificant. Clarabelle wouldn't be so uncomfortable if the item was merely a lump of wadded up paper. Bernie wouldn't be so grim if one of the feet had come loose from the bottom of the machine and dropped to the floor. Dreadful as that might have been, it could have been easily explained, given the Smith-Corona's age. It was practically an antique.

I knew the item was relevant. The ladies knew it. I felt suddenly queasy. It was just as well I hadn't had any lunch.

"Let's have it, then." I was looking at Bernie. She'd taken

possession of the typed pages. I knew she must also have custody of the object.

Bernie reached into her folio again, and this time she withdrew a common, zip-sealed sandwich bag containing a very small ivory-colored item in one corner of the bag. Otherwise the bag was empty. I was seated five feet away, and I couldn't make out the object.

"It's a tooth." Bernie held up the bag. "A single, human tooth. Who knows how long it's been wedged in there."

A tooth? What would a tooth be doing in a typewriter?

Lots of creatures have teeth, though.

"Bernie, how do you know it's human? Could this be a dog's tooth? Or perhaps some other animal's?" I thought desperately. "I mean, what if the machine was stored in a shed at some point? Couldn't it belong to an animal of some kind who broke into a storage shed, chased a mouse to the typewriter, tried to take a bite, and lost a tooth?"

I was grasping at straws. Even I couldn't really envision the scenario I'd just hypothesized. I also knew that for the past forty years the typewriter had sat silently in Otto Lockwood's bedroom. Still, the tooth could have landed in there even *before* Otto vanished. It was worth investigating. "It could be an animal. Right?"

"Not," Bernie looked at the tooth, and then back at me, "unless your dog or other animal had excellent dental care." She turned the baggie over. "See the gold on the back of the tooth, Shae? This tooth has been subjected to some fairly modern dentistry."

We sat in silence for a few moments. My kitchen clocked ticked. Herc looked up at me and whimpered. He needed to go out. At last I found my voice.

"Did either of you touch it?" I asked.

"Nick of time, Shae, dear. Nick of time." Clarabelle enthused, as her bubbly nature rising to the surface. "I had just noticed it, and I was bending down to pick it up and see what it was. Just then Bernice opened the door, and well," she cast a guilty glance at Bernie, "well, she saw my pages, all the fun I'd been having…"

"And I told her to stop whatever she was doing immediately." Bernie refolded her arms. "I said, 'Clare, you know Shae works in legal matters, and you ought not to bother her things.'"

But Clarabelle had been interrupted, and now she seemed eager to go on. "Anyway, we both bent down to get a good look at it, and we could see, plain as day, that it was a human tooth."

"Hmph!" Bernie rolled her eyes.

"Let's not bother with who saw what first, Bernice. You know how that tries me. I was about to point out the crown myself. You beat me to it by a hairsbreadth, that's all. We knew it was human at the same time."

Bernie shrugged. There was no point in driving Clarabelle into a pout.

I'd heard enough. My head was reeling. A *tooth*. A human *tooth*. One of the pointy ones, by the look of it. "So you *didn't* touch it?"

"We certainly did not." Clarabelle looked insulted. "We got two sandwich bags. We used one of them to pick up the tooth, and we dropped it into the other one. It's pristine." She beamed.

"Hardly." Bernie had watched all the right cop shows. "It'll have your carpet fibers on it, Shae, but at least it won't have any of our fingerprints."

Well, that was something. Even so, and in spite of my love for her, I wanted to throttle Clarabelle Darling.

I am not a cop.

I am not an attorney.

I am not an investigator.

I am a court reporter. My job is to get the record down and take care of the exhibits.

My shoulders slumped. I didn't know what to do about this. Sure, someone could have innocently dropped their tooth into the typewriter years ago and forgotten to retrieve it.

Really, Shae?

What if someone had been fighting in the vicinity of the little machine? My imagination immediately produced an image of people playing a literal game of "Rock 'Em Sock 'Em Robots," blackening eyes and blowing out teeth.

Don't be absurd, Shae. Why would anyone position themselves over a typewriter in a fist fight?

I rubbed my eyes, reminded of the dull ache lingering in my right hand. I needed to call it a day. The tooth was safe in sealed plastic. Nothing more could be done for now. I held my hand out for the baggie, and Bernie gave it to me. I turned it this way and that, hoping this tiny object hadn't just ruined my life.

I stood slowly and scooped up Hercules. I reached behind the door, to where his leash hung from a coat hook. It had been there in view the whole time. Clarabelle stood too, unsure of herself again. I crossed the small space and gave her a hug, with Herc squeezed between us.

"I'm going to take Herc out and then come and make some dinner." *If I can manage to eat anything.* "Let's leave this for now and get some rest. I have to be up early tomorrow to get to a job in Pocatello."

She nodded. "Just drop Herc through the dog door when you leave."

"I will. Oh, and Clarabelle?"

"Yes, Shae, dear," she whispered.

"I trust we've had enough fun with typewriter reminiscing?"

"Of course. Oh, yes, of course. I promise I won't touch anything ever again." Tears welled in her eyes again. "I'm sorry, Shae. You know I'm sorry. Right?"

"I know, Clarabelle. I know."

The ladies left and I dropped the baggie into a small, lockable drawer in my coffee table. The moment I turned the lock and withdrew the key my knees buckled and I slumped into the nearest chair. A tooth. A human tooth had been lodged in an exhibit for which I had sole custody and responsibility. It seemed such a tiny item to carry with it such enormous implications.

CHAPTER 18

POCATELLO DRIVE

My Pocatello job consisted of six attorneys, one deponent, one videographer, and four onlookers. As parties to the case, the observers had every right to be there, but our hotel conference room was small. By 10:00 a.m. we were all sweating bullets as the crowded room overheated.

At lunch time the hotel maintenance man had turned the A/C on full blast, hoping to cool the room down. It was as much as he could do though, since the videographer didn't want noisy air-conditioning running during the actual deposition. His mics were sensitive, and the A/C fan overlaid his audio with a loud background roar.

And so, amidst heat, nonstop objections, and a poor attitude from the deponent, we all suffered through the day. It was late afternoon by the time the depo concluded and I was able to pack up and hit the road. I had a long way to go.

That morning I'd been up at five, gotten ready, and driven the 152 miles to Pocatello. I often worked in this medium-sized city located down in the southeast corner of Idaho. I'd slept only fitfully the night before as thoughts of the typewriter and tooth haunted me. I was exhausted as I heaved my equipment into the car and settled in for the 2.5-hour drive home. I was thankful I'd filled the tank when I'd arrived in Pocatello earlier that morning. Long experience had taught me that when a job was finished, I'd be like the horse headed for the barn. I wouldn't want to make any stops.

I drove home in absolute silence, having turned the radio off shortly after leaving town. Though it was after 4:00 p.m., the sun was still high in Idaho's summer sky. I anticipated a peaceful, quiet drive. Plenty of time to think. Plenty of time to ponder the dark cloud that had draped its ominous arms so thoroughly around my life.

I spent the entire trip mentally chewing over the tooth-related problem. What was I to do about an item, *a human item*, that had fallen out of a deposition exhibit?

My smile returned unexpectedly as a thought occurred to me. *What would my ethics professor say?*

Ethics? As court reporting students, we first learned steno theory, or language. We then studied medical and legal terminology. We took English and vocabulary courses. At last, when our brains were stuffed to bursting and our fingers were gaining momentum, we found ourselves facing questions of dos and don'ts, of rights and wrongs.

We were told we might find ourselves in questionable situations where we would have to decide what our own behavior should be. Battling our way through school, safe in our academic world, we hadn't yet experienced the real-life drama of legal proceedings – proceedings in which we would play a vital part.

I had landed in just such a questionable situation now. Out on the lonely highway, I set the cruise control and allowed my mind to take me back to school, back to my ethics class.

I longed for my fellow students as I grappled with my problem alone. I wished I could stand before them and say, "I have an exhibit, a tooth, and a question."

My smile broadened as my mind conjured images of our

classroom setting, complete with our very own Professor Roswell and her slightly unusual teaching style...

CHAPTER 19
ETHICS

Funny the stuff you remember from college courses. My biggest takeaway from Ethics class was that we never *resolved* our ethical dilemmas. I remember our class batting around make-believe ethical quandaries, wracking our brains for first this solution, and then that. I don't remember ever reaching any firm decisions when it came to, "This you *must* do, and this you must *not* do."

I could still hear Professor Kendra Roswell's mischievous voice as she paced the room, posing various ethical problems to us. This was a fun deviation from a normal school night. Professor Roswell was our English professor, but it fell to her to set aside a few evenings each semester and tackle the jungle of ethics with her English classes.

A product of the 1960s, Professor Roswell remained a picture of loose, flowing earth tones and wavy, waist-length hair. She had long since ditched her hippy beads and had donned a bra, in deference to her place of employment. All the same, anti-establishment sentiments were often evident just behind her classroom banter. It begged the question: Why was Kendra Roswell teaching ethics to court reporting students?

None of us cared, mind you. We loved her and her idiosyncratic ways. Class was never boring. I smiled as one particular ethical evening came to mind.

***

"You are in a deposition," Professor Roswell announced, "and multiple exhibits have been produced. When a break is called, Attorney A leaves the room with his client. Attorney B waits until they are out of sight, and then begins rifling through Attorney A's files. It is obvious to you that Attorney B is examining documents that have not yet been produced in the deposition. They are," she raised an eyebrow in our direction, "the confidential property of Attorney A."

She then stood still, waiting as our gasps of horror calmed into muted murmurs. Satisfied that we were suitably outraged, she resumed her pacing.

"*Where* does your ethical duty *lie?*" she trilled.

"You have to tell Attorney A," offered one forthright student.

"No," asserted another, "you tell Attorney B you see what he's up to and make him stop."

"Oh!" Professor Roswell spun to a stop, eyeing them both. "And *who* made *you* the depo police?"

The two girls squirmed in their chairs as another shot her hand into the air.

"Pretend you didn't see." she offered.

"Are you *blind?*" pounced the professor, whirling around. "You're an officer of the court. You've just witnessed an illegal act. Will you now play *dumb?*"

The third student quickly studied the floor, cheeks burning.

A fourth student, Sally Bly, lazily slid her hand into the air. Sally *Sly*, I thought. That girl had street smarts. Sally could always be found at the back of the class, slouched low in her chair. She sat with her long legs straight out before her, ankles crossed. Sally favored dark clothes, leather jackets, and body piercings. Sometimes I overheard tittered comments from other students, as people wondered why a girl like her was attending court reporting college.

I never asked that question. Sally and I had started school the same night, and the two of us had kept pace the past three years. Sally was brilliant in academics, she flew effortlessly through her speeds, and she showed fellow students more respect than they sometimes displayed toward her. I was eager to hear what Sally would do with our ethical question.

Professor Roswell clasped her hands and smiled widely as though she, too, were eager to hear Sally's response. "Yes, Sally? What would *you* do, if confronted with such a naughty attorney?"

"Mind my own business," Sally drawled slowly. Her answer seemed a little anticlimactic until she straightened in her chair and smiled wickedly. "At *first*." Leaning back, she brought in her legs and crossed her knees. She grasped a nail file and stared a while at her fingernails, giving a nonchalant touch here, a small smooth there. I imagined her in professional clothes, *sans* personal hardware. She'd be a stellar court reporter.

"I'd just stay in the room," she went on, "taking care of my nails, like this," she demonstrated another caress with the file. "I'd stare at him 'til he noticed me." Sally looked around the room, allowing her eyes to fall upon each of us in turn. Most of us fidgeted nervously beneath her piercing gaze, but we didn't look away.

Noting our rapt attention, she went on. "Then I'd stare at the files he held. Finally, I'd look right at him and ask, 'Read anything good in there?'"

The class erupted into laughter as Sally dropped her nail file to the desk and resumed her slouch, wicked smile still in place.

"Bravo!" applauded Professor Roswell. "That's the most courageous answer I've ever heard to that question."

"I'll bet he'd drop those papers like they were on fire!" someone said with enthusiasm from the front row.

"So which is right?" I spoke at last. "What *should* we do if we're confronted with a situation like that?"

An undercurrent of agreement rippled through the class. Some students wanted an answer, and others raised more questions …

"Yes, is Sally's way best?"

"Is confrontation wrong?"

"Is telling the other side also wrong?"

But Professor Kendra Roswell was on to bigger and better ethical puzzles. She left depositions behind and put us in a courtroom where a criminal trial was taking place. We were to imagine ourselves as the court's official reporter.

"It's your lunch break," she began, flowing around the room as she posed the question. "As you walk through the hallway, you overhear a whispered conversation in a room where someone has failed to close the door. It's the defendant in the very case you're working on in court. Criminal court. And he's confessing his guilt. 'I killed the guy!' says he.

"To your horror, you realize that he's not speaking to his attorney. Nor is he speaking to his wife." She paused and scanned the class. Reassured that we were keeping up with confidentiality issues pertaining to attorneys and spouses, she finished with a sweeping, "NO, dear students! He's confessing his ghastly crime to his *friend*!"

She stopped her pacing and turned to us, opening her arms wide to encompass all of us.

"And now, my young court reporting friends, what do you doooo?"

A student jumped right in. "Go straight to the judge and tell him what you heard."

"Ah-ha!" Professor Roswell said, triumphantly. "And do you think your judge will thank you for presenting evidence outside the presence of counsel? Do you believe he'll be happy now that you've given him cause for bias?" None of us could escape her demanding blue eyes. "Ask yourselves this question. Does the judge *investigate* cases, or does he simply preside over them and apply the law to the evidence and arguments of counsel?"

Another student blurted quickly, "Go to the prosecution. Talk to the dead man's wife. Tell them what you heard, so *they* can investigate it."

Professor Roswell's eyes positively gleamed. "Ever heard of a thing called hearsay? Did you record what you heard, my friend? Your word against the defendant's. Are you sure you want to get the hopes of the victim's wife involved in this quagmire? Hmmm? Are you ready for the prosecutor to now put *you* on the stand, requiring a replacement court reporter to be brought in? My goodness! Has it occurred to you that your judge, who is fond of you, might have to recuse himself, and that change could cause a mistrial? Do you *desire* a reputation in the courthouse of being an eavesdropping, interfering busybody?"

And on it went. No absolutes. No answers. Just questions. Always questions…

CHAPTER 20
ROCK THROUGH THE WINDOW

I dragged my mind back to the present. *Ah, Professor Roswell. What questions would you ask me now?*

She would surely point out the pitfalls of any action or inaction upon which I decided. Not that I needed any help. I wasn't having any trouble imagining all kinds of pitfalls, all on my own.

My jumbled thoughts had carried me all the way home, but they hadn't helped me solve my problem. I'd found no more answers now than I had at the end of my ethics class. I'd learned that Professor Roswell had never intended to provide us with absolutes. For instance, if A is absolutely *right,* it follows that B is absolutely *wrong.* Perhaps she was just teaching us to *think.* Perhaps her real intention had been to clarify our job description. My big takeaway from her class was that I should mind my own business, play no favorites, and do an excellent job at the thing that *is* my job, and that is to just to get the record down.

But that all blew up yesterday.

I thought of the old typewriter. I thought of the tooth and how it had been discovered. I was no longer a mere spectator to a lawsuit that involved very rich and very powerful players. I now had a secret. A secret that had resided within the first and most important exhibit in the case. And I had no idea if the secret was mine alone.

As I pulled into the garage at home, the question loomed large before me – *what should I do?*

* * *

I'd leave my machine in the car overnight. I was tired, and unloading it could wait for once. I stepped out of the car and shut the door. *Complete silence.* No happy Chihuahua bounding to greet me. No Clarabelle fussing about the courtyard. No sign of life anywhere.

Clarabelle and Herc must be on one of their walks. I glanced at my watch – six forty-five. Hmmm. Seemed late for a walk.

The front door to the Darlings' part of the house was thrown wide open. That was unusual. The ladies loved sunlight and always kept their windows open in the summertime, but never the front door. The front door had no screen, and Clarabelle disliked insects.

It must have swung open by mistake. I stepped through the courtyard to pull the door shut, but I heard muffled voices from within the house. Was someone *crying?*

Alarms went off in my head. Had old Mr. Gruber caused more trouble? Was Clarabelle still upset about playing with the typewriter? Was someone hurt? I didn't want to intrude, but I cared for these ladies. I needed to make sure everything was okay.

I removed my shoes and padded softly through Bernie and Clarabelle's spotless living room. This room was the farthest I'd ever ventured into their home. There'd never been a need to move into the hallway and through to the bedrooms in the back, but that's where the voices were coming from, so on I went. I opened my mouth to call out and ask if everything was okay, but closed it abruptly.

"*Whyyyy?*" Clarabelle cried. Her voice could be heard clearly for the first time, and she was sobbing uncontrollably.

I crept closer, hoping I'd be able to find them and catch Bernie's eye before Clarabelle saw me. I wanted to watch for her signal on whether I should stay or go. I passed one bedroom, and then a second. The ladies were not in either of those rooms. I carried on to an open door at the farthest end of the hallway, squinting my eyes against a sudden, unexpected brightness. Shards of light drew my eyes to the floor.

There, in the middle of the floor, lay a pile of freshly broken glass. The sun, beginning its final descent in the western sky, appeared through a broken window, flooding the room with brilliant rays. They bounced off the tiny crystals on the floor, temporarily blinding me.

I adjusted myself out of the way of the strongest reflections. My hand flew to my mouth in shock as I took in the scene before me. Clarabelle sat on a bed, clutching a picture frame in one arm and a stuffed gorilla in the other.

Squeezing both objects to her chest, she again sobbed, "*Whyyyy?*"

Bernie sat near Clarabelle on the bed, making soft, soothing sounds. Her arm moved rhythmically as she rubbed Clarabelle's back, trying to calm her.

And there was Herc, curled up on Clarabelle's lap, offering what comfort he could. He looked up and whimpered softly at her lament.

"How could someone *do* this, Bernice?" Clarabelle hiccupped twice. "What did Danny ever do to anyone? Poor sweet Danny! His *things*, Bernice!" Clarabelle's body was wracked by fresh sobs. She rocked back and forth on the edge of the bed. "There's glass all over his *things!*"

His things? Whose things? Who was Danny? I glanced around the room, noting a bookshelf that held battered copies of *Tom Sawyer* and *Huckleberry Finn*, various comic books, and several baseball cards. The baseball cards were arranged neatly to display each player's face to advantage. The comic books and the novels looked well-loved and thumbed through. Small flecks of glass could be seen overlaying the entire assortment.

Opposite the bed and nearest to the door where I stood sat a beautiful oak dresser, its surface polished to a lovely, soft glow. Typical male bedroom items, such as a hairbrush, a rolled up leather belt, a watch, and an autographed baseball were arranged on top. In one corner of the dresser stood a photograph of a happy threesome. I could make out the faces of a younger Clarabelle and Bernie. The third face belonged to a smiling young man who displayed the unmistakable characteristics of Down syndrome. Was that Danny?

I tore my eyes away from the photograph and looked back to the two sisters I'd grown so fond of. I could now see a thin line of blood weeping its way down Clarabelle's arm. Some of the window glass had found its way onto the gorilla she held so tightly.

I was frozen, appalled. A brick sat in the middle of the pile of glass. Someone had deliberately smashed their window. Who would do such a thing to these nice ladies? And why pick on *this* room?

A thought struck me, and I swayed on my feet, feeling suddenly sick. Could this be related to the break-in two weeks ago? Had my intruder returned as we'd feared and found my side of the building too difficult to get into?

The brick had been lobbed through the window from the backyard. I stepped into the room, wanting to look into the yard and see if anything looked out of place, but Bernie motioned me back. I looked at her, my eyes questioning, but she simply shook her head slightly. I could tell she knew something, and she didn't want to mention it in front of Clarabelle.

Clarabelle's eyes were closed as she sobbed, so I mouthed silently to Bernie, "Another break-in?"

Bernie answered me with a small nod.

My stomach clenched again, and an unfamiliar heat flowed through my body. I had told myself, enough times that I almost believed it, that my own break-in had nothing to do with the typewriter that was Exhibit A. I'd met all of the parties in the Lockwood/Kensington litigation, and not one of them seemed capable of breaking and entering. With this new development, the question roared back to life in my head. Was someone after the typewriter?

In all the years I'd lived with the Darlings, we'd never experienced a lot of trouble. The area was so safe that no one on our street had even had a package stolen from their front porch at Christmastime. It was unthinkable that the same home had been the victim of *two* violent intrusions in as many weeks. Since there was nothing new in our lives – no new purchases, no lottery winnings, no vast inheritances – I could only conclude that the events sprung from the large case I was working on.

The first incident had occurred mere hours after I'd brought Exhibit A home. And though the intruder couldn't know it, this second attempt at criminal trespass had happened only one day after Clarabelle had discovered that the typewriter held a secret. A human body part secret.

I am not given to high temper, so a sudden protective, simmering anger took me by surprise. How *dare* anyone harm these two innocent women just to gain an advantage in a lawsuit!

The more I thought about it, the surer I became that these intrusions were linked to my exhibit. I needed to get away by myself and *think*. I was overcome by a sudden desire to be alone and mull through my suspicions.

I knew I should leave. The ladies could tell me about this incident in their own way later. I suddenly felt intrusive, a peeping Tom into an area of their lives so private they'd never shared it with me. They'd never mentioned this bedroom or its apparent former occupant. This was very private stuff. I turned and tried to slip quietly back down the hallway.

"Shae, please stay."

I hesitated for a moment, but returned per Bernie's request.

"Shae," Bernie said, never taking her eyes from Clarabelle. "It's high time you were introduced to our darling brother, Danny."

* * *

We sat in the Darlings' living room awaiting the arrival of Sergeant Landers. Bernie had skipped 911 and had called him directly. Clarabelle had agreed to leave Danny's bedroom, though she still held the stuffed gorilla tightly to her chest. She'd allowed Bernie to shake it thoroughly and inspect it for glass shards, but apart from that, she wouldn't let it go. The picture frame she'd been holding was now resting on the coffee table. It was an eight-by-ten of Danny in a high school graduation gown, and he looked radiant. With his right hand, he held his brand new diploma. With his left, he flashed the camera a big thumbs up.

Clarabelle had relinquished the photo only so that we could all see him equally as we gathered round.

"Danny was born to our parents late in life," Bernie began. "I was twenty-one years old, and Clarabelle twenty, when news of Danny's imminent arrival stunned our parents. They'd already raised their family, and retirement was supposed to be just around the corner."

She looked lovingly at the picture. "Our parents knew their pregnancy was high risk, but in 1961 it wasn't that unusual for a couple, even in their mid-forties, to find themselves expecting. They held on through a difficult pregnancy, hoping for a son."

Clarabelle, calmer now, managed a watery smile. "And what a beautiful son he was," she marveled. "Our personal piece of sunshine from the moment he was born. We all just doted on him. Oh, Bernice!" Clarabelle wept afresh. "Do you remember? No matter how much we spoiled him, he just stayed so sweet and out-loved us all."

"Shae will think Danny walked around wearing a halo," Bernie said fondly. "But he was capable of his antics too. I seem to remember a time he dressed the cat in your underwear, Clare, right in the middle of a visit from the minister."

Bernie turned to me. "Mother became ill with cancer when Danny was just ten years old. Lung cancer, though she'd never smoked a single cigarette. The minister was a frequent visitor, and Danny thought he could lighten the atmosphere by dressing up the cat. Clarabelle was fit to be tied."

"I didn't care!" Clarabelle's cheeks bloomed pink. "I *shouldn't* have cared. He didn't mean any harm."

"Mother died within six months of her diagnosis," Bernie said, cutting to the chase. "Father followed shortly after of a purely broken heart. It was up to Clare and me to finish raising Danny and make sure he was always taken care of." Bernie appeared lost in the past for a moment. "We were adults by then, but we had no families of our own. Caring for Danny was no trouble. With Danny in our home, our lives were delightful."

"We lost him when he was only thirty-two years old," whispered Clarabelle. She stroked the gorilla, nuzzling it to her cheek. "His heart had never been strong. He tried – he tried to stay with us." Fresh tears. "But then he t–t–told us not to be sad, that he was going to be with Mother and Father soon, and he was glad we had each oth–oth–other! Ohhhh!"

I jumped up for a box of Kleenex as Clarabelle hid her face in her hands.

"Danny left us on New Year's Day, 1994," Bernie said, taking up the story now that Clarabelle was incapacitated. "We've left his room as it was. Clarabelle can't bear the thought of removing his belongings. It's all we have of him now, you see." Even Bernie's strong composure was showing signs of strain. She patted Clarabelle's hand.

"But we know he's in heaven, don't we, honey?"

"He's an *angel* in heaven," Clarabelle wailed rebelliously.

Bernie grasped the hand she'd been patting, firmer now. "Clare, *angels* are angels in heaven. Danny is Danny, and he's far too busy enjoying his life with God to worry about trying to become an angel."

We were all silent for a moment. What a rich life these sisters had led. Their joys – and their sorrows – were palpable. Their love for their younger brother did not appear to have diminished with time, but their grief seemed to have softened. The breaking of the window was horrendous, but perhaps it had served a purpose, in the end. Danny's door was open. The ladies were speaking of him to me for the first time. Those seemed like good things to me.

"What's the gorilla's name?" I asked with a grin. It was a cute thing, after all, maybe fourteen inches tall, and it held a partially peeled banana.

"Chocolate," Clarabelle stated proudly, sounding stronger. "We gave him to Danny for his tenth birthday, which was just before we three lost both of our parents. Danny always took such good care of Chocolate. He never took him out in the rain." Her breathing grew less ragged as her eyes softened. "Our sweet brother slept with the stuffed animal until he was grown. Then Danny claimed it wasn't manly to sleep with toys, but Chocolate always had a place on his bed." She managed a grin of her own. "Even if it was on top of the covers."

She patted her puffy face and tried a real smile. "Sergeant Landers will be here any moment, and I look a fright. Perhaps some cold water on my eyes…" Clarabelle rose to her feet.

I stood and gave her a squeeze. She sniffed loudly and took herself down the hall while Bernie motioned me to be seated again.

"Clare will be all right, Shae." She paused thoughtfully, gazing at the photograph. "I want you to know that I've been after her for *years* to tell you about Danny. His life isn't a secret. He was our delight and joy. But it's just been too painful for her to talk about. Clarabelle has deeper waters than I sometimes give her credit for." She glanced at the doorway through which Clarabelle had disappeared. "But that isn't all I wanted to talk to you about. The reason this incident hit Clare so hard was that it happened right after she'd received some rather difficult news."

I frowned. Difficult news? And then Danny's bedroom violated, all at once? "What happened?"

"Well, Clare took Herc for his normal afternoon walk over to Nettie's, and I'm afraid Nettie had to tell Clare that she'll be moving to River Grace soon."

I had to catch my breath for a moment. "The assisted living facility?"

"The same." Bernie exhaled deeply and rubbed her thighs. "It's for the best, Shae. Nettie's been struggling for some time to keep up with the shopping, cooking, and cleaning. Now she needs a hip replacement and will have some ongoing needs as far as her care. She's made a good decision for herself, but you know how Clare counts on their daily visits. I'm afraid she spent the visit today trying to change Nettie's mind. Nettie is firm, though, and has already begun making arrangements."

"Poor Clarabelle," I whispered. Something occurred to me. "Bernie, I know you ladies share the car, but I don't think I've ever seen Clarabelle actually *drive* it."

"Oh, she has a license, Shae. I've just coddled her too much, and I drive when we go somewhere."

"Will you drive her to go and visit Nettie?"

"You and I must both encourage Clarabelle to drive herself, Shae. The place is only two miles away. Can I count on you?"

"You got it. What's my role?"

"Just don't offer to drive her. You can offer to accompany her while *she* drives, but don't let her turn you into a chauffeur. She's a perfectly capable driver. She's just gotten out of the habit."

I raised my hand to my forehead as though I were saluting. "Aye, aye, Captain. We'll get her back behind the wheel."

"Thanks, Shae."

"Sure." That settled, I needed one more thing from Bernie while Clarabelle was away. "Bernie, how did you know the broken window was a break-in attempt, and not just some kid throwing a brick for fun?"

"Ladders," Bernie stated matter-of-factly. "Two of 'em. One going up to the top of the decospikes, and one meeting it nose-to-nose from the backyard. It wouldn't have been hard to lower a ladder into our yard from the alleyway, in spite of the spikes. All someone had to do was climb up one and down the other, and they'd have been in."

"In broad daylight?" I couldn't believe it.

"It's pretty quiet back there. Guess they took a chance. They might have finished breaking the window and come on in if Clare hadn't been here and started yelling."

Clarabelle had been here when the brick had come through the window. It was too much. The unfamiliar anger resurfaced, and my blood reheated uncomfortably.

I needed to fix this. That this had happened to Clarabelle on top of her other difficult news was more than I could stand, especially since I feared that the vandalism had to do with my job.

It was nearly 9:00 p.m. I couldn't do anything this evening. Clarabelle emerged from the hallway with her face still puffy but freshly powdered. With one last hug for her and a pat on the shoulder for Bernie, I made my escape. Sergeant Landers would be here to speak to the Darlings at any moment. Since Clarabelle was doing better, Hercules happily trotted before me as we crossed through the courtyard and entered my apartment. We were both hungry. I poured some food into his tiny bowl and threw a frozen dinner into the microwave for myself. As it heated, I stepped to where the typewriter sat silently on my table.

Ha! I thought joylessly. *Silently.* The name of the typewriter was a Smith-Corona Silent.

But you aren't so silent, are you? Oh, I think you have lots of stories to tell. And I'm going to find out what they are.

I hurriedly unlocked the private drawer in my coffee table and withdrew the plastic bag that held the tooth. I stared at it – I studied it. I was still considering it when the microwave beeped that my food was hot.

Tomorrow…tomorrow I am going to get some answers.

I put the plastic bag in my purse as an image of Professor Roswell swam to the forefront of my mind. I could envision her with an arched brow and a piercing gaze as she asked the question, "Ms. Rose, whatever are you going to *do*?"

I'm going to protect my friends. If that typewriter is the reason for these intrusions, then I need to get to the bottom of it, ethics or no ethics, and I'm starting with that tooth.

CHAPTER 21
RIDE TO THE LAB

The next morning dawned bright and sunny. Now late August, the air might be not only nippy, but cold enough to form frost on car windshields. There wouldn't be many more motorcycle riding days left this year. I had a ride planned with my friend Kelly for this Saturday, and the Poker Run was next weekend, Labor Day. And that would probably be it for the year.

For today, I had a different kind of bike ride in mind. I donned my bicycle pants and a riding jacket, and pulled my regular bike out of the garage. I'm particularly fond of my bike, a brown Townie with turquoise rims, white seat, and an ideal—for me—seven gears.

The Wood River Valley boasts over thirty miles of perfectly paved bike paths. If you ride any distance at all, you'll find yourself encountering slopes of varying inclines and declines. I'd tried tackling those paths with a one-gear bike. I'd tried the same rides with a twenty-one-gear bike. In the end, like Goldilocks, I'd found the bike that was "just right." Seven gears.

I put a jacket on Hercules and placed him in the basket attached to my handlebars. He settled into his cushion and let me cover him with a small blanket. He was well-used to this routine. His cushion included a raised, zippered compartment where I was able to put my cell phone. This morning I carefully dropped the baggie containing the tooth inside next to my phone and zipped it closed.

I decided we could ride all the way to our destination, a distance of eleven miles. We were headed for a business located at the very southern tip of Ketchum and could rest there before tackling the return journey.

It was a chilly start, and I was glad I'd brought the extra blanket for Herc. Slowly, as I gained momentum, I warmed up. The past weeks had been filled to the brim with work, fear, stress, and, as of yesterday, concern for loved ones. I needed the release of mindless activity. I rode as fast as I could, exhilarated with the freedom of being outdoors. I pushed myself harder, relishing the sound of my tires, the pumping of my legs. I felt alive!

Alive! The word struck me so hard that my right foot flailed right off the pedal, and I swerved violently, narrowly missing a cyclist in the oncoming bike lane. I refound the pedal and yelled a "Sorry!" to the other person.

Alive, as opposed to dead!

What if the owner of the tooth had been *alive* when the tooth left his mouth, but *dead* immediately thereafter? I'd been searching for reasons that a tooth could have come to rest in the typewriter. I'd played with the words *argument* and *fight*. But my mind had deliberately skirted round the word *death*.

Oh, no. Wobbling, I eased my Townie to the side of the bike path, and then onto the shoulder. There was only one person on the Lockwood Estate who I knew to have died around the time Otto had vanished. The family's patriarch, Myron Lockwood. My mind flew back to Dalton Lockwood's deposition. What had he said?

"As to your reference to an accident, Father's death was always questionable, in my mind. I never felt I got a proper explanation.

It's hard to credit the falling-down-the-stairs story. Father knew those stairs like the back of his hand."

And then Otto's sudden disappearance right after the funeral. My bike was standing still, but the wheels of my mind were working on overdrive. Had Otto killed his father, and then fled the country? Was that why he'd never been able to come home? Could that be the reason he'd asked a friend to mail his letter to Cheeky Peaks, aka Aurora, five years ago? Had he wanted to assure her he was okay, but he couldn't reach out in a more substantial way?

Oh, help! Did Aurora *know*? Was that why she was fighting so fiercely to prevent Otto being declared dead? Did she know for a fact that he wasn't? Was sweet, blind Aurora Kensington an *accomplice after the fact*?

The implications were mind-boggling. I was supposed to be involved in a *civil* case. I looked again at the zippered compartment above Herc's cushion. Had a tiny tooth just infused *criminality* into these proceedings?

Stop! There will be no more conjecture. I was letting my mind run away with itself. The Lockwood v. Kensington case was about two wills, whether the wills were legitimate, and whether the time had come to implement the instructions in those wills. It was not about a murder.

I took myself "firmly in hand," as Bernie would say. First things first. I would see what could be learned about this tooth. If any interesting or revealing information was forthcoming from that, well, *then* I could decide what my next move should be.

CHAPTER 22
GABE'S ANALYSIS

I caught my breath as I waited to cross the highway. I'd finished my ride without further incident, and now I was directly across the street from a dental laboratory owned by a friend, Gabriel Lawrence.

I almost regretted the decision to ride my bike, because now I had to enter a business sporting only a riding outfit and helmet hair. I felt suddenly self-conscious in my padded cycling pants, fearing my derriere looked duck-like. I grimaced at the thought of waddling into a dental laboratory with my makeup sweated off and my hair in the shape of the Liberty Bell.

I tried in vain to fluff my unruly, and now flattened, curls. *Oh, well.* Gabe had seen me with squashed hair plenty of times. Aside from being my friend, Gabriel Lawrence was also one of my Harley riding companions. I never rode alone, and Gabe and his friends were usually good natured enough to let me tag along. On the rare occasions that his friends didn't want me to go with them, Gabe would, without fail, tell them *sayonara* and ride just with me. Although Gabe wouldn't be joining Kelly and me on our ride this weekend, he was going with me to the Poker Run next Saturday.

I opened the zippered compartment in Herc's basket and withdrew the baggie with the tooth. I didn't know what Gabe might be able to tell me just by looking at a single tooth, but making crowns and bridges was his business. He was my best bet at solving at least a part of my tooth's puzzle.

When the coast was clear, I walked my bike across the road, into the parking lot, and around to the north side of the building. Gabe had built a state-of-the-art lab in what had once been a restaurant. The space's former occupation had suited Gabe just fine, he said, because of the water lines and ducting that were already present. It wasn't hard for him to adapt the suite to his needs.

I leaned my bike against the building and lifted Hercules out of his basket. His ears instantly shot up, and he swiveled his head rapidly in all directions, assessing possible threats or interests. He seemed disappointed there was nothing in the immediate vicinity from which he could protect me.

I opened the door and set him inside, whereupon he took off to investigate every corner of the lab. He'd been there before, so he wouldn't be happy until he found Gabe. My friend was maybe fifty-two, a big guy, and probably six-foot-three. His broad chest and arms were covered stem to stern in a variety of tattoos. He looked just like a stereotypical, hardened Harley rider, especially in his biker gear. His size and his booming voice intimidated some people, but not me. I knew there was a softy in there somewhere behind the biker's beard, and I got along well with him, even when that meant tolerating his relentless *naughtiness*.

Closing the door behind me, I heard a long, slow whistle coming from the direction of Gabe's main workbench. There sat the man himself, already holding Hercules, and giving me a thorough once over.

"You should never wear anything but spandex," he said, grinning.

"You're impossible, Gabe," I said, my thoughts returning to the extra padding behind my derriere. "Haven't you ever heard of sexual harassment?"

"You're turning red. Way cute." His smile widened. "Anyway, how can I harass you? I don't employ you. Can't a man pay a compliment anymore?"

"Okay, okay. Just behave yourself. I'm here on business."

"Oh, so serious." He held up Hercules and looked him in the eyes. "What's Mommy been up to? She break a tooth? Lose a crown?"

Herc licked his face.

"Not me. But someone lost a tooth *with* a crown. I was wondering if you'd take a look at it and see what you think."

"How did you get ahold of someone's tooth, Shae? That's just weird, if you ask me. You working on a dental case?"

"No. It's a different kind of case, and I can't talk about it. But I came upon this tooth by accident, and I need to know if I need to know anything about it." My hands felt suddenly clammy and I knew I was babbling. "Because maybe I need to say something to someone, or maybe I don't, and maybe I can just leave it alone, but it all depends, really, on the *tooth* – "

"Whoa, whoa, whoa! Slow down, Shae, you're making me dizzy." Gabe leaned back in his chair so far that Herc laid right down on his expansive chest. He reached up to stroke Herc's belly, whereupon Hercules promptly closed his eyes and stretched himself out more fully.

I could slow down, but not that much. We weren't there for a puppy play date. I strode to the workbench, hands outstretched. "Sorry, Herc," I said, lifting him from his happy place and setting him on the floor. "I need Gabe's full attention."

Gabe reached into a drawer and found a dog biscuit, which he broke in half, then threw a piece for Hercules.

"That should keep him busy. Okay, Shae, let's see what you've got."

I had set the baggie down when I'd lifted Hercules out of Gabe's arms, but I retrieved it and held the possible evidence out to Gabe, warning him to only look.

"Don't take it out. I don't know what we've got there, but I sure don't want to touch it."

"Hmmm." He was thoughtful. "Sure sounds like you've got a theory, though. Otherwise, why be so careful with it?"

"Well, I guess I can tell you that it sort of fell out of an exhibit. I don't think anyone knew it was there, or if they did, they probably didn't mean for anyone to find it. But now I *have* found it, and I can't just put it back. I'm not saying there was foul play or anything, but – well – anyway, I can't just ignore it."

Gabe held the baggie up to the light, turning it this way and that, as I had done. The difference, of course, was that Gabe knew what he was looking at.

"Ah, an adult upper canine. Tooth number eleven, to be exact."

A *canine*? My mind got confused, and my dog theory rushed to the fore. *Wait. No.* Human pointy teeth. They were called canines. Momentary lapse. Good thing I hadn't mentioned "dog tooth" out loud. He'd never let me live it down.

"What's the first thing you'd like to know about this tooth, Shae?"

"Its age," I answered promptly. "Can you tell anything about when that crown might have been manufactured? Or how long it's been on the tooth?"

"From looking at this, just at first glance," Gabe said thoughtfully, "I'd say you're looking at a restoration that was done in maybe the early seventies."

My mouth gaped. How could he even *know* that? I'd asked the question, of course, but I was impressed all the same that he had an answer. And did he say early *seventies*?

"Furthermore," Gabe said, studying the tooth, unaware of my shock, "this tooth was an anchor tooth. It was used to hold an upper partial denture in place."

Denture. The word sent a jolt through me. The tooth's owner had worn a denture. I'd heard testimony that Myron Lockwood's dentures had flown right across the room on the day of his tragic fall. Swallowing hard, I refocused my eyes on the baggie that Gabe held.

"You can tell all that," I stuttered, "just by looking at the tooth for two seconds? Or is it something about the crown?"

"First of all ..." Gabe was in his element now. "Let's call it what it is. It's a reverse three-quarter crown. See the gold on the lingual side?" My face must have been blank. "The tongue side." He smiled. "That's called lingual. The outside of this tooth, the side that sat against this person's lips, is called the labial side."

"Got it." I kept up, concentrating furiously. "Gold on the lingual side. And that says a partial denture to you?"

Gabe laughed aloud. "Patience, patience. I was about to show you. See this little ledge here? That's called a lingual arm rest. And this indentation," he pointed with his little finger, "is for a facial I-bar. Those say partial denture to me."

"Okay." I had to ask the question. "But how can you possibly place the manufacture of this crown in the early seventies?"

"Two things." He grinned. "The type of restoration, and the alloy."

Hercules had finished his treat and was back for more. Gabe reached for the other half of the biscuit and lobbed it across the lab. Herc scampered after it.

Gabe focused on the tooth again. "This was a conservative design used to achieve the retention and stability for holding a partial denture in place, prior to the advent of precision attachments that came on the market later in the seventies."

He was going to lose me quick, talking like that. He knew it. He was enjoying this!

"Okay," I said, "the crown probably wasn't made after the early seventies. How can you be so sure it wasn't made in the sixties? Or even the fifties?" I raised my eyebrows in what I hoped was appropriate professional skepticism.

"Ah." He waved his hand through the air, and I knew he already had an answer ready.

"My visual inspection makes me suspect that the gold could have been created by Dr. Richard V. Tucker, who ran a study group out of Washington that concentrated on the design and composition of this very alloy. I was in college at that time, and we studied this particular alloy at length. It's called JRVT, and I'd know it anywhere. It didn't exist until the early '70s."

He glanced at me and burst into laughter. "If you could see your face, all scrunched up, trying to figure it out. Guess I won't confuse you with an explanation of mesial and distal planes." Gabe gave another belly laugh.

"Guess I won't confuse you with brief forms and CAT software," I muttered.

"Aw, take it easy, Shae. I'm just playin' with you. I can't tell you how long this tooth was in the mouth, but if you say I'm forgiven, I'll tell you what I think is the most interesting thing about it."

"You're forgiven," I said, slightly mollified. "And I'll bite. What is the most interesting thing about this tooth?"

He laid the baggie on his workbench and grabbed a flashlight. Holding the plastic down tight so the tooth was more visible, he shined the light so I could see it in detail.

"The most interesting thing, Shae, is this fine line that's running vertically up the entire length of the tooth. That's a crack, Shae. This tooth isn't stable enough to hold even a partial denture in place, though it had to have been at some point. Also the root is missing its tip."

He shut off the flashlight and turned to me, suddenly serious.

"What are you mixed up in, honey?"

"Wh – what do you mean?" My insides quaked as Gabe confirmed my worst fears.

"I could be wrong." He seemed to be choosing his words carefully. "But if I were a betting man, I'd bet that this tooth left its owner's mouth violently. Could have been a fall, could have been a blow, could have been a car accident, even. But something or someone knocked this tooth right out of some poor sod's head."

CHAPTER 23

RIDE

My alarm woke me at eight o'clock on Saturday morning, reminding me to get up and get ready for my motorcycle ride. I'd slept only fitfully the last three nights, but not because I was worried about another break-in. Bernie had called a security company to come and outfit both parts of the duplex with an alarm system. The broken window in Danny's room was only boarded up for the time being, but that felt almost safer than glass. Any other disturbance of doors or windows while the alarm system was on would trigger a call to the security company and set off enough noise to wake the dead.

I should have slept like a baby, but Gabe's words persisted in haunting my every thought. *"Something or someone knocked this tooth right out of some poor sod's head."*

Myron was dead from a suspicious fall. Otto had vanished almost immediately thereafter. Aurora insisted that Otto was alive. I was no detective, but it was becoming clearer in my mind that one plus one plus one equaled Aurora helping Otto to evade the police. Had she been sending him money all these years? Was *that* where her certainty came from?

I liked Aurora. The thought that I was even *considering* that she might be an accomplice to murder sickened me. The thought of what could happen if I opened my big mouth sickened me even more. I could see the headlines:

LOCAL COURT REPORTER TAKES DOWN VALLEY'S BELOVED CHEEKY PEAKS

I'd be tarred, feathered, and chased from town.

For the moment, I felt safe within my confidential court reporter cocoon. I wasn't *allowed* to talk about the case with anyone.

I needed to quit thinking about it and put my mind on something else. Like the fact that Kelly would be here in two hours, and I needed to be fully awake, dressed, and ready to go.

* * *

Shortly before ten o'clock I laced up my riding boots, snapped on my chaps, and left the house. I slipped into my leather jacket as I walked, stepping into the garage via its side door. I had just pushed the garage door opener button when my phone rang. Reaching into my pocket, I pulled the phone out and saw Kelly's smiling face on my screen. I frowned. Kelly shouldn't be *calling*. Kelly should be *arriving*. She was supposed to meet me here at ten. I swiped the phone to accept the call.

"Won't your bike start?" I teased. "Thought you'd be pulling up right about now."

"Oh, Shae, I'm super sorry. I'm not able to go."

"Why not? Something happen?"

"Just work. Maria's son broke his leg in a skateboarding accident, and she needs to stay home with him. I have to get to the hospital and cover her shift. I'm really sorry."

Kelly was a nurse at our local hospital. I completely understood her situation. I'd often been called to cover depositions for other reporters who'd had emergencies. Hazard of the trade. I was disappointed, though. I hadn't warmed my bike up yet, but I had spent some time last night grooming it. I'd been looking forward to taking it out. This was the second ride in as many weeks to be canceled, and there was very little warm weather left in the year.

"I have a solution for you if you still want to ride, Shae," Kelly offered.

I perked up a little.

"Yeah? What kind of solution?"

"My brother and his friends are riding to Challis. He said they'd be happy to come by and get you if you'd like to join them."

Oh, boy. I didn't like the idea of riding with a group of people I'd never ridden with before. Everyone has their own style, and I liked Kelly's. I also liked Gabe's. I'd never met her brother.

"Ohhhh, Kelly, that's really nice, but – "

"You never ride with strangers. I know. I get it. But Justin said they aren't speed freaks. They like to chill and enjoy the view. I know you're probably all geared up and ready."

I glanced down at my jacket, chaps, and boots.

"So why not give it a try? If you don't like riding with them, you can always turn around and go home."

I looked up at the cloudless blue sky. The temperature today was supposed to reach seventy-nine degrees. I couldn't have asked for a better riding day. I was all ready to go, and the guys were willing to let me ride with them. *Why not?*

"Know what, Kelly? I think I will. It'll be great to meet some new people. Does your brother know where I live?"

"I'll draw him a map," she said, laughing. I could hear the roar of motorcycles in the background. "They're getting ready to go. I'll let Justin know, and they'll be there in a few minutes. Man, I wish I could go. Have a blast, Shae!"

"I'll miss you, Kelly. Don't work too hard."

"Maybe it'll be a slow shift. Dunno. Gotta run, Shae. Bye for now."

"Bye."

I disconnected, zipped the phone back into my jacket pocket, and waited for the guys.

* * *

Justin was younger than Kelly and I by a few years, but most of his friends looked at least thirty. One guy was on a Kawasaki, but the rest were on Harleys. There were six of them, and when they came to pick me up, I suspected that many of my neighbors were sneaking peeks out of their windows. It wasn't every day that six beefy motorcycles came rumbling down our quiet street.

We all introduced ourselves to each other, mounted up, and headed out. I stayed at the rear of the pack, but the group set an easy pace up through the valley, as Kelly had promised. The morning chill was still in the air, but I had layered up for it, and as we left Ketchum behind and headed north, I began to relax and enjoy myself. The highway was unusually quiet this morning, and we had no difficulty getting around the few RVs that we came upon. We passed Galena Lodge, headed into the forest, and in no time began our steep ascent up to Galena Summit.

Everything was rolling along just fine until the gang pulled off the highway to take in the view. I'm a fan of stopping at the top of Galena to enjoy the breathtaking scenery, but I've always preferred to stop at one of the *paved* lookout points. Justin, however, in the lead, passed right by a very nice spot and stopped at a smaller, and most definitely *unpaved*, place along the left side of the highway.

The place was large enough to accommodate our seven motorcycles comfortably, but it had a downward slope to it. I pulled in behind the other bikes and killed my engine with some trepidation. I didn't like stopping on dirt, and I definitely didn't like stopping on *steep* dirt. Dirt that was steep in a leftward, roll-off-the-mountain direction. Kickstands are on the left side of motorcycles. When I put my kickstand down, my bike leaned heavily upon it, causing it to sink at least an inch into the ground before stopping and holding the bike steady.

I carefully dismounted from my leaning motorcycle and went to join the guys. They were having a good time, joshing around, taking pictures, checking phones. All of their bikes were leaning hard on their kickstands, too, but none of them seemed worried about it. This was why I enjoyed riding with Gabe. He would never have led me off the highway onto a small, unpaved, sloping turnout. I feared I would have trouble getting the bike upright again. Gravity would be against me, and I'd have nothing grippy for my left foot to push it up with.

Such a small thing, the decision about where to stop on a road trip. I couldn't blame the guys for not thinking about what a *girl* might need when they made that decision, but I didn't want to head further into the day and risk similar decisions.

I'd ride along with them until we got to Stanley, where we would stop for gas. I'd say goodbye there and turn around and head back. So much for never riding alone. But Stanley was less than an hour and a half from home. I'd be okay.

I went back to my bike and climbed on, hoping that if I couldn't get it up out of its hard lean, one of the guys would be willing to help me out. I'd strapped my helmet on and was just pulling on my gloves when Justin and his friends started piling back onto their own bikes and revving them up. Justin turned around once, apparently to check on me, and gave me a wave. He had his helmet on, the other bikes were roaring, and he never heard me yell, "Hey!" He mounted his own Harley fluidly, checked that the coast was clear, and led the pack back out onto the highway. They didn't even know I wasn't with them.

Hoping against hope, I planted my feet the best I could and tried to push the bike up.

It wouldn't budge. Nine hundred pounds of Harley-Davidson Road King was leaning too far over, and my single female left leg, with my left foot slipping around in the dirt, couldn't do a single thing to lift the bike.

I sat for a moment, feeling stranded. When Justin had looked back, he must have seen a woman on her bike, ready to go. This wasn't his fault. I should have said something before I'd gotten on the motorcycle. Deciding not to blame Justin didn't help me, though. I wasn't leaving this place unless I flagged down a motorist or another biker and asked for help. How embarrassing. I'd never been in such a pickle on a ride, but then again, to beat the deadest of horses, I *never rode alone*.

Sighing, I pulled my phone from my pocket. No signal. I don't know what I'd hoped to do with it anyway. I was sitting on a perfectly good Harley on the top of a very familiar mountain. I should never have let myself get into this mess. I should have kept riding when I saw where they'd stopped. *Bah!*

I was still staring at my phone and berating myself when I heard another motorcycle round the turn behind me. There was no time to flag anyone, as I was still on the bike, but I heard the other biker slow. A crunching of dirt and rock told me that the rider had pulled off into my turnout. Unable to turn around very far with my helmet on, I fumbled with the strap's release loop. It seemed that colonies of wiggle worms sprang to life in my stomach as I heard a familiar voice.

"Are you in trouble here, Shae?"

It was none other than Hailey Police Department's very finest, Sergeant Jackson Landers, and my reaction to seeing him was much the same as when I'd dropped my Chihuahua. I couldn't seem to help myself.

"Sergeant Landers!" I gasped, hoping he would attribute my suddenly flushed face to the afternoon heat. I pulled my helmet off and steadied it, and my hands, in my lap. "How did you know it was me?"

He had dismounted, and he reached a hand to touch the curls at the nape of my neck. "Your hair peeks out from beneath your helmet. Did you know?"

"My hair?"

"Plus, I recognized your bike."

Caught off guard by that statement, I nearly forgot the jitters in my stomach and the embarrassment that my predicament offered. "How did you know what my bike looked like?"

"I saw it when Bernie and I checked your garage after the break-in. So what happened here? I was a little surprised to see you here by yourself. It's always a good idea to ride with company." The sergeant cocked his head. "Are you resting?"

I looked down, too mortified to point out that *he* wasn't riding with company. There was a big difference between he and I, and I knew that.

"Shae?"

"'M stuck," I mumbled.

"One more time?" He bent low in an effort to make eye contact. "I couldn't hear you."

"I'm stuck," I said more clearly, risking a look at his face. He wasn't laughing, at least.

"Can you not get your bike upright?"

"Nope."

He still wasn't laughing. Straightening up, he looked at where I was parked, looked around in all directions, clearly puzzled.

"There are lots of safer places to pull off the road, Shae," he said, sounding very cop-like.

"Well, I didn't really *choose* it," I admitted. "But it was my fault. I was stupid to follow the guys when they stopped here. I should have just kept going."

Sergeant Landers became very still. "You were with a *group*?"

"Yeah. Today is the first time I've ridden with them. They didn't realize I needed a boost because of this slope. They saw me on my bike, and I guess they thought I was good to go." I glared at my left leg. *Why aren't you stronger?* "They're probably nearly down the mountain by now."

He looked sharply in the direction my fellow riders had gone, eyes narrowing.

"It's no good, Shae. Maybe you shouldn't have pulled off here, but you can stop trying to defend a group of bikers who left a rider behind. Were there other women in the group?"

"No. Just me. But listen, they didn't have to let me come. They were really nice – "

"Shae, every biker knows, or *should* know, that you have to have a strong rider ride at the back when you have a new person in the group." I started to speak, and he held up a hand. "It's not because you're female, Shae. It's because you're *new* to them. They should have had someone behind you at all times to make sure you didn't fall too far back, or like this, get left behind altogether."

He rubbed his jaw, his expression grim. Angry, even.

"I'm really sorry, Sergeant – "

"Jax," he interrupted, still rubbing his jaw. His expression relaxed a little. "Just Jax, Shae. Okay?"

"Okay." I mumbled self-consciously. I felt like a little kid, stranded as I was on my huge Harley.

"And you have nothing to be sorry for. I'm not mad at *you*. I'm wondering what you'd have done if I hadn't come along, though." He gestured to my cell phone. "I'll bet that doesn't have a signal."

"Not a single bar." Fidgeting in my seat, I turned the phone's screen on, then off again. "I just figured I'd have to flag a passing car or another biker." It would have been embarrassing, but I was confident someone would have stopped to help me.

"Someone you wouldn't know." *It's like he read my mind.* But I could tell he didn't think much of that plan. Jax drew a deep breath and exhaled slowly. "Well," he said finally, "I'm here now, and I'll help you get your bike up, but no more riding with those clow—"

"They were my friend's brother and his friends."

"Okay, Shae. You want to be nice. But I'll be giving them a talking to if I get the chance."

All cop again.

"Where were you all riding to, anyway?"

"We were going to Challis, but I had already decided to turn around and go home once we got to Stanley."

His cop demeanor slipped some and he smiled, brown eyes crinkling at the corners. "Would you still like to go to Stanley, Shae?"

My breath caught, but he must have interpreted that as indecision.

"It's still a nice day," he pointed out, "and that's where I was headed. We can grab some lunch there if you want."

Things were looking up! My spirits lifted at the thought that I could still get a nice ride in, and this time with someone I could trust completely. And lunch with Jax? My heart stuttered again. I'd have to keep my wits about me to avoid staring at him like a school girl and slobbering into my soup. On the other hand, maybe I could figure out a way to ask him how important the typewriter tooth was – without revealing anything about the case, of course.

"You're on," I said happily.

"Great." He smiled again, even more broadly. "Get your helmet and gloves on, and tell me when you're ready."

I did so and gave him a thumbs up.

He came around to the front of my bike and straddled my front wheel. Then he took a firm grip on my handlebars. "Okay, Shae, push the bike up." I did so, and with his help, it came up easy as could be. He moved over to his own Harley, and I started my engine.

I kicked my kickstand up and out of the way, ready to go. Jax scanned the highway in both directions and headed out, with me close behind him.

This was turning into a good day, after all.

CHAPTER 24

STANLEY

Forty-five minutes later, Jax was ordering a pizza for us at Stanley's favorite pizza place.

The sergeant had set a nice pace on the road, and I'd enjoyed the ride as we traveled down the other side of Galena, through Smiley Creek, along the Salmon River, and then on into Stanley. We'd stopped for gas before finding a place to eat, and I'd seen, to my chagrin, Justin and his friends huddled together not far away from where we were filling our tanks. Jax had followed the direction of my eyes and put two and two together.

"Is that your group?"

"Yes. I expect they're trying to decide who should go back and look for me."

"I'll take care of this, Shae."

"It was an honest mistake," I'd reminded him. "Go easy on them."

"I'm just going to talk to them."

Jax had strolled easily over to the huddle, introduced himself, and gestured back at me. As one, all of my former riding companions looked over in my direction, and I waved. Then they turned their attention back to Jax, and I saw attentive listening and much nodding of heads. When Jax had walked back to where I waited, Justin had come with him. Justin had looked thoroughly embarrassed and thoroughly relieved.

"Man, I'm glad you're okay," he'd said. "We got here and freaked out when you weren't with us. I tore into Robby, because he was supposed to be keeping an eye on you, and he forgot. We're really sorry, Shae. Sergeant Landers told us what happened, and we're gonna be a *lot* more careful in the future."

I'd assured him that everything had ended well, and that I wouldn't get him into any trouble with his sister, Kelly. He'd told me that now, knowing they hadn't lost a member of their party, they were all going to continue on to Challis. I wished him safe travels and turned to face a still stern-looking Jax.

"Think they got the message?"

"I think so. They seemed receptive, at least." Jax shook his head as if still in disbelief that they'd left me behind, then smiled. "Let's find some lunch."

The pizza place had been fairly busy, but we'd had no trouble finding a nice window table. When Jax had placed the order, I'd been trying to figure out how to bring up the tooth without giving too much away. I didn't want to rouse his curiosity. I just wanted to know if cops considered a tooth to be the same as any other body part. I finally came to the conclusion that there was nothing for it but to pull out the well-worn, "asking for a friend" cliché.

Our pizza arrived, and we each grabbed a slice. Then I decided to dive in before other casual chit-chat interfered.

"Can I ask you a cop question, Jax? I mean, I know you're off duty..."

"Sure, Shae. What's on your mind?"

"Well, you know I'm a court reporter. Right?"

"Yeah. I was going to ask you about that. I haven't met many court reporters other than the one who is always in court."

"Right. So – see – " How should I phrase it?

"Hard question to ask?" That was a smirk. He was definitely *smirking*.

"Kinda." I ignored the insolent smile. "You know the things that happen in depositions are confidential, right? We can't talk about the depo, we can't show the exhibits around, that kind of thing."

"I hadn't thought about it, but it makes sense."

"So, I have this friend in Boise," I said, cringing inwardly at the make-believe friend, "who was responsible for a deposition exhibit for the duration of a large case. The exhibit was a thing, not a document. Okay?"

"I'm with you."

"My friend, let's call her Lori, has a nosey roommate named Molly. One day Molly got curious about Lori's exhibit, took it out of its box, and checked it out." My thoughts traveled back to the night I'd learned about Clarabelle's typewriter antics, and I shuddered.

Jax looked closely at me as if he'd noticed my shudder. "Sounds like Lori needs a new roommate."

"I'm not really focusing on the roommate."

"Okay. Sorry. Continue."

"Anyway, while Molly was looking over the exhibit," I looked down, but peaked at him from beneath my lashes, "a human tooth fell out of it."

Jax's eyes widened. He put his pizza down, leaned back in his seat and crossed his arms. His face inscrutable, he simply said, "Go on."

Okay. I'd gotten the hard part out, so I raised my eyes to meet his. "The question is, what should Lori do about it? It's a confidential exhibit. She can't just ask any old person for advice…"

"How does she know it's a human tooth?"

"It's got a gold crown on it."

"And what type of object did it fall out of? Just what is the exhibit?"

"She couldn't tell me, but she said it's an item that is central to a high-dollar lawsuit."

That did it. Jax pushed his plate away, and I could see the muscles in his arms tensing. I feared that I'd raised Jax's foul-play radar to the hilt. I probably should have left out the words "central" and "high-dollar," and just said, "an item in a lawsuit." *Shoot.*

Jax leaned forward over the table as I fidgeted nervously with a fork.

"Shae."

I looked up and found his liquid brown eyes locked onto mine. I tried to make my voice casual. "Yes?"

"I really hope that this is a *friend* you're talking about, Shae." He sounded concerned, but also very cop-like. Sergeant Jackson Landers was a highly trained law enforcement officer, and I suddenly realized he could probably tell when he was being lied to.

I rallied, desperate to stick to my tale for now. Beyond expressing the narrative vaguely as the story of a *friend*, however, I wouldn't lie to him.

"I can't tell you who it is, Jax. I just kind of wanted to know if a tooth mattered so much. It's not like it's a finger…"

"It might matter, Shae, and it might not. I'm afraid it really is up to the police to decide. Your *friend*," I wasn't sure I liked how he emphasized that word, "is going to have to take the tooth, and the object it fell from, and show them to the police."

CHAPTER 25

TROW

Jax's words stayed with me as I set up for a deposition on Monday, two days later, but I was no closer to a decision about what to do with the tooth than I had been before our talk.

Today's job was a video deposition, meaning the testimony would all be videotaped. I made the usual small talk with Cal, the videographer, as we set up. It was almost a relief to have another job outside the Lockwood/Kensington dispute. Today would be a normal day, an uneventful, unexciting day with no suspense and no drama whatsoever. (Said no court reporter, ever.) Still, the job was estimated to last only two to three hours, and I welcomed it.

Cal had arrived at least thirty minutes before I did because he had a lot more prep work for his role in the depo. I knew this videographer, having worked with him a number of different times. I unzipped my machine case and hauled out my laptop, setting it on the table and opening it to wake it up. We chatted lightly as we went about our work, inquiring after family and commenting on the weather as we organized our gear and did systems checks.

Our small talk was cut short by some of the parties entering the room. Three big-gun, suit-and-tie attorneys briskly entered as a team, the youngest of them weighed down by a heavy records box. *Honestly! Out-of-town attorneys do stick out!* Their client was not with them. This didn't surprise me. There was no requirement that a defendant come to the deposition.

I'd read over my notice. All of the defense attorneys were important lawyers from big firms who represented even bigger insurance companies. No wonder they were videotaping this proceeding. One, they could afford to include that step. Two, they could review the deponent's demeanor later in the luxury of their own offices. Three, they could use it to impeach the deponent should his story change at trial. And four, they could play it at trial should the witness become unavailable. That wouldn't happen in this case, though. This deponent would show up for trial, as he was the plaintiff, aka the one who'd brought the suit.

I had already clicked my machine onto its tripod and plugged its cable into my laptop. Finally, I opened my software and made sure it was communicating with my machine.

I was in the middle of creating briefs for all of the names on my documentation when an angry-looking man burst through the door, along with a casually dressed gentleman who carried an even more casual briefcase. Clearly, this was the deponent and his attorney. The guy with the briefcase had to be the lawyer, who at least seemed to be familiar with Idaho small-town dress codes. Nice shirt, khaki slacks, no tie. The deponent was more casual still, wearing a red flannel shirt and blue jeans held up by the biggest belt buckle I'd ever seen.

I looked at my notice. The deponent was Carl Rutger, so I entered that into my job dictionary.

KARL
RUT
GER

I didn't want to spend the whole day writing his last name with two strokes, though, so I created the brief:

R*UT

and defined it as Rutger. The attorney with the last name of Castleton became:

KA*S

And so on. I gave briefs to every name I could find on my notice, and then I stood up to introduce myself to all the players. The case appeared to be a medical malpractice case, and the insurance company representing the defendant, a doctor, had sent in three powerful attorneys to watch out for its interests. The deponent just had his one local lawyer, who seemed relaxed and unintimidated by the force sent against him.

I approached him first.

"Shae Rose," I said, holding out my card. "Pleased to meet you."

"Gordon Flagstone, counsel for the plaintiff." He took my card and set about the laborious process of peeling the back off.

I then approached Mr. Castleton and offered my card. "Shae Rose," I said.

"Rich Castleton." He stretched his hand out to shake mine.

I smiled brightly and jabbed the card into his palm. I wanted nothing to do with another knuckle crunching. He finally got the idea and simply accepted my card. The other two defense counsel dropped their own cards near my laptop, but otherwise completely ignored me. One of the cards had blue writing on it, and the attorney who had dropped it was wearing a blue suit, so I mentally tied the two together. But for that, I wouldn't have known which card represented him. I could have asked, of course, but now I didn't have to. I sat down and identified each of them as potential speakers in the deposition.

As everyone was present, we wasted no time starting. Angry Mr. Rutger sat at the head of the table so that he was in direct line of the camera. I sat to his right, and his attorney, Gordon Flagstone, to his left. Mr. Castleton sat on my other side. He would be asking the questions. The other two attorneys took places farther down the table.

Cal did his normal videotape read-on, and I asked the deponent to raise his right hand as I administered the oath.

CARL RUTGER,

First duly sworn to tell the truth relating to said cause, testified as follows:

EXAMINATION

QUESTIONS BY MR. CASTLETON:

Q. So give me a little bit of background. What is your age?

A. Man, that's a tough one.

Q. There will be harder questions.

I stifled a laugh. Not an auspicious start.

A. I was born in March of '72, so whatever that makes me.

Q. Forty-four then. Thank you. And where were you born, Mr. Rutger?

A. Twin Falls, Idaho.

Q. Did you finish high school?

A. You makin' fun of me?

Q. I am not, sir. These background questions are normal.

    MR. FLAGSTONE: It's okay, Carl. Just answer his questions.

    THE WITNESS: No, I did not finish high school. Got my GED, though.

BY MR. CASTLETON:

Q. Any college?

A. Nope.

Q. We're here today, Mr. Rutger, to discuss an accident that took place on April 14, 2014, and the surgery following that accident. Do you understand that?

A. I know why we're here.

What followed were two of the most contentious hours I'd ever experienced as a court reporter. Mr. Rutger remained angry and belligerent, refusing to answer even the simplest question without a poor attitude and a hostile retort. His attorney repeatedly admonished Carl to just answer the questions, but the reprimands weren't working. Mr. Rutger had been gored by a bull while working as a ranch hand, and in his opinion, the surgeon (the defendant in this case) had made things far worse with the surgery he'd performed.

All of that was understandable. What surprised me, though, was that Mr. Rutger didn't seem to care that every angry utterance was being videotaped and would likely be played for a jury.

Surely his attorney had told him it would be important to appear *sympathetic* to a jury and not antagonistic.

The depo was mercifully short, and I could tell, after two hours, that Mr. Castleton was wrapping up his questions. He had just gotten to his end-of-depo, quality-of-life questions when a difficult deposition evolved into the bizarre.

> Q. And now, Mr. Rutger, you are two years post-surgery. Can you tell me how your quality of life has been affected by this goring incident and the surgery you received?
>
> A. You want to know how I've been affected? I'll show you how I've been affected.

And right there, on videotape, Carl Rutger stood up and grabbed for his belt buckle. *Oh no, you don't!* I was seated less than two feet away from him.

> Q. Are you going to show us your scar, Mr. Rutger?
>
> A. You bet I am. Getting gored in the pelvis was bad enough, but Dr. Freaking Hacksaw mutilated me. This scar's so tight, I got a permanent limp. Take a look at this.

Whatever Mr. Rutger's injuries were, I didn't want them implanting themselves into my brain. I dropped my eyes to my machine and kept them locked there as Mr. Rutger's jeans dropped to the ground. I focused only on my fingers, trying to ignore the peripheral vision that revealed to me a pile of denim surrounding some rather skinny ankles.

The attorney never missed a beat.

MR. CASTLETON: I'll just ask the videographer to zoom in so the jury can see what Mr. Rutger is, ahem, so helpfully showing us.

I couldn't breathe. My eyes watered as I stuffed down laughter and sucked in my cheeks to avoid smiling. I'd managed to maintain my composure while the deponent dropped his drawers, but the unflappable Mr. Castleton's request for a close-up nearly sent me right over the edge. After some moments, while presumably the videographer complied with the attorney's request, Mr. Rutger pulled up his pants and reaffixed his massive belt buckle. I felt it was safe to straighten my head up again and check my computer screen, where I'd inserted the wildly understated parenthetical:

(Witness provides demonstration.)

THE WITNESS: So now you can all see what I've been dealing with.

MR. CASTLETON: Indeed we can. Thank you for your candor and your willingness to talk to us today, Mr. Rutger. I have no further questions.

MR. FLAGSTONE: And I have no questions. We'll read and sign.

(Deposition concluded at 11:05 a.m.)

(Signature was requested.)

* * * * *

Mr. Rutger and his attorney left the room promptly, the big-city hotshots close on their heels. I risked a peek at the videographer, and the maniacal laughter I'd been suppressing suddenly burst forth. He was sitting in stunned silence, having forgotten his read-off. Unlike myself, he'd been unable to look away from Mr. Rutger's demonstration.

"A first," Cal said at last. He looked at me. "You?"

I wiped my eyes and sat back in my seat, barely in control of myself.

"Total first. I've been reporting for eleven years, Cal. And never once in all that time has a deponent, during deposition, video or otherwise, ever dropped trow."

Cal, recovering from his shock, laughed deeply as he stood and began packing up. "Definitely one for the books." He continued chortling to himself as he gathered mics and wound up cables.

I, in the meantime, couldn't resist shooting off an email to Annie in the office in Boise. She always liked to hear about crazy stuff that happened in depos, and she was really the only person I could safely tell. She'd probably proofread the transcript for me later, so there were no rules of secrecy there.

By the time I finished putting my equipment away I had her reply, richly sprinkled with laughing emojis, informing me that my story had made her day. She finished with, "Oh, and three more jobs at the Lockwood Estate day after tomorrow. They've already confirmed, so I'm attaching the paperwork. At least you know at these jobs everyone will keep their clothes on. (More emojis.) Cheers!"

CHAPTER 26
FIRST DEPOSITION OF HAWK RIVERS

On Tuesday I traveled the now familiar road to the Lockwood mansion. The typewriter was in the back of my car, and the tooth remained in its baggie in my dresser drawer. Laughter, they say, is good for the soul, and my laughter at Mr. Pants Removing's deposition had rejuvenated me. I had decided to let the rest of the depositions unfold in the Lockwood/Kensington drama before I thought further about the tooth, Myron, or any of it.

Hawk let me in as usual and followed me to the house in his golf cart. Today was his day to be deposed, and he was quiet as he carried my gear up the stairs. Rather than proceeding into the house, he stopped quite unexpectedly on the top landing. I nearly ran into the back of him, and he put a hand out to steady me. Setting the case down near the mudroom's entrance, he turned and surveyed the spacious grounds. His face was somber as he pulled his Stetson down in front, covering his eyes.

"Well, I always did like this time of the morning in the late summertime." Lifting his gaze, he took in the view as though he might never see it again. "Seems a shame to waste a morning like this, sitting inside a house. I don't know as I've ever found myself in such a place, where I was to be surrounded by lawyers and people with poor intent."

"People with poor intent, Hawk?" I laughed aloud and reached my elbow up to jab him lightly in the ribs. "It's just a deposition, you know. There are only *two* lawyers, so you'll hardly be surrounded, and the people are all practically family to you."

But Hawk simply surveyed the beautiful lawn, the immaculate flower beds, the pristinely-paved footpaths, and the mountain views beyond.

"Guess I'm just nervous," he finally confided. "I never wanted anything to do with family tussles. They're grown people. They should work it out. I just can't think why they want to talk to me."

He looked so profoundly unhappy, I stopped laughing and took his arm.

"Let's go in and face the music together, Hawk. You don't talk fast, so you're already assured of one super fan in the room."

"Yeah?" He squinted down at me. "Who's that?"

"Me!" I beamed and pulled on his arm. "We need to go in now, Hawk. And don't worry, it's routine to talk to *everybody*. They're even deposing Geoffrey Jenkins today, and I've never seen him at all."

"Huh. Can't say I'm surprised you haven't met him. I guess. He keeps to the background, does ol' Jenkins. The family calls him the butler."

A butler. I had truly entered a world previously unknown to me. Never before had I participated in the deposition of a butler. To Hawk I simply said, "And there you have it. They're speaking to *everyone*. So this is perfectly normal. Everything's going to be okay."

His return smile resembled a grimace more than anything else, but at least he was trying. He picked up my bag and carried it through the mudroom, past the over-sized pantry, and beyond the little nook. We reached the dining room and saw that we had a full house. Everyone was there early, even Spencer.

I'd yet to hear Spencer say anything, but he hadn't missed a minute of the proceedings. He'd arrived each morning without fail, taken his place in his shadowed corner, and listened to every word. When the proceedings concluded for the day, he'd slipped out noiselessly, before anyone had a chance to wonder where he was off to.

Hawk set my case down. He looked self-conscious and out of place until I gestured to the chair he should occupy. Seating himself, he removed his hat and placed it on his lap. I supposed that fidgeting with it would give his hands something to do as he answered questions.

Coop Rickman was taking the lead in today's depositions. In addition to Hawk and Geoffrey Jenkins this morning, we would be deposing Spencer Lockwood this afternoon. I would hear him speak at last, and I was curious to hear about his role in the family's legal battle.

Coop looked at me and nodded. I returned the gesture, then faced Hawk.

"Hawk, will you raise your right hand for me, please?" He complied, and we were off.

HAWK RIVERS,

First duly sworn to tell the truth relating to said cause, testified as follows:

EXAMINATION

QUESTIONS BY MR. RICKMAN:

    Q. Good morning, Mr. Rivers. Is it okay if I call you Hawk today?

    A. Sure, Coop. That's what I go by.

Q. Thanks. Hawk, what's your date of birth?

A. December 25, 1945.

Q. Christmas baby?

A. Yep.

Q. How old were you, Hawk, when you came to work on the Lockwood Estate?

A. I was eighteen when Mr. Lockwood hired me.

Q. And to be clear, when you refer to Mr. Lockwood, you are, in fact, referencing Mr. Myron Lockwood, father to Otto, Aurora, and Dalton Lockwood?

A. The very same.

Q. And you began working for him in 1963?

A. That's exactly right.

Q. So if my math is correct, Hawk – and correct me if I'm wrong – you would have been working for Myron Lockwood for twelve years before his death in 1975?

A. That's true.

Q. And similarly, Hawk, you'd been working here for twelve years at the time of Otto Lockwood's disappearance?

A muscle in Hawk's jaw twitched, and his lips thinned. Even after so many years, talking about these events seemed to pain Hawk, even as these topics had pained Aurora.

A. That's right. Twelve years.

Q. Forgive me, Hawk, but I have to ask. Were you a witness to Myron Lockwood's fall down the stairs?

A. No, I wasn't. I was clearing a beaver dam out of

a ditch on the back of the property that day. I didn't know anything about the accident until I came back that evening and saw all the police and the medical examiner's van.

    Q. That must have been a very difficult time for you.

    A. Difficult time for everyone.

    Q. Was it also a difficult time when Otto left, Hawk?

    A. I found it very hard, yes, sir.

    Q. Hawk, when is the last time you saw Otto Lockwood?

Hawk stared at his hat, which was now clenched tightly between his two large, calloused hands. He swallowed three times in rapid succession, seeming to will himself to hold his emotions in check and carry on.

    A. The last time I saw Otto was when he was in the family car and headed for the airport.

Hawk drew a shuddering breath. *Poor Hawk.* This was clearly harder for him than even *he* had envisioned.

    Q. Forgive me, Hawk, but my question seems to have struck a nerve. Can you tell me why speaking of the last time you saw Otto is distressing to you?

    A. Yeah, I guess I can. It's just that he didn't say goodbye. He and Jenkins drove right by me when they left through the main gate. He had his hat pulled down, you know, so I guess he didn't see me. But I was always sorry that I didn't get to say goodbye to him then, since he never has come back.

    MR. RICKMAN: Hawk, thank you for your time. I believe those are all the questions I have for you for now.

I'd like to keep Mr. Rivers' deposition open, in case we need any clarification on anything. Dom?

MR. FLYNN: I think you covered everything I wanted to ask, Coop. We're done.

(Deposition adjourned at 9:35 a.m.)

(Signature was requested.)

* * * * *

I looked at Hawk, who had just replaced his nearly crushed hat upon his head. "All over, Hawk. You did great."

"Thanks, Shae. Sure don't like talkin' about that stuff."

He rose, and I decided to stand up as well. We hadn't been on the record for very long, but I took the opportunity to stretch my back out anyway. I didn't know how long the *next* depo would be.

"And thanks, Shae, for trying to cheer me up," Hawk said shyly. "I mighta bolted right outta here if you hadn't helped me out."

"No problem. See you at lunch?"

"I'll be there. And Shae," he pushed his hat back just as I picked up a pen to make a note in my notebook.

"What is it, Hawk?"

"Well," he patted his shirt pocket and then withdrew a fresh toothpick, "I'll just be working right outside here this morning. The lawn and flower beds need tending."

I waited while he stabbed his toothpick into his mouth, my mind on the thumb drive in my steno case. I wanted to back up Hawk's depo…

"Guess I thought," he said at last, "if this next deposition ain't too long, you might maybe like to see the winter house when it's done."

He had my full attention now. I felt my eyes widen and I was pretty sure my heart skipped a beat. My curiosity had been piqued when I'd first seen the cozy smaller structure, and it had grown exponentially as testimony in the case unfolded. Poor Myron Lockwood had met a disastrous end there. Dalton had allegedly found two wills hidden in a neglected cupboard five years ago in that very house. Of course I wanted to see it! "Hawk," my thumb drive forgotten, "I'd love to."

He nodded as though to himself and pulled the brim of his hat back down. "Well, you just come find me outside when you finish, and I'll walk you on over there. See you then."

Hawk sauntered from the room amidst the casual chatter of all the other parties, and I tried to turn my attention back to what I'd been doing. The moment for making a backup had passed, however. I sensed that our break was over as the chit-chat died down and Coop pulled his legal pad closer. I resumed my seat and simply saved my file to the laptop's hard drive. I then scrolled down a few spaces to gain digital distance between each deponent's testimony.

I was making a small adjustment to my machine's height when my peripheral vision sensed movement. I glanced absently at the archway on the far side of the room – and froze. A man had just entered the dining room through the archway – a man I'd seen before, but never met. Before me, just at the other end of the table, stood the stranger who had stared at me from among the lengthening shadows on my first day here.

"Hey, Shae," Levi drawled lazily, "have you met our butler, Geoffrey Jenkins?"

CHAPTER 27

DEPOSITION OF GEOFFREY JENKINS

Not an exceptionally tall man, I judged Mr. Jenkins to be of an age with Dalton Lockwood, perhaps somewhere in his mid-seventies. I'd noticed no white hair on the twilit evening when I'd first glimpsed Mr. Jenkins for the simple reason that he had none. His hair, whether from a bottle or from naturally good genes, was a deep, slightly oily brown. His form was slender but his face had grown pasty and soft. He exuded none of Hawk's rugged strength or weathered features, though he seemed to share the groundskeeper's disquiet at finding himself in a deposition setting. His eyes twitched quickly to each person in the room before they came to rest on me.

He covered the distance between us easily and reached for my hand. Thoroughly nonplussed, I lifted my hand and shook his, remembering my own handshake reticence too late. No harm, though. Geoffrey Jenkins seemed friendly enough. Overly friendly, in my mind.

"How do you do, Ms. Rose? I've heard a great deal about you."

"Heard about me?" Did he think to win me over so quickly? If so, why did he even want to? I withdrew my hand, feeling grumbly and disquieted. *You could have met me weeks ago if you hadn't been so busy looking scary.*

"Yes, indeed, Ms. Rose. Levi is quite fascinated with what you do. He assures me that you're very good at it."

"Just Shae, Mr. Jenkins, and yes, Levi was an apt pupil."

"If you are to be Shae, please call me Jenkins. Everyone else does. Where am I to sit?"

Coop was taking the depo, so I motioned to the seat on my left that Hawk had just vacated, next to Mr. Flynn.

"Ah. Thank you, Shae."

Jenkins took his seat as I eyed him slyly, still uncomfortable. His manners were impeccable, but there was something *off* about how he carried himself. His eyes continued to jump around to each person in the room, confirming to me my initial thought that he was ill at ease in these surroundings.

I was probably letting my imagination run away with me again. Even if Jenkins *was* ill at ease, there was nothing *sinister* about him. His suit was clean and neat, but not expensive.

And if I thought his hands twisted nervously as we began the deposition, what of it? Nervous deponents were the *rule*, not the exception. I asked him to raise his right hand, and placed him under oath.

GEOFFREY JENKINS,

First duly sworn to tell the truth relating to said cause, testified as follows:

EXAMINATION

QUESTIONS BY MR. RICKMAN:

    Q. Good morning, Mr. Jenkins.

    A. Good morning.

    Q. Have you ever had your deposition taken before?

A. No, sir.

Q. It's a simple process. I'll ask questions, you'll provide answers. I would only ask that you don't talk when I'm talking. That's to benefit our court reporter here. She can only take down one person's words at a time.

A. Very well.

Jenkins smiled at me (*obsequiously,* or so it seemed.) I tried to shake it, but found myself incapable of charitable thought where Jenkins was concerned. *Sure, you're nice in a crowd, but you didn't look so friendly when no one was around...*

Q. When were you born, Mr. Jenkins?

A. June 9, 1941.

Q. So you are currently seventy-five years old?

A. Yes, sir.

Q. And still working as a butler on the Lockwood Estate?

A. My duties are considerably lighter than they once were, but yes. I mainly oversee others now.

Q. Mr. Jenkins, I know a lot of time has passed, but what do you remember of the events that occurred in August 1975?

A. My memory is clear, Mr. Rickman. I will do my best to answer your questions.

Q. Thank you. First, where were you when Myron Lockwood fell down the stairs in the winter house?

A. I was here in the main house, attending to my duties.

Q. What do you remember of that day?

A. It was mid-afternoon, if I recall correctly. We have a direct phone line that runs between the houses, and I received a call on that line from Otto. He was quite frantic, said his father had fallen, and he asked me to call an ambulance.

Q. And do you recall where Dalton and Aurora were at the time you received this call?

A. They were here as well. I believe they were in the kitchen, going over proposed articles and advertisements for the paper's upcoming edition.

Q. Thank you. So I'm clear, do you remember the date of Myron Lockwood's fall?

A. It was August 12, 1975.

Q. And his funeral was held just three days later?

A. Yes. The service was on August 15.

Q. And was August 15 also the day that Otto left the estate?

A. Indeed it was. He left the evening after his father's funeral.

Q. And how are you so sure of this?

A. I drove him to the airport, myself.

Q. Were you aware, Mr. Jenkins, that Otto didn't even tell his own sister that he was leaving?

A. It was not my business to be aware of that, sir. It was my job to drive him, not to question him.

Q. We've heard testimony that, as you and Otto were leaving the grounds that night, you passed by Hawk Rivers. Did Otto not request that you stop for a moment, so he could bid Mr. Rivers farewell?

A. I have no recollection of seeing Mr. Rivers that night.

Q. Is this the first you're hearing of it?

A. Very much so.

I thought Jenkins had looked startled at the mention of passing by Hawk on the night in question, and his testimony had just confirmed it for me. Why would that information be unsettling to him? My opinion of him was not improving.

Q. And again, your destination that night was the airport?

A. Yes, sir. I dropped Otto at the departures gate.

Q. Did you see him go inside?

A. Indeed I did.

Q. And then what did you do?

A. I came home. I recall having some chores to finish up.

Q. You recall that, after all these years?

A. Yes, I do. The reason being, I was working in the winter house when Aurora phoned, looking for Otto. Dalton was there with me, and he knew that Otto had left. He told me to leave it up to him to inform Aurora, and he departed to do just that.

Q. Are you aware, Mr. Jenkins, that Otto has written to Aurora three times in the years he's been away?

A. Oh, yes indeed. Mrs. Kensington was delighted with each letter and told the entire household about them.

Q. Did you ever see the letters personally?

A. I did not, and it wasn't my place to request it.

MR. RICKMAN: Thank you, sir. I have no

further questions for you.

        MR. FLYNN: Just a couple for me.

              EXAMINATION

QUESTIONS BY MR. FLYNN:

    Q. Do you enjoy working here, Mr. Jenkins?

    A. Yes, I do. There is no place I would rather be.

    Q. And do you consider yourself to be loyal to each of the family members?

    A. I do. I hope they all feel the same.

    Q. And you were loyal to Otto?

    A. I like to think so.

    Q. So if he asked for a ride to the airport, you wouldn't have felt the need to pry, or to ask him why he was leaving on the day of his father's funeral, or whether he had told his sister goodbye?

    A. Certainly not, sir.

    Q. And even if you had seen Hawk Rivers as you exited the grounds, you wouldn't have felt that you should press Otto to stop, say goodbye, or explain himself?

    A. Never. He asked for a ride, and I drove him. Period.

        MR. FLYNN: Thank you. That's all I have.

        (Deposition concluded at 10:45 a.m.)

        (Signature was requested.)

              * * * * *

Jenkins wiped his (*clammy?*) hands on his trousers as he rose from his seat. He loosened his tie slightly as if he felt relieved that his deposition was over. With a nod to Dalton and a slight bow in my direction, he made a hasty escape.

I watched him hurry away, my feelings of unease intact.

CHAPTER 28

THE WINTER HOUSE

The air outside maintained just a hint of its morning briskness and I welcomed the change in atmosphere as I stepped outside. Meeting Geoffrey Jenkins had unsettled me. I shook myself slightly and turned my face towards the sun, savoring the warmth that reached through the cool air and touched my skin. I decided it was too bright and sunny to think about Mr. Jenkins. After all, he'd done nothing more sinister than stare at me on my first evening here, and there could be an innocent explanation for even that.

The grounds were tranquil and quiet, with an occasional bird call only enhancing the stillness. Where was Hawk? He'd said he'd be tending the flower beds, but he was nowhere to be seen. My searching gaze took in Hawk's cabin, away and to my left as it hugged the drive leading back to the highway. The little house appeared to be as still and vacant as the untended flower beds.

Looking the other way, I observed a similar quietude enveloping the cozy winter house where it sat to my right. Hawk had promised to take me over there, but he'd also promised to be working right outside the main mansion. Something had held him up, but I hated to lose my opportunity. Curiosity raged within as I took in the mudroom door Jenkins had exited from on that eerie evening. I tried to imagine an elegant curving staircase within the home that had meted out the demise of poor

Myron Lockwood, but couldn't. I had no information at all concerning the interior of the house, except that it did, indeed, have a staircase of *some* sort.

Surely it would be okay if I moseyed over for a look around, even without Hawk. Right?

* * *

Without pausing for second thoughts, I began strolling casually in the direction of the winter house. Along the way I admired another of Hawk's hand-carved benches and breathed deeply of the rich mountain air. By the time I had gained the mudroom's entrance there was still no sign of Hawk. My stomach fluttered slightly as I reached for the door's latch, but I ignored it. I'd been offered a tour of the place. My left hand lifted the latch even as my right pushed on the solid oak door. The door, though obviously quite heavy, swung open easily on well-oiled hinges. I slid quickly inside and closed the door behind me, suddenly aware that I'd been holding my breath.

Pausing for a moment in the semi-darkness, I realized this mudroom bore little resemblance to its sister chamber in the big house. Simple coat hooks adorned the walls in place of intricately carved animal faces. Where the floor in the larger room was a buffed hardwood, this floor was comprised of stones that appeared to have been hand-hewn and shaped expertly into place. I wiped my feet carefully on the doormat, hoping to leave no mark on the floor's immaculate sheen.

Directly opposite where I now stood was a heavily framed opening into some room beyond, and to that opening I tiptoed silently. Placing my hand upon the thick mantel, I peered into what I could now see was a great room—a room that surely used up the majority of the ground floor's real estate. All of the furniture was draped in dustsheets, a spooky testament to the fact that this house was little used at present.

The hair on my arms prickled as I stepped further into the room. The shades were drawn and the room was a quiet, almost neglected gray. *Almost* neglected, but not quite. The hardwood floor, maple by the look of it, had no look of dust, and a huge chandelier, suspended from the ceiling's central peak, bore no cobwebs. Even an old black globe that rested upon a dustsheeted desk shone as though it were cleaned regularly.

But for these touches, I'd have assumed no one had ventured into this house for years. At least *five* years, at any rate. Dalton Lockwood claimed to have found the wills of both his father and his brother in a cupboard in this very place just five years ago.

I stepped into the great room slowly, allowing my eyes to adjust to the gloomy light. Though I couldn't see actual furnishings as they rested beneath their sheets, I could see that the first item one would encounter upon entering from this direction would be a large desk. Beyond the desk, sofas and armchairs sat in a cozy cluster nearer to the fireplace. My interest, however, did not lie with the furniture, and I scanned the room's walls carefully.

Aurora had said that Dalton's discovery of the wills had taken place in an old cupboard in the winter house. To my mind, a cupboard suggested something built *in* to the home, so I'd start my search with any of those that I could locate. There was nothing I could see on *this* side of the room, so I moved quietly beyond the desk, around the furniture cluster, and to the walls near the fireplace.

Sure enough, I saw at last that the walls flanking the fireplace were filled with bookcases above and cupboards below. A quick peek at the cupboard doorknobs dashed any hope of seeing which of them might have been most recently disturbed. There wasn't a trace of dust on any of them. *Well, at least no one will know I've been here if I touch them.*

The bookcases that lined the walls on either side of the fireplace began at waist height and reached all the way to where they met the ceiling's downward slope. Every inch of space was filled with books, and I nearly yielded to the temptation to explore each title. My interest, however, did not lie with books, either, so I reluctantly left them alone and bent to look at the cupboards that supported them.

Pulling open door after door, I discovered such usual odds and ends as Christmas stockings, candles, and sofa throws. One contained nothing but an old box of fishing lures. I discovered no documents at all until I opened the final one, furthest to the right from the fireplace. Inside this cupboard lay a single document, comprised of three sheets stapled together. I looked quickly around the room to be sure I was alone, and drew it from the cupboard.

Chills engulfed me as I read the words *Last Will & Testament* emblazoned at the top. I grabbed hold of the bookshelf above the cupboard to steady myself and perused the first page. *Huh.* It was only a template, with lines to be filled in with names, dates, bequests, et cetera. No personal information had been provided at all. The final two pages were more of the same, with signature and witness spaces provided at the end of the third page.

Closing my eyes, I tried to envision Exhibits B and C. My memory told me that they were identical to this document, but all of the spaces were filled in and the signature lines were not blank. *Hmmm.* I couldn't remember any witness signature lines on the exhibits, so that was another difference.

Had *this* been the cupboard where Dalton had found the wills? If so, had Otto used this template as a guide to his creation of what were now Exhibits B and C? Perhaps he'd thought witness signatures were unnecessary.

I was so engrossed in my thoughts that I didn't register the shuffling of feet or the opening of a door upstairs. A sudden, accompanying creak of a floorboard, however, broke through my concentration and I jumped so violently that the will template flew right out of my hands. *Someone else is in the house!*

Stooping as quietly as I could, I retrieved the document from the floor and replaced it in its otherwise empty cupboard. If this were the cupboard in question, it seemed probable that Dalton really *had* done some cleaning and discovered the wills. I knew I'd be hard-pressed to find a cupboard so tidy in my own home.

Another creak, followed by a muffled voice. I'd been certain that all of the parties had been conferring together, preparing themselves for Spencer's after-lunch deposition. Who would be here in the winter house?

I crept over to a thus-far unnoticed staircase on the far right of the room. Far from the elegant winding steps of my imagination, these stairs were made of wood and led straight up to a landing I could just make out up above. The ascent seemed unusually steep to me, and, thinking of Myron, I was possessed of a sudden desire to view the *bottom* from the *top*. I could still hear a single muffled voice in a room somewhere above me, so I assumed someone was on the telephone.

Hoping their phone call would last a while, I cautiously tried the first step, and then the second. Hearing no complaint from the wooden stairs, I made my way to the very top and turned around.

Vertigo!

As suspected, the staircase was very steep and, in my mind, quite narrow for a home built on such a luxurious estate. Small wonder Myron had met his death when he'd stumbled on these stairs. What a horrible plunge that must have been as he'd known, for a brief second, that he must surely impact the hard floor below with nothing to aid him or cushion his fall.

Cringing inwardly, I decided it was high time I got myself *out* of the winter house. I moved carefully, but as I shuffled forward on the landing the wood beneath my feet finally betrayed my presence with an old-home groan. My breath caught and I stood absolutely still, certain that my unaccompanied snooping was about to be discovered. My stillness only brought the muffled conversation into greater clarity and I listened, my trepidations forgotten, to an unfamiliar voice. *Could that be Spencer?* I leaned toward the sound, careful to keep my feet in place and thus avoid further protestations from the floor.

"Yeah, it's my turn after lunch," said the voice. "I just wanna get this over with."

Definitely Spencer, then. I listened more closely, aware that I was hearing only one side of a conversation. I'd seen an old-fashioned rotary phone near the bottom of the stairs and wondered if Spencer was using a landline. If so, why?

"No, nothing's finalized yet, and all this secrecy is making me nuts."

A pause as the person on the other end spoke.

"No. I told you, no one's aware of any of that. I came up with it and did it all on my own. Everyone knows about it, but no one knows I'm behind it. What's that?"

Another pause, and I longed to reach the other phone so I could hear the response. Spencer was behind *what?* I listened closely as he spoke.

"Listen, nobody can find out about any of this until the case is over, okay? I'm only trying to do what I think is best for the family, but they won't all see it that way."

I held my breath as the other party spoke into Spencer's ear, then waited for his reply.

"I don't know when it'll be over. It could go all the way to court, for all I know. No one seems willing to concede anything. I mean, Aunt Aurora and my cousins aren't in any hurry to end this. I think they actually look forward to the little court reporter showing up."

Gasp! How had *I* come into this? I strained my ears.

"I'll deal with that. I've been working on it, and I'll have another go soon. I mean, *everything's* at stake, as far as *I'm* concerned. For now it's important that they don't suspect anything. Hey, did you get Jen's invitation to that concert next month?"

Another pause and I turned away, sure that the conversation had changed tack.

"Yeah, I think I'll try to go if I have the time. Look, man, I have to meet up with our lawyer before I answer questions this afternoon. Call ya back later? Thanks. Bye."

My suppositions about landline use were confirmed when I heard a handset being replaced onto its cradle. *Why use a landline clear over in the winter house, Spencer?*

Well, privacy, obviously. And here I was, intruding on it.

I looked dizzily down the steep staircase and inhaled deeply. Gripping the rail tightly and stepping only on the balls of my feet, I made my way quietly to the bottom, exhaling only when I arrived there. All the hairs on my neck were raised at the certainty that at any moment I'd hear Spencer's voice behind me, saying, "Hey, what are *you* doing here?"

A thump and a jingle of keys. I hadn't thought it unusual to find the door unlocked when I'd arrived, but now I realized that Spencer must have gotten here first and opened the door. Now he was going to exit the house at any moment. If he spotted me, he might assume I'd overheard his conversation. Would that trouble him? *What* was he working on, that he'd try again soon? *What is it that no one can know about until the case is over?*

Suddenly, the room tilted slightly as air seemed to *whoosh* right through my head. Could Spencer possibly be talking about the intrusion at my home? The brick through the ladies' window? Could he believe that retrieving the typewriter would somehow be "best for the family," even though they might not all see it that way?

Might I, at this moment, be alone in the house with a crowbar-wielding, lamp-smashing, brick-throwing bad guy?

I couldn't know, of course, but I found myself thinking about Spencer and his quiet sullenness in a new light. I glanced frantically around the great room, seeking a place to conceal myself, but found nothing. The room was large and open, with a door on the opposite side that led to what I could see was a small kitchen. I didn't want to get trapped in there. Apart from that and the staircase, there was only furniture and open space.

Heart thudding, I quickly bent down and removed my shoes. My footsteps now softened by my socks, I scurried as quickly as I could through the great room, beneath the mantel, and into the mudroom. I could hear footsteps on the wooden stairs even as I squeezed myself out of the mudroom's exit. I'd be seen—and what an odd sight I'd be—if I tried to return to the main house by way of the drive and in my stockinged feet. I leaped from the porch and skipped around to the rear of the winter house just as I heard the slamming of the mudroom door and the jingling of keys.

CHAPTER 29

DEPOSITION OF SPENCER LOCKWOOD

After lunch I'd made my way back to the dining room of the main house and taken my seat. I'd tossed my ruined socks in my car before heading down to Hawk's house to eat. He'd apologetically informed me that he'd been called away by Jenkins after his deposition this morning. Jenkins had wanted Hawk to have a look at the water heater. My freshly-heightened radar pinged me again as I asked myself if Jenkins had overheard Hawk's offer to show me the winter house. Had he deliberately called Hawk away so I couldn't visit the place?

No, that was carrying things too far. Speculation about Spencer's conversation had thrown my thoughts into overdrive, and I was seeing shadows everywhere.

The lunch hour over, the parties began to trickle back into the room and take their places. As usual, Spencer was the last to arrive, and I watched him obliquely as he forewent his accustomed path to the seat beneath the fern. He seemed almost bashful as he made his way to the chair on my left. He smiled at me diffidently and I nearly questioned the entire conversation I'd overheard.

My previous observation of Spencer had been that he was a man who seemed reluctant to be here. He was sometimes sullen, often slouching, always taciturn. He never participated in any of the family banter before or after depos. Rather, he was always last to arrive, first to leave, as though he wished to be invisible. I'd viewed him as completely unthreatening. Until the phone call.

He took his seat beside me and I found that I could assign no prior label to him at all. The air he exuded didn't feel morose *or* dangerous. I double checked my equipment and decided that the man before me was either truly bashful or a very good actor.

Coop shuffled some papers out of his briefcase before turning to me with a nod. He was ready to begin.

Spencer swiveled in his seat so he could face me, his hand already in the air for his oath. He'd been present for six depositions already, and he knew the drill. I stuffed my questions down, swore him in, and we were off.

SPENCER LOCKWOOD,

First duly sworn to tell the truth relating to said cause, testified as follows:

EXAMINATION

QUESTIONS BY MR. RICKMAN:

    Q. Do you mind if I call you Spencer today?

    A. I don't mind.

    Q. Great. When were you born, Spencer?

    A. May 20, 1987.

    Q. Making you twenty-nine years old today?

    A. Yes.

    Q. Spencer, were you raised here in this house with Aurora Kensington's grandchildren, Levi and Amy?

    A. They're a little bit older than me, but yes.

    Q. I understand that your father was approaching middle age when you arrived?

A. He was forty-seven.

Q. And was he married to your mother?

A. Yes.

Q. And what happened to her? Why is your mother not in the picture?

A. She and Father got divorced when I was a baby.

Q. And she never tried to gain at least partial custody of you?

A. I don't know. I've never heard from her, and Father won't speak about it. If she tried, I don't think she tried very hard.

I tried not to stare at Spencer. I knew how it felt to be motherless, though I, at least, had grown up under my mother's care. How horrible it must have been for him to have never known her. I next glanced quickly at Dalton's formidable features. Had Spencer's mom even had a chance in court against this man and all his money? Had Dalton deliberately kept his son from knowing his own mother?

Q. I'm sorry to hear that, Spencer. If you wouldn't mind, now, I'd like to hear about the rest of your family. For example, how would you characterize your relationship with Levi and Amy?

A. First cousins once removed.

There were several chuckles from various parties and Spencer flushed. Coop didn't laugh, though. He smiled at Spencer as if to encourage him.

Q. Thanks for that, Spencer. That stuff always confuses me. More to my point, though, do you get along with your cousins?

A. Yeah, I guess so. We like different things.

Q. Will you give me an example of something you like?

A. Computers.

Q. And what do they like that's different?

A. They like outside stuff. Hiking, biking, skiing. You know.

Q. Okay. How about your Aunt Aurora? Do you get along with her?

A. Yes. Aunt Aurora's always been nice to me.

Q. Spencer, I'm not sensing any hostility from you toward your Kensington kin. Am I correct about that?

A. I'm not hostile toward them.

Q. Then why are you suing them?

The room went completely silent and I held my breath. I sensed that everyone shared my surprise at the bluntness of Coop's question, but we *all* wanted to hear the answer. Spencer swallowed several times and looked at his attorney, who remained quiet. Nothing objectionable here.

A. It's just a legal thing.

Q. I'm sorry, Spencer. Can you speak up? I didn't catch that.

Spencer, eyes on his lap, had mumbled almost unintelligibly.

I'd written what I thought I'd heard, but I was happy when Coop clarified.

    A.   I said, it's just a legal thing.

Much better.

    Q.   Perhaps you can explain it a little bit better for me, Spencer.

    A.   My grandfather, Myron, is dead. My father found his will, and he wants the will executed.

    Q.   Thank you, Spencer. And that's not unreasonable. But it's not just your grandfather's will that brings us here, is it?

    A.   No. It's also because he found my Uncle Otto's will, and since no one knows where Uncle Otto is, Father wants to execute his will too.

    Q.   And you're supporting your father in those wishes?

Spencer looked at his father and then at Aurora before returning his gaze to his lap.

    A.   Yeah.

    Q.   Your father mentioned, Spencer, that the Kensingtons wish to modernize the newspaper, and he does not. Do you remember that testimony?

    A.   Yes.

    Q.   And do you agree with your father, or would you like to see some changes as well?

    A.   I wouldn't mind a few changes.

Q. What would you like to see changed, Spencer?

For the first time Spencer's eyes lit up, and he became more animated.

A. I'd like to see a blog become an official part of our online version.

Q. Any particular kind of blog?

A. Well, I like that Badger Thicket guy.

Q. Remind me of who he is.

A. He takes all of the stories in the regular paper and turns them into something funny. People really like him, and I think including him or someone like him in our online version would really give the paper a boost.

Q. Great, Spencer. Thanks for your candor. I'd like to change topics for a minute now, if I can.

A. Sure.

Q. Were you with your father, Spencer, when he found the wills he alleges were drafted by Otto?

A. No.

Q. So you have no proof that he found them where he says he found them?

A. I guess not. But he's my father. I believe him.

MR. RICKMAN: Thank you, Spencer. Those are all the questions I have for you today.

MR. FLYNN: And none for me.

(Deposition concluded at 1:25 p.m.)

(Signature was requested.)

* * * * *

I wasn't surprised that Mr. Flynn had no questions. Why ask his client questions that could give rise to still *more* questions from the other side?

It was only one-thirty in the afternoon, and as I packed up, I began making plans for the rest of the day. I had transcripts to work on, laundry to do, and bills to pay. I wanted to stop at the pet store to get Herc some food, maybe even a new toy. I wanted to make the most of my time and get all of my chores out of the way before Saturday morning.

"Hey, Shae?" It was Coop.

"Yes?"

"We may be finished with depositions in this case."

"Okay, Coop." *Oh, no.* The day of reckoning regarding the typewriter was at hand.

"But we aren't absolutely sure," he went on. "Would you mind hanging on to the exhibits for just a bit longer?"

Relief flooded over me. "No problem, Coop," I said, keeping my voice casual. "Just let me know when you think you're really, really finished, and we'll wrap things up then."

"Thanks, Shae. By the way," he said, grinning at me, "you're moving like your hair's on fire. You in a hurry?"

I stuffed my laptop cord hastily into my bag and reached for my steno machine.

"Yep. Got a lot to get done before Saturday, so I'm happy we finished early today."

"What's Saturday?"

I crammed my laptop into my poorly packed bag and zipped it closed. "Saturday is the day of the poker run."

Coop laughed aloud and Mr. Flynn, all business, frowned over at us.

"Maybe I'll show up for that, Shae, just to see you on your

Harley." Coop laughed again. "I know you ride, but I can't picture it. You're so little!"

"Am not. In my boots, I'm nearly five-seven."

"So you went for the boots with the big heels?"

I *hmph'd* as he chuckled again.

"It's still hard for me to imagine you riding your own Harley. But hey, have fun. We'll call your office if anything comes up."

Hawk materialized just in time to take my steno case from me. As we walked through the kitchen, he shook his head as though to clear it.

"Did I hear that right, Shae?"

"Hear what right?"

"That you ride a *Harley?*"

"Yep. Going out on it tomorrow."

He carried my bag down the steps and over to my car.

"Well, I guess I'm about as surprised as I could be. Never woulda thought it."

He was staring at me as though he'd never seen me before, and this time it was my turn to laugh.

"I'll take a picture for you."

"You do that." His eyes crinkled as he smiled and popped a toothpick in his mouth.

I smiled at him even as my stomach clenched. I was nearly out of time. I was going to have to come to a decision about the mystery tooth, *and soon.*

CHAPTER 30

POKER RUN

I was excited. I'd had more than the usual on my mind in recent weeks, and now I had decisions to make. Ethics? Tell the cops? I told myself I was eager to finish the case and return to normal. Was that really true, though? I'd grown fond of the lovely estate and most of the characters involved.

But today was not a work day. Today was the Poker Run, and I'd been looking forward to it for weeks. I'd flown out of bed at 7:00 a.m., yanked open the front door, and stepped into the courtyard. *Yes!* The sun was shining, not a cloud in the sky.

Icy concrete beneath my feet reminded me that this was late August in the mountains, and I hugged my arms to my chest as I scurried back inside. No matter, though. The forecast promised a reasonable warm-up later, and the run wasn't to begin until one o'clock.

I bundled up in a comfy jacket and Ugg boots, calling to Hercules as I rounded up his leash and a plastic bag. Must pick up after our pets. He bounded to me, sensing my excitement and lending some of his own as I clicked the leash into place. Almost as an afterthought, I grabbed a hat and a pair of large sunglasses. There aren't many certainties in life, but there was one thing I knew I could count on. Hailey is a small town, and when you leave home in pajamas, an oversized jacket, and just-rolled-out-of-bed hair, you are bound to meet at least five people you know. I was probably kidding myself that the hat and sunglasses would help, but they made me feel more put together. *Or semi-disguised, at least.*

After a quick walk around the block, Herc and I both felt awake and refreshed. Naturally we had run into old Mr. Baker and his German Shepherd, Duke; we'd greeted Julie Anne, Pilates instructor, out for her morning run; Stella Baumgartner had asked after the Darlings as she surveyed her end-of-summer petunias; Eddie Blake from the local produce department tooted his horn on the way to work, waving a hello from his vintage 1957 Chevy pickup; Frank Gruber had shaken a fist at Hercules as he stood in his yard next to Ziggy; and we'd nearly been plowed down by ten-year-old Isaac Parker as he lit out for who-knows-where on his bicycle. Six people, not five. Maybe Isaac didn't count, though. He'd yelled a quick, "Sorry, lady!" but hadn't seemed to recognize me. I waved back at everybody, even Frank Gruber. The air was warming up already. The day was glorious.

Back in my living room, I picked up Herc and twirled him around playfully. "Mommy gets to go for another ride today, Herc. And Clarabelle is taking you to Nettie's. You know how Miss Nettie spoils you."

I was ready for coffee, and he was equally eager for breakfast. When I set him down he rushed to his mat and waited expectantly. I poured his food into his bowl, then added coffee and a sizeable amount of hazelnut creamer to my mug.

I carried my creamy coffee into my bedroom and took stock of my denim selection. I'd been riding in the same pair of Levis for years. I'd worn them a week ago when I'd had my chance meeting with Sergeant Landers on Galena, and there was never really any question that I would wear them again today. I twiddled my hands through several others on the freshly-laundered pile, then grabbed my favorites, along with a white T-shirt and my leather vest, and headed to the shower.

Once I was clean and dressed, I put my Ugg boots back on. No need for riding boots yet. I made my way to the kitchen and filled a large bowl with hot water. I found some soft rags under the sink, as well as a cannister of foaming glass cleaner. Thus armed, I headed to the garage and opened the door.

"Hello, beautiful." I stood back and admired my Road King. "Let's get you spiffed up." Not that she needed much. I just needed to remove a layer of dust and some dead bugs from my last ride. I had very hot water, a towel to wipe, a towel to dry, and a towel to clean the windshield and polish the chrome.

I was nearly finished when the phone rang. It was Gabe, saying he'd swing by at noon. He wanted to know if I'd started the bike up yet and made sure everything was in working order.

"About to," I answered. "Just had to shine her up first. Wanna listen?"

"Sure." He chuckled. "Lay the phone down and light 'er up, and don't forget to hold the clutch in."

"Ha ha." Gabe insisted on being over-protective. "Hang on."

I set the phone on the ground as instructed, then swung my right leg over the saddle. I regretted the Ugg boots. I would have preferred more grip on my feet, but I had no trouble getting the bike upright. I could have left it on its kickstand, but this was more fun. I leaned down and pulled the choke all the way out with my left hand. I'd skipped my normal pre-ride routine last week when I'd been expecting Kelly, but I didn't want to make a habit of that. And so to business.

Clutch in first, always. No exceptions. I turned the power knob to the "on" position, verified the bike was in neutral, and hit the start button. Overkill, yes. I didn't need to hold the clutch in, because a bike won't jerk while in that gear. Still, that was my process. Clutch gripped firmly *in*, bike in neutral before hitting the start button. I am nothing if not cautious. As a woman alone in a garage with a nine-hundred-pound Harley-Davidson, I knew that extra care was just smart.

The motorcycle wheezed and stuttered in the still cool morning air. I opened the throttle and fed it some gas. *Rumble.* That was better. I waited a moment longer so it could really wake up. I opened the throttle twice more and the bike growled and coughed hoarsely. After thirty seconds or so I felt the bike begin to idle more smoothly, like it no longer wanted to go back to sleep. I cranked the throttle way open and the roar was deafening. As it should be. Loud bikes are safe bikes.

I let it idle a bit longer, giving it an occasional burst of open throttle, and then I killed the engine. I pushed the choke back in. The bike wasn't fully warmed up, but it was in good shape to begin our ride. I'd open the choke again when we were ready to go.

I hopped off the bike and picked up the phone.

"Satisfied?"

"Yep. Good girl. I've always liked how that bike sounds."

Me too!

"Now go and have yourself a good breakfast, Shae, and I'll be 'round at noon."

"Aye aye, sir." It was still early, but I was already enjoying the day. I'd been working hard lately, and I was ready to blow off some steam.

* * *

Gabe arrived as promised, promptly at noon. I'd already

pulled the Harley out and closed the garage door. I'd started the bike back up and now it chugged beside me in neutral, patiently waiting for me to don the rest of my gear and hit the road. I was already outfitted in my scuffed riding boots, my worn leather chaps, and my favorite leather jacket. All I needed were my gloves and helmet, and those were in my hands.

Gabe is a guy who looks like he's been astride a motorcycle since birth. Tattooed, gray-whiskered, and knuckle-gloved, he arrived with his long-ish hair waving out slightly from beneath his Harley half helmet. A jacket was strapped to his luggage rack, but for now he wore a black T-shirt and black leather vest. As he cruised neatly up to the curb near my garage, I admired, not for the first time, how at home he looked in his low-slung Corbin seat.

I gave him a thumbs up so he'd know I was ready and he wouldn't need to dismount. I was sure he saw me, but he killed the engine and hopped off the bike anyway. Approaching my bike, he took a look at everything from my gas gauge to my saddlebag buckles. He tested my lights and turn signals. *Overprotective.* At least he knew he didn't need to check me. I always wore a full helmet with face shield and a jacket armored with Kevlar, no matter how hot the weather.

Finally satisfied with my motorcycle, Gabe ambled over to me and hitched his thumbs in his vest's pockets. "Ready to go, darlin'?"

I grinned. "Yep! Let's go play some poker!"

Gabe's laugh resonated deeply, and he mussed my hair. "Helmet on, kiddo, and remember how we ride in groups. I don't want anyone else lane sharin' with you, so you'll ride beside me, on my right, instead of just behind. I'll be keepin' my eye on folks, and if I see someone ridin' stupid, I'll get us away from him. You just stick close. Capeesh?"

"Got it."

"Okay, then. Shoshone, here we come!"

* * *

The bar's parking lot was already teeming with every kind of motorcycle imaginable, but by far the largest number were Harleys. Gabe's eagle vision found space for us somehow, and we backed our bikes in and shut them down. Swinging my leg off the bike, I promptly removed my helmet and clamped a hat down on my head. I dropped my gloves into my upside down helmet and then hung it from one of my handlebars. Gabe, quicker than I, was ready to go and waiting.

We entered the bar and found it jam-packed with bikers. The place was filled with raucous voices, country music, and a sea of leather. We scanned the crowd, hoping to see friends and acquaintances. Finding none, we headed to the back to pay our entrance fee and register. Actual *gambling* would have been illegal, so everyone, rather than betting as they drew each card, simply paid twenty dollars to participate. Seventy percent of the money would go to charity, with 30 percent being divvied up among people with the first, second, and third best hands.

I paid up, signed my name, and received my first card. I was utterly disgusted. A two of clubs. Gabe showed me his and my ire grew. At least *he'd* been dealt a king.

We made our way back outside to await the commencement of the run. There were a few tables scattered around, and we sat down and simply enjoyed the pretty day. It could just have easily rained and ruined everything.

"So," Gabe said, breaking the silence, "what ever became of

that tooth you found, Shae?"

I should have known he'd be curious, and I contemplated my hands as I searched for an answer. I could probably speak more freely with Gabe than with anyone else, simply because he already knew, for example, that the tooth may have been knocked violently out of someone's skull.

"I still haven't decided yet what to do about it, Gabe," I said honestly.

He squinted in the bright sunlight. "You talk to the cops about it?"

I thought back to my 'asking-for-a-friend' conversation with Jax. "Not really."

He raised his eyebrows in some surprise. "You gonna?"

But I didn't want thoughts of the tooth ruining the poker run, so I just shrugged and said with a smile, "Not today, Gabe. Tomorrow, who knows?"

Gabe took my cue and patted my hand. "Gotcha."

He rose to his feet and stretched mightily, saying, "You'll figure it out, Shae. I'll go get us a couple waters."

Determined to cast work-related thoughts aside, I stashed my completely lame playing card into my bag and pulled out some lip balm. Ah, that felt better. Riding always dried out my lips. Focused as I was on my lips, I failed to notice a small, midday shadow come to a stop near my feet.

"You're gonna lose, darlin'."

My head snapped up. The sun shone directly into my eyes, and I couldn't clearly make out the lone figure standing over me. "I beg your pardon?"

"You're *all* gonna lose. Pot's mine today."

I didn't like the way he was leaning over me, so I stood and moved away. He followed, looking me over. *Yuck!* Annoying.

"You're aware it's a *charity* run, right?"

"You'll be a good lookin' loser, though," he said, ignoring my question. His words sounded greasy, and my skin crawled. Still, who was he to act like a bully, especially when the game had barely begun? And what kind of a bully could he really even be? He was maybe five-ten and crazy skinny. *Scrawny* even. He didn't scare me.

"Day's just starting, dude, and I don't know you. See ya." I walked toward the bar, no longer happy to be alone in the sunshine.

He stepped in front of me, blocking my path. I could smell alcohol on his breath, stale and bitter. The creep yanked a leather pouch from a pocket in his jeans and dangled it before me. "This'll be full of my winnin's later today, sweetcakes, you'll see." He stepped forward, bringing his stink with him. "And people like you should be more polite to people like me." He reached forward a bony finger, as if to make his point by poking me in the chest, but his arm was whipped backward through the air, his entire body following suit. Gabe had grabbed the offending arm and flung it so far back that the skinny man flew at least two feet backwards.

The guy lost his footing and landed hard on the concrete. Scampering up like a wiry prize fighter, he took a good look at Gabe's size and sudden ferocity. He stepped back farther and raised his hands in apology. "Hey, man, no harm, no harm. The lady and me was just predictin' the outcome of the game today."

I knew it. Wimpy bully.

"Get away, worm." I'd never seen Gabe angry before, and it was a sight to behold. Two hundred forty pounds of solid biker meat and muscle towered over the scrawny offender as he scurried away, and it was all I could do not to stick out my tongue.

"I'm leavin', I'm leavin'. But that don't change the fact that I'm *winnin'*, so I guess we'll see who's the big man at the end of the day!"

Gabe took a single step toward him, and the man hurried off, glancing back once to be sure Gabe wasn't giving chase.

I nudged Gabe in the ribs with my elbow. "Thanks, big guy."

Gabe stared after the arrogant stranger as the skinny man approached another group of people and swung his leather pouch around.

"Man's making a pest of himself." He turned to me. "And he's been drinking. We'll make sure he leaves ahead of us, Shae. I don't want him behind us."

I nodded, sad that the unpleasant man had robbed Gabe of his good humor. He hadn't responded at all to my "big guy" comment. Determined to restore Gabe's spirits, I pulled him in the direction of the parking lot. Directing his attention to his own bike, I asked if I could try out his new Corbin seat. My ploy worked perhaps just a bit too well. Gabe roared with laughter when I threw my right leg over the saddle, relaxed back into the seat…and couldn't reach the handlebars. The seat looked comfy from a distance, but the thing was just too low for me. Not to mention the fact that his mini apes were adjusted for *his* size and reach.

"You look like a kid on that bike, Shae," he teased, adjusting his hat.

"Hey, I have no trouble on my own bike," I retorted, secretly pleased. He'd forgotten the skinny man. "And women have a different center of gravity. You guys can lay back into your bikes and look all Joe Cool. I have to be more upright. My seat works great." I hopped off. "My bike is perfect for me."

"Your bike is way too big for you."

Ah, this was more like it. Gabe was always trying to talk me into trading down into a more manageable Softail, but I liked how my Road King handled on the highway. I'd been awed by its power the first time I'd ridden it, and it had stolen my heart.

Our companionable banter was cut short by the sound of many engines starting up. People were mounting bikes all over the parking lot. I stashed my bag and hat, slid my gloves on, and pulled my helmet on to my head. I sat on my own bike and got it up off its kickstand, which I then kicked out of the way. This was more like it. A perfect fit.

Gabe held up his right hand, fist closed, and I waited for his signal. Finally, after two-thirds of the bikes had already left, he twirled his index finger in the air to say, "Let's roll."

And we were off.

* * *

Sadly, the arrogant man made his presence felt throughout the day, to the whole party. And while he didn't *completely* ruin the day for all of us, he certainly tried. He could be seen at each stop, beer in hand, waving his dratted pouch around and telling one and all that he'd be the winner of the pot. First place was to win 15 percent of the total purse, with second place getting 10 percent, and third place getting five. With so many bikers, the "pot" was therefore going to be at least three hundred dollars for the best hand.

It was a significant enough amount that there was a great deal of grumbling when the skinny man produced four aces when we reached Hailey, our final destination. Accusations of cheating were leveled, but no one really wanted a brawl. Most of us had been out to have a nice ride, enjoy good company, and raise some money. No one drew a weapon and said, "Roll up your sleeves, mister."

"I'll bet someone lets the air out of his tires if he shows up next year, though," I whispered to Gabe.

"Count on it." Gabe looked at the man who was strutting around, pushing his luck beyond all reason as he bragged about how he'd beaten them all. Gabe shook his head. "If he lives that long. How dumb can you *be*?"

CHAPTER 31

CHEEKY PEAKS

Dear Cheeky,

Oh, I need help! My very best friend is planning to move herself into River Grace. We've known each other all our lives, and we're just as close as two people can be. I take another friend's dog and we go see her every single day. And now she's moving! Oh, Cheeky, she isn't old enough to live in an assisted living facility, she just isn't. And how can she leave me this way? River Grace isn't even walking distance from my home. I'll be bereft. What does one say to a person who is taking this step too soon?

Please tell me how to persuade her to stay.

Desperate in friendship,

Clare D.

My Dear Clare,

How very touching that you love your friend so well. True friendship can be hard to find at any age, and it seems that yours has endured, nay, strengthened, through these many years. I dare say that you and your friend have shared many joys and hardships together as you've traversed the dusty trails of life.

Sweet Clare, you have loved your friend well, and now you must show your love more fully than ever before. You must support her decision. River Grace is a beautiful home, and I am sure she will be very happy there. I honor your friend, Clare, for facing a difficult decision so courageously. Help her move, dear one. Find ways to visit her frequently. Hold your grief away from her eyes, lest you sadden her for taking a step she feels is timely. And take heart. This is but a new season in your lives.

 Most tenderly yours,
 Cheeky Peaks

--∞--

CHAPTER 32

CLARABELLE CAUGHT

"Clarabelle Darling!"

It was Sunday morning on the day following the poker run, and I was enjoying coffee and blueberry danish in the ladies' kitchen. Bernie had been with us earlier, but had taken Herc for a walk to the store. She'd told me she had missed the *Valley Scribe's* Friday edition, and she hoped there were still copies available.

"How is that even possible?" I had helped myself to more danish as Bernie laced her walking shoes. "Clarabelle hasn't failed to pick up that paper even one time in all the years I've known you."

"Don't know," Bernie had returned crisply. "But I guess we'll live, as long as there are copies left. Come on, Herc."

And so they'd gone, and Clarabelle had risen and raced 'round the kitchen, setting things to rights more roughly than was her wont. She'd filled the sink with water and started plonking every dish in sight beneath the suds. When she'd grabbed for my danish plate, I'd held on fast.

"Whoa, Clarabelle! Not done. What's got you so jazzed up?"

Clarabelle had released my plate and gone back to the sink. "Sorry, Shae." And she cast me a glance that had looked positively...*guilty*. She had continued to putter around the kitchen, shining objects that already gleamed, straightening mugs that were perfectly aligned, until Bernie had burst through the door and all but shouted her name. At that, Clarabelle dropped the plate she'd been inspecting for the third time, and it shattered.

"Do you think Nettie doesn't read the paper?" Bernie was out of breath and flushed. Herc trotted in after her and began inspecting the floor beneath the table. He knew Sunday mornings meant danish crumbs.

"Oh, Bernice, I—I—oh, it'll be all right! I disguised my name."

Bernie just glared at her, so I grabbed the paper right out of Bernie's hand. It was open to the Cheeky Peaks column. I read through the letter quite obviously written by one Miss Clarabelle Darling, my eyes wide.

"You disguised your name as *Clare?*" I asked incredulously.

"Well, I didn't know what else to use!" Her voice rose defensively as she blocked Herc from walking towards the broken plate. "No one calls me Clare but Bernice, and I don't know if Nettie's ever heard her use it. It was all I could think up."

Bernie took the paper back from me and sat down, her burst of steam evaporating.

"Clare," she asked, her voice puzzled but kinder, "is this why you didn't bring the paper home on Friday? You didn't want me to see it?"

Clarabelle wrung her hands. "Well, no—I mean, yes. I—no, I didn't want you to see. Yes, that's why I didn't bring it home. I didn't really think my little letter would make it into the *column*, Bernice. I was just so upset because Nettie is moving away."

"River Grace is two minutes by car, Clare."

"Yes, well, Herky and I like to *walk* to see Nettie for iced coffee. We go ev—we go every d-d-d-daaaayyyy!" Clarabelle scooped Hercules to her chest and bawled.

"Why didn't you tell me how upset you were about this, Clare? You'd have felt better."

"Because Cheeky's *right*, and I'm being selfish, and I didn't want you to know how selfish I *am*. And now you know, and Shae knows, and I just know Nettie knows too."

I handed her a tissue, and she sniffed dramatically into it. The storm had passed. Clarabelle, incapable of keeping secrets, had hidden this from us for nearly two whole days. It was a wonder it had taken her this long to boil over.

I stood and grabbed Herc's leash. "Come on, Clarabelle. Herc gets another walk."

She looked at me through puffy eyes. "Where are we going, Shae?" Her voice was almost childlike.

"We're going to Nettie's. I'll bet, if she's seen this, all she's thinking is what a wonderful friend you are."

"Do you really think so?"

"Of course I do. But we don't want her worrying about you, do we?"

"No! Never!"

"Right. Let's go encourage her. You can tell her you think Cheeky Peaks was spot on."

"Shae's right," said Bernie briskly. "Let's not allow any more water under this bridge. Be sure to give Nettie my best."

* * *

Later that evening, as I sat at home indexing the exhibits from my Drop Trow case, I had to smile as I thought about how the visit had gone. Nettie had indeed read the paper and had been unsure of whether she should let Clarabelle know she'd seen it.

Clarabelle had apologized profusely, with many tears, assuring Nettie that she was *happy* her friend could move into such a fine facility. Clarabelle confessed she'd been selfish at the thought of Nettie moving away, and she asked if Nettie could *ever* forgive her.

Nettie had allowed Clarabelle to gush until she was spent. She'd known that her friend just needed to "get it out."

When Clarabelle's tears had dried at last, Nettie had produced a brochure and some actual photos Jax had helped her take of her new room. While Clarabelle and I exclaimed over the brochure and admired the photos, Nettie had leaned in and whispered conspiratorially, "It won't be all fun and games, though, I'm told."

"Well," I'd said, "at first you'll be healing up from your surgery, of course."

"No, no," said Nettie. "My surgery isn't scheduled until next year. I'm moving now so I can get settled in well ahead of having a hip replaced."

"So what do you mean, not all fun and games?" Clarabelle had asked. "I see lots of opportunities to play, Nettie. This Lazy Eights Bingo Club looks fun. I could come and join you!"

"Yes, yes, do, Clarabelle. But I'm not talking about *those* games." She'd leaned in closer, as though afraid to be overheard in her own home.

"I've spoken to some of the residents there." She'd looked at each of us, eyes dancing. "They've warned me that there's a certain nurse there who goes by the name of Sybil Le Doux. The residents call her Duckie, but not to her face. Apparently she's a right handful, and not always very nice! Arnold Hayward told me he'd caught her red-handed, stealing ice cream right out of his personal freezer! And one time she hid Mildred Hartford's slippers for a solid week."

"Someone should report her!" I was appalled, but Nettie shushed me with a wave of her hand.

"Some might say," she all but giggled, "that Mildred had it coming. She'd asked her grandson to bring her a realistic-looking rubber mouse, and she'd put it in various places to frighten Duckie. Whenever Duckie would see it and go set mousetraps (the safe cardboard ones, you know), Mildred would move the mouse and put it somewhere else."

Nettie was in fine fettle. This was the first time I'd met her, and I liked her greatly.

"Naughty Mildred," I'd concurred, calming down, "though I hope the ice cream stealing part isn't true. But why do they call her Duckie? Doesn't seem very respectful."

Nettie had nodded. "Arnold said that a former resident by the name of John Haywith had trouble pronouncing Nurse Le Doux's last name. According to Arnold, Mr. Haywith thought the spelling of it looked like Dux, or Ducks, in his mind. After that, he would only ever call her Duckie. She had no choice but to tolerate it from him, and he's gone now, may he rest in peace. But she takes a sharp tone, I'm told, if she ever catches any of the others using it. Since she's rather unpopular on the whole, when she's not listening, no one calls her anything *but* Duckie."

"Goodness," said Clarabelle. She looked back at the photos. "You must behave yourself, Nettie, and not get on Duckie's bad side. The thought of you with no slippers…"

Nettie and I had laughed together. I'd picked up the brochure again, thinking that the home looked charming. Even so I was glad that Bernie and Clarabelle had me to look after them, should the need ever arise. I could only imagine what dear Clarabelle might get up to with a nurse like Duckie ordering her around.

I finished my exhibit index and went in search of an envelope for the documents. Finding one, I then turned on my computer so I could print postage on the envelope and get it ready to mail to Boise. I'd no sooner finished when the phone rang. The display told me that Annie was calling. How odd. It was after 9:00 p.m.

"Hello?"

"Hey, Shae. Sorry to bug you so late. I really hope you don't have plans for tomorrow."

"Just work, Annie. Transcripts."

"Thing is, I just got a call from Coop Rickman. He said they've had to schedule an emergency depo for tomorrow morning. Something about new evidence. Since it's late notice, they aren't going to start until nine o'clock. Can you make it?"

"It won't be a problem, Annie. Who are we deposing?"

"According to the notice that Coop sent, you'll be working on the Volume II deposition of Aurora Kensington."

I thanked Annie and hung up the phone, my mind spinning. I'd told Jax nothing about the actual typewriter or the precise case. This surely couldn't have anything to do with my conversation with him two weeks ago. Plus, Coop had warned me there could be further depositions.

Still, as the words *new evidence* rattled around in my head, I found myself unable to shake the feeling that the case was about to blow wide open.

CHAPTER 33

AURORA'S LETTER

Hawk carried my steno bag into a very quiet dining room the next morning. Coop had arrived first and seemed preoccupied by a sheet of paper he held. A large speaker phone sat within easy reach.

"Hi, Shae." Coop tore his gaze from the paper and lifted his eyes in greeting. "We're gonna be a small crowd today."

"Okay. What's up? Is anyone else coming at all?"

"Only Aurora. No one else. Not even Dom." He gestured toward the speaker phone. Apparently, Mr. Flynn had been unable to travel to Idaho on such short notice. "He'll be joining us by phone. This isn't going to take long at all."

"Okay."

I looked up in time to see Aurora Kensington making her careful way into the dining room. She was making full use of her pearl white cane, with no grandchildren to assist her. Today she looked positively regal in black slacks and a sparkly white, three-quarter sleeve tunic.

I felt I should make my presence known. "Good morning, Mrs. Kensington."

"After all the time we've spent in this same room together, my dear, you must call me Aurora."

"Thanks, Aurora. I'll try to remember."

Our conversation went no further as Coop and Aurora waited for me to finish setting up my equipment. Perhaps it was only because Amy and Levi weren't present, but Aurora seemed more subdued than usual. I stole occasional glances at her as she sat quietly, thinking thoughts I couldn't begin to guess at. All of us jumped when the speaker phone rang.

Coop reached out to answer it and turned the volume up.

"Can you hear me, Dom?"

"Yes. Am I coming through all right?"

"Sounds just fine. Shae's here and ready to go. Shall we get started?"

"That's fine, Coop. Let's go ahead and swear the witness in again."

AURORA KENSINGTON,

First duly sworn to tell the truth relating to said cause, testified as follows:

EXAMINATION

MR. RICKMAN: The first thing I'd like to do is have another exhibit marked. Madam Court Reporter?

I took the single sheet of paper from him, affixed a blue exhibit sticker to it, and returned my hands to the keys.

(Exhibit No. D marked.)

QUESTIONS BY MR. RICKMAN:

Q. Aurora, you called me yesterday and told me that Amy had found something in Otto's bedroom. Is that correct?

A. Yes.

Q. And you asked me to come over and take a look at it with you?

A. Yes.

Q. And after I read it, I told you that I would keep it, fax a copy to Mr. Flynn, and schedule a short deposition for you today. Correct?

A. Correct.

Q. Aurora, I'd like you to tell me what Amy found.

MR. FLYNN: And I'll object for the record. I just received this exhibit this morning. I haven't had a chance to verify its authenticity. I haven't even shown it to my clients yet.

MR. RICKMAN: Your objection is noted, Dom.

BY MR. RICKMAN:

Q. Go ahead, Aurora.

A. As you can imagine, Coop, Mr. Flynn, this case has renewed Amy's and Levi's curiosity about the family. They've been asking a lot of questions about my brother, Otto. I remembered a picture album that Otto used to maintain, but I wasn't sure what happened to it. I asked Amy if she would poke around carefully in Otto's room to see if she could locate it.

Q. Is there a reason it's taken you this long to remember the album, Aurora?

A. Well, it was Otto's. When he first left, I didn't want to disturb his things. Recently, since Dalton has filed this lawsuit, it may have seemed prudent to search Otto's room, but I've been completely blind for years now. Searching for something is beyond me, and it didn't occur to me until my grandchildren started asking questions.

Q. And did Amy find the box of albums?

A. No. But she did find an envelope in Otto's desk that held a picture of my father and his three grown children. The envelope also held the letter you have now marked as Exhibit D.

Q. Did Amy read the letter to you, Aurora?

A. Yes. We were both shocked, I can assure you. It's a letter from my father, addressed to me. My father wanted me to have the letter in case anyone contested his will, which, he said, left the estate and the business to Otto and to me.

Q. Did the letter say what he had left to Dalton?

A. Almost nothing. A condo in Sun Valley. Father said he feared Dalton would contest the will, so he was leaving me this letter as added insurance.

Q. I'll represent to you, Aurora, that this letter is signed by your father and dated August 9, 1975. Is that what Amy told you as well?

A. Yes, it is.

Q. And according to my notes, your father's tragic accident happened just three days later, on August 12, 1975?

A. Yes. That's right.

Aurora grew very quiet and I had to strain to hear her.

It's almost as if he knew...

Q. Just a bit more, Aurora, and we'll be done. I have to ask, do the sentiments and wishes expressed in this letter bear any resemblance to the will that we've marked as Exhibit B in this case, wherein Dalton inherits half of everything, and you get almost nothing?

A. It bears no resemblance whatsoever.

Q. Can you think of a reason, Aurora, why this letter would be among Otto's things when there's no sign of the will to which it refers?

A. I just don't know, Coop. Perhaps Father had expressed his wishes to Otto, written this letter according to those wishes, but died before Otto could complete the actual document.

Q. And that's a theory, but you're only guessing?

A. I'm only guessing.

    MR. RICKMAN: Thank you, Aurora. I have nothing further.

    MR. FLYNN: Just a few follow-up questions, please.

EXAMINATION

QUESTIONS BY MR. FLYNN:

Q. Mrs. Kensington, you've been told that this letter was typed and not written by hand. Correct?

A. Correct.

Q. What kind of paper was it typed on?

A. It feels like a normal sheet of paper. It's been folded for many years. I can feel the indentations where the folds were.

Q. It's not thick paper, Mrs. Kensington?

A. It is not.

Q. It doesn't smell of cedar?

A. Why no, Mr. Flynn. My father wrote this letter. Since it's typed, I imagine he used Otto's typewriter. But he wouldn't have necessarily used Otto's paper supply. The cedar paper was all Otto.

MR. FLYNN: Nothing further. I want to renew my objection to this piece of very late evidence, Mr. Rickman, and I can assure you that we will be subjecting the actual letter to the utmost scrutiny.

MR. RICKMAN: Knock yourself out, Dom. Get a handwriting expert if you want to. This looks like the real deal to me.

(Deposition concluded at 10:35 a.m.)

(Signature was requested.)

* * * * *

Short and sweet, but what a bombshell! This new evidence could, in fact, blow the case wide open, as I'd guessed. I lifted Exhibit D off the table so it could join its compatriots in my exhibit folder. I frowned.

Something about the document had raised a barely whispered question in my mind as I had tucked it away—some thought I couldn't articulate. I opened the folder and looked at the new exhibit again, but whatever the uncomfortable notion had been, it had vanished.

CHAPTER 34

SNOOPING

I didn't know Dalton Lockwood could ride a motorcycle.

Considering his age, I wondered if he even *should* ride. Yet here he was, decked out in blue jeans and an American flag leather jacket. If he owned a helmet, he'd left it at home, and had instead covered his receding hairline with a flaming red bandana. Curved black sunglasses, brand new riding boots, and knuckle gloves completed his ensemble. Everything was too new, too shiny. My critical eyes saw only a tough guy wannabe who'd watched *Easy Rider* too many times. I hoped he didn't know I was there. In fact, why *was* I there? What ride was this, anyway?

I didn't particularly want to get into a conversation with someone who was a party to an ongoing case. I would mingle in another part of the crowd. Did I know anyone there?

Just as I was about to slip away, Dalton Lockwood turned slowly in my direction, his eyes finding and holding mine. He smirked. His expression implied that he knew something I didn't, and his eyes oozed arrogant, condescending victory. I grappled with confusion. What was Dalton looking so smug about?

Then he raised his hands and looked greedily at the playing cards he held. I stared down at the cards, wishing Dalton hadn't come on this ride. He was ruining it with his smirking conceit. Deciding to ignore him, I turned away.

"Hey, little lady."

I turned back, annoyed, but Dalton's face had blurred, re-emerging as the face of the bluffing biker of the recent poker run. The biker waved his cards and leered at me, shaking a full money pouch with his other hand. My stomach clenched, and my heart pounded. In my anger I made to step toward him, but my feet wouldn't move. I tried to signal other people. I wanted to cry out that the man was a cheat and a reckless rider, but my dry mouth wouldn't form the words.

I watched in mute helplessness as the man who had been Dalton, and was now the awful poker run winner, strode to his motorcycle and got away. I willed my feet to move, and screwed up my face in an effort to make my mouth work—and popped awake. I sat bolt upright in bed, heart still thudding.

* * *

It was the smirking that had gotten to me, that had tipped me into full-scale court reporter madness. Fully awake now, my conscious mind completed my dream. I couldn't avoid making a comparison between Dalton Lockwood's smug face and the cocky biker's same expression during the Poker Run. A cocky biker who had swaggered and bragged, tapping his cards in blatant, early celebration. A biker who'd cheated. He'd had the winning hand all along because somehow he'd made that happen ahead of time.

Aside from his arrogance, why did that biker remind me of Dalton Lockwood? Why had I dreamed that they were one and the same person?

And what was that other thing nibbling at the edges of my mind? Something had caught my attention about that last piece of evidence, Exhibit D. I went back, my mind's eye returning to yesterday morning. There'd been a wisp of a half-formed idea, and then nothing. I'd packed up and gone home, the same as every other day.

Now I sat on my bed, and the memory of the ghost thought came back to me. What had it been that had *nearly* aroused my curiosity? The exhibits were mere feet away, boxed in my dining room. I should leave them alone. That typewriter had endured quite enough shenanigans in this house without my disturbing it further. But something was nagging at me, and I'd never get back to sleep until I figured it out.

The temptational pull was startling. I peered over the edge of the bed. Hercules hadn't sensed my wakefulness, and his blanket rose and fell as he snoozed soundly. If I moved, if I actually *got up* and ventured into the living area, he would follow me. I told myself not to disturb his burrowed slumber. I told myself that the lawyers would take care of their own case. I told myself not to meddle.

And I ignored myself.

I turned and stole a glance at the clock—1:23 a.m. I'd gone to bed at ten thirty, but I hadn't been in a hurry to go to sleep. I'd read a fascinating crime novel until nearly midnight, and when I'd turned off the light at last, I'd fallen asleep immediately. For one hour and twenty-three minutes. Just long enough to take the edge off. Long enough for *smirking* to enter my dreams and a forgotten thought to torture my mind.

I grabbed my sweats from the foot of the bed and pulled them on. I was reminded of the last time I'd yanked on sweats in the dark of morning. The very night I'd first begun work on the Lockwood case, an intruder had been in my home. Two weeks later, someone had lobbed a brick through Danny's window, perhaps seeking criminal ingress.

Between those intrusions, Clarabelle had discovered the tooth in the typewriter. And now that *thing*, that wisp of a thought that had teased my mind just yesterday.

It seemed to me that mystery followed upon mystery in this case. I'd asked Gabe my questions about the tooth, had even posited a hypothetical to Sergeant Landers during our chance motorcycle encounter. But my real questions remained. Why had Otto fled the country the very day of his father's funeral? Why hadn't Aurora tried harder to find him five years ago, when he'd written? Was she, as I'd already surmised, protecting him?

I turned on the bedside lamp, unwilling to light the room up entirely. Herc stirred in his comfy cave as I slipped my feet into my slippers and rose. The bed creaked. Herc stuck his nose and eyes out curiously.

"If you get up," I whispered a warning to him, "you'd better stay quiet. If you bark, the ladies will think there's been another intruder." Hercules cocked his head and whined at my hushed tone, but he took my cue.

Our duplex, once a single structure, had paper-thin walls. Bernie had often told me she was a sound sleeper, but I knew Clarabelle suffered wakeful nights. I would try not to disturb them.

I eased my bedroom door open and crept into the living room. Ceiling lights were too harsh for this time of night, so I edged my way along to the end of the wall on my left. Feeling for the light switches, I chose the farthest along the wall and pressed it.

My tiny dining area was instantly awash in warm shadows. I had deliberately rigged my simple hanging light fixture with soft white, forty watt bulbs. I disliked a garish glare above the table. Now the light was barely sufficient. I decided to turn on the kitchen lights as well, dimming them to what felt appropriate for the hour.

Hercules whined, and I found him seated by the front door.

"Oh, no, you don't, Herc." Letting him out wasn't why I'd left my bed. "You'll be fine 'til morning. Go lay down."

I rounded the table and found the small box of exhibits I sought. I'd written *Lockwood v. Kensington* on the front and had placed it on the floor next to the typewriter in its Samsonite case. I lifted the box to the table and withdrew the short pile of documents. There were only three—not many—especially considering the magnitude of the case. Then I picked up the typewriter case and laid it on the table as well. I opened the latches and laid the top of the case back on the table. The Smith-Corona gleamed up at me in the soft light. If I was going to look at the exhibits, I might as well look at them all.

I handled exhibits almost every day in my work. I'd frequently gone through them page by page, inspecting them thoroughly before shipping them off to my firm in Boise. But every time I'd done that in the past, I'd been seeking *spellings*. I had wanted to verify verbiage in a difficult paragraph that had been read into the record. I'd never snooped for the sake of snooping. *Until now.*

Just as I was telling myself that this was different, that the stakes were high, and that my snooping was justified, Hercules whined again and skewered my train of thought. "Buddy, I *told* you—" I stopped short, taking in his tiny form. He looked so hopeful as he hopped from foot to foot. He only did that when his need was dire.

I tiptoed over to the front door and knelt down. "I'm going to open the door, Herc, but you'd better be serious." He reached his nose to my face. "I mean it. Out you go, but no barking, and come straight back in when you're done. Good boy." I released the dead bolt as noiselessly as I could and inched the door open. Herc bounded out into the courtyard, but he'd heard the sternness of my warning. He didn't make a sound.

Assured by the presence of our new wrought-iron gate, I left the door slightly ajar so Hercules could come back inside. Then I returned to the table and looked afresh at my exhibits. I decided to view them chronologically. Picking up Myron Lockwood's will, I laid it to my left.

Next in order came his letter to his daughter, Aurora, the letter that had caused such consternation two days earlier. As I placed it to the right of her father's will, a breeze flowed gently through the partially open front door, and the letter drifted lightly from the table. My fingers reached out as it descended toward the floor, but faltered as I was struck by a powerful sense of déjà vu. Something about this exhibit had pricked my senses this early morning, just as it had yesterday in the deposition.

I looked at the letter where it had come to rest amidst a week's worth of dust bunnies. *What was it?* My mind could just, *almost* catch the thought, but I needed a proper look at it.

I retrieved the letter and placed it again just to the right of Myron Lockwood's will. Finally, I withdrew Otto Lockwood's *Last Will & Testament* from my exhibit box, and laid it to the right of the letter. Three exhibits. Three points of contention…

"The dates are wrong."

I'd have hit the ceiling had Bernie not laid a firm hand on my shoulder to calm me.

CHAPTER 35

DEPUTIZED

"I didn't mean to startle you, Shae." Bernie held Hercules with the hand not resting upon my shoulder and nodded toward the open door. "I was in the kitchen for Tylenol. Must have overdone it in the yard yesterday." Bernie removed her hand from my shoulder and rubbed her lower back, stretching. "I'd no sooner put the bottle back in the cupboard than I noticed this little guy at my feet."

I'd forgotten the ladies' dog door.

"Oh, I'm sorry, Bernie. I forgot. I should have stayed outside and watched him." Turning to Hercules, I tried to scold him. "Little rascal! We had a deal. You were to be serious, do your business, and come back home."

Hercules, happy in the crook of Bernie's arm, gave a doggie grin and wagged his tail. *Incorrigible.*

"It's no trouble, Shae. He lives there as much as he lives here."

That was true. All the same, no point rewarding him. I took him from her and put him on the floor, telling him to go to bed. This time, he complied.

I pointed to the exhibits.

"You weren't supposed to see these, Bernie. They're totally confidential, so mum's the word. Don't even tell Clarabelle about them."

"Can't you deputize me or something?"

I laughed. "I can't *deputize* you, but I can *trust* you. You can't unsee them, I know, but this is top secret depo stuff."

"Got it," she said. "Sorry, Shae. I didn't know not to look."

But Bernie didn't look sorry. She actually looked rather excited.

I smiled. "Great. So tell me, what did you mean when you said the dates are wrong?"

"Well, you had them sorted by date, but how do you know all of the dates are correct? It looks to me like at least one of them is off."

I'd only looked at the wills once so I could identify them for my transcript's index. I'd brought them to each of the case's depositions, and I'd seen them lying on the dining room table, but I hadn't studied them. Now, Bernie lifted and held Myron Lockwood's will under the light.

"It's a fairly straightforward document," she said, adjusting her reading glasses. "I, Myron P. Lockwood, being of sound mind, do hereby state my wishes and bequests."

"Go on."

"The Q in bequests is raised, just like in the pages that Clarabelle typed."

"Yes, well…" I was confused. "It would be, wouldn't it? Doesn't that just prove it was typed on this typewriter here?"

"It would seem to." Her eyes took in the remaining two documents. "And you'll see here," she said as she lifted Otto's will, "this has the same simple language, and the same raised Q."

I was mystified. "Yes, they match. But what is your *observation*?"

"Myron's will, Shae, bears the date of July 30, 1975. Otto's will shows a date of August 15, 1975, nearly two weeks later."

"Okay, Bernie, and they both have the raised Q. They were both typed on the Smith-Corona."

"Yes, but when?" Bernie lifted the letter Myron Lockwood had written to his daughter, Aurora, shortly before his death. "This letter, Shae, is dated *between* the writings of each will. In the top left-hand corner we see that Myron typed August 9, which was only three days before his death."

"How did you know Myron died on August 12?" I asked, startled.

Bernie just tapped her head. "Even then I read the papers, Shae. Good memory, I guess."

"You never cease to amaze."

"Anyway, take a look at this." She held the letter out for my inspection, and I gasped. Click, click, click. This is what my peripheral vision had caught, what had troubled the edges of my mind. Bernie had found the thing I had almost, but not quite, noticed as I'd been stacking the exhibits into their folder after the depo. I now read the letter quietly to myself.

There, in the second paragraph, Myron had written to his daughter,

"It is my hope, Aurora, that this letter will equip you with the strength you need in order to hold your place in the family business. I trust Otto implicitly, and I have no concern that he would ever try to shunt you aside. I am concerned, however, that Dalton may not wish to leave things as I have decided. I fear that Dalton will not quietly accede to my wishes that you always have equal authority. Produce this letter as you must, daughter, that any discord among you may be quickly quelled."

Five Qs, just in that paragraph, and not a single one of them was raised. They fit in line perfectly with the rest of the letters.

"I don't understand, Bernie." I set the letter back down on the table. "How can the same machine have typed a will with *raised* Qs on July 30, a letter with *normal* Qs on August 9, and then another will with *raised* Qs just days later, on August 15?"

"Precisely my point! And don't forget, Shae. Clarabelle's *Agatha Christie* pages all exhibited the raised Q, as well, forty years later."

Confused and a bit frustrated, I raised my hands in the air.

"It's possible," Bernie mused, "that Myron used a different typewriter to type the letter, though the typed words look identical but for the Qs."

I was shaking my head, remembering some of my lunchtime conversation with Hawk. "Hawk told me there had never been another typewriter on the estate. He also said that, in his later years, Myron didn't leave the grounds at all. He couldn't have used a typewriter at, say, the newspaper office. Even if he had, it would have been a more modern instrument by 1975, like an IBM Selectric, and there would be a difference. This makes no sense."

"I thought as much. That's why I said the dates are wrong." She lifted the August 9 letter and placed it to the *left* of Myron's will on my dining room table.

"If I'm correct," she said thoughtfully, "then Myron's letter to his daughter was typed *first*, before anything had damaged the Q in the typewriter. That would mean..." Bernie stopped speaking as she perused the wills.

"Mean what?" I asked, holding my breath.

"Have you read these, Shae?"

"Not the wills. I've heard the testimony."

Bernie nodded once to herself.

"Right. Here's my theory. The letter to Aurora was written *first*. Then something happened to the typewriter, damaging the Q—"

"And *then* the wills were typed, and Myron's was *dated two weeks earlier*," I finished in a whisper.

"Yep."

"Bernie," my voice trembled as I voiced my growing suspicions, "what if Otto killed his father?"

Bernie looked up sharply, pursing her lips. "Is *that* what you think happened?"

I told her that Myron's cause of death had been called an accident, a fall down the stairs, but that Dalton questioned that. I also told her that Otto had disappeared the very night of Myron's funeral. Hawk had seen him leave. Aurora had heard from him, but refused to speculate as to his exact whereabouts.

"I think perhaps she's been protecting him, Bernie. Maybe even providing for him."

"If Otto Lockwood killed his own father, Shae, then he certainly had the means to construct a will, backdating it to some weeks earlier. It also tells us that the typewriter was damaged sometime between August 9 and August 15, 1975."

I looked at her. "Because?"

"Because the letter shows an undamaged typewriter—that's the ninth—and the wills show damaged Qs, damage that remained. We know that from Clarabelle's typing. So the typewriter was fine on the ninth and not fine thereafter. The wills would have to have been created by the fifteenth, which was the day Myron was buried and Otto vanished."

"But Myron's will favors Dalton, Bernie. I know that much. Wouldn't Otto have written his father's will more favorably toward himself? Toward Aurora?"

"Perhaps not, if he was fleeing the country. And if, as you suppose, Aurora was protecting him, Otto may have felt that a will in Dalton's favor would be less obvious. It would raise fewer questions for his sister to answer."

Bernie yawned, pointing a final time at Otto's will. "This," she said, "could have been written at the same time as Myron's will. If this is indeed Otto's work, he apparently dated them two weeks apart and forged his father's signature. The newspaper business is left largely to Dalton, with Otto and Aurora playing a minimal role on the board."

"Maybe that's why Dalton is so sure of himself." I spoke slowly, visualizing his arrogant, angry face. "No other wills have been produced, Otto isn't around to explain, and Aurora can't see. She wouldn't have noticed anything odd about the Qs in the documents." My shoulders sagged. "Amy and Levi would have seen that the letter looked different, but they weren't there when it was produced yesterday."

"Neither of the attorneys mentioned that the documents held discrepancies?"

"Can't say any more, Bernie." Talking about a possible *crime* with Bernie was one thing. Discussing what attorneys had said in depo proceedings was another.

She arched a querying brow as though to say, *we've gone this far...*

I sighed. "Okay, listen. I'll say this much. I think sometimes attorneys hold some things back for trial. Coop produced the letter. He doesn't have to reveal all of its secrets. And Mr. Flynn hadn't any time to study it. He objected to it. He's probably playing his cards close right now too."

Bernie nodded. "Fair enough. But Shae?"

"Yes?"

"Do we know what the typewriter types like now that the tooth is gone?"

"I close my mind to such questions." Another arched eyebrow from Bernie made me smile. I felt my cheeks heat up.

"Well..." I stalled.

Her brow edged up even more.

"Okay." She had me dead to rights. Who *wouldn't* want to know what the typewriter typed like with the tooth gone? "Obviously I've been curious, but I can't—"

"*Crime*, Shae. There could be a *crime* involved."

"All right, all right. I'd love to know if the tooth was the reason for the wonky Qs."

There. I'd said it.

"One way to find out!" Bernie immediately whisked the Smith-Corona out of its case and peered at the wooden box it always rested upon therein.

"This is a paper holder, Shae."

"Bernie, no! Don't touch—"

But her fingers had already pried the top off of what I'd assumed was just a platform to hold the typewriter in place. I quickly moved to her side and stared at a small stack of cream-colored, thick vellum paper securely ensconced within four carefully lined, one-inch-high walls. The storage area had been closed for a long time, so the aroma of cedar was powerful as it exited the little chamber. With trembling fingers, I lifted a sheet of paper and walked to the far end of the room, away from the box. Holding it near my face, I breathed deeply. Unmistakable. Indisputable. We'd found Otto's paper supply.

CHAPTER 36

BERNIE TYPES

Tap, tap, tap, tap, tap, tap, tap, *pling*. Tap, tap, tap, tap, tap, tap, tap, tap, *pling*.

I swirled around. Oh, no! She knew better! Bernie had drawn up a chair, inserted one of Otto's sheets of paper, and was typing like mad.

I stormed across the room just as she withdrew the paper from the machine. What was that I'd said about *trust?*

She studied the paper for only a moment before handing it to me with a "Well, well, well, what have we *here?*" expression.

I took the letter and glanced down, half fearful of what I would see. Bernie had copied the paragraph I'd just read from Myron's letter to Aurora. The truth was inescapable. In the document that Bernie had typed, all five Qs were perfect. They lined up just as they should with the rest of the letters.

"Mystery solved," said Bernie with satisfaction. "That tooth gummed up the works. Made the Q look funny."

"It must have been Myron Lockwood's tooth," I breathed.

"One more time?"

"The tooth. It had to have been Myron Lockwood's. The tooth belonged to a denture wearer. Myron wore dentures."

"Many people wear dentures." Bernie played along.

"Myron fell—or was pushed—down the stairs in the winter house. The typewriter was in the winter house. That house has just one large great room on the first floor, and Myron fell down the stairs leading into it from the second floor. Aurora testified that the fall was so violent, poor Myron's dentures flew across the room. If he had an anchor tooth, like my friend Gabe told me about, that tooth could have flown too."

"And landed in the typewriter?"

"Exactly."

Bernie nodded thoughtfully. "So Myron writes the letter on August 9. Then Otto kills him on August 12. He creates a will for Myron and backdates it to July 30, two weeks before the murder. He creates his own will, concurring with his father's 'wishes.' He dates it August 15, the day he plans to leave forever."

I nodded, enjoying none of this. From all I'd heard, Otto had been a good man. Both Aurora and Hawk had expressed kind words about him. I felt miserable with my growing certainty that he was a killer.

"He would have then had to hide the letter his father had written to Aurora," I said. "It was in his desk, so surely he knew about it."

"I wonder why he didn't just destroy it?"

I shrugged, baffled. "Maybe he wanted to leave some kind of leeway for Aurora in case anything ever happened to him."

I turned my attention again to the wills.

"So far," I struggled on, "we've explained why the wills may have been dated the way they are, and why they both have unusual Qs. They were both typed *after* Myron died, and *after* the tooth became lodged in the typewriter."

"I'm afraid so, Shae."

"It doesn't explain what I'm to do now, though, Bernie. Deposition exhibits are sacrosanct in my world. That you've seen them is bad enough. I can't just go running to the police with this. It's all just conjecture on my part, anyway…"

Bernie took the thick sheet of paper back from me and moved to tuck it into the leather folio with Clarabelle's *Agatha Christie* pages. Straightening back up, she yawned mightily. It was by now two o'clock in the morning. I needed to let Bernie get back to bed.

She approached me, and laying both hands on my shoulders, said quietly, "You'll find it, Shae."

I felt my brows furrow.

"Find what?"

"The right thing, Shae. You'll find the right thing to do. Right now, go and get some sleep. No problem solves itself at two in the morning."

My own eyes felt suddenly scratchy, and I knew she was right. She bid me good night and reminded me to lock up after her. Good old Bernie. Consistent as ever.

But I didn't sleep even a few minutes the rest of the night. I lay in bed, unable to escape images of a man falling, a man fleeing, and a strange little typewriter typing strange little Qs…

CHAPTER 37

BOOBY TRAP!

Two days later found me knee deep in deposition exhibits and personal testimony on an unrelated case. It had been three days since the last Lockwood/Kensington depo. Three days since the admission of Exhibit D, Myron Lockwood's letter to his daughter, Aurora. Two days since Bernie and I had concluded that it was very possible that Otto Lockwood had murdered his father. The days had been fretful and the nights sleepless as I had tried to come up with the "right thing" that Bernie was so sure I would find.

I couldn't reveal my deposition exhibits to the police. If I did, I could lose my license and find myself the target of a lawsuit myself. And did I even *want* to reveal what I believed? I liked Aurora Kensington. I didn't want to make trouble for her.

The "right thing" was proving as elusive as ever, but I couldn't think about it now as I bit my lip to keep my emotions in check in my current depo. Today's testimony was tough to hear, and my stoic, professional court reporter mask had all but crumbled. In a moment, I feared it would slip from my face entirely.

I was in Twin Falls covering a deposition for a law firm that specialized in medical malpractice, horrible accidents, and wrongful death. People awash in life's most dire circumstances sought counsel here and found the very best. We were in their comfortable conference room, with late afternoon sunshine streaming in through the windows, as a devastated widow told a story of what she believed was preventable loss.

The attorneys were all somber, respectful. My demeanor matched theirs as Mr. Lotham's questioning continued.

    Q. So no one in the hospital asked your husband if he'd taken his medication that day?

    A. All I know is that nothing was written down. If they'd asked, if they'd cared, they would have known what medications he was on. They could have checked for harmful interactions—

    Q. I'm just asking for what you know personally, ma'am.

    A. I know they didn't write down that they asked him. There's nothing anywhere, noth—noth—nothing we've s—s—seen—all they had to do was ask—

    Q. Do you need a break, ma'am? I know this is difficult.

    MR. BRECKAN: Here's some tissue, Wanda. Want to go outside for a minute?

    THE WITNESS: No. I—I'd like t—to just f—fin—finish.

    MR. BRECKAN: Okay. Al, you can resume.

BY MR. LOTHAM:

    Q. Wanda, I'd like you to tell me in your own words how your life has changed since George passed.

Wanda looked stricken, and I waited, hands poised over my keys. It seemed that even my heart's beat was slow, quiet, mournful in the grief-thickened atmosphere. A clock ticked. A fly buzzed against the window, seeking ingress into the cool room. Wanda lifted her red eyes and her drenched, forty-something face to the men gathered around the table. She wrung her hands, shredding her tissue.

> A. How can I explain the loss of my other half? How can I face morning coffee now, when I always shared it with him? How can I go to bed at night, knowing he's not there, and never will be? How can I garden, knowing he won't be there to point out the weeds I missed? How can I do anything alone, when before I did everything with him? He was my best friend.

Her chest was heaving now, and great sobs wracked her narrow frame. She seemed so frail, so broken. I'd seen grief before. I'd heard sad, sad stories. But today my slow, quiet, mournful heart hurt for this woman, and my eyes betrayed me and stung as I continued writing.

Not allowed, Shae! No tears! Think of something funny. Lighten up and do your job.

The testimony carried on for a little while longer. I knew that when attorneys asked about a person's current life situation, it often signaled a winding down of the deposition. We were nearly finished, and I needed to back burner my emotions. I forced myself to think about Hercules prancing around Clarabelle's feet; of her sneaking him a morsel of cheese when she thought I wasn't looking; of Mr. Gruber's apoplectic face, almost comical in its rage. I thought about the drive home this evening and how beautiful the twilight sky would be. I thought about anything but the lump in my own chest and the thought of people who have gone on too soon.

This deposition had started late in the day. It would be dark when I got home, but still warm. I would get into some stretchy clothes, find a book, maybe have a nice glass of—

> MR. LOTHAM: Those are all the questions I have for you, ma'am. Thank you for your time.
>
> MR. BRECKAN: And I have no questions. You're all done, Wanda. We'll read and sign.
>
> (Deposition concluded at 7:15 p.m.)
>
> (Signature was requested.)

* * * * *

I looked closely at my transcript to make sure I hadn't missed anything due to being distracted. Everything was there, down to the letter. Mr. Breckan quickly escorted Wanda out of the conference room, and Mr. Lotham packed up his things and left.

I observed a pile of rumpled tissue on the chair Wanda had vacated, and my chest squeezed. I knew what it felt like to be alone. I had the Darlings, but with my parents gone, and no extended family… I didn't like to dwell on it, but this case had touched a nerve. More than a nerve. Drat! It had hurt my heart. *Not for myself,* I lied. *For Wanda.*

I packed up quickly, making sure I had all of my exhibits. They were numerous due to the nature of the case. The exhibits included medical records from the deceased man's life, pictures of the couple in happy times, and affidavits from neighbors—people who wanted to attest to the man's good health prior to his hospital stay.

I left the conference room with one final look around to be

sure I hadn't missed anything. The room was untidy because we'd been working for several hours, but my end of the table was completely empty. I hadn't overlooked any of my things. I headed to the lobby and stepped out into the cooling, twilit air. A breeze burned my still stinging eyes, and they watered.

I'm not crying. It's been a busy few weeks, today's depo was unusually sad, and this wind is being mean…

Comfort food! Yes. I stuffed my gear in the car and got behind the wheel.

Blue Lakes Boulevard in Twin Falls is full to bursting with fast food restaurants. It was well past my normal dinner hour, I felt sad, and my internal autopilot led me straight to my favorite burger joint. Then, cheeseburger in hand, I sat in my car, played happy music, and began to feel the day fade into history. I'd be home in no time, and tomorrow was a day off. I was tired, but that thought perked me up considerably. Also my burger was a rare treat and absolutely delicious.

My junk-food-induced euphoria carried me all the way home. I didn't even think about the possibility of wildlife bounding onto the darkening highway. My phone rang just as I was entering the outskirts of Hailey. The number appeared on the car's hands-free display, but I didn't recognize it. I was nearly home and didn't want to get into a conversation. If it was important, they would leave a message.

It was nearly nine o'clock by the time I eased my car into the garage and killed the engine. I sat in the car for a few moments, absorbing the stillness. Traveling days always zapped my energy, and even my burger buzz had faded. I was contemplating the cooling, clicking sounds of the engine when my phone rang again and startled me. Since the car was not running, the hands-free display didn't respond. I quickly fished through my bag for my phone and saw that Annie from my firm was calling. At nine o'clock at night. Never, ever good, for either one of us. She wouldn't be calling unless something had come up. I swiped the screen to answer the call.

"Hi, this is Shae."

"Hi, there. Glad I caught you. Are you home from Twin yet?"

"Just drove into the garage. I'm still in my car."

"I'm glad you got there safely. My phone's about to die, so I tried you from my daughter's cell." So *that* was the call I'd ignored. *Oops.* "Listen, I just got a call from Coop Rickman. He said he's sorry for the late notice again, but he's scheduled another deposition for tomorrow at 6:00 p.m."

"Another depo?" Tomorrow was Friday. It was supposed to have been a day *off*, and now there was an evening depo? Were there more surprise documents in store?

"Hello?" Annie asked. "Shae? Are you there?"

I recovered my composure and reminded myself that having a job was a very good thing, even on a Friday evening.

"I'm here, Annie. I'm just surprised, you know? Did Coop give the name of the deponent? I thought we'd already covered everyone there was to depose."

"Sorry, Shae, he didn't say. But Coop said he's putting a notice together. I'll send it along to you when I get it. He just wanted to make sure you were available. He mentioned bringing the exhibits along."

"No problem, Annie. I can get there. Maybe it'll be short."

"Hope so. Sorry about that. Thanks a bunch, Shae. I owe you. I'll send the stuff as soon as the email comes through."

"Thanks, Annie. Enjoy the rest of your evening."

"You too, Shae. Night."

We disconnected, and I opened my car door, my curiosity piqued. What had come up? Would Mr. Flynn be able to attend the deposition, or would he appear via telephone again?

As to my day off, it wasn't really such a blow. My day "off" wasn't ruined. "Day off" was a misnomer anyway. Most court reporters have home offices, and freelancers like me knew that *non* work days were really just *home* work days. I could still have my small sleep-in. I could walk Herc. I could have lunch when I wanted. But I'd be busy.

First I would index my exhibits from today's job and mail them off. I was expecting another transcript back from my proofer, so I would make my corrections to that job, finish the worksheet and transcript cover pages, and turn all of that in. Then I would get a head start on editing today's transcript.

I gathered my handbag and my burger wrapper and climbed out of the Juke, heading to the hatch to get my gear. I spied the large stack of exhibits where they lay next to my machine case. Way too much to carry at once. I would need an extra trip to the house to get everything inside. I heaved the stack of papers into my arms, then hoisted my handbag onto my shoulder, tipped the trash into the bin, and hurried to the door that led into the courtyard. I didn't want to leave the car hatch and the garage door open for long.

The courtyard lay deep in shadow, quiet, almost ghostly. The Darlings' motion-sensitive light failed to light my way—a first. I always relied on it. I'd trodden this route many times, however, so I forged ahead confidently. Halfway through the journey to my door, my phone rang yet again. Maybe Annie was calling to say there wouldn't be a deposition tomorrow. That wouldn't be so bad, would it?

I juggled the exhibits and allowed one purse strap to fall from my shoulder. Now my bag hung open, and I grabbed for the glowing cell phone within. My huge pile of papers started to shift in my other arm, and I struggled to steady them even as I saw the word, "Restricted," flash across my phone's screen.

I'd seen that once before, when Jax had called me after the break-in several weeks ago. Maybe he was calling again to say that they had a lead. The exhibits slipped even more and I tried to grab them with the hand that had plucked the phone from my bag. I couldn't manage a swipe to answer it, but I didn't want to miss this call. I decided to run for it, get inside quickly, dump the exhibits, and answer the call. Bernice would have been by to unlock my door for me. Now that we had our secure front gate, she did that when she knew I'd be returning after dark.

Cell phone ringing, exhibits slipping, I made a dash for my apartment. Three feet before I'd attained my goal, my left knee slammed into something unexpected—something *hard*, something in the way. Whatever it was crashed beneath me as my momentum flung me forward. With my feet whooshed out from under me, I flew forward like a rag doll. As I hurtled toward the door face first, a deafening series of pops exploded from somewhere within the courtyard. I had only a fleeting awareness of a small blur streaking past me, of footsteps running away.

I hit with a sickening crunch to my face and right shoulder, then slid down the face of the door to a hard landing on my right elbow, knee, and hip. The force of the fall left me helpless, with nowhere to go but all the way to the ground. A moment before, I'd been hurrying inside to answer my phone, but now I lay on my back, my body screaming in agony from every part that I could identify.

My exhibits were strewn about the courtyard, but I couldn't find the wherewithal to even care. I heard myself moaning slightly and didn't care about that either. I was aware of light entering the yard, of voices buzzing. Somehow they seemed distant to me.

I was afraid to move. My brain, unable to direct itself to one particular area of concern, resorted to accepting an exquisitely painful chaos. Back, neck, shoulder, wrists, both knees, right ankle, forehead, right eye, mouth. My spine felt snapped in two, and I didn't know if my toes would work. I wore glasses for nighttime driving, and I hadn't yet removed them. I was sure they were broken and digging into my temple, maybe my eye. I'd heard the crack as my face hit the solid wood. The thought of self-investigation at this moment terrified me—even if my hands could perform the task.

Voices broke the silence just above me.

"Shae, Shae, can you hear me?"

Another moan. Me again. I couldn't speak. *Please be patient, voices.* Gathering my painful courage at last, I wiggled the big toe on my left foot. Relief flowed through me. My toe had responded to my command. I tried my entire foot, and that moved as well. I gingerly tested the toes on my right and found them responsive. I'd wait a moment to move my right ankle about. It was sending leave-me-alone signals to my addled brain, and I heeded them.

"I don't think she can hear me, Bernice. Should we call nine-one-one?"

"She's stunned. Let's give her a moment and see if she answers us."

If my feet were responsive, surely my hands and arms would be as well. I moved my right hand slightly, unwilling to do anything too quickly in case I'd broken bones. But my hand behaved as it should, so I tried the left. It was okay.

"There, Clare. She's moving. Shae, honey, can you open your eyes?"

Now the part I'd been dreading. I reached up to feel my face, certain there would be blood dripping everywhere from gouges caused by my driving glasses. To my utter astonishment, however, my glasses were intact! I felt no wetness at all! I carefully touched my eye and winced. I'd probably be bruised, but really, everything felt just as it should.

Even as I was giving thanks for well-made glasses, my hand moved up my forehead and discovered a large knot halfway between my hairline and eyebrows. I could tell it was swelling by the moment. Further investigation of my face revealed fat upper and lower lips on the right side. I tested my jaw gingerly and flinched, but heard no crunching, no clicking. Sore, then. No breaks or dislocations.

"Oh, Shae, dear, please open your eyes." Clarabelle's voice sounded unsteady and frightened.

I heard further whispered conversation. "Soon as we see how she is, I'll try to round him up."

I was barely able to discern Bernie's words. *Round who up?*

With great effort I opened my eyes. Clarabelle was kneeling down, dirtying her dress, her worried face not twelve inches from mine. Concern puckered her brow as she fluttered her hands over me, not sure if she should touch.

"I see you can move some, Shae." Bernie was standing, but she was bent low, watching me carefully. "Do you think you're ready for us to help get you up? I'd like to get some ice on your mouth and that goose egg you noticed."

"*Ice?*" cried Clarabelle. "We need an ambulance!"

CHAPTER 38

INJURY

"Noooo," I moaned again. "No ambulance."

I pictured local emergency responders, with big hearts and no-nonsense efficiency, flooding our tiny courtyard. My mind conjured images of a gurney, I.V. bags, and the interior of an ambulance. "Please, not that. I wasn't unconscious. I was afraid to move, and everything hurts."

With the ladies' help, I struggled to my feet and warbled into my apartment. I sat on the edge of my couch, head thumping, eyes watering. Bernie left for a moment, then returned with several bags of frozen peas.

"Shae," she said, then waited until I managed to look up. "I want you to put these everywhere it hurts." Bernie handed me the peas, then slipped mysteriously from the room. It was unlike her to vanish in a crisis, but I was too miserable to ponder on it much.

Clarabelle grabbed a throw pillow and slipped it behind me as I tried to lay back. Careful not to jostle me, she sat on the edge of the couch.

"You really should go the hospital, Shae, dear. You've such a nasty lump on your head, and we've all learned about such things. Bleeding brains, I believe. What if you have a bleeding brain?"

My swollen lips managed a tiny smile. "I think you're referring to a brain bleed, Clarabelle, and I think I'm okay. I hit the front of my head." I tapped it. "The hardest part. I've done worse than this to my head as a kid on my bike."

"That was before we knew," she said sagely. "Now we know better, and you should be looked at."

But I knew what CT scans cost. I knew that a trip to the emergency room would put a terrible dent in my small savings account. I patted her hand and tried to brighten up a little for her sake.

"I'll be okay, Clarabelle. I need to make use of these peas, though."

"Oh, where do you hurt? Is it more than your head and your poor mouth?"

I pointed. "Right ankle, both knees, right elbow. I don't know if ice will help my shoulder, my back, or my neck. They're more jarred than banged up. Maybe you can find me some Ibuprofen?"

Clarabelle was already rolling up my stretchy work pants. "Shae! Your ankle is swollen all up, and so are both of your knees!" She sounded horrified at what she'd found. "The right side is the worst. Let me see your elbow." Clarabelle lifted my sleeve with care. "Yes, skinned, it will be bruised. Oh, poor you."

She shaped bags of peas around my damaged ankle and both knees. That left one bag for me to lay on my goose egg and swelling right eye. *Ah.* That felt nice. As I closed my eyes, I heard cupboard doors and a rattling around in the kitchen. Clarabelle must be searching for Ibuprofen.

"In the cupboard above the dishwasher, Clarabelle." My sore jaw made speaking an effort, and speaking loudly enough to be heard was even worse. How had I managed, with one fall, to injure so many areas?

Soon Clarabelle was at my side again with pain killers and a glass of water. Setting the water down, she helped me ease myself up so I wouldn't dribble water down my chin. After I swallowed the pills and lay back down, Clarabelle seated herself again on the edge of the sofa.

"Shae?"

"Yes, Clarabelle."

"I'm afraid Sergeant Landers is on his way here."

I spluttered, nearly choking. I sat up suddenly, unaided, and regretted it at once.

"Why?" I gasped. Hadn't we had enough *real* trouble at this residence? Why would he need to come because I was *clumsy*?

"Because," said a deep male voice, "this was no accident, Shae."

I hadn't heard anyone come in, but I only had to look up to see him. The sofa faces the front door, but I'd been so intent on Clarabelle, Jax's sudden presence took my breath away.

"What do you mean?" I asked, thinking back. I'd tripped on something, then that loud noise, and a blur of motion... *Hmmm*. What *had* I tripped on?

"I need to take a better look around, Shae, but it looks like someone was in the courtyard, waiting for you to get home. They'd moved Clarabelle's garden bench, the low one with the little frogs on it, right into your walkway. I looked around with my flashlight, and beneath the far corner shrub I discovered, among other things, some fresh burn marks and cherry bomb casings. It still smells like flash powder out there."

"Other things?" My mind was too scrambled to take it in.

"Someone wanted to hurt you, Shae."

I'd never seen him more serious, and that was saying something.

"From what I've seen, they waited, then set off the cherry bombs to startle you, ensuring you would fall by way of the strategically placed bench."

"But I'd already tripped before all the noise." This made no sense.

"No one said this was set up by a mastermind, Shae."

"But the new gate—"

He put down his flashlight and notebook, casting an inquiring glance at Clarabelle. She shook her head slightly.

Seating himself on the chair opposite me, he gazed soberly at his hands, clasped together before him. Knuckles stood in white relief as each hand clenched and unclenched around the other. It finally dawned on me that he wasn't in uniform. Bernie must have called him on his private phone. The thought made me squirm. This was his night off. She shouldn't have troubled him.

The peas from my forehead had slipped to the floor when I'd sat up. Jax stood again, picked them up, and handed them to me.

"Best hold this up to your head, Shae. That lump is a doozy."

I complied as he scowled at some dark thought and resumed his seat. By the time he turned to face me, the scowl was gone and his voice was gentle. "Here's what we have so far, Shae. I got most of this from Bernie when she called me." He referred back to his notes. "Hercules was barking, so the ladies thought he must have heard you come home. They waited for you to get your things inside and come to retrieve him. When you didn't come, they opened their door to see what was troubling Herc."

Herc? It sounded nice to hear him use my affectionate nickname. *Wait a minute. Where was Hercules?* I hadn't seen him since that morning.

Jax held his notebook but didn't look at it again. He knew what it said. "The ladies opened their door just in time to see you trip over the bench. That's when the cherry bombs went off. I expect whoever was waiting lit them as you entered the courtyard. His fuses were probably too long for his purposes. Took longer than he expected. You fell, they went off, and he made his getaway."

"But the gate …," I began again, massaging my neck. "We keep it locked tight. How did he get in?"

Bernie stepped out of the night and into my living room, her face flushed as if with exertion.

"The gate was open, Shae," she said grimly as she caught her breath. "The window repairman was here today to fix the window in Danny's room. We gave him clear instructions to keep that gate firmly shut and locked, but he had to have left it open when he finished the job." She looked furious. "Gave some varmint just the opportunity he must have been looking for."

I remembered the blur that had zoomed past me as I struck the door. "Where is Hercules?"

Bernie took a deep breath. "He's gone, Shae. We'd just opened our door when the cherry bombs went off, and he bolted right out that open gate. I've just been all over the neighborhood, but I can't find him." She clutched the doorknob, fury fading, her strong veneer cracking for the first time in my memory.

My heart, one of my few body parts that had remained unhurt, now pounded painfully in my chest. Hercules was too little to be out on his own. He was too black to be seen at night. In his fright, there was no telling how far he would go before he slowed down. He could get lost, run over. He could go a little too far and find himself in the hills with the coyotes and hawks.

Bernie strode across the room, knelt down, and took my hand in hers. "I've told all the neighbors, Shae. There are people out looking for him right now."

"Not in cars!" I cried. "He's black! They won't be able to see—"

"No, no, Shae," she said in a soothing voice. "They know. They're walking. Some are on bikes with headlamps. But I'm afraid it's getting late, honey. They won't be able to look much longer. I had to come home and tell you."

The thought of tiny, big-hearted Hercules out alone in the night was too much to bear. My eyes were well past mild watering now. Hot, round tears boiled over and rolled down my cheeks. Bodily pains receded from conscious thought as I worried about my brave little soldier.

Oh, Herc. Buddy. Where are you?

CHAPTER 39

EXHIBITS

A masculine hand passed me a tissue. "I'll let the officers on duty know about Hercules, too, Shae," Jax said.

I nodded, wondering when enough was going to be enough. Could this still be about the Lockwood case, as I'd suspected before? The timing of this evening's so-called attack was just a bit too coincidental, considering another depo had just set up for tomorrow. But did I really believe this was a deliberate attack, as Jax seemed to think? Could Spencer really be behind an act like this? As suspicious as I'd found his phone call, my brain just couldn't picture him crouched low in the courtyard, waiting to hurt me.

I wished more than ever that I could talk to Jax about everything, but I couldn't.

"Meanwhile, Shae," Jax was still speaking, "I need to ask you some questions and get a statement from you. I know you're tired, but it really is best when it's fresh. You up for it?"

"Okay." I closed my eyes, needing my Ibuprofen to kick in. I wanted Hercules to come charging through the door, excited to see me. But Jax was ready to begin.

"When you got home, Shae, did you exit your car immediately, or were you delayed?"

"I was on the phone. I didn't get right out of the car."

"And when you did get out and entered the courtyard, did you see—"

"Ohhhh, Jax!" Clarabelle squealed.

I opened my eyes at her excited interruption.

Clarabelle clasped her hands and bounced on her toes. "Maybe this is about the typewriter!"

I'd been hoping Clarabelle wouldn't make that connection, but I supposed it was a fair guess on her part. Even so, I wasn't prepared for her sudden further outburst of, "Jax! Ask her about the tooth!"

Jax's head snapped up, and he looked at me sharply. "*Tooth?*"

"Clarabelle, hush!" Bernie cried as I squirmed. *Oh, boy.* "That's Shae's business! You let her—"

"Bernice, I will *not* hush. That's three times now that this house has been disturbed, and this time Shae is hurt. Jax needs to know someone's tooth fell right out of Shae's exhibit."

"I mean it, Clare," Bernie fairly growled. "You mind your business, and for that matter, come with me on home. This is not yours to tell, and you know it."

"I *won't* go home, Bernice." Clarabelle glared mutinously at her sister. "Shae needs me. Jax has to ask her questions and write down her statement. He said that. But then he'll leave, and Shae will be alone. I won't leave her."

Jax snapped his notebook closed, still looking at me. "Ladies," he said quietly, "I need to talk to Shae alone for a few minutes. I promise I'll knock on your door and let you know when I'm leaving. Will that work?"

A still stern Bernice didn't wait for Clarabelle to answer, but crossed over the room to her and grabbed hold of her elbow.

"That'll be just fine, Jax. Come on, Clare. We'll let Shae and Jax handle this. We're only a few steps away when they're finished." I thought Clarabelle might protest some more, but before she could say another word, Bernie said, "Anyway, Clare, I could use some of your special hot chocolate. I've still barely caught my breath."

Mollified at last, Clarabelle allowed herself to be led away. I wouldn't have minded some of her special hot chocolate myself, and the specialer, the better.

When the door had closed behind them, Jax turned his now inquisitive brown eyes on me in full force, uttering just three words. The three words. "Typewriter? *Someone's tooth?*"

I lay back against my cushions, closing my eyes. I was so busted.

"Jax, I know I said my questions were for a friend, and I'd love to tell you all about it, but I can't." I didn't dare open my eyes. I couldn't trust myself when his own were so near.

"Work stuff?"

I nodded again.

We sat in silence for quite some time, my official statement quite forgotten. I'd explained to him already how my work was very confidential. Even so, there was no way he could avoid pursuing information about a human tooth that had been lodged in the typewriter of a missing man. If I wouldn't help him, was that obstruction? If I did help him, would I be sued myself? Lose my license?

His voice startled me. "Tell you what, Shae." Jax had my attention, and I snuck a glance. He was staring at the back of the sofa, deep in thought. I looked at him properly and waited.

"First of all, Shae," he said, his voice kind but ringing with authority, "a crime has been committed here tonight, and it'll have to be investigated thoroughly. However, I'll hold off on asking you any more questions about it for now. I'm going to guess at some things. I don't want you to say a word if I'm guessing right. Not a word. I'm just thinking out loud here.

But if I'm completely off track, maybe you can just ask that we return to your statement."

I opened my mouth, but he cut me off. "Not a word." He leaned back in his chair, thinking.

I waited a good five minutes before I finally saw him nod once to himself.

"I think we can keep this simple, Shae. Here's what I think we've got." He ticked the first point off on his finger. "One, three attacks have occurred on this property in a very short period of time. In such a safe neighborhood, I can only surmise that there is something of interest here, and someone wants to either see it or take it.

"Two, you're a court reporter, and you've been involved in a big case lately. You've collected exhibits. In the first break-in, the intruders were clearly looking for a *thing*. That means they weren't concerned with your personal knowledge about their business. Rather, they were concerned about something you had in your possession, i.e., exhibits."

Things that I'd tried to ignore, like the reason for the intrusions, seemed instantly obvious to him. He ticked off a third finger. "Three, I expect one of the exhibits is a typewriter, and that a tooth has become dislodged from within the typewriter and has fallen out. Clarabelle was clear on that point."

You've done it this time, Clarabelle.

"Four, you've said nothing about the tooth because of the confidentiality provisions of your job."

I opened my mouth but he only held up his hand and shook his head.

"Five, whoever these perpetrators are, they're becoming more desperate; thus, the attack on you tonight."

I sat mutely and watched his brain working things out. He was way ahead of me, and he was in full police form. He'd said nothing that needed correction.

"I think I should tell you, Shae, that these matters cannot be left alone. If I am correct and your exhibits are the reason you were attacked, then we've perhaps only scratched the surface of something deeper that needs looking into."

He moved quickly to help me as I tried to sit up. Alarm bells were sounding in my painful head. It sounded to me like he or someone else was going to ask to see my exhibits.

"Take it easy, Shae." He'd taken Clarabelle's seat on the edge of the sofa, and he laid a warm hand on my arm. "I said no questions. I'm going to work on this and see what can be done. I don't want you to have to talk about it. Hold tight, and let me figure it out."

I had never heard more beautiful words. *Hold tight, and let me figure it* out. Could he really do that? He seemed sure, and his confidence was contagious. The elephant that had seated itself firmly on my shoulders since the discovery of the tooth simply stood up and walked away. Sergeant Jackson Landers knew the stakes, and he was going to figure it out.

I relaxed back against my pillows as he rose to his feet.

"Hey, Jax?"

"Mm-hmm."

"Did you call me earlier?"

"No. Why?"

"Oh, it's nothing." Just a random call then, when I'd seen the word, "Restricted." I'd hurried for nothing. Maybe I'd have fallen anyway, but probably not as hard. I stifled a groan. I had one more request. "And Jax?"

"Yes, Shae?"

I tried a puffy smile. "When you knock on the ladies' door, would you ask Clarabelle to bring me some of her special hot chocolate?"

"You can have anything you want after the doctor clears you."

"What? No!"

"Yes." His voice had a tone of finality to it. "I'll find the on-duty detective and have a chat. Then I'm coming back and taking you to get checked out."

CHAPTER 40

STIP

"Shae!"

I stirred and groaned. Everything hurt.

"Shae!"

I tried moving the other way. Ugh. That hurt worse.

"I'll just get the blinds. Maybe that'll help."

"It's still dark out, Clare. Give her a minute. She's coming around."

Footsteps moved away from the window and toward the bed. Why were the Darlings in my bedroom? A very worried Clarabelle had insisted on plying me with hot chocolate when Jax had brought me home, even though I'd been at the emergency room until nearly 1:00 a.m. I was sure my head had only just landed on my pillow.

"Shae, honey," Bernie said, her voice breaking through my mental fog, "can you wake up? I'm going to turn on the light now, so keep your eyes closed for a sec. The police are on their way, and I'm sure you'd rather not be in bed."

The room brightened, and Clarabelle gasped.

"Shhh," ordered Bernie.

I opened my eyes slowly and found a fully dressed Bernie standing next to my bed, holding a steaming mug.

"It's all so mysterious, isn't it?" Clarabelle's voice was high, and her eyes were brighter than I'd ever seen them at this hour.

What *was* the hour? I tried to turn my head toward my clock and moaned.

"'Time is it?" I asked Bernie.

"It's six fifteen, Shae. Sun'll be up shortly. You want your sweatshirt, or what?"

I peeled back the covers. I'd struggled into my comfy sweats last night while Clarabelle held my chocolate, and I'd fallen into bed still wearing them. I'd been far too sore to worry about changing into pj's.

"I'll splash my face, Bernie. Then, I guess, I'm ready."

"Oooh, but Shae, your hair—" Clarabelle began.

"—is fine," Bernie finished. "Here, Shae, let me help you." And scooping one arm behind my back, Bernie bore some of my weight as I came to a sitting position on the bed. "Are you okay?"

"I'm fine," I lied, moving gingerly.

"Any lightheadedness?"

"No. I'm just stiff, Bernie. The bump on the head is really the least of it," I said. "Doc cleared me."

Looking at me intently, Bernie finally stepped back and pointed to the steaming mug. "Coffee," she said simply. "Nice and hot. We'll wait in the living room for Jax. He said he's bringing a detective. They'll be here any minute."

I hobbled to the bathroom, turned on the light, and saw the reason for Clarabelle's gasp. I had a bona fide black eye. I understood the hair comment too. I looked as though I'd spent the night battling grizzly bears in blizzard conditions. I carefully splashed water on my face and brushed my teeth. I turned away from the mirror and promptly forgot about the state of my hair. Bernie had carried my coffee with her to the living room, and I was grateful to take it from her when I joined them.

I noticed a large stack of papers on my dining room table and remembered my scattered exhibits from the night before. Bernie saw my glance and gestured to Clarabelle.

"Clare picked them all up, and she tried to dust them off."

"I didn't read them, Shae, I promise," piped in Clarabelle.

"Oh, Clarabelle," I said, relief and affection clamoring for equal space within my heart, "thank you, you goose! I'm not worried about what you saw. You've saved my bacon by gathering these papers up."

Clarabelle beamed.

I moved slowly to the couch, coffee in hand. I had just managed a tentative sip when the knock at the door came. Clarabelle was on her feet in an instant, but then stepped back, almost shyly, as Jax escorted a stern-looking man in plain clothes into the room.

"This is Detective Jim Atherton, everyone," Jax said. "Detective, this is Shae Rose and her landladies, Bernie and Clarabelle Darling."

"Good morning, ladies." The detective's words were clipped. "Ms. Rose, I'm told that this is your residence."

"Yes." I hoped I didn't sound nervous.

"Thank you. I have a warrant, Ms. Rose, which requires you to hand over any and all deposition exhibits you have in your possession regarding the Lockwood/Kensington lawsuit. I will also require anything at all that has issued from the exhibits, including any objects or writing."

I stared at him, stunned, assimilating the word *warrant*. I guessed that the Darlings had told Jax about their typing escapades last night when he'd told them he was leaving, but how did the detective know the name of my case? I hadn't mentioned any names involved to anyone but a freshly deputized Bernie.

"Someone was working in your Boise office late last night," the detective said after possibly observing my confusion. "Or at least my call was forwarded to a living person. They were very helpful in providing details about what you've been working on."

I managed a small, "Ohhhh..."

"I also have," Detective Atherton continued, "a stipulation, which has been signed by both of the attorneys involved in that case."

Now he really had my attention.

"I'll let you read it for yourself, but you'll see that you're to be held harmless regarding the confidentiality of the exhibits. You can safely comply with the search warrant and let me have them."

I read the document over carefully, and when I came to the phrase, "We hereby stipulate that we will relieve the court reporter of her obligation to maintain the deposition exhibits in a confidential manner," I was satisfied.

"How did you get them to sign this?" I asked, amazed.

"Better question might be, how did I get a prosecuting attorney to draft this document and a judge to sign the search warrant at this hour." He seemed amused at himself. "But the short answer is that I woke one lawyer up, then had to wait until 8:00 a.m. New York time to reach the other. There's a second signature page, because he had to fax his reply. You are indemnified, Ms. Rose." The detective looked around my apartment curiously. "Where are the exhibits? I'm sure there's no need to actually search for them."

I pointed mutely to the corner of my small dining room. Jax moved to retrieve the typewriter case, the box containing the exhibits, and Bernie's leather folio with the typed pages. I found the scene to be steeped in an irony that would probably be lost on anyone else. *A stipulation had handed me the beautiful Smith-Corona, and a stipulation was whisking it away.*

Detective Atherton observed Jax's acquisition of all of the items and turned as though to bid us a good day. Tired and bedraggled as I felt, I knew something more needed to be done now that I was relieved of my duty.

"Detective?"

"Yes, Ms. Rose?"

"You'd probably better take a seat and let me fill you in on what we've come up with so far about those exhibits."

Atherton raised his eyebrows and sat down slowly in the armchair across from me. He pulled a notebook similar to the one Jax used from his coat pocket, but laid it on the end table and ignored it, at least for now. He leaned back into chair's depths and steepled his fingers in front of him, looking at me as though he were sizing me up.

"Very well, Ms. Rose," he said, his tone highly interested. "You have the floor."

CHAPTER 41

CHEEKY PEAKS

Dear Cheeky,

Just recently my dear husband and I were sued...sued! by our not so dear neighbor. His mean scoundrel of a horse was stealin' our apples, and our dog barked at him to warn him off. Rotten horse nearly kicked our sweet pup to death! Well, naturally the judge saw things our way, and sent my neighbor packin'. "Dismissed," I think my lawyer called it. So now, how do I live next door to that man? His high-falutin' lawyers pressed my husband mercilessly and gave him stress. Such great stress I feared for his health. Now we've won our case, but our sue-happy neighbor still lives next to us. What do I do?

    Faithful Farm Wife,

    Cordelia

(p.s. If you'll post my letter and make a reply, I'll knit you an afghan. Alpaca!)

Dear Faithful Cordelia,

No need to knit me an afghan, though I'd wager your handiwork is second to none. I am most happy to respond to your letter. I am sorry to hear you and your husband were sued. Having heard nothing to the contrary, I trust that this writing finds him in good health. As to your neighbor, my friend, the solution is clear. Kill him with kindness. Do you know his favorite kind of pie? Bake that, and take it over. Take a barrel of apples for the horse, since you know how he loves them.

If your neighbor isn't easily won, don't give up! Greet him in friendship. Help his wife with her groceries. Offer a ride, or a wheelbarrow, or some spare fencing. Mend the relationship if you can, my friend. Do good, even when good has not been done to you. Then you will find peace and earn the respect of all.

 Golden Rule Believer,

 Cheeky Peaks

--∞--

Dear Cheeky,

I come from a family that is, um, comfortable financially. And I wish I didn't. They argue about money, and business, and sometimes I can't believe they're even related. Now they've pulled me into one of their arguments, and I can't win. If I side with Person A, then Person B will never forgive me, because Person B is counting on my support. BUT, if I do side with Person B, then I will die on the inside, because I disagree with Person B. No one is asking my opinion. I don't want to rock the boat by speaking up, but I can't keep this up! I feel like I'm the rope in a family tug-o-war, and I'm losing my mind.

    Friendless in My Family,

    Glum Richie

Dear Glum,

Chin up, young sir! You can never go wrong by staying true to yourself. What one requires in such situations is COURAGE. Yes, indeed. And you have that commodity in spades, I dare say, or you'd not have written to this column. Be respectful, be kind, be courageous, and you can't go wrong. You must live your own life, not the lives of either Person A or Person B. They will strive and bicker if they so choose, but you, you will never allow yourself to be tug-o-war's ungainly rope. Square your shoulders, Knight Gallant. Let your own dreams and convictions guide you, and you'll not only live well, but you'll sleep well while you're at it.

    Your Most Stalwart Lady in Waiting,

    Cheeky Peaks

--∞--

CHAPTER 42

THE DAY AFTER

I stifled a groan as I crawled out of my car. Everything hurt, head to toe. Thanks to Bernie and her frozen peas, some of the swelling had receded from my knees, ankle, lips, and goose egg. Frozen peas couldn't do much about the vagrant blood that had settled beneath my right eye. For the first time in my life, I had a shiner. Nor could the peas' cold comfort assuage the agony embracing my entire back and neck. I'd swallowed three Ibuprofen tablets before I'd left the house. That had been thirty minutes ago. If they were helping, I was unaware of it.

I'd given some thought to calling in the cavalry. This depo was late in the day. I could have called Annie and told her about my accident. She would have found someone willing to come over and help due to a last-minute emergency. Several things stopped me.

One, was it *really* an emergency? I was uncomfortable, but nothing was broken. I was familiar with the case, the players, and the vocabulary likely to come up. By now my job dictionary was huge. I was accustomed to the rhythm, the cadence of these proceedings.

Two, I had to consider the hour. A reporter from another part of the state could get there by six o'clock, without a doubt. But then she must either stay in Ketchum for the night or travel on darkened highways when she was already tired. There were the aforementioned large animals on the roads at night, and I didn't want to put another reporter in a dangerous position. Also, again, there was the sticky question of the exhibits. Another reporter wouldn't have them.

Well, neither do I....

However, while Coop had mentioned that I should *bring* the exhibits, I didn't know for sure that he'd *need* them. I might be betting my career on the chance that he would not.

Three, this was *my* case. I'd been on it from the start, and I was determined to see it through to the end. By now I felt as much a part of this lawsuit's demographics as any of the people involved. It was true that none of the parties knew just *how* involved I'd been, of course.

No, nothing was going to keep me from this deposition. I would come up with a tale rather close to the truth that would explain my slightly impaired state. A simple fall, nothing more. Hopefully, I could pull off a white lie that would spare me too many questions regarding my appearance. I took a deep breath and hobbled around to the rear of my car.

I wasn't surprised to see Hawk standing behind the Juke, but I thought it odd that he didn't make a move to open the hatch. He stood, motionless, toothpick frozen in place between his teeth. Only his eyes moved as his gaze raked over my frame, pausing at each bruise on my face, noting my limp. Beneath his ever-present Stetson, a dark red tinge crept along his skin from neck to eyebrows—except for his mouth. His lips were white, compressed into a grim line. His arms hung straight down on either side of him, fists clenched.

"Breathe, Hawk." I tried for a smile, but my fat upper lip

ignored my instructions and wouldn't move. I could only imagine the grotesque resulting grimace.

"Heard you got hurt, Shae." His voice was gruff, crackly.

My pain-addled brain hadn't seen that coming. How had word of my fall last night already reached the Lockwood mansion?

"Police were here." Hawk's Adam's apple bobbed, and I could see the effort his quiet veneer cost him.

"Ah." It clicked into place. Jax was probably just being thorough. The Darlings and I had seen one too many unfortunate circumstances unfold since I'd taken on this job.

"Sergeant spoke with me, Shae. Told me it looked to him like someone tried to hurt you deliberate. Set something where it ought not to be, made a ruckus with foul intent."

I held on to the car's rear fender for support, unsure of what to say.

"Heard your dog run off too." At this he looked away, a muscle twitching in his jaw.

"Hawk," my voice cracked, "I need to be strong today. You understand? I can't think of Hercules right now or I'll..." I battled with a lump in my throat. That wasn't my only struggle. My entire chest squeezed mercilessly at the thought of tiny Hercules out in the world alone, adding to my other ills. I needed to reassure both of us, so I went on.

"The ladies have the gate open so he can get in when he comes home. The neighborhood has formed a search party. They've been searching all day. The folks at the animal shelter arrived this afternoon, and they're combing through places they know dogs like to hide. Hercules knows the way home." My voice shook again, so I squared my shoulders and said, with more certainty than I felt, "He knows the way home, Hawk."

Hawk stared steadily into my eyes, nodded once, and reached for the hatch.

"Guess you know what'll happen," he said, his jaw twitching again, "if I find the person who did this to you, Shae."

His quiet ferocity both soothed and alarmed me.

"Easy there, Hawk." I stopped myself from attempting another smile. Painful to do, and painful to see, I was sure. I changed the subject. "I'm so curious about why we've been summoned here for this late depo. I thought all of the depositions were finished. I don't even know who we're deposing."

Hawk slammed the hatch, hefted my steno case in one hand, and offered his other arm for me to lean on.

"They didn't tell you?" he asked, taking one slow step at a time with me.

"Nope."

"Well, you're lookin' at him. Funny thing, though. Last time I got that paper thing with the fancy name—"

"A subpoena."

"Yep. Well, I got that from ol' Dalton's lawyer. And you know all about that. You were there."

I nodded.

"Wasn't so bad. He had questions about the night Otto left, and I thought, fair enough. This case is about Otto being gone an' all. But this time I got a phone call from that Coop fella, saying he needed me one more time this evening. He asked could I come again, even without the paper."

We'd reached the top of the stairs and the mud room entrance.

"You hold this rail, Shae, while I get the door. You don't look too steady to me."

"It's really not that bad, Hawk. Truly."

"Huh." He set my steno case down, opened the door, and held his arm out to me again. "Anyway, Mrs. Kensington said she knew Coop was gonna call me, and it was fine with her, so I just said okay, and here we are."

Another deposition for Hawk? A last-minute one, at that. What had come up that Coop needed to speak with Hawk on the record again? He was on the defense side of this case. What could be gained for the defense by calling Hawk back for one more round? My questions were endless.

As he had my first day on the job, Hawk carried my machine right through the kitchen, past the nook, and into the dining room. Without a word, he unzipped the case and withdrew my laptop. Motioning me to my chair, he then handed me my machine and tripod.

"Guess it hurts you to bend down, Shae. You just show me which plug to put where, and I'll do it for you."

My eyes stung rebelliously despite my earlier resolve. I'd planned to give short shrift to my various aches and pains, but the sight of Hawk's toughened, outdoorsy frame, bent over my fragile equipment and myriad cables, moved me. My throat tightened, and I drew a steadying breath. Herc would come home, I would heal up, and there was no need for all this melancholy. I plastered a lopsided smile to my face.

"Thanks, Hawk." He looked up. I'd sounded brittle, so I tried again. "It's all going to be okay. Please don't worry."

I managed to ease myself down onto my gorgeous leather chair, for once lamenting its armless state. I could have used the support, just this once. Hawk bent down to plug in my power cords, then handed me each in turn so I could connect one to my laptop and the other to my machine. Finished with my cords, he stood and patted my shoulder. We grew quiet as parties began to arrive in the room and take their places.

CHAPTER 43
SECOND DEPOSITION OF HAWK RIVERS

Aurora arrived first, as was her wont, accompanied by Levi. She seemed older somehow, more frail. As Levi guided her by the elbow, I noted a protective posture from him that I had not previously observed. Could Aurora be ill? She seated herself in the chair Levi held out for her, uttering not a word.

Moments later, an equally somber Amy moved into the room, exuding a svelte and quiet strength. She put me in mind of a cheetah, her movements lithe, her bearing sure, her gaze watchful. She seated herself next to her grandmother, who whispered quietly into her ear. Nodding, Amy rose from her place and left the room. She returned only a moment later with a lovely chenille shawl, which she draped around Aurora's narrow shoulders.

I saw little evidence of the mighty matriarch with whom I'd become acquainted throughout these proceedings. Perhaps she knew she was defeated. If I was correct and she'd been helping Otto all these long years, it stood to reason that this case had worn her down. I yearned for a glimpse of the valley's plucky Cheeky Peaks columnist, but that fair matron had withdrawn. Before me sat an elderly woman who was clearly abiding in pain.

Here I was, feeling sympathetic toward someone who could well have been aiding and abetting a murderer for forty years. But he was her brother. If she *had* been helping him, perhaps her actions were understandable, if not justifiable. I took in her down-turned mouth, her hands as they clenched the arms of her chair, and I hoped things would not go badly for her.

If things *did* go badly for her, it would be because of the evidence I had turned over.

You had no choice, I reminded myself. Even now, the now-familiar queasiness revisited me as I sat in the leather chair Aurora had insisted upon. Considering the wretched state of my face at the moment, surely no one would notice a fresh pallor on my cheeks as nausea rolled over me. I wanted to be wrong. I'd grown fond of Aurora Kensington.

The quiet scene was shattered by the arrival of Dominic Flynn, his 6:00 p.m. shadow the only evidence of a harried, unexpected travel day. It was surprising he'd been able to arrange a flight at such late notice. He'd been in New York early that morning, signing a stipulation.

At Flynn's side walked Dalton Lockwood, surly, scowling, his angry eyes scouring the dining room table. When his gaze came to rest at last on my face, he sat down, hard, in his seat. Did my fat lips and blackened eye come as a shock to him? Had the police failed to speak with him during their inquiries earlier in the day?

His eyes soon moved away, however. I knew he had important things to occupy his mind, but could he not spare a single civil comment? A simple, "Where'd you get the shiner?" would have been preferable to silence. I looked away and tried to quell a burgeoning dislike. Soon he was leaning in whispered conversation with his attorney, pausing occasionally to cast venomous glances at his sister. Aurora, although visually unaware, tensed and reached for Levi's hand.

I squirmed in the smothering atmosphere as the tension in the room reached unprecedented levels. Spencer's quiet arrival received no attention as he slouched to his favorite chair in the far corner and took his shadowed place beneath the hanging fern.

We awaited only Coop Rickman who had, until this evening, always arrived early. I fiddled with my notepad. I tried to think up more briefs that I could enter into my job dictionary. I checked my machine's connection and double checked my power cords. *Let's get this show on the road!*

To my astonishment, Jenkins entered the room and paused at the head of the table. He'd attended no depositions thus far except his own.

"You requested my presence, madam?" His voice quavered slightly, surprising me even more. Why would Jenkins be here? Why would Jenkins be *nervous*?

"Quite right, Geoffrey," Aurora replied, her voice soft and rough. "Thank you for joining us. Please take a seat anywhere. I expect Coop will be here any minute."

"I'm here now," Coop said briskly, breezing in from the kitchen entrance. He laid a hand on Aurora's shoulder and set his briefcase on the table.

Jenkins quietly seated himself in the back of the room, near Spencer's hidey hole. While Spencer melted into the background beneath his fern, Jenkins sat on the edge of his chair, bolt upright. He smoothed his jacket and adjusted his tie, an image of misery.

What is going ON here?

I turned my attention to Coop, who said simply, "Ready when you are, Ms. Rose."

I looked at Hawk as he hovered in the background. Catching his eye, I gestured with my head toward his seat. He grimaced, but lowered his sinewy frame into his chair, pulling his hat down into his lap. I administered the oath, and we were off.

HAWK RIVERS,

First duly sworn to tell the truth relating to said cause, testified as follows:

EXAMINATION

QUESTIONS BY MR. RICKMAN:

Q. Thank you for coming at such short notice, Mr. Rivers.

A. Sure.

Q. I only have one line of questioning for you this evening, so I'll get right to it. You testified in your previous deposition that, on the night Otto Lockwood disappeared, you saw Mr. Jenkins driving him away, presumably to the airport. Correct?

A. That's right.

Q. Mr. Rivers, I know the night in question was forty years ago, but considering that you were younger, I assume that your eyesight was probably pretty reliable.

A. Always had good vision.

Q. Okay. I need to know, though, how you were so sure it was Otto in the back seat of the car.

Hawk scratched his head, obviously perplexed by the question.

A. How did I know it was Otto?

Q. Yes. For example, did you speak to him?

A. No. No, I never did speak to him that night.

Q. Then what made you believe it was Otto?

A. Had to be. He had that Indiana Jones hat on that he loved so much. Plus, he's taller than Dalton. I seen so many comings and goings of this family through the years, got to where I knew who was in the car by their stature. Yes, sir. That was Otto, I'm sure of it.

    Q. But you didn't speak to him?

          MR. FLYNN: Objection. Asked and answered.

          THE WITNESS: No, I didn't speak to him.

BY MR. RICKMAN:

    Q. Were you able to see his face clearly?

    A. I was not. He had that hat on his head, kinda pulled down in front, and he was facing the other direction, out the window that was away from me. Already told you I wished he'd at least've said goodbye.

    Q. Thank you. And are you sure, as you sit here today, that it was Mr. Jenkins who was driving the car?

    A. Yep. Driver's side was what I could see best from my front porch there, and I could see the driver. Thought nothing of it. Jenkins drove the family all the time.

          MR. RICKMAN: Thank you, Mr. Rivers. I have no further questions for you at this time.

          MR. FLYNN: And I have no questions.

          (Deposition concluded at 6:15 p.m.)

          (Signature was requested.)

          * * * * *

Dominic Flynn was apoplectic. "Coop, I flew all the way from New York for this charade! A five-minute deposition? What are you playing at?"

"You got off easy, Dom. I'd actually planned to re-open the depositions of both Dalton and Jenkins. That's what I'd originally scheduled for tonight, but I'm afraid the events of the past twenty-four hours have thrown all of that out the window. New information revealed that I only needed to speak to Hawk. Beyond that, I think we're really well past the deposition level now."

He turned to the kitchen entrance. "Gentlemen?"

Jaws dropped as Sergeant Landers and Detective Atherton entered the room. Dalton spluttered in surprise, but I had a feeling that Aurora, though sightless, knew exactly who had arrived. I swallowed hard at seeing Jax carrying my exhibit folder and the old Samsonite typewriter case. As the detective introduced himself, I thought about the stipulation, sitting even now in my machine case, and relaxed somewhat.

The deposition was over, but this was no moment for me to begin packing up and stowing away my gear. I sat, quiet as a mouse, eyes wide, stomach in an uproar.

Detective Atherton took the Samsonite case from Jax, and Jax, one hand now free, gave my shoulder a quiet squeeze. I looked up at him but his eyes were intently scanning the room. Very cop-like.

Atherton laid the case on the table and opened it. "As all of you are aware, this typewriter was placed into evidence at an early stage of the deposition phase of this lawsuit." he said, breaking the stunned silence. "I was mystified as to whether it was a plaintiffs' or defendants' exhibit, considering that it was delivered to a law firm in Hailey prior to the commencement of depositions.

"I've since come to learn some of the history surrounding that transaction. Mr. Flynn and Mr. Rickman were both informed via a third-party attorney that they were to go to that law firm and stipulate that the court reporter could take possession of the Smith-Corona. They did as they were asked, and they required Ms. Shae Rose to sign a receipt accepting custody of the typewriter."

No one fidgeted. Not even Spencer looked bored. I alone knew what had fallen from that typewriter and what news may be coming. A dull throbbing commenced in my head. The tension was amplifying my injuries. I listened hard as the detective continued.

"While the typewriter was in Ms. Rose's possession, she observed that an object had fallen from the interior of the machine."

That wasn't quite right, but I blessed him for leaving Clarabelle out of it, at least for now.

"During the time that Ms. Rose had sole custody of this old typewriter, misfortune visited her home three times. The most recent of those was just last night." He nodded to me. "We didn't know, because she didn't mention such concerns, that Ms. Rose's job might be at the center of one successful and one attempted break-in at her place of residence.

"After the personal attack last night on Ms. Rose, however, Sergeant Landers learned that, indeed, the very exhibits from this lawsuit might be at the bottom of Ms. Rose's misfortune. He deduced this on his own, as Ms. Rose remained, as of last evening, unwilling to discuss any aspects of her work here. He contacted me, and I believed his case required immediate attention. I acquired a search warrant and a stipulation so that Ms. Rose would be held harmless in turning over these deposition exhibits."

Hawk, who'd been slouched in his chair, now sat upright and rigid. "What do you mean, misfortune visited Shae's home *three* times?" he demanded. "You mean last night wasn't the first?"

He'd snapped a fresh toothpick in two as he searched my face for answers.

Jax squeezed my shoulder again but looked only at Hawk. "Easy, Mr. Rivers."

Dalton's face flushed instantly. "What's so compelling about our lawsuit?" He was all but shouting. "And *why*," turning to Mr. Flynn, "did you sign that stipulation? Those are *our* exhibits!"

"Calm down, Dalton." Dominic Flynn, harried and over-traveled, appeared to be losing patience with his client. "The detective had a search warrant. He was getting the exhibits one way or another. He told me Ms. Rose had been hurt and how it had happened. Did you want me to risk him throwing an injured court reporter in jail for obstruction?"

Dalton threw me a look that told me he'd probably consider it, but he said no more.

"As to what's compelling about the case?" The detective eyed each person in turn. "This is an ongoing investigation, but I can share a few things with you."

His eyes rested on me for a moment before he continued. "A large portion of the information I'm about to share with you came from observations and deductions Ms. Rose herself had made. Without her assistance we'd be, as they say, behind the eight ball in this case."

With a slight bow to me he said simply, "In your debt, young lady."

He then returned his attention to the room's waiting occupants. "Here's what I can tell you so far.

"One, the object that fell from the inside of your Exhibit A was a human tooth."

An audible gasp echoed from around the room.

"Two, when we examined the typewriter case, we found a false bottom containing a stash of typing paper. The compartment was lined with cedar, and the papers carried that scent. I mention it because I am assured that all of you will appreciate the significance of that discovery."

I glanced furtively at Aurora, but this news elicited no response from her at all. If anything, she slumped farther into her seat. Amy edged her chair closer to her grandmother.

"Three, the break-in attempts and the personal attack that took place at the residence of Shae Rose and her landladies, Bernice and Clarabelle Darling."

Atherton paused for a moment as Hawk grumbled under his breath.

"Four," he then went on, "the typewriter itself. I understand it is an exhibit in your civil case. I'm afraid I must inform you that both of Ms. Rose's landladies, Bernice and Clarabelle Darling—

(*uh-oh*)

—may have overstepped themselves by typing on the typewriter."

Detective Atherton raised a hand to his mouth—to hide a smile? Maybe he knew the Darlings. That was a safe bet in our small town.

"Miss Clarabelle Darling experimented with the typewriter *before* the tooth had become dislodged. The sheets that she typed, and which are currently in our possession, demonstrate a raised Q deformity. Conversely, in the document that Miss Bernie Darling typed later, with the tooth gone, the Qs line up perfectly with the rest of the letters."

Dalton started to rise from his seat, blotches forming on his neck, his eyes blazing. "Now see here! No one had any business—" Mr. Flynn grabbed his arm and yanked him forcefully back into his chair. Dalton sat, muttering something about exhibits that ought not to have been messed with.

Detective Atherton raised his eyebrows, waiting to see if Dalton was in hand. "It should be noted," he said quietly, "that the police department considers the discovery of the tooth to have been *beneficial*." Dalton's color deepened further, but he said nothing as the detective continued.

"Five, we've checked the dental records for both Myron and Otto Lockwood. Ms. Rose had clued us in that the tooth had belonged to a person who wore dentures. Though both Myron and Otto, sadly for them, wore dentures, Myron's dentures were a full set. He had no natural teeth remaining to him. Otto, on the other hand, had a partial upper denture, anchored to a single tooth, tooth number eleven, which was consistent with the tooth that fell out of the typewriter."

The room swam briefly as I searched for air. The tooth was *Otto's*? Not Myron's? I peeked up at Jax, who nodded slightly. He knew of my theories. I'd been so sure that the tooth was Myron's that I'd never considered the possibility that Otto might also wear a denture. I turned and stared outright at Aurora, only to find that gentle tears now streaked her regal face. But Detective Atherton wasn't finished.

"It's too soon to say for certain, but we've sent the tooth off for DNA testing. We'll be able to match it if it's Otto's, because Mrs. Kensington (a nod in her direction) provided us with hair from her brother's hairbrush just this afternoon. She's kept his room ready for his return all these years, so his things are still there."

No wonder Aurora looked so terrible! She'd been so certain that Otto was still alive. But was he? How had he come to part with his tooth? His one remaining upper tooth?

Aurora and Detective Atherton had so captivated my attention, I'd forgotten the other players.

"What exactly are you saying, Detective?" Amy's silky voice was firm. Angry. "I don't think anything you've said so far gives us any certainty about Uncle Otto's situation. He may have lost a tooth, but we all know he's still alive." She looked round the room, chin lifted. "I mean, he wrote to us just five years ago!"

A scuffling sounded from the far side of the room as Spencer raised himself in his chair. "I wrote that letter, Amy."

Stunned disbelief trembled through me. Probably through everyone. I shuddered as I took in the shocking implications of this news. My shiver grabbed my tender lower back and nearly caused it to seize. Clutching the table before me, I drew a ragged breath, which Jax apparently noticed. He bent down to my ear and whispered a barely audible, "You okay, honey?"

My cheeks warmed. *Honey.* Pretty word, that. Beautiful, even, when *he* used it. I nodded slightly and eased myself back into my into my chair, suddenly feeling much better.

To my right, Aurora raised a feeble hand to her chest. "Oh, Spencer! That was *you?*" Her head moved about, as though she wanted to look directly at him but was unsure of where to fix her eyes. "*Why*, Spencer? *Why*? I've had such hope, been so sure...."

I thought for a moment he might hang his head in shame, but his facial muscles worked as though he were building up the courage to do otherwise. He glared at his father, and Dalton glared right back, his eyes leaving no question as to the depths of his anger and sense of betrayal.

Spencer stood, and with uncharacteristic clarity he announced to the room, "I'm sick of doing everything your way, Father. Yes, *yes*, I absolutely wrote that letter. Aunt Aurora, I'm so sorry. I kept thinking if you knew *why*, you'd understand."

Turning back to his father, Spencer's voice rose measurably. "You wanted to sell the paper even then! Oh, yes, everyone.

That's what this is all about! Father's wanted to sell this town's paper to a huge newspaper conglomerate. They've had their eyes on our paper for *years*, and not to make it grow. They want to shut it down. They want to force feed valley residents their own huge production."

Spencer started pacing. I sat, enthralled. I'd never seen him so animated.

"And that's not what the valley wants. People here want to hear about things that concern *them*. They want to discuss their own politics and tout their own events. People want to read local stories about local people. And yes, Father, they want a *blog*. I'm Badger Thicket! I have a following of thirty-seven hundred people!"

So *that's* what the secretive phone call was about!

A small grin played at Levi's mouth. *Spencer* was Badger Thicket, the anonymous local satirist. Had Levi suspected as much?

Spencer took a breath and looked around the room, imploring. I saw at last that Spencer didn't want to *betray* his family. He wanted to *belong* to the family, to be a part of the family business. And that meant keeping the *Kensington* side of the equation strong and on track.

"Father wants to sell out." His voice had dropped, and his shoulders were nearly slouched. With clear resolve, he managed to retain his erect posture and continue. "He wants to close up and move to Florida, but he could only sell if both of the wills were executed and he owned one hundred percent of the paper. He's been trying to sell off all the other papers too. He just hasn't found any other willing buyers yet."

He looked at Aurora, and had she been able to see him, she'd have viewed a young man begging for understanding. Perhaps she could hear the plea in his voice. I could.

"That's why I wrote the letter five years ago, Aunt Aurora. I thought if Otto wrote home, Father would quit trying to gain control of the company in order to sell it."

Spencer almost looked surprised at himself, but then he lifted his chin even more, as though pleased with the courage he'd mustered. "But I won't sit quietly any longer! You can take my name off of those lawsuit papers, Mr. Flynn. I'm out. I'm backing Aunt Aurora and Levi and Amy, if they'll have me."

"Why, you little—" and Dalton was off, hauling his seventy-two-year-old frame from his seat with surprising agility.

He launched himself at his son, who had stopped his pacing near the fireplace. Still a very strong man, Dalton lunged for his son's throat. Spencer side-stepped him at the last moment, and Dalton threw his hands up to catch himself, barely avoiding a headlong crash into the mantel.

As he swung back around to see where Spencer had gone, his flailing arms swept across the mantel and caught the bust of dear old Myron Lockwood.

Time slowed, the very air taught with horror. Jax, who had taken a quick step toward Dalton, froze in place. The marble bust, which had proudly surveyed the doings of this family for forty long years, toppled from its lofty perch and dropped with agonizing certainty to the stone floor below. Upon impact, the imperious head separated itself from its shiny plinth, rolled, and slammed into the granite fireplace surround.

Levi leaned over to tell Aurora what had just happened, but his words froze on his lips as the bust, now removed from its base, battered by its fall and the resultant collision with the granite, broke cleanly in two.

An inner chamber, now exposed to the elements, disgorged papers that had been tightly-rolled for too long. As though sensing their new freedom, the documents unfurled slightly of their own accord. A warm aroma delicately teased my olfactories as the documents partially revealed themselves to the shocked occupants of the room.

CHAPTER 44

WILLS

"That says *will* on it!" cried Spencer.

The documents, having been ensconced within their marble tomb for some time, did not unfurl completely, but Spencer's position in the room allowed him to glimpse one word at the top of the uppermost page. He made a rush toward the papers, but his father was nearer. His bony hand shot out greedily.

"Stop! Don't move another inch!" Jax's tone was firm and commanding. "Leave the papers where they are and back away, Mr. Lockwood."

Dalton wavered. His hand shook as he licked his lips, and his eyes darted first to Jax, then back to the documents. Suddenly, his face smoothed and he straighted up, his shoulders relaxed, and he held his hands out as though in gentle entreaty.

"Ah, gentlemen, ladies," he attempted a smile. I thought his cheek twitched a bit. "You misunderstand my intent. I'm afraid I suffered a strong reaction when I saw Father's bust so violently damaged. I merely meant to gather up the pieces…"

"Touch nothing. The only gathering to be done will be done by Sergeant Landers." Detective Atherton's voice rang with authority. He was making notes in a small spiral notebook, not even bothering to make sure his order was complied with. He must have assumed it would be followed.

Dominic Flynn spoke up at last. "Let's bring things down a notch, shall we, please?" He pointed his narrow face in Detective Atherton's direction and waited until he had that gentleman's full attention. "There's been no *crime* here, Detective. Unless of course you would like to charge young Spencer with something for the dreadful deceit he inflicted upon his own aunt with that fake letter."

Detective Atherton resumed his note taking. "You'll have to point me to the law that says it's illegal to impersonate a family member, Mr. Flynn."

I stuffed down a smile. Who could laugh at a time like this? But the atmosphere in the room was surreal, and I looked at each player in turn. Round the table to my right, starting at the far end, were Amy, Levi, and Aurora, with Coop between Aurora and myself. To my immediate left stood Jax, and just the other side of him Hawk sat as though he were made of marble. I had thought he'd been about to intervene in the event Dalton had actually tried to strangle Spencer, but when the bust fell, he'd turned to stone. He hadn't moved or spoken since.

Next to him sat Dominic Flynn, his small eyes flitting to each party, just as surely my own were doing. Dalton stood between Flynn and the fireplace. Spencer was several feet away from his father, near the far end of the table. Standing slightly to the right behind me, still in the place he'd stopped after entering the room, stood Detective Atherton.

Finally, all but forgotten in the commotion, Geoffrey Jenkins sat ramrod straight on his perch near the hanging fern. The table being in the way, I couldn't see his hands. I could, however, see that his normally imperturbable appearance now glistened, and drops of sweat were rolling down the sides of his face. Curious, I examined him further. His shirt, what could be seen of it beneath his suit jacket, was plastered to his chest. His Adam's apple bobbed repeatedly as he swallowed again and again.

I was shaken from my observations by Detective Atherton's voice. "Sergeant, let's have a look at those papers, please."

Jax had already pulled gloves on, and he strode forward to retrieve the documents.

"Don't step on anything!" Dalton's voice was edgy, querulous. His hands gestured toward the broken pieces of plinth and bust, but his eyes remained fixed on the partially unrolled sheaf of paper. "And I want to look at those right along with you. You can't stop me!"

The detective raised his eyebrows and studied Dalton's defiant face. "Very well, Mr. Lockwood. This is your home, and for the time being, these are your documents. Let's clear some table space here, and we'll all look at them together. I'd ask that none of you touch them, though."

Hawk and Flynn rose simultaneously and pushed their chairs aside. Amy and Levi, on the other side of the table, pulled glasses and pitchers of water out of the way. With table space now available, Detective Atherton walked to my left, where the chairs had been cleared, and carefully laid the papers out on the table.

Everyone leaned in for a look. I probably should have kept my professional distance. We weren't on the record, after all. But who's kidding whom? I was neck deep in this case. I leaned stiffly forward, as unobtrusively as I could, straining to see.

Levi plucked some smooth stones from a decorative glass vase, and Detective Atherton placed the stones on the four corners of the papers to hold them flat. Gooseflesh prickled my skin as I read the title page and realized these weren't documents, *plural*. This was a *single* document, comprised of several pages.

Eerily similar to our Exhibit B, we now had before us a document entitled, *Last Will & Testament of Myron P. Lockwood*. The document was dated May 25, 1975. Levi whispered quietly into Aurora's ear. The will was neatly typed on crisp, thick, cream-colored vellum paper.

"Cedar." Aurora's voice was little more than a whisper. "Even after so many years, I'd know that smell anywhere. That's Otto's typing paper. That's why Father brought Otto home from the rain forest he loved. He needed him to create his will. I just never knew they'd…they'd…" Aurora drew a deep, shuddering breath. "I never knew they'd actually accomplished it," she finished simply.

"Now hold on, Aurora!" Dalton was fuming again. "I don't know what you think this is, but—"

"Wait, Dalton." This from Mr. Flynn. "Don't get into a needless argument," he said. "This will is dated earlier than the will we've produced as Exhibit B. That means that the will we've produced is the most recent, and therefore supersedes this one."

"Supersedes?" Dalton furrowed his brow.

"Ours is newer. It carries the date of July thirtieth, 1975, and it's the one that counts," Mr. Flynn said.

Turning to Detective Atherton, Flynn waved dismissively at the will laying on the table. "That will won't hold up in any courtroom, Detective. It's moot. Useless."

"You don't even know what it says."

"It doesn't matter. It's of no account. The wills we've produced in this litigation are the documents that count, and their authenticity will be a matter for a judge to decide. I personally have no doubt—"

"Wills!" Aurora bolted upright in her seat. Her cheeks flooded with color as all signs of a frail, disheartened woman disappeared.

"Wills, indeed! Compare them, Detective. My brother Dalton has produced *two* wills, yet Father's head disgorged only one. If there's been sneakery and skulduggery, a comparison should clear it up. I would contend that the papers smelling of cedar are far more likely to be authentic than anything yet produced in discovery."

"It still doesn't mean Otto's alive, Aurora." Dalton was glaring at the will in the center of the table.

"I thought I'd lost him once today, Dalton, when Detective Atherton arrived and asked for samples from Otto's things. I will soldier on, whatever the outcome. I for one am eager to see what Father had to say about his estate in what I contend is his authentic *Last Will & Testament*. Let the comparisons commence."

"Yes," said Detective Atherton. "Sergeant, would you bring the documents labeled Exhibits B and C here, please?"

Jax returned to my end of the table. I scooped up the folder containing the documents and passed it silently to him. His hand was warm where it brushed mine as he took the exhibits, and my skin burned quite nicely.

Returning to the center of the gathering, Jax pushed the will, complete with its stone paperweights, farther across the table. He then carefully laid Exhibits B and C beneath it, so that all three documents were visible to all parties.

Exhibits B and C seemed flimsy, pale, and unspeakably *ordinary* when placed near the thick, creamy vellum of the will from the bust. The difference in the paper was self-evident. "The Q," Amy breathed. "The Q is just fine, not raised up like on Exhibit B." Her face paled as realization took hold. "So the will from the bust…"

"…was typed *before* the tooth became lodged in the machine," finished Levi.

"You are exactly right, Ms. Kensington." Atherton agreed. "The raised Q does indeed place Exhibits B and C in time. As Mr. Flynn has so astutely pointed out, the exhibits they produced were drafted at a later date than the will we discovered this evening."

Coop, who had remained silent to this point, said at last, "Detective, we're all here. Let's see exactly what the will from the bust says. Who knows? Maybe old Myron cut Otto and Aurora out completely and left everything to Dalton after all. Might not be much left for us to fight about if that's the case."

The detective nodded. "That's not what I came here for, but I believe the discovery of this document can only shine more light on a previously murky situation. Have a seat, everyone."

CHAPTER 45

CUT OFF

"Cut off?" Dalton blustered, his face reddening. "This is appalling! A travesty! Father would no more have cut me off completely than he'd have cut off his own leg."

"Look at you, dear brother, now that the shoe's on the other foot." Aurora was returning to her matriarchal, authoritative, no-nonsense self, and I was happy to see it. "The very thing you expected me to believe—that I'd been cut out of Father's will entirely—is what you, yourself, must now swallow. There is no doubt in my mind that the will encased in Father's bust is his true and legal *Last Will & Testament*."

Aurora turned to Hawk. "Levi tells me that you signed the bust's will as a witness in May 1975."

"Yes, ma'am. I remember it clear."

"Do you know what became of it?"

"No, ma'am. Mr. Lockwood just told me he planned to put it away safe and sure until he could visit his lawyer at some point."

"Didn't you realize, Hawk, that after Father died, no will was brought forth?"

"Not my business to realize anything like that, Mrs. Kensington. No one came and asked me about it, and I didn't know what it said. If I thought about it at all, I thought it was good luck the will had been finished before the accident. I mean, I knew it had, 'cause I'd witnessed it. Guess I just assumed you were working out its intent. Looked like you and Dalt—Mr. Lockwood took to running things as a team. Seemed about right to me. I'm sorry about not mentioning it, though. If I'd've known you were so stuck…"

"Thank you, Hawk. I can see that you didn't know. Except for Otto's absence, there were no major changes around here. As to the will, was there just the one? Did he ever ask you to witness another?"

"No, ma'am. Never."

Aurora turned her attention to Detective Atherton. "I also understand, Detective, that Exhibits B and C, the wills Dalton has produced, have no witness signatures."

"That's right." Atherton extracted the final document from the exhibit folder. "And this might be an opportune moment to bring up the letter that you have marked as Exhibit D in your civil case."

"And why is that?" Aurora

"It has normal Qs too," said Detective Atherton simply. "Like the will from the bust, it was typed before the typewriter was damaged."

Turning to Coop, Aurora nodded to herself. "Coop, I do believe our case is won. Exhibits B and C are on the wrong paper, they don't smell of cedar, and in the case of Father's will, Exhibit B is such a far cry from the bust's will that it is nonsensical. My father would not have created such diametrically opposed documents within such a short period of time. The bust's will also lines up perfectly with the letter he wrote me."

Aurora moved in her chair so that she could face the room at large. "Father called Otto home from the Amazon to help him set his estate in order. Otto did so and created the will we discovered in the bust. How like Father to hide it away like that. Perhaps he hoped to see some changes in Dalton before he finalized it by giving it to his attorney. We'll never know."

"Who knew he even *had* an attorney, Nana?" queried Levi. "You always said he didn't like them."

Aurora nodded slowly and tugged the chenille shawl more snugly against her shoulders. "He never said a word about it. Having taken such care, however, to have Otto create a will, to have Hawk witness it, to have an attorney standing by to receive it…well, I don't believe that any other *real* will was created before his untimely demise.

"As for Otto," she reached out a hand that Amy quickly captured and held, "I don't believe he created a will for himself at all, which relieves Exhibit C of all credibility. Young men at the tender age of thirty-four rarely want to prepare end-of-life documents, even if they do travel to unusual places."

She patted Amy's hand and released it. "Throughout these proceedings I have held that the documents tendered as exhibits are false," she continued, her tone rich with confidence, "and I am more certain of that now than ever."

"Conjecture and assumptions!" cried Flynn. "You are hardly in a position to play judge and jury here, Mrs. Kensington!"

"Watch your tone in this house, mister." Hawk had emerged from his apparent shock and looked positively menacing.

Mr. Flynn drew a breath. "No disrespect intended, of course," he said, throwing a completely disrespectful sneer at Hawk, "but this case goes forward. You can't prove that the July thirtieth will isn't authentic, and that will clearly names Dalton as Myron's sole heir and executor. The fact that the earlier May twenty-fifth will bequeaths nothing to Dalton is entirely moot. Forgive me, but we stand by Exhibit B, your father's most recent will. It was your father, not I, who cut you and Otto out. We'll see you in court!"

Dominic Flynn turned to me with an imperious, "Madam Court Reporter!"

I nearly jumped out of my skin, and I saw Jax's eyes narrow.

"I want this on the record!"

My hands shook as I struggled back to my machine. Long minutes of sitting still had rendered my sore muscles nearly useless. I feared I wouldn't be able to write accurately.

"Enough." Detective Atherton caught my eye and shook his head, motioning my hands away from my writer. Given the choice of obeying an irate attorney or a police detective in full investigative mode, I decided I'd go with the cop. I removed my hands from my keys gratefully.

"I waited outside the room just as Hawk's deposition was concluding," said Detective Atherton. "I waited, because I needed to be sure of Hawk's testimony on a key component. Hearing testimony, however isn't what brought me out here this evening. Nor was discovering a will in a marble bust the thing that commanded my presence, although that was certainly an interesting development."

Detective Atherton backed away from the table slightly and nodded to Jax, who stepped forward.

"I'm afraid my real purpose for traveling out to this estate on a Friday evening was to make an arrest."

No one breathed. My heart thudded, unsure where this new tone was going to take us. The grandfather clock ticked.

"Geoffrey Jenkins," said Atherton, "please stand up. I am arresting you for the murder of Otto Frederick Lockwood."

"Jenkins!" exclaimed Levi.

"Otto!" cried Aurora.

"Idiot!" huffed Dalton.

I looked from one to the other, shocked.

"Sergeant Landers," Detective Atherton continued, "please take Mr. Jenkins into custody."

Jax approached Jenkins, who was still in his position on the far side of the room. Jenkins tried to stand, but his legs buckled. He barely caught the edge of his seat, sitting half on, half off, his hands held out beseechingly. "P—please," he entreated Jax, his bald pate glistening, "there's been a mistake. You can't arrest m–m–me!" He squirmed away from the handcuffs Jax held, his eyes imploring each of us in turn until he reached the detective.

"I thought we had an—"

"Enough!" barked Detective Atherton. "Read him his rights, Sergeant, and maybe he'll shut up."

Dalton seemed unmoved by the arrest of his decades-long faithful servant. He merely flicked a piece of lint from his sport coat and gazed back at Jenkins with great disinterest. "Can't help you, Jenkins, if you were stupid enough to kill my brother." Dalton backed away from the table, as though to make room for people to pass by. "Go on, then," he growled at Jax. "Get him out of here. The sight of him sickens me."

"Stand up, Mr. Jenkins," said Jax, not unkindly.

Jenkins wobbled to his feet. Dalton continued backing away. Everyone's eyes were on the pathetic sight of Geoffrey Jenkins, whose trembling arms were held behind him as Jax secured the handcuffs.

I thought I alone noticed Dalton's surreptitious movements toward the rear exit. He had passed the great fireplace and backed up against the wall near the archway, where he felt his way along until he reached the archway and slipped around the corner and out of sight. The man had never paid me much attention, and apparently he still thought I was of no consequence. He didn't seem to notice me watching him.

"And everything becomes clear," muttered Detective Atherton. I glanced up. I'd been mistaken in thinking no one else had observed Dalton's departure. The detective was staring keenly at the archway. Speaking into his walkie-talkie, he asked, "You there, deputies?"

"Affirmative," announced at least two unseen voices.

"Round him up, then."

"Copy that."

The detective nodded to Jax. "Sergeant Landers, please be so kind as to remove the handcuffs from Mr. Jenkins. I trust that he will keep to his end of the agreement." He seemed to take in Jenkins' pallor. "Sorry, Mr. Jenkins," he said. "You probably thought I was reneging on our bargain, but I needed your alarm to be authentic. Our arrangement is still in place."

Exhaling profoundly, Jenkins dropped weakly back onto his chair. A stunned Spencer resumed his seat next to him.

My head was reeling. Jenkins arrested. Jenkins released. Dalton sneaking off. And now, here was Dalton being returned, escorted by two uniformed deputies. His usual sour expression had morphed into unadulterated panic. He looked at first one deputy, and then the other, as though wondering if he could take them. Clearly, he could not.

One of the deputies tossed upon the table a clear plastic bag that contained rolls of cash and what looked to be a U.S. passport.

"He'd just retrieved these from a safe, sir," reported the officer.

Detective Atherton grunted in acknowledgement and shook his head.

"Sorry for the charade, folks." The detective stowed his notebook in a pocket and took in the entire gathering. "I had to be sure, and Mr. Lockwood's hasty exit has confirmed a story I heard only just this afternoon." Tilting his head, he sought Jax's eyes. "Sergeant Landers? If you would?"

Jax approached the petrified Dalton and seized first his left arm, and then his right, pulling them behind him. I found Jax to be alarmingly, *magnificently* professional as he expertly clamped handcuffs on to a struggling Dalton's wrists.

"Dalton Lockwood," Jax commenced, "I am placing you under arrest for the murder of your brother, Otto Lockwood. You have the right to remain silent. Anything you say can and will be used against you in a court of law."

"You can't arrest *me*!"

"You have the right to an attorney—"

"I'm Dalton Lockwood! That *means* something in this town! You're making a big mistake!"

"—if you cannot afford an attorney—"

"Do you *hear* me? I'm guilty of nothing! Whatever Jenkins did, I had no part—"

"—one will be provided for you."

"I already *have* an attorney, and he'll have your badge. Uncuff me this instant."

"Do you understand these rights as I have read them to you?"

"I understand that you've kissed your career goodbye!"

Unperturbed, Jax turned toward Detective Atherton and raised an eyebrow. The detective rubbed his eyes with one hand and reached around to massage his neck with the other.

"Take him away, Sergeant. I've heard enough from him for now. I'll be along shortly to interview him at the station."

Nodding, and with an almost imperceptible wink in my direction, Jax took Dalton by the elbow and escorted him from the room.

CHAPTER 46
THE DEAL

"Nana, Detective. What is this?" Amy stood, appearing agitated, first placing her hand on Aurora's shoulder, and then pulling it away as she paced several small steps in each direction. "What has happened? Why did you believe you'd lost Uncle Otto, Nana? And now, why is the detective sure of it?"

"I sure hope someone is going to explain things to us," said Levi, frowning at the wills spread out on the table. "Who broke into Shae's house? How do we get to the bottom of the wills? Is Uncle Dalton really going to jail?" His brow furrowed even more, and I knew I was staring. Bewilderment suited him.

"All right," Detective Atherton said, raising his hand. "I'll explain what we know for now. We don't have everything nailed down yet, but we have a very strong case against your uncle, Levi. I'm so sorry, Mrs. Kensington. If you'd rather not hear some of this…"

"I'm staying." Aurora's voice did not quaver. She'd refound her strength, and I knew it wouldn't leave her again. She was the head of the family now. *Always had been, really.*

"Very well," said Detective Atherton. "As I've already explained, while the Smith-Corona was in Ms. Rose's custody, a tooth became dislodged and dropped right out of it. Ms. Rose and the ladies had the sense not to touch the tooth, but bagged it up. Ms. Rose was unsure of what to do with it, as she didn't want to interfere in a case with which she had only professional and confidential involvement."

"Here, here," growled Dominic Flynn.

Atherton ignored him. "We've seen that shortly after the discovery of the tooth, there was a second break-in attempt at her home. Only this time, the perpetrator broke the window in her landladies' portion of the house. It's one building, and it's possible the miscreant didn't know in which precise area Ms. Rose lived. As this was the second such attempt to gain entrance into the house, Ms. Rose became suspicious that an exhibit she was holding might be what the intruder or intruders were after."

A nod in my direction.

"Ms. Rose, not wanting to raise undue alarm, showed the tooth to a dental technician, who advised her that it was tooth number eleven, and it had held a partial denture in place. This information, in and of itself, did not reveal any foul play. Ms. Rose, seeking to guard the confidentiality of deposition exhibits, decided to hold off on approaching the authorities. People lose teeth for many reasons, after all."

"But if the tooth had been in the typewriter for years," interrupted Spencer, "why did it suddenly fall out at Shae's house?"

"My very question!" said Mr. Flynn.

"I understand." The detective wiped his brow. "I was certain that question would come up. I assure you, Ms. Rose did not meddle with the exhibit. I told you earlier that Miss Clarabelle Darling experimented with the typewriter. I have spoken to Miss Darling, and I feel certain that it was only nostalgic curiosity that drew her to type on the Smith-Corona. Unaware that the typewriter should be left alone, Miss Darling spent an afternoon typing, *ahem*, portions of an *Agatha Christie* novel."

My puffy lips nearly smiled at the detective's bemused tone. Would he have preferred her to type portions of *Moby Dick*?

"She tells me that," he went on, "when she realized it was getting late, she picked up the typewriter to put it away. I believe that all of her typing had loosened the tooth from its resting place, because it fell out as soon as she lifted the machine."

More gasps and titters could be heard around the room. Mr. Flynn was livid. With his mouth slowly opening and closing soundlessly, he looked like a freshly caught trout. Coop chuckled low into his chest. Amy stared at the detective, seeming to reserve her reaction, while Levi's lips twitched in a suppressed grin. Aurora remained ramrod straight in her chair. Spencer and Jenkins sat watchful from their place beneath the fern.

Finally, Dominic Flynn pounded the table, finding his voice. "Is there nothing to be done about this improper handling of a *deposition exhibit*?"

Coop merely shrugged.

"It is an imperfect world, Mr. Flynn," the detective reminded him. "Clarabelle Darling didn't know any better, and Bernice Darling was trying to help Ms. Rose." He glanced around the room. "If I may continue?"

Mr. Flynn huffed back into his seat.

"When Bernice Darling investigated the typewriter, she actually discovered two things. Her first discovery was a false bottom in the Samsonite case, complete with a cedar-lined compartment that was filled with cedar-scented, heavy vellum paper, quite similar to the paper used to create the will that was located in the bust this evening. Using some of the paper she found, Ms. Darling made her second discovery. With the tooth now absent, the typewriter no longer had its idiosyncratic Q."

Detective Atherton stopped his narrative and stepped to the foot of the table to pour a glass of water.

"Fast forward to last evening, when Ms. Rose got hurt. Remember, this was the third incident involving an intruder at an otherwise unmolested residence. When called to the scene, Sergeant Landers believed that someone had been lying in wait for Ms. Rose to get home. Setting off cherry bombs could possibly distract her enough that she wouldn't notice the bench, and would trip over it."

"Glad you weren't hurt worse, Shae," Levi said.

"Yes!" Amy agreed enthusiastically. "I feel terrible about all of this, Shae. You didn't deserve any of it."

I looked down quickly, mumbling a grateful, "Thanks, guys," before the detective resumed his explanation.

"And so we became involved in the case last evening at around 9:00 p.m."

The detective turned to me, and my face flushed hot. I didn't like being in the center of this. Coop looked on approvingly. Encouragingly, even. Dominic Flynn had virtual daggers flying from his eyes, as though willing them to tear me apart. He probably regretted signing the stipulation that held me harmless regarding the exhibits.

"When Sergeant Landers learned of a human tooth being found, he contacted me, and we all know what followed." The detective took a breath. "I obtained a search warrant and a stipulation. I then collected from Ms. Rose the tooth; the typewriter; Exhibits B and C—which are of course the wills being disputed in this lawsuit; Exhibit D, the letter to Aurora from her father; the Agatha Christie papers typed by Clarabelle Darling; and the single sheet of paper typed by Bernice Darling.

He had lifted each document in turn as he spoke, and now laid Myron's letter next to the other exhibits.

"This afternoon, Sergeant Landers came here to the estate to conduct interviews and to collect something of Otto's that we could use to compare to the tooth's DNA. While he was here, I made some phone calls and learned the identity of Otto Lockwood's dentist. The good doctor is retired now, but he passed his practice on to his daughter, who has carefully maintained their records all these years. It was a simple matter to discover the truth about Otto's partial denture and the anchor tooth that held it, tooth number eleven. It was also a glaring fact that Otto had never reported a problem with his denture or his tooth. This is something the daughter assured me that Otto would have done immediately if he'd lost such an important tooth in innocuous circumstances."

I listened, spellbound, happy that I didn't have to take any of this down. I would have been too distracted.

"Because of the exhibits we had retrieved," Atherton continued, "Sergeant Landers knew of the Lockwood/Kensington lawsuit. He knew there were claims as to Otto's situation. Some claimed he was dead in the Amazon. Some claimed he was alive and writing home. I'm happy to say that Jackson Landers is an excellent police officer, and he began to ask himself whether Otto Lockwood ever made it out of the valley in 1975 at all."

Detective Atherton drank some water and gathered his thoughts. I secretly thought he was enjoying this. I hoped he would explain later why he was revealing so much about his case. Didn't the police usually hold their cards close to their chests during an investigation? I put my questions aside and tuned back in.

"The typed papers we collected proved that the disfigured Qs were only present when the tooth was lodged in the Smith-

Corona. The wills we collected from Ms. Rose, Exhibits B and C, were therefore typed on the typewriter when the tooth was in it. Should the tooth prove to belong to Otto Lockwood, as we suspected, and considering that he had to have lost it here, in the valley, where the typewriter was located, and that he hadn't sought any dental care after the loss of it…I'll be frank. We believed that Otto was no longer alive."

"In which case, he couldn't possibly have authored either Exhibit B or Exhibit C." Amy appeared to be thinking aloud. "But there does remain one very pertinent question."

"Quite," asserted Aurora, almost as firmly as she might have done a week ago. "Spencer may well have written the letter we thought was from Otto five years ago. But let's not forget Otto's *first* letters. I received one just six months after his return to the Amazon, and then I received another two years after that. Spencer certainly didn't write those. He wasn't even born until 1985! That's ten years after Otto left, and eight years after I received the second letter…" Aurora seemed to run out of steam as she trailed off.

Detective Atherton was shaking his head, but of course Aurora couldn't see that. My own head was swimming. Those letters had convinced me that Otto was receiving help from his sister. But to my ears now, she almost seemed to be searching for an explanation as to why Otto had written twice, then stopped writing. *Was she truly not involved at all?*

"We are agreed that Otto could not have created the wills that have been proffered in this litigation," Aurora said, her voice growing quieter. "But that doesn't mean he's dead for sure. Mightn't he have made do, somehow, with his dentures, even without the tooth?"

"But how did he lose the tooth in the first place, Nana?" Levi laid a hand on her arm. "How did it end up in the typewriter *after* he wrote up the will we found in the bust, and *before* he vanished?"

"I have answers for all of your questions," Detective Atherton. "As I said before, I came here for a purpose this evening. I was coming here to arrest your brother Dalton, Mrs. Kensington, but I needed to verify a few facts first. You see," he looked to the back of the room, straight at Jenkins, "Sergeant Landers learned some very important information this afternoon during his visit here. I'm afraid Mr. Jenkins has some unpleasant news to tell you, Mrs. Kensington. He has now told us everything in exchange for leniency for his part in some terrible actions. Mr. Jenkins?"

The atmosphere thickened noticeably, and I reminded myself to breathe. Aurora raised a hand as though seeking support, and Levi grasped her hand in both of his, drawing his chair nearer to hers. Where Aurora's tears had dried since the discovery in the bust, I now noted fresh wet tracks shining on her lovely face.

"Mr. Jenkins," she managed calmly, "is Otto dead?"

Jenkins uttered a single croak and reached for a glass of water. Mopping his brow, he loosened his tie and took a sip. "Yes, Mrs. Kensington. Otto has been dead since 1975. He died here on the estate." He was sweating profusely now, with rivulets running down his neck and throat. His shirt clung to his body.

"But the letters…"

"I—I—I wrote— Mrs. Kensington, I'm afraid I wrote those early letters."

Spencer jerked away from him. "What are you saying? Why have they arrested my father instead of you? Did you kill Uncle Otto and write to Aunt Aurora to cover it up?"

"No, no, no, no!" Jenkins was pleading with the room at large to believe him on this point. "No, no, I didn't kill him."

"But he did write to cover it up." Detective Atheron turned to me. "And I'm afraid he's been behind all of your difficulties at home, Ms. Rose—the break-in, the window smashing, and most unfortunately, the event last night where you were injured."

My skin instantly turned clammy. *Jenkins had been in my house? Jenkins had traumatized Clarabelle? Jenkins had deliberately booby-trapped my walkway and set off cherry bombs, all in hopes of* hurting *me?* My heart thudded painfully as my mind tried to grapple with this information.

"You dog." Hawk was on his feet, his voice a throaty growl.

Jenkins cringed, and Detective Atherton looked up sharply. Jax and the two deputies were gone. Atherton clearly couldn't afford to have things get out of hand.

"Easy does it, Mr. Rivers," he sounded much like Jax, even as Jenkins cowered in his corner. "Jenkins will be held to account. Don't do anything you'll regret later."

"I won't regret it." Hawk's expression was fierce, and his hands clenched into fists.

"But I will, Hawk." Aurora's words rang with clear sincerity and drew Hawk's gaze. "We've just learned that Otto is truly gone. Dalton has been arrested. Jenkins will serve time, Hawk, surely. The detective only said leniency, not free passage. Jenkins will never be allowed back on this estate. We can't lose you, too, you great leathery lug. Let the law deal with Jenkins."

Hawk tore his gaze from Aurora and turned to me. Looking fiercely into my eyes, he said not to me, but to Aurora, "I told Ms. Rose what I'd do when I found the man who did this to her, and I meant it. She coulda broke her neck, plunging into her door like that."

I had to jump in here. "But that doesn't mean you get to break *his* neck, Hawk." I clamored to my feet and limped over to him. Never had I had such a champion! But I couldn't let him get himself into trouble. I laid a hand on his arm.

"I'm going to be fine, Hawk. Just picture Mr. Jenkins in a prison cell and be satisfied." A yelp sounded from the far end of the room. "He'll be miserable. Don't you dare get into trouble by hurting him."

"You heard the detective. He cut a deal," Hawk said stubbornly.

"He won't face life, Mr. Rivers, it's true," Detective Atherton said. "Although ten years, at his age, could well be a life sentence." His walkie-talkie squawked, and he spoke into it briefly, telling someone to come inside.

I gave Hawk's arm a tug and felt his muscles relax slightly. The thought of Jenkins receiving a ten-year sentence seemed to have mollified him.

"My letters." Aurora sat, staring quietly into a blackness that must surely now be filled with memories and images of Otto. "Geoffrey, do you know what happened to my letters?"

Jenkins' posture sank, if anything, even lower.

"Mrs. Kensington," he managed, "you know by now that they weren't real…"

"Did you take them, Geoffrey?"

"I—I—"

"I'm sure you had a key, Geoffrey. The desk used to belong to Father. I never suspected you. Never."

"Forgive me, Mrs. Kensington!" he cried, seemingly undone by his own betrayal of her unwavering trust.

At last I sensed from him a deep remorse, not only for himself and his own consequences, but for the pain he had inflicted on someone with whom he had lived for decades—someone who had only treated him with kindness and respect.

"*Why?*" One simple word bore the colossal weight of her regal sorrow.

"Dalton wanted Otto declared legally dead," Jenkins whispered. "He was going to file. You'd told him about the letters. He knew Otto couldn't have written them. He didn't know who had, but he wanted them gone, just the same. He was afraid they would have complicated and prolonged matters in court."

"I see," Aurora said stiffly. "I'm afraid hitching yourself to Dalton's wagon has been your undoing, Geoffrey. I only hope you can find peace somehow, now that you no longer need to do damage and bear secrets. It brings me no joy to see you come to this end. No joy at all."

Another deputy now entered the room from the kitchen entrance, and Atherton motioned him toward Jenkins. The officer withdrew handcuffs from his belt and approached Jenkins, who gripped his chair, clearly terrified.

The detective shook his head at the deputy. "He's a cooperating witness, Deputy. We can do without the cuffs this time."

Surprised, the officer stowed his handcuffs back away.

"Wait!" Jenkins cried. "What about our deal? Why are you arresting me now? I'll keep my word!"

"I'm sure you will," the detective said grimly. "But this is a murder case. No one agreed to your remaining free pending sentencing. That's not how it works at all. You won't be housed with Mr. Lockwood. I'll be by later to explain how things are going to go."

"Noooo," Jenkins wailed desperately. "I'm not ready! Please, I'm not ready!"

The deputy ignored Jenkins' pleas and led him from the room. As they passed by me, I squeezed closer to Hawk, the better to reassure myself and to restrain him.

"Ms. Rose," Jenkins bawled, "I'm so s–s–sorry! I never meant to hurt you! I just had to get the typewriter back for Dalton." Dalton. Always for Dalton.

I shied away from Jenkins, and in seconds they were gone.

CHAPTER 47

THE FACTS

Crickets.

Isn't that what people call it when the silence in a room is deafening? I heard no real crickets, but I was sure I could hear Hawk's heart as it thumped mere inches away from my head. I'd known he was tall, of course, but close proximity now revealed that the top of my head barely reached his shoulder.

"So let's have it," Levi said, breaking the silence as everyone exhaled. "You know a lot. You must have evidence since you arrested Uncle Dalton. We want the story. Nana wants answers."

"Yes," Aurora said firmly. "One needs facts. You seem certain that dear Otto is dead, and that Dalton is responsible for it. Let's have the truth as you understand it, or in the morning, I shall have to see what I can do to bail the bum out."

"Nana!" gasped Amy.

"Why?" This from Levi. "Let him cool his heels while this gets sorted out. Maybe we can all relax around here for a change." Levi raised his eyebrows at Spencer. "Yes?"

"Yes!" agreed Spencer enthusiastically. "I swear, I never wanted to be part of Father's lawsuit. I was just—just afraid…" He looked at Aurora. "Did you know, Aunt Aurora?"

"That you were Glum Richie?" she tutted. "Of course I did. And I've been pulling for you. I knew you had copious quantities of courage lurking beneath the surface. Welcome back to the family, Knight Gallant."

Spencer actually blushed and scuffed a toe on the carpet, but his eyes were shining.

"Thanks, Aunt Aurora."

"But back to the story…" Levi.

I looked hopefully at Detective Atherton while nestling beneath Hawk's arm. I didn't want to be noticed and have someone ask me to leave. If there was a story coming, I was all ears.

The detective massaged his neck again and looked at Levi.

"All right," he said. "There are some things I can tell you, because I have a written confession from Mr. Jenkins, as well as some other hard evidence. Everyone go ahead and have a seat."

He turned and looked directly at me. "Ms. Rose, I'm afraid this no longer concerns you—"

"Aw, let her stay." Coop had remained quite comfortable in his chair, and he now leaned back, a picture of easy confidence. "She's the one who made this discovery possible, after all. Plus, she won't tattle before the trial. We already know the girl can keep a secret, eh? And somehow or another, this is still a deposition, I think." He hiked a thumb at Hawk. "Deponent's still here." He grinned mischievously and winked at me.

The detective's lip twitched mysteriously, but he just motioned me to my chair in a you-may-stay-if-you're-silent kind of gesture. Hawk took my hand and helped me to my seat, clearly still mindful of my date with a doorway last night. My body was screaming for more Ibuprofen and my bed, but I wasn't about to miss this.

"Okay," Detective Atherton said, "I'll go over the case as we now know it. We'll know more when the hair we collected and the tooth," he nodded to me, "come back with their DNA analysis complete. But this is what we learned from Mr. Jenkins this afternoon, and we believe it to be the truth.

"In August of 1975, on what was apparently a very stormy night…"

CHAPTER 48

BACK TO THE PAST
AUGUST 1975

Otto reached out and idly began to spin an old black globe that occupied the upper right corner of his desk. Stopping the globe suddenly, he pointed to South America. The Amazon. Of course.

"I'm heading back," he said. "This is where I've been, and to there I shall return. I left the biggest part of myself there four months ago when Father sent for me." He contemplated the great room. His eyes fell upon a stack of old newspapers near an armchair. Father's chair. He cleared his throat.

"My heart was never in the newspaper business. But then I expect you know that." He chuckled. "Or at least you *hoped* it. You never cared for my ideas." He set the sheaf of paper down. "I've left everything in order. I've booked a flight for first thing tomorrow morning."

The storm raged outside, while the storm inside Dalton grew quiet. He smoothed his own hair now, dark and lank after his dousing.

"Please tell everyone I love them," Otto continued, "that I hate goodbyes, and that I'm off to my life's calling. The rain forest, indigenous tribes." His expression grew wistful. "I must go and do what I can. I'm sure everyone will understand."

Dalton looked down at his dripping clothes. His wet hair chilled him, yet his heart thrilled. He'd plowed through a fierce storm, snuck into the winter house, soaking himself through so he could confront his brother, and for *what*?

He'd already won! Otto was leaving.

"Only thing is," Otto's musing tone interrupted Dalton's quiet exultation, "I can't find the will I drew up for Father."

Dalton started. There'd been no sign, no mention of a will in the days since Father's passing. He'd dared to hope that a legal document hadn't been accomplished before Myron's untimely accident. It would mean a long probate, but Dalton was willing to allow state law to determine the estate's outcome. He'd take his third and build his own empire. But now Otto was saying the will had come to fruition after all. He threw a sidelong glance at the *Last Will & Testament* he'd seen Otto studying when he'd arrived moments ago, but closer inspection revealed that it was only a blank template.

"What will is that?" Dalton muttered. "Some guy at the funeral said he was Father's attorney, but I didn't believe him. Didn't even mention it to Aurora. We knew Father didn't like lawyers."

"Guess the guy didn't take it personally."

"Didn't say a word about a will, though," Dalton persisted.

"Exactly." Otto spun the globe around thoughtfully. "After Father and I finished up the final document, he said he was going to put it in a safe place until he could take it to his attorney, who I'd never heard of, either. Apparently, he trusted the attorney to *keep* the will. He just wanted me to *draft* the thing."

Dalton shifted his feet, his earlier edginess returning. He just wanted Otto to leave and be done with the family.

"Well," he said, "if the attorney doesn't have it, and you can't find it, Father'll have died intestate. State can deal with it. Happens all the time."

"Not so much to the wealthy and famous, I think." Otto furrowed his brow. "Can't imagine where he put it, though. The one time he committed something to writing, rather than just keeping it in his head, and it's gone missing."

Otto's chair creaked and Dalton jumped. Beads of rainwater splashed from his jacket, and some of the droplets sprayed the template on Otto's desk.

"You were studying that thing just now," Dalton accused. "You sure you weren't planning to re-write a will for Father?"

Otto raised his eyebrows and surveyed his younger brother's face. Contemplating the papers lying on his desk, he reached a hand to touch them, almost tenderly.

"Ah, yes, brother," he sighed. "I can see how you would leap to that conclusion. But no. I was simply looking at it, remembering Father's wishes as expressed in the document we made, and wondering where the dratted thing was."

Dalton crossed his arms and frowned stubbornly. *What if Otto is lying to me?*

But Otto could read his younger brother all too well. "Listen, Dalton, I know you may not believe me," he said kindly, "but I really wouldn't forge a new will and pass it off as Father's. You might think I'd do that and treat you poorly in it. But the truth is, little brother, that Father's *actual* will already did you plenty of damage. Since I can't find it, and since I want to leave anyway, I may as well tell you not to put too much effort into looking for it."

Dalton's heart thudded as he stared at Otto's face. He saw no malice there. Only pity. How dare his weak, spineless, irrational older brother pity *him*? Otto didn't know anything about anything, except tree hugging and saving the whales or some such.

"I'm trying to tell you, Dalton,"—Otto's voice was soft, even gentle—"that Father cut you out. I'm afraid he left you nothing. No money, no authority in the business, no ownership interest in any of his properties, including this estate. He said you could keep the condo in Sun Valley. He didn't want you homeless. But he included provisions wherein you must purchase the condo over a period of thirty years, like any homeowner. Aurora was to hold the note, and you'd have made payments to her."

Dalton stood silent, blood whooshing through his ears. Veins stood out hard in his neck, and his temple throbbed.

"You! You put Father up to this!" He could barely see. Otto's face blurred before him as Father's ultimate betrayal sank into his heart and found its mark. He swayed where he stood.

"No," Otto almost whispered. "No, that's not my way. I'd have sought another solution."

Of course you would. Dalton's thoughts were venomous. *Always like to see yourself as so fair! It's sickening.*

Finally finding some sense of his own feet, Dalton backed away, unconsciously moving toward his Father's marble bust that Otto had contemplated such a short time ago. Reaching it, he turned and stared at it in agony.

"But look, Dalton…" Somehow, Otto's voice penetrated the frenetic pumping and whooshing of Dalton's blood. "As of now, there is no will. I truly can't find it. I suggest you run things amicably with Aurora, and perhaps everything will turn out all right."

"Probate," Dalton spluttered. "I'll insist we hurry it along."

"Well, careful there, bro. I wouldn't rush into asking the courts to decide anything that could be overturned if the will showed up. Run the business. Work with Aurora. She has full signatory authority over everything. We can try to delay. I'll keep in touch."

Dalton's fingers caressed his father's likeness. *I can't even sign anything...*

The marble felt cool, heavy beneath his touch.

"And if I don't want to work with my dear sister? If I think she's meddlesome, and I'd rather she stay well out of things? Then what?" If Otto noticed Dalton's menacing tone, he didn't reveal it.

"Then I'll have to come back and help straighten things out, I'm afraid." Dalton cringed at his brother's words. "Since I'm the eldest, I can initiate probate proceedings that will have some clout, and I'll testify as to what was in the will I drafted. I wrote it on this typewriter, Dalton. I'll hang on to the ribbon. It won't contain a signed document, but it'll be strong evidence." Otto looked into Dalton's eyes, imploring him. "Please don't push me into doing that. Get along with Aurora. This business of trying to thwart your family at every turn has got to stop."

With that, Otto turned, and opening a drawer in his desk, he slid the template he'd been perusing neatly inside.

Perhaps it was the simple task of casually stowing away a sheaf of paper. Perhaps it was the fact that Otto had turned *away* from Dalton for a moment, as though this had been a trivial chat, which was now concluded. Perhaps it was the *pity* from a few moments earlier. Perhaps it was Otto's threat to return if Dalton didn't play nice. Whatever the final straw actually was, it broke all reason within Dalton's head. Without a moment's thought, he grasped the marble bust in both hands, took three rapid steps toward his brother, and smashed the bust into the back of Otto's skull.

A soft crunching sensation reverberated through the bust and into Dalton's hands. The room tilted oddly, and surprise took him as he, in an instant, contemplated the damage he had inflicted. Some other version of himself noticed that the violence of the blow had dislodged Otto's upper partial denture, which had flown right out of his mouth and landed on the typewriter. That same disjointed other version noticed a sudden warming of his own chest.

At last, after what seemed an eternity, Otto's body slumped forward and collided with his desk, finally sinking all the way to the floor. The blood flowing freely from the back of his head quickly pooled around him, spreading forth like syrup.

Dalton managed to set the heavy bust down on the desk, his fingers nearly numb with shock. As the fog started to clear, he began to absorb the reality of the scene before him. Looking on in abject horror, he stepped back slightly, even as sudden inner voices quarreled in his mind.

Good riddance! He was going to make your life a misery.

No! What have you done? He was your brother. You've got your own brother's blood all over your chest.

You're doomed. You're going to spend the rest of your life in prison.

Even as the inner voices tormented Dalton after murdering his brother, a real voice spoke from the direction of the mudroom. This voice managed to permeate Dalton's stunned consciousness as Jenkins said practically, "We're going to need to clean that up."

CHAPTER 49
THE CONSPIRACY
AUGUST 2016

"So Jenkins has been in on it the whole time?" Levi asked as Detective Atherton finished.

"I'm afraid so." Atherton's voice was clipped, grim. "Mr. Jenkins made a full confession this afternoon."

I looked at Aurora. She sat unmoving in her chair, her face completely white.

"Poor Otto," she whispered. "Such a happy, kind young man. He never deserved that. And to think," she said, gripping Levi's hand, "we've been living with a murderer for all these years. It defies my imagination. Dalton's known all along what he did, and he played his part to the limit."

"Including suing us to get control of the estate," Amy inserted indignantly. "There are simply no words to describe any of this."

"I have words, Amy," Levi said angrily. "I hope he rots in prison." Levi suddenly looked at Spencer and said contritely, "Hey, Spencer, sorry. I know he's your dad."

"I don't want him as my dad anymore." Spencer dropped his grief-stricken face into his hands. "I didn't know." His words were muffled. "I promise, everyone, I didn't know."

"No one is blaming *you* for any of this," Levi said. "Okay? I mean, you weren't even born yet when it happened."

Amy turned to Atheron. "Detective?"

"Yes?"

"Did Jenkins say anything else? I guess I can't imagine how Uncle Dalton had the nerve to bring this lawsuit, knowing what he'd done."

"Yes, Ms. Kensington, there is more. I'll tell you what Jenkins told me. On the night of the murder, Dalton and Mr. Jenkins cleaned up the blood stains in the winter house and took Otto's body out into the woods to bury him. He's going to attempt to lead us to the very place tomorrow."

"I'd like to go too, please," managed Aurora.

I thought Atherton was about to turn her down when Levi piped up. "We'll help her, Detective, and we'll stay well back."

After a moment's consideration the detective gave Levi a curt nod and resumed his narrative.

"After everything was clean," he told them, "Dalton and Jenkins loaded Otto's body into the trunk of the car. Dalton put Otto's *Indiana Jones* style hat on his head and sat in the back passenger seat. Shorter than Otto, he sat on two phonebooks to create the effect of a taller man. When they passed the gate, on their way to dispose of the body, it was a simple thing for Hawk Rivers to assume that it was Otto in the car. Jenkins cemented the assumption later when he told Hawk he'd driven Otto to the airport. Hawk never had a reason to doubt that it was Otto in the back seat."

Atherton took a seat now, sighing as if the day had finally caught up with him.

"Jenkins explained that, within the next few days, Dalton decided that he would create two wills, one for his father and one for Otto. He used Otto's typewriter, and even went so far, after the wills were typed, as to remove the ribbon from the Smith-

Corona. He asked Jenkins to dispose of the old ribbon. Jenkins, feeling that he really ought to provide himself with an insurance policy, held on to it. It's now in our possession, and technicians have confirmed that three wills and one letter were the last things typed on it."

He motioned to the cedar-scented will from the bust. "The second two wills on the ribbon match your Exhibits B and C to the letter. It will be short work to compare the earliest typing on the ribbon with this document."

"And the letter was the one from my father?" Aurora's voice had slipped to a whisper.

"Yes, Mrs. Kensington," affirmed Atherton equally quiet. "It's there, right in line after the real will that Otto typed, the one we found in the bust tonight."

Spencer came to stand next to his cousins and his aunt, as though he wanted to seal his allegiance to them. Head down at first, he smiled when Levi slapped him on the back and Amy gave his waist a squeeze.

I felt suddenly intrusive, but I still had questions. I felt thankful when Spencer voiced one of them for me.

"Sir," he spoke from Amy's side, "if you knew Father killed Uncle Otto, why did you arrest Jenkins first?"

"Ah," Atherton actually smiled. "Just a little strategy I wanted to experiment with. I had Mr. Jenkins placed under arrest *first* because I needed to see Dalton's reaction. Jenkins could have acted alone in murdering Otto, after all. I had only his word that it was Dalton who had delivered the blow. When Dalton tried to leave quickly the way he did, he confirmed every word of Jenkin's story.

"Mr. Jenkins, by the way, never actually touched the typewriter ribbon spools. He handled them with a handkerchief.

We've dusted the spools that Jenkins had for prints. We were able to confirm his prints were not on them. As we'll soon have Dalton's prints available to us, we'll be able to compare with what we've found. I expect we'll have a match."

"But why didn't Uncle Dalton *use* the wills he'd created?" Amy asked. "He supposedly 'found' them just five years ago. Why not bring them out forty years ago, when he made them?"

"Jenkins talked him out of it," the detective said. "He feared that an attorney might show up one day with a *real* will. Remember, Otto said it existed. He just didn't know where it was. So Jenkins wrote the two earlier letters to Aurora to keep her satisfied that Otto was well, and they bided their time. The real urgency only arose five years ago when the newspaper conglomerate approached Dalton about buying the paper. Dalton knew Aurora would never sell, so he 'found' the wills and set about wresting control of the company away from her."

"Why did they break into Shae's place?" Hawk asked another of my questions. He had been silent while the detective explained their findings, but now clearly still seemed rankled. "That's what I want to know. Why attack her last night? Wasn't one murder on Dalton's conscience enough?"

"Jenkins told me they simply wanted the typewriter back." Atherton shrugged. "Dalton hadn't known that Aurora was going to admit it as a deposition exhibit, though he should have, since the wills he'd produced in discovery had been typed on it. When he learned that Shae had been given possession of the machine, he ordered Jenkins to do everything he could to get it back."

I couldn't stand it anymore, sitting here silently. I'd been through a lot with this case. "But *why?*" I blurted out. "What good would it do to get the typewriter back?"

If the detective was surprised to hear from me, he didn't show it. "Dalton knew about the odd Qs, you see." Another shrug. "He didn't know the tooth was in there, but he knew Otto's partial denture had landed on it. And he knew it didn't type the same after that. The Qs were higher than the rest of the letters. Jenkins told me that Dalton feared a comparison of his 'wills' with any other document typed on the typewriter. With good reason, as we've seen."

So I'd been right all along. The break-in, the smashed window, the attempt to hurt me (and get by me and into my apartment, no doubt), had all been because of the typewriter. Exhaustion washed over me, and I suddenly wanted to close my eyes to the world and sleep.

Aurora stirred, and I decided to move as well. I was aching from sitting too long in one position. I needed to get home. I needed to find Hercules. I looked at my trusty steno machine and decided to start packing up.

"Spencer." Aurora's tone was warm and loving.

Spencer reached for her hand. "Yeah, Aunt Aurora, I'm here."

"I'm adopting you, young man."

Hope touched his face fleetingly, but then he looked at his cousins. They might object. Far from it. They were both beaming.

"Not," continued Aurora, "that we need to do anything on paper, Spencer. You can keep your name. But you are part of *my* family now. You shall join us in the business, and you shall have your blog. Allow me to be the first to congratulate you and welcome Mr. Badger Thicket to the newspaper that is staying very much in this family, where it belongs—our very own *Valley Scribe*."

"Great news!" Levi grabbed Spencer's free hand and shook it vigorously. "Welcome home, cuz!"

"And I've just thought of something," Amy said, as all eyes turned to her. "The true will was discovered in a bust of Grandfather Myron's."

"Yes." Aurora. "And?"

"It occurs to me how true it is, what everyone has said all along about your father, Nana. He really did keep everything important in his head!"

CHAPTER 50

LAST WALK

I packed up quietly while the family continued processing all that had unfolded that evening. Detective Atherton filed the documents away while Hawk hovered close at hand, helping me unplug and stash everything away.

Levi approached as I tucked cords into my bag. "Did you ever finish your video game, Shae?"

"Nope. I got to Level Four, though."

"Good job, but it's too bad we won't have more depos. There are a lot of levels left. You'd have enjoyed them."

I laughed. "One day maybe I'll get an iPad. I'll be able to finish it then." I stretched out my hand. "It was great meeting you, Levi." I turned to face the whole gang. "It was very nice to meet *all* of you."

"I'm so sorry about all that happened to you because of us." Spencer spoke to a general murmuring of assent from everyone else.

"It wasn't the fault of anyone here," I assured them. "I wish you all the very best, and next time I'm in trouble, I'm sure Cheeky Peaks will be hearing from me. Goodbye, everyone!"

Hawk carried my bag a final time as he walked beside me to my car. Detective Atherton joined us, leaving the family to assimilate all they had learned that evening. As we approached my car the detective slowed to a stop and turned to face me.

"I am beholden to you, Ms. Rose."

"To me?" I was surprised. He had things so well in hand.

"Yes, indeed. Like I said inside, all of the information you were able to provide me this morning enabled us to move very quickly and, after interviewing people here, to put the rest of the puzzle together easily. I thank you, and I would ask that you thank the ladies for the part each of them played, as well."

"Even though they both typed on the exhibit?" I grinned wickedly.

He laughed aloud, a first. "Oh, yes. I've known the Darlings for years. My mother used to ski with them."

"All right, then." I grinned again, but didn't move. I still had one pressing question for the detective.

"Can I ask a question, Detective?"

"Certainly, Ms. Rose."

"Why reveal so much? I mean, we loved hearing the whole story, but even *before* you arrested Dalton, you'd told us quite a lot. Is that normal?"

"Not always." He walked on thoughtfully for a moment. "Thing is, I needed to see how Dalton would respond, and that old saying occurred to me."

"What old saying?"

"Give a man enough rope and see if he hangs himself."

CHAPTER 51

RETURNED

I rounded the corner onto my street and saw, again, lights and lots of activity in front of my home. The driveway was once again blocked, so I parked at the curb and hobbled my way up to the crowd. There was Mr. Gruber again. I sighed. What now?

"Ohhhh, there she is! Shae, dear, hurry, hurry." Clarabelle waved as though I should move faster. "Frank Gruber is here."

Along with half the neighborhood. Approaching the group, I saw neighbors from all up and down not only our street, but some from several streets away. Most had bikes, but some were simply wearing stout walking shoes.

"Meet your search party, Shae." Bernie grinned. She certainly seemed to be in a better mood than when I'd seen her last. "Everyone's been searching for Hercules all day. We just gathered back here to make some sandwiches and carry on."

"But then Mr. Gruber showed up," Clarabelle gushed. "Ohhhh, show her, Frank. Show her!"

The crowd parted slightly, and Frank Gruber stepped forward with a wriggling bundle in his arms.

"Show me what?"

A tiny black head popped out from beneath a folded blanket.

"Hercules!" I reached for him even as Mr. Gruber moved closer so Herc wouldn't fall in his excitement. "Oh, thank you,

Mr. Gruber!" Hercules was soaking my face in kisses and wiggling so much I could barely hold him. "Where did you find him?"

"Vell, all day I didn't see my Ziege. He only stayed in his pen in the yard. It is covered, to protect from sun. Tonight, I go to find him to see if he vod come eat. I look in his pen, and I see your very small dog." He pointed to Herc. "He vos in Ziege's bed, and Ziege vos vit him, laying vit him, keeping him varm."

I looked around at my neighbors' joyous faces in amazement. Everyone was clapping Frank Gruber on the back, thanking him, marveling at the nurturing instinct of his pet goat. Mr. Gruber tried to brush away the attention at first, but eventually he warmed up and laughed with the rest of us.

Stella Baumgartner from down the street invited Mr. Gruber to have dinner with her family the next evening, saying, "And bring Ziggy. I can't wait to meet him. And what a cute name. Wherever did you come up with it?"

I listened with interest. The ladies and I had often wondered how the (once) cantankerous old Mr. Gruber had arrived at such a darling name for his pet.

Mr. Gruber looked confused for a moment, as though he didn't understand the question. "Ziege? It is simple. Ziege is German for goat."

CHAPTER 52

FAMILY

Two and a half months had passed since Dalton Lockwood's arrest and the end of my work on the case. My injuries had healed, and I rarely thought about the dark day that Jenkins had lain in wait in order to take me out of action and steal the little Smith-Corona.

I lifted a glass baking dish out of the oven, savoring the smell of beautifully candied yams. I'd used my dad's favorite recipe, happy to share some of my own family's traditions with the Darlings as we celebrated Thanksgiving this year.

"Come on, buddy," I said to Herc as I edged out the door with my yams. "Are you ready for a nice Thanksgiving?" He wagged his tail enthusiastically and followed me to the Darlings' front door.

"Oh, how pretty," I said when I saw the table.

"Shae, you can set your dish right here," Clarabelle said, pointing to an open space. "It does look nice, doesn't it? And you're just in time. The others will probably be here any minute. Bernie has left the gate open for them."

Clarabelle bustled off to the kitchen and I hugged my arms around myself, relishing the scene. The table cloth was made of a burnt orange background, overlaid in random patterns with multi-colored autumn leaves. The ladies had retrieved their best china from the ornate cabinet near the kitchen door, and cutlery rested within carefully rolled, deep green cloth napkins. At the head of the table, in place of a dinner plate, sat the cheerful photo of Danny as he played to the camera on his high school graduation day.

A silver lining, then, I thought. The dreadful brick through the window had brought Danny back to center stage in the ladies' lives, and talking about him had been cathartic for Clarabelle. It seemed that her grieving heart was able to let him go at last, even as she shared him with all of us. My heart squeezed within my chest as I took in the loving scene, awed at my own inclusion in it.

I swallowed the lump in my throat as the doorbell rang. I opened the door and smiled warmly at Frank Gruber and Hawk Rivers, both dressed in their finest and smiling shyly.

Clarabelle hurried to take Mr. Gruber's hand and show him the table and the wonderful feast laid thereon. I threw my arms around Hawk and buried my face in his chest. It was my first in-person glimpse of him since the night of Dalton Lockwood's arrest, and my chest squeezed again.

I mumbled into his shirt. "I'm so happy to see you, Hawk."

He patted me on the back awkwardly, but when I pulled away his face was split with the biggest grin I'd ever seen him wear.

"Thanks for inviting me, Shae." He looked more closely and nodded. "You're looking better."

"Yeah, shiner's gone." In an effort to quell the still-present lump in my throat, I reached up to jab his ribs playfully with my elbow. I'd forgotten how tall he was. "Thank *you* for coming, Hawk. *We* get to feed *you* this time."

"Brought you a present from the family, too, Shae." He grinned again, more secretively this time. "Kinda early for Christmas, but Levi says go ahead and open it up anyway."

I took the giftwrapped box that Hawk handed me, mystified, and read the card.

Merry Early Christmas, Shae!
Come back and see us any time.
Aurora, Levi, Amy, and Spencer

Tearing off the wrapping paper I discovered, in the box, a brand new iPad. It had a sticky note on top which said only, "Game's loaded. You got this, Shae! Levi."

An iPad. My own iPad. I stuck out my arm to Hawk. "Pinch me."

His grin broadened even more. "Levi said you'd like that."

"Okay, you two, let's eat!" Bernie called us to join her, Clarabelle, and Mr. Gruber at the table.

There followed two wonderful hours as old friends and new sat around an Idaho Thanksgiving feast. Clarabelle regaled us with stories about her visits with Nettie over at River Grace. Bernie recounted some of the recent projects she'd undertaken, including having Mr. Ivory back out to remove all of the decospikes from the back fence.

"Deco my foot," she grumbled lightly. "Ugliest things I ever saw."

I spent most of the meal glancing around the table fondly. Family. I'd never thought I'd find real family again, yet here they were. Friends, neighbors, landladies, sure. But we were knit together with the strongest of bonds, and my heart swelled. A true *Thanksgiving* Day.

At last, when we couldn't eat another bite, Bernie went off to the kitchen to make coffee.

The ladies still had a land telephone line, and when it rang she answered it promptly. I heard a moment of subdued conversation before Bernie reappeared in the kitchen doorway and motioned for everyone's attention.

The look on her face held a warning, and some of my joy drained quietly away in alarm. "What is it, Bernie?"

"I'm sorry to have to end a lovely Thanksgiving meal this way, but Jax is on the phone. I'm afraid there's been an incident at the assisted living home, River Grace."

Clarabelle's hand flew to her mouth. "Is Nettie okay, Bernice?"

"She's fine, Clare." In spite of her words, I thought Bernie looked awfully grim. "But the nurse, the one they call Duckie, is dead under suspicious circumstances."

We all sat in shocked silence. Suspicious circumstances? In *Hailey?*

"Shae?" Bernie's voice startled me.

I barely heard her, my mind astir and incredulous, but at last I answered, "Yes, Bernie?"

"Jax would like to speak with you."

"Oh, okay."

I rose on suddenly numb legs, went into the kitchen, and found the telephone laying on the counter. I picked it up.

"Jax? It's Shae. Bernie just told us what happened. I can't believe it."

"Yeah, horrible thing to happen any time, but even worse on Thanksgiving." I was sorry to hear him sound so harried on a day when everyone else was celebrating. I'd hoped to see him later. He had promised to bring Nettie and come for pie this evening.

"What *did* happen, Jax?"

"I'll fill you in on some things later, Shae." He sounded odd, almost muffled for a moment. "But I can tell you that it was a hit and run."

I gasped, looking toward the very somber crowd now occupying the dining room.

"Here's the thing, Shae. We've got twenty-three residents and five staff members over here, and we need to get statements from every one of them while events are still fresh in their minds. We just don't have the personnel to do that quickly. I was wondering if you'd be willing to come over here with your machine. You could sit with my officers and take down everyone's statements. You wouldn't have to put them under oath or anything, but you're so fast with that writer of yours, it would really help us out."

I was actually relieved there was something I could do to help. My thoughts zoomed to my brand new iPad. I would be able to bring it and provide realtime. It would be an honor to do that for him. He would be able to listen to one person's statement in one part of the building, and then come and scroll through other statements on the iPad. Efficient. Perfect.

"You bet, Jax. I'll be there in ten minutes."

"Thanks a million, Shae. See you then."

Hanging up, I stepped back into the dining room.

"What did he want?" asked Hawk.

"Jax needs me to help get everyone's statement down, guys. I'm going to have to get over to River Grace right away."

"Oh, Shae," Clarabelle clasped her hands against her chest, "how wonderful that you can help."

"No one better for the job." Hawk nodded soberly and pushed his plate away.

"That's right," affirmed Bernie. "Off you go, Shae. We'll clean up here and save some pie for you."

I took in the faces still gathered round the table and wished them all, once again, a very happy Thanksgiving. Telling Herc to stay with the ladies, I headed out the door to my apartment. I would gather my equipment and be on the road in no time.

I smiled softly to myself.

Duty called.

WANT TO BECOME A COURT REPORTER?

Check out the **National Court Reporters Association** (NCRA's) A to Z program at **DiscoverSteno.org**.

Then reach out to **Project Steno** at **ProjectSteno.org**.

They will match you up with a school and can provide tuition assistance. Project Steno's goal is to get students in and out of school in two years.

MY THANKS

I am indebted to my beta readers, Judy Pisani, Veronica Williams, Doreen Sutton, and Elaine Childs. They took time from their busy lives to read through my story with court reporters' eyes and to provide me with invaluable feedback and encouragement.

I would like to thank Deanna Warner for helping to name Ziggy the goat. I put a plea out on social media, asking for help with naming him. I received many wonderful suggestions, but Deanna's idea was perfect and I ran with it immediately.

Thank you, Larry Weinberger, for providing me with invaluable expertise in all things related to teeth!

To my daughter and Muse-in-Chief, Amy Wojkowski, thank you. You are my biggest cheerleader, book reviewer, and safety net. You never let me stray into the mire of too much information; nor do you allow me to skimp where I've missed a flavor that is crucial to my story.

This book would not be what it is without the invaluable contributions of my editor, Dawn Kinzer. Thank you, Dawn, for your hard work, your ideas, and your wonderful suggestions.

Finally, there would be no book without my publisher, Suzanne Parrott. All the months of encouragement, hand-holding, and just plain believing in me are what finally brought a raw manuscript to life. Your design work dazzles me.

THANK YOU!

ABOUT THE AUTHOR

Diana Kilpatrick has led a varied, adventurous life, from her days with Youth With A Mission and Mercy Ships to her never-dull career as a court reporter and her work in prison ministry. When she isn't traveling for work or for speaking engagements, Diana devotes her free time to her writing, her family, and her affection-seeking cat Bella.

Follow Diana at:

Website: DianaKilpatrick.com
Facebook: @diana.kilpatrick.9

DIANA **KILPATRICK**